WILD BLUE

*Saving the World with Duct Tape
and WD-40*

EARL TROUT

Isabella Media Inc

Wild Blue : Saving the World with Duct Tape and WD-40 by Earl Trout
Published by Isabella Media Inc
Copyright © 2020 Isabella Media Inc

This book is a work of fiction. Names, characters, businesses, organizations, places, events and incidents either are the product of the author's imagination or are used fictitiously. Any resemblance to actual persons, living or dead, events, or locales is entirely coincidental.

For information contact:
Isabella Media Inc
270 Bellevue Ave, Suite 1002, Newport, RI 02840
www.isabellamedia.com

Book and Cover design by Isabella Book Design
ISBN: 978-1733041683

First Edition : Month 2020

CAST OF CHARACTERS

The Good Guys

Theophilus (Theo) Spivak — Recently hired physicist at Pasadena Institute of Technology.

Kevin Oxley — Electronic genius rocket scientist, Theo's best friend.

Dr. Francis Noah Weksler — Physics Department Chair at Pasadena Institute of Technology, inventor of stealth technology, Theo's boss.

Dr. Dianne Wright — Assistant Dean at Pasadena Institute of Technology.

Dr. Sarah Norton — Nobel prize winning physicist, Dr. Weksler's recently deceased wife.

Ms. Zambini — Manager of Kagel Canyon Estates Mobile Home Park.

The Bad Guys

Professor Pul — Leader of the S.O.L.

Bahadur — One of only two S.O.L apprentice terrorists.

Mikhail — The other S.O.L apprentice terrorist.

His Supreme Eminence — Leader of the Holy Garduña, Professor Pul's superior.

The Kinda-Sorta Good Guy

Leonard Ostermann — Federal Communications Commission (F.C.C.) Under-Assistant West Coast Field Director.

###

1

PASADENA, CALIFORNIA — 2003

"It was spring, the time when [would be] kings go off to war..."
— 2 Samuel 11:1

You should know that I am not brave, and the bomb really scared me. Yes, I always used to enjoy those cool explosions in movies and TV shows, but not anymore. Those aren't real, and they don't actually explode right in front of you. The real thing is not cool at all. That bomb blew up a two-hundred-foot-tall broadcasting tower, sending pieces flying in all directions while the attached warehouse detonated into a huge black smoke storm launching car-sized fireballs. Any closer to the explosion and I would have been impaled by a flying, white hot, steel beam just before being roasted alive. I still have nightmares about me as the protein in a gigantic shish-kabob.

The explosion launched one of those infamous California forest fires you hear about every year. The official, convoluted, and improbable explanation for the blast blamed it all on an illegal campfire. That's because our government felt compelled to cover up the terrorism.

My close encounter of the terrorist kind absolutely terrified me, which I suppose, is the whole point of terrorism. That, along with a vile, psychopathic desire to hurt, maim, and kill. Oh, and of course, *Terrorist Job One:* forcing other people to pretend they worship the same way as the terrorist.

Those terrorists, a depraved religious cult, did their first attack on American soil in West Los Angeles, on Christmas Day, 2002. You never heard anything about it because the power elite redacted the truth. On a Sunday just two months after that Christmas Day viciousness, I found myself in a deadly situation. Actually ... more than merely deadly. It was also sticky, stinky, icky and gross. And it moved really fast.

I am not a fan of chaos theory and I don't believe in coincidence. I believe things happen because somebody made them happen, especially stupid things. Early in childhood I realized I had a congenital need to place blame. In this case, however, because my deadly situation began to pick up speed, I couldn't devote adequate time to guilt analysis. So, I just quickly decided to blame Santa Anna for my lethal circumstances.

That seemed to make at least a modicum of sense. You see, Antonio López de Santa Anna, the handsome, rich, politically astute, and almost completely incompetent eleven-time Presidente and/or Dictator of Mexico convinced himself that *chicle* (the white goo from sapodilla trees) could be formulated into artificial rubber. During one of his many exiles, Santa Anna rented a room in the U.S. home of wannabe inventor Thomas Adams. In March 1867, El Presidente somehow managed to get two tons of *chicle* shipped to Mr. Adams in New York City. This is a true thing.

Adams never created even so much as a single successful application of *chicle*-based artificial rubber. While on his way to dump the last bits of the worthless glop into the East River, he became aware of a new paraffin wax-based confectionary fad called "chewing gum". He rushed back home, warmed up the *chicle*, added a bit of sugar, and personally launched the world-wide chewing gum industry. This is also a true thing. So, I also blamed Thomas Adams for me being trapped in the deadly device.

But then ... it really didn't seem fair to blame either Santa Anna or Thomas Adams without due thought process. Nevertheless, it became obvious I would soon crash and be splattered to death before I had enough data to assess culpability. Accordingly, despite my discomfort with making a judgment call based on feelings instead of facts, I just blamed everything on William Wrigley, Jr. That kinda-sorta worked for me because Mr. Wrigley, the most successful, zillionaire, chewing gum magnate in the history of the world owned the big unstoppable trash dumpster in which I was trapped. It escaped from the Wrigley Mansion.

Now, regardless of what you may end up thinking by the time you hear our entire true-life adventure, I want you to know that Kevin really was a good friend. However, he— quite frequently—also managed to be my worst nightmare. Though basically a good guy, my assumption is, he never inherited the responsibility gene. By way of example ... there I was ... trapped in the large Wrigley Mansion dumpster, rolling downhill insanely fast—totally out of control—in the richest part of Pasadena. The dumpster and I rushed past stately old-money mansions as rapidly as my 29-year-old life appeared to be rushing to its end. At the bottom of the steep hill, the oak tree-canopied boulevard made an acute turn to the left. My dumpster had no steering wheel.

Using structures on terrain as baseline, I calculated my street at a twenty-eight-degree descent. Maybe even twenty-nine. Very scary. My eyeglasses were caked with grime. I fingernailed off a bit of gunk and squinted downhill.

Okay... there's an old guardrail down at the dead end. Oh, don't even think dead end!

The cliff on the other side of the guardrail dropped a hundred yards straight down to the Rose Bowl parking lot. The crumbling wooden guardrail wouldn't even stop a skateboard from going off the cliff. It occurred to me that my immediate future would consist of disgusting video on the eleven o'clock news.

Now I'm not a rocket scientist, but—well actually, Kevin *is* a rocket scientist—I'm just a physicist. In any event, I instantly analyzed my situation and then settled on the only logical course of action: I squealed. "Aiieee!" I found it comforting.

I do not even remotely resemble an athlete so, escape from the dumpster seemed unlikely. My body type is "scrawny side of five foot-eight". When it comes to things like baseball and football, I can't even catch a cold.

Through exhausting effort, I clawed my way semi-upright. My throbbing fingers barely gripping the grimy edge of the runaway monstrosity, I frantically looking around, trying to find a savior. As if in answer to an unspoken silent prayer or, more likely, in answer to my loudly spoken scream, Kevin's "classic" 1983 GMC van rolled up alongside my dumpster.

Kev originally wanted to make the old beater a replica of the *A-Team* van, but he settled on plain white in order to protect his goofy secret identity. Actually, his first choice for a classic ride had been a 1986 Ferrari Testarossa, like the one Sonny Crockett drove in the last two seasons of *Miami Vice*, but Kev couldn't stuff his illegal television broadcasting gear and the instant hot water heater into a Ferrari.

I immediately recognized the van as Kevin's because of the five small aerodynamically correct bumps for antennae housing on the roof. Also, when I looked really closely, I spotted one of the many micro spray nozzles positioned all over the windowless exterior. He imbedded each nozzle in a miniaturized, one-sixteenth-inch-wide, low-drag NACA duct. The nozzles and ducts, of his own design, were the same white as the van, rendering them essentially invisible. His ducts had no aerodynamic function and I never asked if they served some other function, but he received pleasure from thinking of them as stealth rocket nozzles. Because that would be cool.

I can't believe I still remember his stupid home-made bumper stickers:

I ♡ Board Meetings

And...

The Pirate is Watching

The passenger side window slid down and Kevin turned his head to look out at me. He Smiled, and crooned, "Hi sailor. Want a lift?"

Ah ha! Now I knew precisely who to blame for being trapped in a gigantic garbage can: Kevin. As usual. Guilty as bare feet on a snow day. I yelled, "Ox, you were supposed to hold onto this thing."

"Sorry," he shrugged. "Minor distraction."

"I saw her, Kev. She had *major* distractions."

The dumpster and my anger both gained momentum as I coalesced into my frequent state of dread. He glanced at the end of the street, down at the bottom of the hill, and said, "Hey, listen, do you want a ride or not?"

I thought it important that I be clearly understood over the annoying clanging and banging of the dirty dumpster, so I screamed, "Kevin Oxley, I wouldn't ride with you if my life depended on it!"

"I think it does," he smirked, wriggling his eyebrows toward the guardrail above the parking lot of death.

I cleverly responded, "Aiieee!"

Jumping as high as panic permitted, I grabbed his passenger-side rearview mirror, grunged myself up out of the dumpster, and threw myself toward the van's open window. He made a hard-left turn. The passenger door flew wide open with me stuck half-way through the window while my stomach tried to get a grip on the windowsill.

"Aiieee!"

He jerked the steering wheel to the right, making the passenger door fly back and slam shut. The impact shot me down to the van floor. The van roared up Arroyo Drive, tight roping the edge of the cliff.

The dumpster splintered through the guardrail and soared out over the canyon. Seconds later it made a trash landing in the parking lot. Twisting metal, breaching welds, and shattered wheels screeched like a tortured metallic creature.

My face pancaked on the floorboard and my feet terror-twitched out the window. Kevin looked down at me with a quizzical stare and mildly said, "Theo, you look tense."

"Aiieee!"

With my nose still pressed against the floor mat, I mumble-shouted, "I could have been killed trying to save this stupid old record album from that dumpster for you." Spitting out floor mat morsels, I shook the '60s vintage vinyl at him ... *Woman, Woman* by Gary Puckett and the Union Gap. At least I think I shook it in his direction. Having only one eye available, I was forced to squint sideways past my nose and crumpled corn chip bags. I couldn't really use the eye stuck to the transmission hump.

"It's a classic," He said indignantly.

Then, his demeanor softened. He seemed to finally grasp the enormity of his best friend lying face down on the floor of his van, terrified. A look of genuine concern flooded over him as he said, "You didn't scratch the vinyl, did you?"

"That record has considerably fewer scratches than my face."

"Oh, good."

2

GREATER LOS ANGELES — A COUPLE OF HOURS LATER

The rest of the runaway dumpster day did go better. For a while.

Being the first Sunday of the month, it was our "hit all the hobby shops in L.A. day". I left my car in the Pas Tech staff parking lot and we were on the road again. First stop: Burbank's House of Hobbies for me (I collect little HO-scale automobiles). Then, Toys R Us for Kevin (he collects Hot Wheels). For a late lunch we grabbed street tacos from a Victory Boulevard roach coach before Kev headed us across the girth of L.A.

About an hour later he dropped me at Allied Model Trains in Culver City while he continued on to Los Angeles International Airport (LAX) to do his latest good deed.

He didn't return on schedule (what a surprise) and my long wait in the hobby shop became awkward. There are only so many stories one can share about little toy cars before the hobby shop natives get restless. I retreated to the Coffee Kettle Café, about a block down Sepulveda Boulevard. There I sat, sucking up room temperature backwash in my formerly iced mocha coffee, worrying about being late for my mandatory participation in "Sunday at Seven".

Once he finally picked me up, I remained quiet as he drove west toward the 405. Then his customary, incessant, punching of radio buttons began. I delivered a highly caffeinated complaint. "I don't know why I let you get me into these things. I am going to be late for work—again. I do not appreciate it when you make me late for work—again."

"Well now, Theophilus Spivak," Kevin said, "in the words of esteemed country philosophers, Alan Jackson and Jimmy Buffet..." he sang, "...it's five o'clock somewhere."

I said, "It is five o'clock right here. Right now. In Los Angeles. And you can't possibly get me from here all the way across the megalopoli to Pasadena by six-thirty o'clock, at which point I will officially be late. And anyway, with all due respect to Mr. Jackson and Mr. Buffet, that song makes absolutely no sense. It cannot be half past twelve where they are drinking and also be five o'clock somewhere else, unless somewhere else is an obtuse mango republic where they do time zones in half-hour increments."

"Relax, Theo," He said soothingly, "Being late is relative, is it not? For example, if your job was in Pago Pago, you'd be really early."

"My job is not in Pago Pago and the only thing relative about this is that you're my relative. I think I need to change families. You're just not responsible."

Sudden silence. Kevin sucked in a slow, deep, ragged breath followed by a hushed, deep exhale. His lips quivered. His eyes moistened. He rolled the back of his head on his shoulder muscles and sniffed.

"Very well," he said. "Let's talk about responsible. A Lufthansa jumbo jet relied on me to transport Ms. Heidi von

Kleinschmidt to international flight 633 no later than 4:47 p.m." His voice became shaky. "Her presence at LAX being critical, I am proud to say I delivered her on time."

Even though I had seen his crushed psyche act before, he still almost sucked me in. He's good. I studied him closely. Kevin's core is too honest to maintain a poker face. I detected an infinitesimal curl of a smile.

So, I protested. "She's a flight attendant. You took her to work."

"Hah. True. Oh ... but Theophilus ... a gorgeous, five-foot-nine, strawberry blonde flight attendant *mit grossen blauen Augen.*"

Yeah, okay, so she had big blue eyes. Normally, I would have accepted Fräulein von Kleinschmidt as a compelling argument for making anyone late, but not at that point—against my will—again. I looked straight at him, past my now permanently floor mat-warped nose. "You don't get it, do you? *Some* people have goals. *Some* people have jobs. And the way this day is going I will soon be able to say that I am *some* person who *used* to have a job."

He pondered for a few moments, tapping his fingers on the van's unique steering wheel. Kev personally rescued the steering wheel—actually a control yoke—from the skeletal remains of a 1943 C-47 "Gooney Bird" cargo plane he found while four-wheeling in the upper Mojave. The gray WW2-era "Bakelite" (polyoxybenzylmethylenglycolanhydride) wheel was cool, but, mostly, it allowed Kev to pretend he was flying.

"I do have a goal," he said, with a tone somewhat noble. "My goal is to... have no goal." Then, pushing a button on the steering wheel, he firmly announced, "DONUTS." A map showing all donut shops within ten miles of our location instantly projected inside the windshield.

Kevin's Head-Up Display (HUD)—his own design—synched with a military grade GPS unit in one of those aero bumps on the van roof. He voice-controlled it via the new wireless connection technology called Bluetooth which was then only a year old (and not fully reliable). Kevin worked out the bugs and perfected his own Bluetooth connection.

At Kev's voice-activated option, his display could project the then new GPS navigation, weather alerts, mechanical diagnostics, and reruns of *Scooby-Doo*. Few vehicles in the entire world could do any one of those things in 2003, and none could do them all. Except Kev's van. Everything in his van was faster and more advanced than NASA. In the hot-rod, rock 'n' roll lyrics of Brian Wilson from *The Beach Boys*, "If it had a set of wings, man, I know it could fly." Kevin's van may not have even needed wings.

He created his super-sized head-up display in our apartment garage right after being fired from Rocket Force Laboratories (RFL). He developed it for three reasons:

1. He was bored
2. He liked high definition anything
3. He really, really liked donuts

I clearly stated, "No, I do not want a donut."

"Hmm, perhaps you're right," he said. "This late in the day we need more substantial nourishment. BIG MAC."

Little golden arches flashed in convenient locations all over the floating map.

"No. I do not want a burger."

He cheerfully asked, "Emergency root canal?"

My face scrunched. "What?"

He announced, "HAPPY TEETH."

Instantly, little "happy teeth" icons zoomed up in front of the windshield showing dental office sites throughout Los Angeles. I shook my head and looked out the side window.

"Relax, Theophilus," He said. "Cryogenate, dude."

"What?"

"Get fridged."

"Excuse me?"

"Chill."

I nodded. "Chill. Okay, chill I understand. I used to watch *Miami Vice* too, when we were in high school. Chill it is. Right. Okay. Uh huh. Chill." I continued looking out the side window, resolute to never ride with him again.

After a few more minutes of his evasive fun, he finally gave me his usual faint apology. I accepted his peace offering: a cup of hot cocoa delivered from the dashboard dispenser. It went well with the donuts he forced on me.

He glanced at me, smiled, and said, "Everything's chicken?"

I could never stay mad at him for very long. We had had too much history and too much fun. I snorted, "Yes ... everything's chicken." We learned that quaint phrase from our paternal grandfather when we were quite young. It just meant everything's okay.

We moved eastward—microcosmically slow—on the ten. (I-10) Depending on which direction one is traveling that's either the San Bernardino Freeway or the Santa Monica Freeway.) I cannot understand why anyone still refers to that time of day as "rush hour". A stupid misnomer like "rush hour" makes me anxious. But then, just about everything makes me anxious.

I calmed down a bit, only wheezing occasionally, while we crawled along with thousands of other cars. Half an hour later, somewhat content with my fate, we were finally moving in the general direction of Pasadena as Kevin sang along with Gary Puckett's *Young Girl* on "K-Gold", the oldies radio station.

The extremely hot weather combined with the van's very cold air conditioning and excellent hot chocolate epitomized my Cali bliss. I also loved driving through freezing winter at Lake Arrowhead with my convertible top down and the heater turned up full blast. Or being on the beach looking up through palm trees at snow on top of the mountains. Except for corrupt politicians, I loved L.A. I would be at least an hour late for Dr. Weksler's seven o'clock Pas Tech lab demonstration but... life was good. Dr. Weksler knew Kevin by reputation. He would, hopefully, be understanding.

"How do I get a refill?" I asked.

Through a mouthful of donut, it sounded like he mumbled, "D7."

I pressed D7 on the old, but newly rechromed Wurlitzer jukebox control panel mounted in the dashboard. A mirrored ball and disco lights dropped from the van ceiling and hung over our heads. It scared me.

"Aiieee!"

I hadn't seen that trick before. Weird, but considering Kevin, not surprising. Unfortunately, when I pushed that D7 button, *Stayin' Alive* by the Bee Gees overrode *Young Girl* on the twenty-three-speaker audio system. A Kevin crisis. He liked Gary Puckett more than donuts.

"Wrong button," he mumbled. "<u>B</u>7, not <u>D</u>7."

I tried again. The disco nightmare retracted, and a panel whirred open in the dashboard revealing two dispenser nozzles. I refilled my cocoa and added extra whipped cream.

As the song began to fade out on the radio, the DJ did his back-announce, "That's Gary Puckett and the Union Gap with *Young Girl*. Ooowhee that is one moldy oldie. That girl must be at least seventy by now. Hey Puckett, it's okay. She's a seasoned citizen."

Kevin scowled. "Sacrilege," he mumbled forcefully, spraying donut drops.

The DJ continued his spiel, "It's five thirty-seven. This is kindly beloved Uncle Earl LeRoy Trout the Third and you're drivin' the Trout Route, with more on the upcoming Rock Legends concert at the Hollywood Bowl—"

Swallowing quickly, Kevin pointed to the radio and shouted, "Gotta go to that!"

The DJ continued, "—starring Three Dog Night, Paul Revere and The Raiders, and these guys... Simon and Garfunkel... from 1966, with... *I Am a Rock*. Don't take me for granite."

"What?" Kevin yelled. "Excuse me? Aren't we forgetting somebody? Aren't we forgetting the greatest living voice in rock 'n' roll history? Mr. Gary Puckett."

Kevin's eyes glazed over as he slipped into a different reality. I had seen that look before. First, his face reflected a faraway serenity. Then, his jaw jutted out. Eyes became fearsome piercing rays. I would swear his eyebrows became bushy when he said in a low, gravelly voice, "Avast there matie."

I moaned, "Oh, no."

"Somebody is just going to have to point out the error of their ways."

I drooped into my seat and dropped my face into my hands.

He chanted, "Yo-ho-ho-ho," and radically dived into an unannounced exit from the freeway. I straight-armed the dashboard with my left hand and gripped the back of the seat with my right, keeping me somewhat secure as he juked northeastward on Crenshaw Boulevard, heading toward Hollywood. I knew our next stop would be the pinnacle of Mount Wilson (no relation to Brian).

Like a true L.A. native, Kevin optimized the ever-changing traffic flow patterns by heading north on Rossmore Avenue past Wilshire Country Club and "The Ravenswood" (Mae West's apartment building), then deftly avoiding Sunset Boulevard tourism by taking Fountain Avenue east, eventually winding his way to California State Highway 2, whose always-empty five lanes dead-end in the small residential neighborhood of Silver Lake.

Powerful political forces had prevented Highway 2 (the "Beverly Hills Freeway") from ever being built through or even *under* Beverly Hills. Quietly, in 1975, the "pliable" California legislature canceled the project after one-hundred-and-ninety-eight million dollars had already been spent (six-hundred-ninety million in 2003 dollars). The rest of the freeway that was supposed to go all the way to the Pacific Ocean is still unfinished. And forgotten.

Angered by the radio station, Kevin pounded his fist against the dashboard, which dislodged the disco ball.

"Aiieee!"

The mirrored silver ball rotated above my frightened brain, immersing us in twirling, multi-colored, disco lights as

Kevin The Pirate augered the van through traffic. He growled along with the Bee Gees loudly singing, "Ah, Ah, Ah, Ah, Stayin' Alive, Stayin' Alive".

And then he snarled, "Arrgh".

That made my incarceration official.

3

ANOTHER HOUR LATER

Our trek ... north on the two freeway, then the two-ten, passing the backside of Jet Propulsion Laboratory, and then up Angeles Crest Highway, added at least an hour to Kevin's new crusade. No hope now. I would be conspicuously absent from Dr. Weksler's Sunday at Seven demonstration.

* * * * *

If one suddenly awoke in the middle of the antenna farm on top of Mt. Wilson, the not-of-this-world surroundings would be unnerving. Scores of radio and television broadcast towers, some rising up more than two hundred feet into the thin mountain air, grow out of a thick forest of pine and cedar. They share turf with the domes of Mt. Wilson observatory. Close by, an old hundred-foot-long, narrow, aluminum structure stretches across the mountainside. Scientist George Ellery Hale erected that odd vision of the future in 1904 with the aid of mule teams that drug the arcane Snow Solar Telescope up the mountain. The unusual name (Snow) did not refer to cold white stuff. It honored Helen Snow, the lady who donated construction monies.

All this strangeness huddles together in a mathematically perfect, chaotic maze of red, white, and black steel beams, silver cables, and blinking red lights in an area smaller than two football fields. All bathed in the eerie yellow glow of low-pressure sodium lamps. *Star Trek* should be so lucky.

* * * * *

Arriving at the pinnacle just after sunset, Kevin parked in a smallish forest clearing less than a quarter mile from the tower field. We had a clear line-of-sight to the top of the huge Channel Eight broadcast tower.

A small rise between us and the road down below meant anyone at the tower footing who happened to look up the mountainside would not see us parked in the clearing. Being, as I am, cautious (read: panicky), I scoped out the situation by standing on tippy toes on a picnic table.

A dark gray sedan sat with its motor running, just outside the antenna farm chain-link perimeter fence. Normally, this would generate enough concern for Kev to terminate his "mission". But this time, he continued his Pirate passion.

Kev popped open a utility panel on the right rear of the van, reached in, and snap-released a hand crank. As he wheeled it counterclockwise, things began to whirr and click. The van's large, triple-hinged, clamshell back doors ominously opened like the covers on an ICBM silo. Together, we deployed the stabilizer struts below the van, and then manually slid out, rotated, and extended the master control panel into operational locus. The whole process required an anxious, fear-inducing (for me) six minutes. He fine-tuned knobs and sliding potentiometers, then glanced up at the

Channel Eight tower. "Yep," he said, "We should be close enough to transmit a clear signal."

I replied, "And commit at least thirteen of my favorite federal felonies."

"Naw. Nine, tops."

He threw the last auxiliary control board switch. Two segmented roof panels split apart and slithered down into the hollow sides of the van. Our spiffy metalized fabric uplink dish unfurled as it rose through the roof opening. Yes, I said *our*. I am discomfited to admit I did occasionally provide technical expertise for Kevin's machinations.

Shaking my head, I said, "Do you really want to go to prison? You didn't even like graduate school."

Too late. A beaming sound which would have been perfect for a bad black and white sci-fi movie told me our dish locked onto the Channel Eight tower.

Kevin put on his "instant pirate" costume, complete with tri-cornered hat, black eye patch, and gold tooth.

He pontificated. "Theophilus my friend, somebody, somewhere must take a stand for what is good and true. I view this as not only our God-given, inalienable right, but as a solemn obligation. If you're not willing to stand with me on this issue, just say so right now."

"I'm not willing to stand with you on this issue."

Honest insincerity oozed from his lips. "My dear friend, thank you for being so refreshingly candid." He slammed a large stuffed parrot onto his shoulder and growled, "Now get behind that TV camera."

In his best pirate voice (the one that sounded like he gargled with Drano) he added, "It's show time!"

I counted him down. "In five — four — three ..." and cued him with the correct finger.

* * * * *

Dr. Gil, the quirky, mustachioed, KZLA Channel Eight weatherman, blessed with abundant gesticulation, overacted the forecast on the "Early Evening News Zoo".

"Hot and dry again!" Dr. Gil put on a sad face. "Sorry folks, still no rain." He jumped up and down. "We're having another one of the worst droughts in California history. The rainy season just passed and nobody—." The audio went dead. The TV screens of everyone watching Channel Eight went black.

A second later, Kevin's image and gnarly voice commandeered the Channel Eight broadcast signal. "Avast there maties Pirate TV is on the air. We have another wrong to right."

All over Southern California, people shouted, "Hey! The Pirate's taking over again!" Anyone near any television anywhere, crowded in to get a view, everyone wondering the same thing: "What's he up to this time?"

"This is our biggest challenge yet." The Pirate snarled. "This relates to a genuine American hero."

Southern Californians gasped with anticipation.

The Pirate continued, "It has come to my attention that Gary Puckett is excluded from the upcoming Rock Legends concert at the Hollywood Bowl."

All the patrons in all the inns in all the land gasped and grumbled, "Oh, no." and "How dare they?" and "That's not right." Even those who never heard of Gary Puckett were offended. Such was the power of The Pirate.

On all those TV screens The Pirate growled, "Do you know who *is* booked for this concert? Three Dog Night. Give me a freaking break ... there's only one dog left. I ask you; how can you have a Legends concert when you leave out Gary Puckett, the greatest living legend of them all?"

People everywhere nodded at each other, saying, "You can't do that." — and — "That's just wrong." — and — "Shame on them."

The Pirate said, "That's false advertising."

The people said, "That's right."

The Pirate said, "This is worse than a wardrobe malfunction."

The people shouted, "Amen." — and — "Preach it, brother."

The Pirate invoked the federal government, shouting, "Where is the F.C.C. when we need them? This must be reported to the Federal Communications Commission."

All over the southland, thousands of Pirate fans smiled their happy conspiratorial smiles and loudly sang their unification chant (a small portion of the chorus from the Beatles all-time third biggest hit): "Yeah ... yeah ... yeah. Yeah ... yeah ... yeah."

Up on Mt. Wilson, where I still manned the video camera, my terminal case of panic took root. *It's not enough for him to simply do a highly illegal bootleg TV broadcast. broadcast? Must he also ask for help from the F.C.C.?*

I whispered to Kevin, "You are a lunatic."

I knew that, as in the past, people everywhere were grousing along with The Pirate. I knew they all pumped their fists and welcomed the new cause.

I checked my pulse and wondered if Folsom Prison had a golf course.

4

SAME TIME — DOWNTOWN LOS ANGELES

In the dreary ninth floor men's room of the Federal building in the City of Angels, Federal Communications Commission Under-Assistant West Coast Field Director Leonard Ostermann practiced his sneer. At age forty-seven, Ostermann had already spent almost five decades taking himself too seriously. Five foot-six with thinning male pattern red hair and matching freckles on his pasty white face, Leonard (don't ever call him "Lenny") weighed-in at only one-hundred-forty-seven pounds. Still, that was heavier than his voice, which often cracked with a nasal squeak. Instead of crisp, standard-issue, bureaucracy blue suits, Leonard preferred what he considered "old school private eye" ... baggy, wrinkled, brown suits.

He looked sternly into the eyes facing him in the washroom mirror, whipped out his badge, curled his lip and said, in his wimpy voice, "Leonard Ostermann, Federal Communications Commission."

He shook his head. *No ... not quite right.* He returned the badge to his inside suit coat pocket, paused, posed, and whipped out the badge again. "Field Director Ostermann, FCC." *Hmm ... not menacing enough.*

Staring himself down in the mirror, ol' brown suit assumed the shooting stance he saw in so many movies. His body turned sideways, to be an even smaller target, he held his badge in both hands with both arms straight out, aiming at himself. He curled his lip excessively, well past the Elvis zone, added a raised eyebrow, and shouted, "Federal Communications Commission, Ostefer Offerman. No. I mean, Officer Otterman. No. No. No." *Okay ... calm and cool now ...* "Ostefer Officeman. Ahhh."

A flushing toilet reminded Leonard that he did not have a private, ceramic-coated rehearsal hall. Embarrassed, he quickly began smoothing wild hairs in his severe comb-over. A smiling, gray-haired bureaucrat emerged from a stall and went to the sink. Trying to be invisible, Ostermann shuffled backwards to the stalls.

The gray-haired bureaucrat snickered loudly, "By the way, I liked version number four ... *Otterman.* Hah." Leonard slammed his stall door shut. The jolly, gray-haired, bureaucrat laughed hysterically all the way down the hall.

In the FCC offices at the end of the hallway, Ostermann's two elderly secretaries, Cleo and Berlene, were charmed by The Pirate's illicit broadcast on a large projection TV.

"Unity is the key," Kevin decreed. "This is a call to arms."

Cleo flirted with the TV. "Oooo, you can call me to your arms anytime, you little outlaw you." She leaned toward Berlene, "I always did go for the mysterious type."

Berlene gave Cleo the stink eye "Cleo, you know how long Mr. Ostermann's been trying to catch that whack-a-doo."

"Alright, Berlene, alright. Just keep your teeth in."

Cleo grabbed the red key hanging from her desk and unlocked the drawer labeled, PIRATE EMERGENCY ONLY.

The empty emergency drawer contained only a red pushbutton. Knowing the tiresome commotion certain to follow, Cleo sighed. "And the proverbial poo-poo hits the federal fan."

With a dramatic flourish she pushed the button. A blinding red light flashed above every door on the floor, including the men's room. Ostermann rushed out of his stall, washed his hands, flattened his comb-over and, stumbling with belt and zipper, ran down the hall toward the FCC suite.

"Where is he?" Leonard demanded.

"Channel Eight," Berlene said.

Leonard high-stepped it to the dull gray melamine-paneled conference room. Right behind him, Cleo carried the overstuffed file folder stamped EYES ONLY and labeled PIRATE.

Forty-seven television screens covered two walls of the conference room. Each set monitored a different local independent television station, network affiliate, or cable system.

Leonard pointed at the KZLA-TV Channel Eight monitor and shouted, "I'm gonna get you, mister." Grabbing the master remote control unit, he switched every screen in the room to Channel Eight while simultaneously launching ten DVD and VHS recorders. Staring at the entire bank of monitors, he stuck his left arm straight out behind him and said, "Cleo, get me—"

"—your file on The Pirate." She interrupted and stuck the fat folder in his hand.

Leonard turned on the audio for all forty-seven television sets. Kevin's Pirate rant could be heard throughout the entire FCC headquarters in a weird, multi-tracked voice. "... to bring forth upon this concert a new notion. A notion conceived and dedicated to the proposition that Gary Puckett is a legend."

Leonard muted all forty-seven televisions, shook the file folder at them and, with a great deal of personal satisfaction, spoke directly to all forty-seven. "I've got enough here to put you away for twenty years. You are going down."

For dramatic emphasis, he then tried to lower his voice one octave for each word as he said, "Way, way, way down." His voice wasn't deep enough, and it cracked on the third "way". He did an irritated prissy shake and started over again at a higher range. This time he got all the words out but fell considerably short of being dramatic with his semi-squeaky "Way, way, way, down." Sipping helium would be an improvement.

He waved an accusatory finger at all the screens. "Hah. Mister Pirate you are med deet. No. You're dead beat. No, no, no." He paused, composed himself, concentrated really hard, and slowly said, "You ... are ... dead ... meat. Hah." He sneered and growled. Squeakily.

Because all forty-seven TVs in the conference room were muted, Leonard did not hear The Pirate shout, "Can I count on your support?"

Mr. Ostermann also did not hear the thousands of Southern Californians who cheered and sang, "Yeah... yeah... yeah." to their televisions. Nor did he hear the hundreds of thousands of motorists—whose favorite radio stations carried the audio portion of The Pirate's broadcast—as they lowered their car windows and cheerily sang to each other, "Yeah ... yeah ... yeah."

Nor did Leonard realize that "Yeah ... yeah ... yeah." was now the battle hymn of disenfranchised Gary Puckett fans, as well as the million left-coasters who never heard of Gary Puckett but who really enjoyed supporting irreverent, underdog, lunatic-fringe conspiracies. Television station managers prayed for The Pirate to hijack their station because he got bigger ratings than a high-speed freeway chase. Southern Californians loved their Pirate.

Cleo and Berlene watched the very small TV built into the cabinet between their desks. The Pirate said, "Will you embrace my cause?"

Cleo looked at the TV dreamily. "Oh, I embrace it, baby." Then they both softly sang, "Yeah ... yeah ... yeah."

5

I met Kevin on our first day of kindergarten. Amazingly, (considering all that happened over the years) we were still friends in 2003. We went in and out of each other's lives for twenty-something years, sometimes not seeing each other for weeks or months, because as an adult he kept going places unidentified. Whenever we got together again, we just picked up right where we left off, as if our lives had simply been recorded and fast forwarded.

The friendship had a rocky start that first day of kindergarten. He convinced me the pink finger-paint was bubblegum flavor and the blue tasted like a raspberry slushy and eating them both at the same time would be the most wonderfullest thing ever in the whole world. Not.

Ox always felt it acceptable to push my buttons and bend my boundaries, just because we were cousins. He got away with it in three different decades so, I guess blood is thicker than finger paint.

With help from Kevin's parents, my mom and dad moved from South Central (not a great place to do a childhood) to South Pasadena at the start of our high school freshman year. Back then, I wore small round-lensed glasses because I thought they were cool. But I'm a geek and I seldom actually know what cool looks like. And I'm hard of seeing.

Kev, the good-looking, fun-loving, total babe magnet, quarterback of the South Pasadena Tigers *varsity* football team (as a *freshman!*) took me under his wing. Being his cousin meant I got to hang with him on the sidelines. Being his best friend meant I became eligible for female fallout. A blessed wingman.

An athletic rarity, Kevin had world-class natural talent without an ego issue. To him, football was just a game. He played the game so well in fact that, at age fourteen, he was already being scouted by USC, UCLA, and several U's to be named at a later date.

However, in the fall semester of our South Pasadena High School sophomore year we both took advanced placement physical science as an elective. (We were both brainiacs). That ended the Ox's athletic career. Hooked on physics, he hung 'em up and never looked back. After high school, we roomed together at M.I.T. on full *academic* scholarships.

Even as adults in 2003 He and I were still very much alike in every way. Well, except that he was tall, muscular, and athletic. Other than that, we were twins.

Oh, and I was black (on my mother's side) and he was white. I was dark mocha with chocolate eyes. He was vanilla over blue. We still are.

Basically, a good guy, Kevin practices honesty, kindness to strangers, and support of the underdog. He has a sense of adventure and a sense of humor. But no sense. He responds to his own drummer who has a bizarre cadence, which frequently impacts my own fine and lovely, perfectly normal day. Like, for example, the Mount Wilson Sunday surprise.

* * * * *

Still manning the video camera in Kevin's van, I became increasingly uneasy about his exceptionally long bootleg broadcast. Given enough time, the FCC would establish our location. My usually sweaty palms had broadened their coverage pattern to include all extremities.s

Kevin The Pirate shouted at the camera, "Are you with me?"

"Absolutely not," I said, quietly.

The Pirate continued, "We must get Gary Puckett into that rock legends concert at the Hollywood Bowl. Send protest letters to the radio stations. Boycott the Hollywood Bowl. Girlcott the Hollywood Bowl. Most importantly ..." He leaned solemnly into the camera. "Never ... never ... ever start your lawn mower before ten o'clock on Saturday morning. Thank you." Then he growled his signature closing, "Yo ho ho and a battle of fun."

Kevin dragged his index finger across his throat as a signal for me to "cut". I hit the kill switch. Both metaphors scared me.

Kevin stared at me, beaming in his own glory, seeking my never-ending adulation.

I stared right back. "A verrrry long speech, Kev."

Thoroughly immersed in his performance afterglow, he ever-so-slowly removed the pirate costume. Meanwhile, I scrambled to pack up equipment and get us on the road. He just kept beaming and basking.

"Our finest hour," he said, "We have just begun another great service to all mankind."

"*We* is one of those *group* words, Kevin. I don't want to be part of your *we*."

"Deny it if you must, Theophilus Spivak, but you have been an integral component of all The Pirate's great humanitarian campaigns."

"Like, bring back the McRib sandwich? That was heart-warming."

He stepped out the back of the van to join me in the peaceful forest. "Hey, we got the people Classic Coke, didn't we?"

"Well ... yeah." I had to agree that was a major societal accomplishment. "But I am seriously worried, Ox. You've never jammed a transmission for that long before."

He reassured me. "Nothing can possibly go wrong."

BOOOM! A huge explosion threw us both off our feet.

I started to stand up, but Kev shouted, "Get down!"

I ducked just as a seven-foot-long, flaming section of the Channel Eight tower sizzled over our heads and speared the trunk of a sugar pine. THWUMP!

"Incoming." he shouted. We both flattened out and covered our heads with our hands. *Yeah, like our hands are gonna save our brains.*

ZOOSH!

A four-foot section of black and red tower strut flew over us at what would have been gut level had we not been pancaked on the ground. WHANK! It impaled the side of the van. A couple feet remained sticking out.

The van rocked as we staggered up and looked down at the Channel Eight tower, just in time to see it split in two. The top hundred feet broke off and crushed the nearby maintenance warehouse. It exploded just as the bottom half of the tower fell across the road like a redwood in a forest fire. Huge fireballs rolled up out of the warehouse and shot into space. Flames at the tower base crackled forty feet into the air.

Kevin said, "Aiieee."

I replied, "Aiieee!"

We closed up the van quicker than possible. Kev removed his Pirate gear and dove onto the driver's side. I clutched the bottom of the seat and stared straight ahead, not daring to look either right of left for fear of seeing something else we might have destroyed. Pinecones and forest floor debris flew up from behind the rear wheels as the van spun out of the clearing and down onto the mountain road, sidestepping flaming wreckage.

Through sheer willpower I calmed myself to the point where my wheezing was not quite so annoying. "Kevin," I wheezed, "How ... did we ... blow up ... the tower?"

Deep in thought, he stared into the rearview mirror at the blazing rubble behind us. "Technically, there is no way we could have caused that explosion."

"I know that, and you know that. I don't think the tower got the text."

"You're a scientist, give me a scientific explanation."

I wheezed.

"You're absolutely right," He said. "We didn't do it. We have nothing to worry about."

Through clenched teeth I rasped out, "Step - On - The - Gas."

Accelerating down the mountain, I finally dared to look back. Most everything at the antenna farm consisted of metal and did not burn. Some flames could still be seen but, nothing like the original conflagration. Then I semi-panicked.

"Oh, my gosh, Kevin," I shouted. "We're in a forest."

"Well, duh. Clever observation, Doctor Watson." He looked at me with his right thumb and forefinger making an "L" in front of his forehead.

"No—Kev—we're in a dry, brushy, Southern California forest on a hot summer night."

"And ...?" He still didn't get it.

"And there is a *fire*.

"Oh ... yeah." He got it. He tossed me his cell phone. "Call it in." I got as far as dialing nine-one before he yanked the phone away from me.

He held his palm up to me. "No. Wait."

"What do you mean?" I scolded. Kevin was an Eagle Scout for God's sake. The man had integrity. I could not believe he would fail to report a potential forest fire.

"Not the cell phone." He pointed to the microphone hanging on the side of the center console. "Use the CB. There's no caller I.D."

I just finished up with the Forest Service when the dark gray sedan that had parked next to the tower roared past us on the right shoulder, almost sideswiping the van. Kev reflexively jerked the steering wheel to the left, but that segment of Channel Eight tower sticking out the side of the van degraded its already top-heavy handling. He overcorrected to the right. The van rose up on two tires, on the verge of rolling over. We slid way out onto the shoulder of the highway, fishtailing in the loose gravel along the brink of an eight-hundred-foot drop. We did a three-sixty, then a one-eighty in the opposite direction.

Oh my God. X-games in a van.

Ox barely bumped and jumped the van back onto asphalt. The dark gray sedan continued to rush down the mountain in front of us. I squeezed the bridge of my nose and blinked. From my angle the driver appeared to be a giant orange.

I shrieked, "That maniac—that idiot—that—that —that thing—it—he—it—could have killed us."

6

Peeled and burnt rubber made a permanent record of our fishtails on the asphalt as Ox regained control and pursued the hit-and-run bad guys down Mt. Wilson. Though tricked out with a genuine 1957 DeSoto Adventurer, 345-horsepower Hemi, Kevin's van was still a van, not a Ferrari. Hairpin mountain curves are not the forte of a custom van stuffed with electronics. And a broken section of TV tower.

We couldn't catch the dark gray sedan, but because Kevin drove like a maniac (well-practiced), we kept its headlights and/or taillights in sight on the switchbacks below. Each time I spotted the car through dark tree silhouettes, something troubled me. JDLR. (Just Don't Look Right.) But I couldn't figure out what.

At the base of the mountain, Angeles Crest Highway levels out at the twin upper-crust bedroom communities of La Cañada/Flintridge. We knew traffic lights, crosswalks, and such would slow down the gray sedan and, eventually, we'd catch up somewhere on the streets above Jet Propulsion Laboratory. The evil sideswiping car slowed for an intersection and Kev closed the gap. I did a double-take and realized what hadn't looked right. The car we were chasing was red. It was supposed to be gray.

"Give it up Ox man," I said. "We're chasing the wrong car."

"The heck we are. Those jerks almost killed us. Hang on." He accelerated even as the criminal car braked for a stop sign.

"Kevin, that car is red. The car that sideswiped us was dark gray."

"Low-pressure sodium, Theo."

I thought he was making an obscure Star Trek reference which I couldn't recall. That troubled me because, I never want to forget any obscure Star Trek references. Then, I got it. Those icky, glowing yellow, low-pressure sodium lamps at the Mt. Wilson antenna farm shift the color spectrum. Red becomes dark gray. So, chasing a red car is what we were supposed to be doing!

We would eventually learn (after becoming their prisoners) that Mikhail, the short, round, bald man in the orange jumpsuit, who looked like a giant orange, drove the red getaway sedan. Bahadur, the dirty thin man in the passenger seat appeared to be in charge.

If you've ever tried to follow badly translated instructions in order to assemble an item manufactured in China (e.g., a barbecue, a model car) then you would have felt right at home with the strange syntax of Bahadur and Mikhail. As Kevin pulled up beside the car, Bahadur shouted to Mikhail, "Down slow. Attract the attention to us selfs do we not want."

Kev pointed his finger out his window right at Bahadur's head. "Hey you."

Bahadur and Mikhail snapped their wide-eyed faces toward Kevin.

Kevin shouted, "You almost killed us. That's a moving violation—leaving the scene of stupidity."

Bahadur shouted at Mikhail, "You must him lose."

Mikhail slammed on the brakes.

Bahadur slammed into the dashboard.

"Ow! Idiota you are."

We rolled past their car, giving Mikhail an escape opening. He made a hard right, hopped a curb, dug trenches by accelerating across ritzy backyards, and then emerged out onto Foothill Boulevard.

When Kev caught up, Mikhail crashed through a barricade and drove into a night-lighted construction site. The red sedan went in, out, under, around, and through a maze of wooden framework erected on a seemingly never-ending slab of cement. Kevin followed. I held my breath and my armrest. *Oh Lord, what am I doing here?*

The top of the van skimmed under a massive laminated wooden roof truss not yet raised into position. If the truss had been an inch lower, the van would have been peeled open like a sardine can. I exhaled, then held my breath again, and then perfected enhanced wheezing.

Glancing around, Kevin murmured, "Hmm, I didn't know they were building a shopping mall here." He looked at me. "Good location don't you think?"

I wheezed, profoundly.

A hundred yards ahead, the smarmy sedan roared out of the unfinished mall's wooden skeleton and u-turned to a sliding stop, raising a cloud of sawdust, dirt, and gravel.

"Alright. They want to be reasonable," Kevin said. "Let's talk this out." He slowed down and stopped outside the mall framework.

Mikhail opened his door and stepped out of the car.

"He's got a gun," I yelled. "It's, it's, it's a... uh, an Uzi... uh, AK-47... K-9... one of those things."

Kevin squinted, looking carefully. "No, it's a FAMAS F1. French made. Cheap weapon. Sheet metal body." He curled his nose in disgust and with a French accent, added, "We are not impressed."

Why would I care if bad guys have a cheap gun? Is that a macho man thing I don't get?

Mikhail raised his gun and got into position to fire over his car roof.

Kev flipped open a spring-loaded safety cover on his door armrest, saying, "Hemi don't fail me now."

He pushed a recessed blue button and the nitrous oxide pump did its thing. The van shot off like a bat out of purgatory. The Hemi roar and nitro-boosted RPMs, combined with blue flames shooting out quadruple exhausts, must have surprised Mikhail because he sprayed bullets in non-lethal directions.

Kevin had clocked his van in a mid-eleven-seconds quarter mile at Pomona, with a top speed of 118 mph. This time, his incredible van saved our lives. We dodged a bullet. No... a flock of bullets. The blue flames, by the way, had nothing to do with nitro injection. Just another fun-filled Kevin Oxley movie-style special effect.

Mikhail jumped back into the gangstamobile and Bahadur yelled, "Now go. Now go."

Their right front fender clipped a major supporting player in the construction site drama. That support beam slowly fell over, followed by the entire 2.3 acres of completed wooden mall framing collapsing onto itself like an enormous domino parade. The falling lumber sounded like applause as Bahadur and the giant orange sped away with Bahadur shouting "Idiota! Idiota! Idiota!"

Our van flew over several bags of something and then smacked bottom in a drainage ditch. The jarring blow ejected that chunk of Channel Eight tower. Kev stopped about a block away, shook his head, flipped his hand at the red sedan speeding away, and said, "What a discourteous driver. Probably from New York City."

He picked up his mobile phone, pushed a button, waited three seconds and said, "La Cañada/Flintridge — FAMAS F1 — 31 rounds — Town Car — Autumn Red." He pushed the 'end' button and turned to me. "Everything's okay, Theo. No danger. Don't worry about it. Everything's chicken."

I looked at him, speechless, trying to figure out who he really was.

He shrugged, and said, "What?"

"What? What do you mean, what? What do you know about exotic guns? What was that with the phone call?"

He hit the palm of his hand on his forehead. "Oh, that's right. I am sorry. I never told you. I have a secret identity." He did his Sean Connery voice, "The name is Bond. Kevin Bond, international secret agent and—"

"Ox, what are you doing?"

"Theo, I am pushing your leg. I used to play paintball, remember? And then I moved up to airsoft because the airsoft weapons are way fine, 'cause they're modeled after the real things? And I still read the magazines? And they have military news?"

I remembered. "Yeah, okay."

"Yesterday, I read that sixteen FAMAS F1s were stolen from the Gendarmerie at Sainte-Chapelle in Paris. I recognized the weapon from the pictures in the magazine."

"And the phone call?"

"It's a toll-free public number for reporting suspicious activity. You want the number? I'll text it to you. I was an Eagle Scout, remember? I take civic responsibility seriously."

"And, as a former Eagle Scout, you just happened to know the *precise* color of the sinister sedan?"

"Well, if you must know, the *precise* color is actually Autumn Red Crystal Pearl Coat, special order code BDB17. I am a car freak, remember? I read the new 2003 Lincoln Cartier Town Car brochure last night. EPA estimated *precise* mileage is 17 city, 25 highway. It even has a *precise* 21.3 cubic feet of trunk space which is the *precise* size needed for transporting a *precise* three and a half dead bodies."

"Kevin," I said gently, "please take this in the spirit in which it is offered. DON'T EVER GIVE ME A RIDE TO WORK AGAIN."

He shrugged, crinkled his eyebrows, raised his palms in bewildered innocence and said, "What?"

7

With Kevin deep in thought and me deep in sulk, we did not talk at all on the short drive back to the Pasadena Institute of Technology. He dropped me at the staff parking lot, dimly lit by a solitary streetlamp on the edge of Los Robles Boulevard, far across campus from Pheltor Hall. Then he headed home, leaving me alone in the dark with my Mustang convertible, the only vehicle remaining in the spooky lot.

I bought my Mustang from a little old lady in Pasadena. Seriously. Parked in her rickety old garage was not a shiny new Super Stock Dodge. Nope, instead... a hardly used 1964½ Mustang. It hibernated for twenty-seven years, ever since the little old lady bought it new in '64. She used it only for going to church on Sundays. That's a true thing. Oh, and her Wednesday night Bible study, too.

When I bought it from her in 1992, the odometer showed only 6,318 and six-tenths miles. Imagine, a twenty-seven-year-old—but still brand new—Mustang. All original. It even had the optional color-keyed "pony" interior. Ford called my yellowish-greenish color, Aztec Gold Metallic. Her body still glistened. (The car, not the little old ... never mind).

I bought it for only $573 because that's all I had saved-up by age 17. It was my kinda-sorta high school graduation present.

The little old lady from Pasadena was my grandmother. In 2003, I still had the Stang and, thankfully, I still had grandma in my life. I didn't believe in God, but I did believe in driving granny to church once in a while. Go granny, go.

Widely spaced antique lamps dotted the gloomy campus with diffused circles of pale light. The 1920s acorn-shape frosted globes sitting on fluted green metal lampposts supplied lovely ornamentation but, very little illumination.

Worried and frightened on more levels than usual, and even though it was after nine o'clock, I opted for the slim hope that Sunday at Seven might have run late and I could catch Dr. Weksler still wrapping up at the lab. My being there for his public demonstrations was mandatory for my position as his sole lab assistant.

It'll be okay. I'll just tell him what happened and face the dire consequences. At least I'll be interacting with a somewhat normal human. That'll be a nice change from my previous ten hours. Though, Dr. Weksler has his own deadly issues. Oh my gosh, why do I get all the crazies?

I took a few cautious steps into the dark campus. A loud crackle and pop startled me.

"Aiieee!"

Snapping my head toward the sound, I glimpsed a high-bar Harley downshifting its way south toward Colorado Boulevard. *Great, now I'm going to be attacked by a motorcycle gang.*

Wow. Really dark. I never realized how scary the empty campus could be at night. Charming narrow walkways with delightful shrubbery in the daytime turned into black holes with grotesque creatures at night. Something skittered through the bushes. I reassured myself.

Oh ... it's probably just a cute little bunny or lizard. Ahh ... lizards aren't cute. I don't like lizards!

I made an historic decision to calm my heart rate and be brave, compelling myself to maintain a moderate, self-assured, steady pace. Then I changed my mind and ran as fast as I could.

* * * * *

I had started work at Pas Tech only two weeks earlier, at the beginning of the spring semester. My first assignment was to construct a quaint Midwestern town square for Dr. Francis Noah Weksler, head of the Physics Department. Dr. Weksler, seventy something, had been a full professor at Pas Tech for more than forty years. A "stealth pioneer", he owned one of the formidable brains that helped end the cold war. He still had those giant shoulders upon which several generations of physicists stood.

Six feet tall with angular cheeks, Dr. Weksler closely shaved (0.4 centimeters) his gray beard and any remaining gray hair. Mirrored yellow-lensed sunglasses with white thick plastic frames rode on the shiny skull. The entire "do" went well with his overly dramatic lecture style. The mirrored lenses hid the emotions.

Dr. Weksler's occasional one-hour Sunday night lecture/demonstrations, open to the public, were famous in the San Gabriel Valley. His "showmanship" however, had become hollow in the two months since the Geneva catastrophe, his demeanor now indicating he would rather be anywhere else other than alive.

When DVD player/recorders were introduced in 1997 at a thousand dollars per unit, Dr. Weksler bought two; one for the lab and one for his home office. He archived every lecture, demonstration, and experiment on both DVD and the soon-to-be-antique VHS video tape cassettes. Very helpful for reference. And occasional lawsuits.

* * * * *

Though out-of-breath from running across the dark campus, I felt safer when I arrived at the elaborate beaux-arts west entrance to Pheltor Hall. Not a living soul could be found. Nervously looking around, I spotted an icepick stabbed through the heart of a DVD and into the trunk of the massive twisted oak tree which draped over the building's portico. A hand-scribbled message on the disk read, "Watch it, Theophilus". I didn't know if it was an order or a warning.

Dr. Weksler had a reputation nearly as gnarly as that twisted oak. His strange, wide-open eyes in the yearbook photo made him appear faintly nutso. The quote under his yearbook picture read, "Hell hath no fury like mine."

I unlocked the ornate door, and tread softly toward the back of the wood-floored lecture hall. Echoes of my own footsteps scared me, so I began to run. Which, of course, made the scary echoes louder and faster. *Great. Now I'm chasing myself.*

Slapping the disk into the player, I exhaled and saw what I missed by being late... two dozen attendees—mostly under-performing students trying to notch up extra credit with Dr. Weksler—gawked as a tornado touched down at the far end of Main Street. Dr. Weksler narrated in ominous tones. "The tornado. A violently destructive funnel-shaped cloud that reaches out, grabs, and destroys things created by mere humans."

Dr. Weksler's shiny head and mirrored-yellow sunglasses unexpectedly appeared above the town square; his craggy face almost as large as the entire business district. He loved the drama he created. "A single tornado carries more explosive force than mankind's largest nuclear bomb. Humanity remains absolutely vulnerable to the ultimate WMD... Weather of Mass Destruction."

The tornado was merely eleven inches tall. The small Midwestern town square was the miniature I created inside Dr. Weksler's Norton Chamber. All my years of building model cars and airplanes finally proved useful.

Each side of the Norton Chamber measured a precise two-feet wide by two-feet tall because the Heisenberg Uncertainty Principle suggests that any such containment device must be a near perfect cube in order to maintain control of induced, captive weather. No lid or covering existed on top, due to safety issues associated with absolute suppression. The chamber's sides were clear, constructed from Glasonate, a seven-millimeter-thick, layered, polycarbonate-glass laminate. Robust, bullet resistant Gluconate Glasonate could, in some applications, be considered bullet-*proof*, dependent upon caliber and distance to target.

Dr. Weksler had me mount the Norton Chamber, with my town square inside, atop a scruffy wooden cabinet. He positioned the chamber at the east side of the physics lab, in front of a student seating semi-circle.

In the video, Dr. Weksler manipulated the control panel at the rear of the chamber. The coolest control was the chrome-plated T-bar handle which had been the original automatic transmission floor shifter in my Mustang. I installed a shiny

NOS shifter in my Stang, donating the old one to the control panel.

Leaning backwards from the Norton Chamber to avoid overspray, Dr. Weksler snapped a switch and slowly pushed the T-bar, thereby creating a miniature rain cloud on the opposite side of the small-town square from the tornado. The fascinated audience leaned in for a closer look.

"As you can see," he announced, "creating weather within the synthetic environment of the Norton Chamber is not a problem. However, if we remove the artificial parameters, we can no longer control that weather."

He pulled a lever. The front and side clear Glasonate panels dropped. The tornado and the rain cloud attacked each other, spewing wind and water on everyone within ten feet, each of whom shrieked and grumbled.

"If science learns to control the elements," Dr, Weksler continued, "imagine the benefits to humanity. We can send rain to the wastelands and bring forth abundant crops. Hunger, floods and devastation can be abolished." The entire audience bolted, more interested in getting out and getting dry, than getting lectured. Grasping for attention, he added, "We could insure fresh powder at Aspen during spring break." No reaction.

Over the departing babble, Dr. Weksler loudly squeezed in, "He who commands the weather commands the planet. If anyone sees Mr. Spivak please inform him that his absence is noteworthy."

Clearly, I was in trouble. I immediately sent an obsequious text to Dr. Weksler. (Known on campus as a *WeksText*.)

After an uncomfortable scamper back to my car through the scary dark campus, punctuated by my occasional squeal, I drove home to our South Pasadena apartment. It was late on Sunday night, Kevin's bedroom door was closed, and we both had work in the morning.

I went straight to my room, collapsed on my bed, and stared at the cottage cheese ceiling. Ox apparently had no trouble going to sleep. I couldn't even go to drowsy. I tried counting sheep. No, that's not true. I never count sheep to relax and drift off. Instead, in my mind, I count little cars in my model collection. Or sometimes, molecular formulations. That night, I just kept counting everything that happened during the long, terrifying day. And placing blame. I finally drifted off at one in the morning. Then I awoke at two and started counting again.

Never did get any quality REM that night due to my brain re-runs of Kevin's bootleg Pirate broadcast ... the Channel Eight tower explosion ... the car chase down the mountain ... missing Dr. Weksler's Sunday at Seven ... and Kevin and I stupidly bringing only hot chocolate and a disco ball to the machine gun fight.

8

TWO MONTHS EARLIER (CHRISTMAS NIGHT) — WEST LOS ANGELES

Yes, this could have been a prologue, but I don't like prologues. I don't read prologues. I don't think anybody does. I don't even like the concept. I always just want to get right into reading the story instead of wasting time on a prologue. That's because my personality has all the calm and thoughtful qualities of a coffee-drinking Chihuahua.

If you wish to pretend this is a prologue then, go ahead. But it isn't.

* * * * *

L.A. had its own twin towers but, not "skyscrapers", due to the ever-present threat of earthquake. Though only twenty stories tall, Fox Hills Towers were impressive by Southern California standards when constructed in the 1970s. Not far from 20th Century Fox movie studios, the gleaming beige and silver towers faced each other from opposite ends of a hundred-yard-long shiny marble courtyard. A pseudo-religious cult calling themselves the S.O.L. decided to bring one of them down.

The cult leader assigned Bahadur and Mikhail, two new Anti-Christian, Anti-Semitic, apprentice terrorists to get the job done. Bahadur and Mikhail chose Christmas Day for the attack. In the S.O.L., they were known as *el macho cabríos* (Billy goats), the standard title for entry-level goons. As you already know, in a couple of months, they would become unpleasantly familiar to Kev and me when we chased them down Mount Wilson.

Each tower had an actual thirteenth floor, albeit architecturally disguised so as not to be noticed from the ground and, of course, no thirteenth floor appeared on elevator buttons. Access originated solely in the underground industrial parking garage.

Not designed for human occupation, visionary architects designed the thirteenth floors for a labyrinth of heavy duty, three-phase, electrical Pyro cable and outlets handling everything from 115/230 to far above 415v, accompanied by massive heat-transfer air conditioning. All calculated to house... the Big Iron.

In the mid-1970s, a twenty-four-month waiting period existed for customers to purchase a two-million-dollar IBM 7000 series mainframe computer (the Big Iron). Developers of Fox Hills Towers became the first builders ever to incorporate dedicated mainframe space into a commercial building. Those "stealth" thirteenth floors promised an extraordinary competitive edge when it came time to lease office space to high rollers.

* * * * *

In addition to their loathing of Christians, Bahadur and Mikhail chose Christmas Day 2002 because both towers would be closed with only a solitary rent-a-guard on duty. In the previous week, they attended trade school to learn all about the ViaDev 2360 Skystand window-washing platform, which incorporated both manual and wireless remote control.

The deadly dumb duo spent the night before Christmas morning on the roof of the north tower, hiding among building mechanicals. They devoted most of their activity that night to shivering, because they forgot their jackets.

Bahadur, the skinny one who hadn't shaved in five days, stood five-feet-eleven. His long greasy, grimy, brown hair overflowed onto boney shoulders revealed by his sweat-stained, faded red tank top. Bahadur was as seedy as parrot poop.

On a different build the shirt would be a "muscle shirt", but no discernable musculature adorned his desert-baked epidermis. A two-inch scar set his puffy lips in a permanent sneer, making him look as if he despised everyone on earth. Not far from the truth.

Bahadur displayed a teardrop tat under his left eye. In the gang culture of his younger days, that pictogram indicated he murdered someone on command. Bahadur had not actually done so. He merely bought the tattoo to augment his street cred. His only actual murder was that of Roscoe, his mother's cat.

Mikhail's face, except for the bushy unibrow, was cherubic. Soft. Round. Welcoming. He looked to be a gentle soul and, indeed, acted as such until ordered to become a ball of hate inflicting immeasurable pain and suffering, which did not occur often enough to keep him satisfied.

As always, Mikhail wore his favorite attire, a dirty orange jumpsuit. Aside from that, nothing really made Mikhail stand out from the ordinary, everyday terrorist crowd. Except—for this assignment—he also wore a shiny green turban.

Green is the sacred color of Islam. Green represents flowery fields and eternal oases in paradise. Those achieving paradise will wear green robes and recline on green cushions. Green is the life-giving color of desert peoples.

* * * * *

The pre-dawn Christmas Day sun beyond the eastern horizon gave a spectacular golden glow to each of the dozen high altitude aircraft contrails unfurling in every direction. Bahadur and Mikhail didn't notice. As they climbed aboard Skystand number four, anchored at the top edge of the north tower, all they noticed was enough light to do their job. But not enough for them to be seen from the ground. Bahadur initiated their quick seven-story descent down the rear face of the building.

They stopped at the windowless thirteenth floor to insert and set off a low-tech electromagnetic bomb. E-bombs do not explode in the traditional sense. Instead, they greatly increase the intensity of a magnetic field and thereby induce a massive current in all electrically conductive objects. The mammoth electrical spike would fry the mainframes. At the very least, those huge multi-million-dollar big iron computers would become scrap metal tombs for years of destroyed data.

With luck, the electronic spike might travel beyond the thirteenth floor and destroy everything electrical in the entire building, making the tower a good-looking, lifeless shell. The building might even burn itself to the ground. Bahadur and Mikhail loved the possibilities.

Inserting the small, convenient, travel-size, sneak-across-the-southern-border-without-detection e-bomb into the thirteenth floor required only that a smallish hole be drilled from the exterior of the tower through to the interior of the subfloor. Reaching into his ditty bag, Bahadur retrieved the mini-drill and did the job in less than a minute. Together, using their window-washing pole, they pushed the e-bomb through the wall and into the building. They squealed with delight when it thudded on the floor.

Gleefully lowering themselves down the side of the tower, they stopped outside the fourth floor where they could safely and remotely set off the bomb. Mikhail unlocked the remote detonator and flipped a switch. Bahadur dutifully said a prayer. Mikhail pushed the red button.

* * * * *

The myth of the thirteenth floor being stuffed with super computers originated from an article Bahadur saw in an old 1978 issue of *Mechanics Illustrated* found in a Bedouin tent.

In reality, by the time Fox Hills tower construction ended, the PC had taken over the business computer market, replacing main frames with inexpensive, personal computer workstations. The super wiring, plethora of electrical outlets, and humongous air conditioning never existed. The thirteenth floors of both towers were never occupied because they had no windows, no convenient human access, and were not suitable space for any tenant. Only empty boxes for Christmas and Hanukkah decorations hung out on the thirteenth floor. The e-bomb, of course, had no effect on those.

The e-bomb, however, loved the ViaDev 2360 Skystand's remote control. The two connected instantly and fried the remote control in Mikhail's hand. Glee turned to screams of horror as the window-washer platform plummeted to earth. Because they were only four stories up, the Skystand's safety brake didn't have time to completely stop the fall, but it did slow to a non-lethal crash landing. Though not physically hurt, Bahadur soiled his britches. (Not really noticeable, considering his personal hygiene.) Mikhail sprained an ankle when he slipped on the polished marble as they ran away like scared cesspool rats.

Thankfully, the S.O.L. Christmas Day attack failed due to incompetent Billy goats. At five-feet-five and 279 pounds, Mikhail's obese body was as quick as his mind. So round that, in his orange jumpsuit, from a great distance he could be mistaken for a basketball. Mikhail had never heard back from the Wizard about someday getting a brain.

Mikhail's handler, Bahadur, was a dim bulb apparatchik. Had military rank been determined by lack of hygiene, Bahadur would have been a general. If stupidity was an iron girder, Bahadur would be the Eiffel Tower.

* * * * *

Federal ghosts swept the scene first, sharing little with L.A.P.D. The left-behind shiny green turban, initially a major clue, got redacted before L.A.'s finest were even allowed inside the yellow tape.

9

MARCH 3, 2003

Monday Morning after the Sunday Tower Explosion, Car Chase, Machine Gun, et al.

No way to know if those volatile Sunday events frightened Kevin. He mastered fear internalization years earlier. The only clue came when he decided he needed to be late for work that Monday. So, he decided to have a board meeting.

Board meeting is Kevin Code for going surfing at Surf City USA© (the copyrighted nickname for the City of Huntington Beach). He called Ms. Sipes and let her know he wouldn't arrive at the corporate office until two o'clock.

* * * * *

Pulling into his executive parking spot at Extrapolated Electronics on Brand Boulevard in Glendale "right on time" (2:00 pm), he changed into business attire in his van. That meant replacing the neoprene wetsuit with cut-off jeans and swapping his Hawaiian shirt of many colors to a trustworthy, IBM-blue Hawaiian shirt. Regardless, the flip-flops remained the same. Employers overlooked the ensemble in exchange for access to the brain.

He paused to peel and stick his latest homemade bumper sticker onto his battered briefcase. Sauntering into the luxurious lobby, he held the case at an awkward angle which assured Ms. Sipes could read his new creation:

> Geoelectrophysicists Receive
> Forward Transfer Resistance

Kevin really liked his made-up word, "geoelectrophysicist". It accurately described his skillset but ... he made it up. The "receive forward transfer resistance" part was Kevin Code for his non-relationship with the beautiful Ms. Sipes, receptionist at Extrapolated Electronics.

When Kevin arrived, Ms. Sipes, of the short skirt and tight sweater school, stifled a small yawn and exaggerated a big stretch. She always seemed to have a need for stretching whenever Kevin showed up.

You could hear the smile in his voice. "Good morning Ms. Sipes."

She admonished, "It's two o'clock in the afternoon."

"Afternoon?" He looked at his wristwatch, did a cartoon double take, looked at it again with wild-eyed surprise, then held the watch up to his ear and tapped it three times. "Well then, this stupid watch is absolutely correct."

Ms. Sipes queried, "Uncle died again? Dog ate your research?"

"Dog ate my Uncle."

She laughed out loud.

Kevin said, "Actually, Theo and I were attacked last night by two goons with a machine gun."

"Oooo. That's a new one." She smiled. She stretched. "Seriously, Kevin, what shall I tell Mr. Grotsky? He's been looking for you."

Kevin gave her a penetrating stare, lowered his voice and said, "Tell him you're running away with me."

She crossed her arms, tilted her head, and pretended to consider the possibility. "Umm ... no. But, thank you for asking."

"Ms. Sipes," Kevin pleaded, "Let me take you away from all this. Whatta ya say? Tonight? You ... me ... a loaf of bread ... a bottle of Cheeze Whiz."

Looking around, she said quietly, "Listen, Kevin, this is serious. You missed a very important meeting this morning."

"Well, I'm sure there'll be another very important meeting tomorrow. Have you ever noticed how they seem to come in flocks?"

She whispered, "Mr. Grotsky said he wants to meet with you as soon as you get here."

"Oh... kay. Duty calls," Kevin sighed. He stood at attention, clicked his heels, and gave her a military salute. "Thank you, Ms. Sipes. As you were."

Walking down the long deeply carpeted, mahogany-paneled, and expensive-art-adorned hallway to his office, Kevin stopped halfway and looked back at her. "Ms. Sipes ... *as you were...* means you were stretching."

Even from twenty feet away she had the ability to look deep into Kevin's eyes. She did her best-ever, long, supple stretch. Kevin smiled, bit his knuckles and continued down the hall, pausing occasionally to kick his heels in the air and let out a happy "Yee haw."

Ms. Sipes grinned in appreciation of his appreciation.

* * * * *

His massive, sculpted mahogany door held a satin-finish brass nameplate:

> Kevin Oxley, Vice President
> Research & Development

He entered the lush office, put his back to the door, and pushed against its substantial weight until the latch snicked in place like a precision Bimmer gearbox. The room's air pressure changed, confirming he had locked out the real world. Hushed solitude comforted him as he thought about the momentous, unfinished task awaiting.

The unique office ambience came from Kev's personally selected blend of 1950s country-maple furniture, 1930s Hawaii posters, car stuff, and animation cells. An autographed picture of Trigger, the most famous horse in motion picture history, sat in a golden frame on the maple coffee table in front of a midcentury Roy Rogers wagon wheel couch. Mr. Rogers, the "King of the Cowboys" signed the picture when Kevin and I met him at the Roy Rogers Museum in 1982, when we were eight years old. We loved that horse.

Kevin's L-shaped desk once belonged to Harley Earl, the car-guy who invented automobile styling. A large framed Carl Barks-autographed poster of *Oncle Scrooge Picsou* (French, for Uncle Scrooge McDuck) hung up behind his desk. Kevin found that personal treasure in a Paris flea market on the *Boulevard du Palais*, not far from *Sainte-Chapelle*.

A dozen identical round black clocks stretched the length of the eighteen-foot-long office wall. A plaque beneath each clock identified its time zone. Instead of actual time zone names, Kevin labeled each clock with a phrase holding personal meaning. Starting with Pacific time on the left and heading eastward (across the wall to the right) his clocks were labeled:

Mickey & Donald — John Elway — Sam Clemens — Never Forget — Queen Mum — Béarnaise — Glasnost — Big Wall — Sushi & Ginger — Shrimp & Barbie — King Kam — King Salmon

Putting his feet on the huge desktop, he opened his briefcase and pulled out the only thing in it: his newest state-of-the-art Personal Digital Assistant (PDA), the Handspring PalmOne Treo 600. The Treo 600 would not be available to the public until November, more than half a year away, but Kevin's Treo already far exceeded 2003 state-of-the-art. That's because, after reporting his long-lead beta tester findings, he hot-rodded it, overclocking the CPU, quintupling the memory, and turning it into a screamin' machine.

He leaned back in his imposing glove-leather executive chair, looking at his clocks, remembering times good and not-so-good. A deep breath slowly let out and then... *Well, time to kick butt and save the world.*

Time to resume Alien Invasion. Kevin tickled the touchscreen on his tuned and flamed Treo 600. Office lighting dimmed, and his suite filled with the theatrical-quality sound of laser cannons in perfect sync with larger than life 3D holographic video of fried green invaders.

That's when Mr. Grotsky walked in.

A ten-foot-tall, snarling, red Maglothian Rexlithar opened its mouth, exposing slimy, razor-sharp teeth surrounding Mr. Grotsky's head. Mr. Grotsky rolled his eyes and continued walking toward Kevin's desk. Above the din of battle, he shouted, "You missed the meeting."

Kevin turned off the game. "I can explain about that."

"No explanation necessary," said Mr. Grotsky with a malevolent smirk. "And, by the way, you won't ever have to worry about being late again."

"Well, actually Melvin, I never really did."

Mr. Grotsky said, "Kevin, I wear many hats here at Extrapolated Electronics. In this meeting I am wearing the hat of your supervisor."

"Oh, so this is an *official* meeting?" Kevin said. "Well then, let me get *my* hat." He reached into his file cabinet (which contained no files), drew out his customized pith helmet, and put it on. At the top peak of the helmet, four miniature halogen spotlights rotated. The hatband, made of a Jerry Garcia tie, hung out the back of the helmet like a neon ponytail. Five-inch-long tassels, strung with genuine 1960s love beads, dangled around the entire perimeter of the helmet. The tassels draped down to the middle of Kevin's nose. Using both hands, he parted the beaded fringe, so he could peek at Mr. Grotsky.

"I'm ready now, sir."

"Based on your track record with previous employers I was afraid your productivity might be somewhat low here at Extrapolated. After all, Mercury Dynamics fired you, RFL fired you, and NASA allowed you to resign somewhat gracefully." Mr. Grotsky took a deep breath. "Kevin, I was willing to take a chance on you because you are a certified electronics genius."

Kevin blinked several times and blew fringe out of his eyes. "Thank you."

"Your theoretical concepts are unique," Mr. Grotsky continued. "You develop new technology from existing componentry. But you make us no money. Will you please take off the stupid hat?"

Kevin took off the stupid hat. "Yes sir. Removing stupid hat now, sir. HUA!"

Mr. Grotsky sat in a guest chair and became very solemn, leaning in toward Kevin. "Your productivity hasn't been low, it's been nonexistent."

"But Melvin, I haven't failed on any project yet."

"That's because you haven't *finished* any project yet. Let's see … there was the Silver Toe Sock. Which I still don't get."

Kevin raised his pointer finger in front of his lips. His voice became hushed. "Silver threads woven into the toe will become the receiver for a subminiature GPS tracking device."

Mr. Grotsky leaned in. "And …?"

Kevin raised up his open palm, signifying caution. His eyes darted about the room. He whispered, "Every home in America has a secret missing sock graveyard. We will finally learn where socks go to die."

The phrase *going postal* arrived in Mr. Grotsky's mind.

Mr. Grotsky said, "And then there was—oh yes—the MARUSS project. What did that stand for?"

"Magnetic Resonance Ultra-Sound Shower."

"Right. And it was … a … shower … without water?"

"Correct, sir. Hair, body, and teeth squeaky clean in 30 seconds without soap or water." Before Mr. Grotsky could respond, Kevin went into his happy-dappy TV infomercial announcer voice. "But wait. There's more. You also get whiter teeth and firmer breasts."

Grotsky sighed. "And why did you not complete that one?"

"I didn't want firmer breasts."

"Kevin, you get bored and abandon every job."

Kevin played his ace in the hole. "Oh, but I'm very close on the ramistat."

"Yes, of course you are," mused Mr. Grotsky. "The ramistat. Your pet project. Tell me again, please, what is its purpose?"

"I haven't decided yet."

"Mr. Oxley—"

Kevin interrupted with a trembling voice. "Oh no!"

Alarmed, Grotsky shouted, "What? What's wrong? Are you all right?"

"Oh my gosh ... Melvin ... you called me *Mr. Oxley*. That's one step away from deleting my security door code."

"Kevin, I have to terminate you."

"Oh, Melvin ... terminate sounds so ... so ... permanent."

"It is."

"How will I feed my wife and kids?" Mr. Grotsky looked quizzical. Kev continued, "I don't have a wife and kids, but I could rent some if that would help."

Mr. Grotsky shook his head.

Kevin did his noble stance and said proudly, "Melvin, I believe you have sorely misjudged me. You see, I have a vision for this company, a vision in which I am on a mission to explore strange new worlds of home electronics. In this quest I require autonomy. I require freedom from the shackles of time clocks and the bonds of expectations. What I want is to boldly go where no small kitchen appliance manufacturer has gone before."

"What you want is a fat paycheck and no responsibility."

"Well, yeah, that too."

Mr. Grotsky stood up. "It's all over Kevin. It's final. Do you have any questions?"

"Well, there is one thing I always wondered about."

Mr. Grotsky said, "And, what is that?"

"Where do babies come from?"

Mr. Grotsky turned and walked away, squeezing his shaking head with all ten fingers. To Kevin it looked like Mr. Grotsky's head was being attacked by a small octopus.

Well, actually... I guess that would be a dectopus. Hah!

Mr. Grotsky walked out of Kevin's office. A security guard immediately walked in. He carried empty cardboard boxes, and sadly said, "Hey Kev."

"Hey, Vincent."

"I'm sorry, buddy." He sat the boxes on the desk and began loading Kevin's *objets d'art*.

Kevin tapped on his customized Treo 600. Haunting theme music from *The Godfather* rose out of the sixteen surround sound speakers and filled the room. Kevin stuck his chin out and slowly stroked his jawbone with the loosely curled fingers of his left hand. He did a pretty good Vito Corleone. "Vinnie, can you get me off on this one? For old time's sake?"

Vincent shook his head.

"Can't you just call one of your capo de tutti fruities?"

Vincent smirked and shook his head.

"How about your own personal goombah?"

Vinnie smiled and shook his head.

"Okay, okay. How 'bout your own personal Gumby?

Vincent shook his head.

"Gumbo? Garbo? Chili Gumbo? Chili Palmer?

Vincent laughed. "I'm Sorry Kev. It's not personal. Just business."

Kev said, "Yeah, I know. I wish it was personal. I hate business."

10

SOUTH PASADENA, CALIFORNIA

Kevin's employment life expectancy had become inversely proportional to the length of time since his college graduation. As he went from NASA to Mercury Dynamics, to Applied Aerospace Arrays, to Rocket Force Industries, to Extrapolated Electronics, he remained in the San Gabriel Valley "Satellite Belt", reasonably close to our apartment in South Pasadena, which was also close to my job at Pasadena Institute of Technology. It had proven mutually convenient to share an apartment to which he could return every time he came back from wherever it was he sometimes disappeared.

Compared to more modern buildings, our midcentury apartment had much larger rooms and no amenities. We were on the second floor with two large bedrooms, a big wooden deck, a huge living room, and a miniscule kitchen. No problemo. You don't need a kitchen to order pizza or bring home Panda Express (which, by the way, was founded in South Pasadena). Kevin did not cook, and I could only make Cheerios. We would have been fully functional with only a microwave and a mini fridge in a broom closet. Come to think of it, the broom closet wasn't all that important either. I don't believe either of us owned a broom. All I remember for sure is that no female visitor ever swept with me.

In 2003, high definition TVs were still new, expensive, and rare. The Ox man, of course, considered them a necessity. He created his multiple screen HD TV by interlacing four sixty-inch screens with an audio/video quad-splitter, like his "inspiration piece", the gargantuan video screen at Dodger stadium.

His five-foot-tall by almost nine-foot-wide screen had wall-mounted floor-to-ceiling speakers at each end and a four-foot-tall cabinet running across the bottom (where his "dog" hung out). The array filled one living room wall. It comforted me to know that he also tweaked the huge TV to be an astounding burglar alarm.

From out on the second story deck, we had a lovely view of crashes down below on the narrow, twisting Pasadena Freeway (the first freeway in the United States). South Pasadena, by the way, is not, as you might assume, part of Pasadena. South Pasadena became its own city in 1888 by seceding from Pasadena, the impetus being residents in the southern part of Pasadena wanted a dry city. To this day, South Pasadena is still dry.

Speaking of dry... when Kevin arrived at our apartment that Monday afternoon of his latest termination, the extremely dry and extremely hot Santa Ana Winds were blustering down from Barstow. One static-filled living room drape stuck to the gigantic TV screen. The other drape flip-flapped out the partially open living room window.

Kev sat his box of job leftovers on the floor next to his well-worn recliner, and he plopped. Fresh new unemployment meant a perfect time to be comforted by a pet. "ROVER," he called out, and then added a cheerless, "Here boy."

A top-hinged, swinging flap in the cabinet below the compound TV opened slightly. Friendly red eyes peeked out to make sure it was the master's voice.

"C'mon ROVER."

The voice-activated ROVER raced out of its "kennel" and across the living room floor on eight knobby low-pressure tires which were perfect for navigating a dusty lunar surface or old shag carpeting. The official federal acronym stood for Remotely Operated Vehicle Extraterrestrial Research.

ROVER had been Kev's last project at Rocket Force Industries, his penultimate employer. Nineteen inches tall, two feet wide, and three feet long, the matte aluminum and shiny silver critter bristled with retractable tools and gadgets in various metallic shades punctuated by an occasional patch of gold foil.

High on the list of things which made Ox crazy were federal employee ego, government incompetence, and wasted tax-payer money, all of which he believed should be felonies. I pretty much agreed.

Sired by a typical self-replicating federal agency budget, Kevin's ROVER had no practical value in space (or other) research. His overuse of his favorite phrase, "My insignificant vehicle for insignificant research", no doubt hastened his termination. RFI insisted he take his one-off ROVER prototype with him. They delighted in getting rid of them both. While at RFI, Kev always had his homemade bumper sticker stuck to the rear of the little vehicle:

$$\boxed{R_{eally} \; O_{btuse} \; V_{ery} \; E_{xpensive} \, R_{ip-off}}$$

Kevin said, "ROVER. Look."

ROVER's two optical receptors perked up and focused on Kevin. The video screen in ROVER's lower front panel displayed a heart-warming Golden Retriever smile. Though not anthropomorphic, ROVER certainly exuded cute.

Kevin said, "Astern 1.5 meters."

ROVER backed up about five feet and stopped.

"Sit."

Based on Skyhook theory, the Kevin-designed adaptive/semi-active and uniquely flexible articulated suspension adjusted perfectly. ROVER's stern dropped down flat to the floor, creating a stable platform. The prow elevated, and ROVER sat at attention

"Launch sequence." Kevin said. He laid his right arm on his chair armrest, lifted his right hand, and waved. ROVER's turret made gentle metallic whirring noises while rotating and elevating in situ until the on-board tracking system locked on Kev's extended hand. A red laser targeting dot centered on his palm.

"Houston, we are A-OK," Kev announced, just for fun. To ROVER he specifically stated, "Remember the prime directive: humans are never injured."

With an Alvin the Chipmunk voice, ROVER squeaked, "Okay."

On top of ROVER, a launch tube telescoped out from the turret to its full 20-inch length and a miniature drag-strip countdown light array flashed to life. ROVER's Alvinesque voice counted down as the lights went from red to amber to green. "... three ... two ... one ... ignition."

WOOSH!

A frosty can of root beer shot out the tube, through the air, and into Kevin's waiting hand.

"The beverage has landed," He said to nobody. He pushed on a short section of the unique soda can rim (which he had patented). The micro-battery-powered can top folded back and under itself to open half the lid, thereby creating an instant, ersatz aluminum mug.

Root beer foam sprayed everything.

"Houston, we have … … … no problem." In his newly unemployed frame of mind, a little overspray simply didn't matter. He took a long, satisfying sip. "One small vehicle for man, one giant leap for refreshment."

He peered over the big padded left arm of his recliner down into the box of odds and ends salvaged from his office. He sat the soda can on the end table, leaned way over and began sifting through personal treasures. Lifting out his brass door name plaque, he sat it beside his Xbox controller on the end table. He sighed. He retrieved a sock with a silver-toe, laid it on his name plaque, and sighed again. Then he pulled out a small—about four inches on a side—complicated-looking electronic device laden with wires, ports, and a cluster of mini sliding potentiometers. It looked like the child of a Rubik's Cube and a *Star Trek* Borg Cube.

Holding it up, Ox looked at it, lovingly. "Alas, poor ramistat, I knew ye well."

11

Dr. Weksler, curmudgeonly at the best of times, softened to let's say ... indulgent ... regarding my missing his Sunday at Seven lecture. He assured me he would remain satisfied with my job performance so long as we, in the words of his favorite Thomas Edison quote, "Make progress every day." Edison had said that to him, personally. Through family connections, Dr. Weksler hung out with Edison quite a bit. He was a five-year-old child prodigy when Mr. Edison passed away at eighty-four years of age.

For the nerdy now trying to figure out Dr. Weksler's age in 2003, I'll spare you the mental anguish. Seventy-seven. Still a prodigy, still going to work every day, and still stubbornly holding onto tenure despite university attempts at forced retirement.

With very little on the calendar that Monday, Dr. Weksler closed the lab early. I, thankfully, went straight home for a siesta, exhausted from nervous tension and lack of sleep. When I walked through our front door, the drapes waved and crackled with static. The TV played very low in the background.

Ahhh, perfect white noise for a perfect nap. I'm alone and I am tired.

I hauled myself toward the living room sofa.

A male voice said, "Hi honey."

"Aiieee!" I jumped sideways. My shoulder bumped into cousin Penny's cuckoo clock, knocking it off the wall. I caught the clock—just barely—and cradled it as I fell to a safe landing on the sofa. Jerry Rice would have been impressed. Well, maybe not. When I stood up to rehang the clock, my peripheral vision saw something move on the other side of the room, which scared me again. "Aiieee!" I dropped the clock to the floor. It sproinged and shattered to pieces. (I bought a replacement before Penny's next visit.) Squinting, I recognized the man in the recliner. "Kevin? What are you doing here?"

"I live here. Remember?"

He fiddled with micro tools and his beloved ramistat.

Why is he home early?

"Don't 'hi honey' me," I said. "Last night wasn't funny, Ox. Dr. Weksler expressed pithy crabbiness today because I missed his Sunday at Seven."

My mention of Dr. Weksler seemed to shake loose some synapses in Kevin's head. His eyes rolled up to the left as he carefully considered his next statement. "Theophilus... what is it... precisely... that you do?"

"I'm a researcher at the university. I do research."

"Lots of pressure? Heavy deadlines?"

"No deadlines. I work at my own pace."

His eyes developed a happy gleam. "No expectations?"

I grabbed for the closet doorknob and got shocked by static electricity. "Ouch! You can't put scientific research on a timetable. It could take years before we finalize something with commercial or military application."

He smiled. "Oh, Theophilus, what a healthy, nurturing atmosphere in which to work."

I figured it out. "Oh, no, don't go there. Don't you even go near there. You got fired again, didn't you? No. No. No. No. And just in case I haven't made myself clear—NO."

A scorching blast of Santa Ana wind blew the drapes in and up and over and around me and the television. The Santa Anas are *katabatic* winds (Greek for "flowing downhill"), a Southern California phenomenon. Every year, the hot, menacing high-desert winds gust down through Los Angeles valleys and villages, making Angelinos feel threatened by things unidentifiable. Santa Anas put everything in life on edge. Including my hair.

The drapes stuck to my head, my clothes, and the TV screen. "Darn Santa Ana winds." Kevin laughed while I struggled to extricate myself from drape confinement.

Then, we were both riveted to our life-size TV as we became aware of dialogue, low in the background, between TV co-anchors Robert Putnam and Audrey Ishimoto.

"—and speaking of static in the air, Channel Eight had some on-air problems yesterday, right Audrey?"

"Actually, Robert, the biggest problem was *off* the air," Audrey replied. "An explosion toppled our own KZLA-TV broadcast tower, putting Channel Eight off the air for sixteen hours."

I shouted, "Turn it up. Turn it up."

Kevin sat rigid and pointed the TV remote. Eyes glazed over; we watched the big screen. My jaw dropped open, allowing me to wheeze comfortably.

Video of a police officer appeared on our huge screen. He held up the black and red tower piece which fell out of Kevin's van. Anchorman Robert Putnam's commanding voiceover made it even more alarming. "In an anomalous, but possibly related story, L.A. County Sheriffs say this section of the Channel Eight tower with white paint scratches was found near a destroyed shopping mall construction site. Officials are hopeful that forensics may shed light on the origin of the white paint."

I muted the TV and gasped.

Kevin looked at me. "Theo, did you have something to add to that story?"

"Your van is damaged, and they can match the white paint to your van."

"No, they can't."

"Ox, I know these things. I am a physicist. I watch C.S.I.—I know they can figure out that the white paint came from a General Motors van."

"No, they can't."

"And just why not?"

"Because it's not GM paint. It's not anybody's paint. I created it. It's my own custom formula. There is no other paint like it anywhere in the world."

"Oh."

"And the damage to my van is superficial. Just sheet metal. A couple hours in our garage with some Bondo, my spray gun, and ... good as new." He nodded at me. "And I thank you for being worried about my van."

"I'm not worried about your van. I'm worried about being waterboarded."

I turned the sound back on as anchorwoman, Audrey Ishimoto, gave additional details about the previous night's destruction of their Mount Wilson broadcast tower. "A religious cult calling themselves the S.O.L. claimed responsibility for the blast, stating they wish to focus attention on their demands for political recognition and a sovereign homeland."

I exhaled and unstiffened.

On screen, Robert Putnam, the Dean of Los Angeles anchormen, segued neatly into the next story. "There was another felonious incident involving Channel Eight yesterday. Just minutes before the blast, a bootleg broadcaster known only as The Pirate, hacked our programming. Our pirate-cam goes live now for this exclusive interview with FCC Under-Assistant West Coast Field Director Leonard Ostermann."

We both restiffened.

In a chroma key window above Putnam's left shoulder, Ostermann appeared, primping. Robert Putnam, in his legendary, beloved, dramatic delivery, spoke to the chroma key image. "Mr. Ostermann—quickly now, Southern California is waiting—give us your observations on yesterday's horrific events."

Ostermann flattened his last wild hair. "A dark day, indeed. The city lost a primary broadcast tower and the airwaves were interrupted by an unlicensed transmission. I feel personally violated."

"That must be uncomfortable for you," said Mr. Putnam. "Any new developments?"

"It is my belief that The Pirate and the terrorist cult are, in reality, one and the same."

"Aiieee!" I dissolved into the sofa and began overtime wheezing.

Putnam cocked an eyebrow into the television camera. His rich basso voice almost made TV screens vibrate. "A most surprising revelation, sir. Research shows that our hundreds of thousands of viewers from the mountains to the sea consider The Pirate to be a folk hero".

Extremely offended, Leonard Ostermann snarked, "Folk hero? He's a common criminal. And last night's bombing proves it."

Mr. Putnam put a warm smile into his voice. "One further question, Mr. Ostermann: Do you support the Gary Puckett crusade?"

Ostermann replied with a confused, self-important, and irritated, "What?"

The chroma key image of Ostermann above Putnam's left shoulder switched to a bikini bottom.

Robert Putnam looked straight into the unblinking eye of the TV camera and intoned a dramatic story ending line: "The Pirate: Folk Hero ... or common criminal?" Next came a dramatic pause during which Mr. Putnam shuffled papers while his facial expressions told the rest of the story, his dramatic timing superb, as always. At the appropriate moment he looked up, smiled his wry, crooked smile and in a lighter tone, said, "Up next, the second installment in our five-part series as Channel Eight investigates bikini wax."

Kevin clicked off the TV.

I shouted, "Oh, my gosh. Did you hear that?"

"Yeah, five days of bikini bottoms. Must be ratings week".

"Ox, we are in deep sushi."

Instead of being worried, he smiled a dreamy smile. "Wow. Imagine that. Robert Putnam called me a folk hero. I've always thought of myself as a ... kind of a ... a rebel. I don't know, Theophilus, what do you think? To me, 'folk hero' connotes an image of a fringy leather coat and a little furry hat that used to be a little furry animal."

"What do I think? I think you are certifiable."

He smiled. "A certifiable pirate? Really?

"No. I think they think you bombed the TV tower. That's what I think."

He shrugged. "That's ridiculous. There's no way they can pin it on us."

"No way they can pin it on ... *us*? Us? That's another one of those *group* words. It indicates a plural. Not a singular, like, I. As in I am innocent. I am not at fault. I did not do it. I will not visit you in Alcatraz."

"And, I believe *you* are overreacting again."

Both living room drapes blew in and stuck to the television with a loud crackle. I jumped. "Ahh." I gritted my teeth, scrinched my eyes closed tight, and covered my face with the fingers of both hands. I mumble-whined, "We've got to go to the police."

Kevin stared me down. "Okay, here are some really important *group* words: We didn't blow up the tower. We don't know who did. We reported it to Smokey Bear. And if we go to the police, we will be arrested."

While I pondered that sober truism, he picked up his ramistat and the television remote. "You know what I really think?" he said.

"What?"

"If I rewire this TV remote with my ramistat, I might be able to get it to control the static in those drapes."

I rolled my eyes up into my head, looking around in there for some hint of common sense. I decided to utilize one of my favorite escape mechanisms. Boldly, I said, "I'm going to do my laundry." And I left him to his madness.

Now deep into his own little world, Kevin didn't merely ignore me—he didn't even hear me. He picked up the TV remote and the emergency roll of duct tape always kept in his recliner side pocket and said, "Ahh, duct tape. Nature's most perfect accessory."

* * * * *

About an hour later, Kev had the TV remote, the Xbox controller and his ramistat soldered, hard-wired and duct-taped together with a module from an old Apple Newton Message Pad, components from a defunct cell phone circuit board, antiquated computer SIMMS, a row of DIP switches, and unidentifiable stuff from the innards of our deceased home air purifier.

When I walked into the apartment carrying my laundry basket, he stood up and said, "Tah-Dah."

He pointed his new, improved ramistat at the drapes and pressed a button. The drapes crackled, released their grip on the TV, and hung straight, at attention. The invisible electronic force of his modified ramistat actually affected the drapes.

I begrudgingly admit to being somewhat impressed. However, as I stood there tired, scared, and emotionally drained, holding my heavy laundry basket full of newly clean clothes, with my hair all squirrelly from static electricity, I could not have cared less about his stupid ramistat. But I did feel a profound need to whimper. "The dryer kept shocking me. I ran out of fabric softener. The clothes are sticking to everything. This is not my century!"

He ignored my plight. "Hey, check this out."

When he moved the joystick on his combination ramistat/ TV remote/Xbox controller, the drapes moved. Using the joystick, he swayed the drapes back and forth in an ever-widening arc and then counted down.

"Three ... Two ... One."

He smacked the drapes against the wall, creating a loud slap and a mighty cloud of dust. Elated, Kevin said, "Theo, do you know what this means?"

"We need to vacuum the drapes?"

He shook his head. "The ramistat signal has a grip on the static in those drapes."

"Congratulations. Another useless invention."

He looked around the room, searching for another target. "Hmm ... what else attracts static electricity?" He spotted my basket full of static-charged clothes and took aim.

"No." I scolded.

Too late. He pressed a button. Laundry flew out of my basket in all directions. I opened my mouth to scream in fear. The scream never escaped because my mouth got filled by a skyrocketing sweat sock. At least it was clean.

12

PASADENA, CALIFORNIA

The Pasadena Institute of Technology looks like an early twentieth-century upscale neighborhood filled with classical mansions and large craftsman homes. Because that's what it used to be. Prior to 1949, every building on campus had been a private residence. An entire two blocks of homes were purchased and converted to classrooms and offices. Immense old California Valley Oak trees rising up to a hundred-feet tall, stand watch over the compact campus located halfway up the mountain foothills, just East of Los Robles Avenue. (*Los Robles* is Spanish for "The Oaks".) It's as if Walt Disney built his own small left-coast vision of an ivy-league college.

* * * * *

Henry Ford, Orville Wright, Harvey Firestone, and Thomas Edison all included Jorge Pheltor on their shortlist of friends. Like Ford and Wright, Pheltor was a relentless, burgeoning industrialist. Like Edison, he was a creative researcher captivated by the seemingly unlimited possibilities of emerging technologies. Like Harvey Firestone, Jorge enjoyed a good party. Unlike Firestone, however, Pheltor was not grounded. Instead, he was airborne. Jorge, the aviation fanatic.

By the late 1920s the "flying machine" had been legitimized. In this roaring era, Jorge Pheltor's stream of new inventions made airplanes more reliable and much safer. Out of touch and parsimonious U.S. President Calvin Coolidge, however, almost single-handedly put a stop to aviation progress.

"Can't we just buy one airplane and have the pilots take turns?"
— Calvin Coolidge

Jorge Pheltor inserted his special gifts into aviation, inventing instrumentalities that made nighttime and inclement weather flying a reality. His genius helped the allies win World War II.

At the time of his death in 1960 (ironically, in a plane crash, at night, in bad weather), Pheltor held some three hundred, mostly aviation-oriented, patents. He left the bulk of his fortune to the Pasadena Institute of Technology. The bequest included construction of an on-campus building designed by Pheltor himself: a two-and-a-half story, reddish-brown brick edifice with ornate marble trim and sculpted details more common to the Gilded Age. A dramatic twenty-five-foot-high leaded glass roof covered the building's auditorium-lecture hall-laboratory, where I worked with Dr. Weksler. It became known as Pheltor Hall.

To receive his munificence, the P.I.T. Board of Regents had to accept—for all time and eternity—the most striking and unique architectural feature of Pheltor Hall. They did. Fifteen feet up on the right side of the monumental main entrance stands a larger-than-life statue of Jorge Pheltor. At the same height, on the left side of the entrance stands a statue of Calvin

Coolidge. The statue of Pheltor sticks its tongue out at the statue of Coolidge. For all time and eternity.

"Wisdom doesn't necessarily come with age. Sometimes age just shows up by itself."

— Woodrow Wilson

* * * * *

Shaking my head and grinding my teeth as we walked along one of the many oak-shaded paths on campus, I muttered, "This is a very, very, very bad idea."

"Careful, you're gonna set off the wailing-and-gnashing-of-teeth alarm."

"Kevin, you do not belong in a university."

"Nonsense. Look at me. I'm lovin' it."

I groaned.

He swiveled his head and spread open arms to his Pas Tech paradise. "Oh, I do love it all, Theophilus. The ivy-covered professors. The pompous circumstances. The curve of twenty-two-year-old thigh."

"Just remember, when you get to the Assistant Dean's office, *do not* use me as a reference. Don't even let anyone know that I know that you know that I know you."

"What a pal."

"Ox, I am serious. I really like my job. Don't mess it up."

"Mess it up? Man, all I want to do is clone it. No responsibility. No deadlines." His tone changed to lustful. "No mercy."

Looking where he stared, I embraced the lusting. Then, as the delightful redhead passed by, we saw her skirt unattractively bunched on one side due to all that static generated by Santa Ana conditions. Quickly and nonchalantly, so as not to attract attention, she tugged unsuccessfully at the misbehaving cloth.

"Tsk. What a shame," Kevin observed. "Embarrassing static cling. Duty calls."

Pulling his ramistat from his pocket, he aimed at the young woman's skirt, and used his invisible beam to smooth out the fabric. Totally unaware of Kevin's actions, the lovely lady walked on down the path, looking prim and well-finished.

He tilted his head and raised his eyebrows and palms at me.

"Okay, Okay. It is *not* a useless invention."

We arrived at the quad where I had to go left to Pheltor Hall, and Kev needed to continue across campus to administration. I pointed the way. "Just go through the little Japanese garden thingy, past the Koi pond, and then keep going straight. The offices are in that multi-colored but mostly green house."

"K. I'm gonna wander a bit. You know, just get the lay of the land. Appointment's not for another hour."

Still concerned, I said, "Well ... please ... be very careful."

"What? Does the koi pond have a mock ness monster?"

"No, I just mean ..." I closed my eyes, swallowed, and sucked in big oxygen. "Okay, I will probably live to regret saying this ... goodluckwithyourinterview." I groaned again.

"Hey, thanks bro."

"And don't embarrass me."

"I won't." He held up the scout salute. "Scout's honor."

"And don't embarrass yourself."

"Never certain of that."

Soaking up character from old wood, brick, and stone, Kevin ambled the full length of the time-sheltered campus.

Upon crossing paths with students, he bubbled over with wannabe-new-professor-babble.

"Hello. Glad to see you this morning. Did you know I'm on staff here?"

– OR –

"Hi there. I'm Professor Oxley and I'm doing long-term research on a big fat grant."

– OR (upon meeting a cute coed) –

"Good morning. Going out for the chess team this year? Do you have a stale mate? Give me a call."

Students just smiled and passed on by, paying little attention. Looney-Toons are indigenous to Southern California.

Still early for the appointment, he sat on a Greene & Greene-inspired, river rock bench in the shade of myriad oaks, luxuriating in faux Ivy League. The Santa Anas dwindled to a gentle breeze. In concert with giggling water from the mission-style fountain, they satisfied body and soul. *This is it. I'm home. The culmination of a life wasted in search of a punch line.*

Then he thought about what he just thought about.

Hmm ... I bet I could make up a joke ... about a high school prom ... where they didn't have refreshments. But it wouldn't be funny ... because ... there's no punch line!

"Hah!" He laughed out loud at his own thought joke.

The sudden laughter from a crazy man on the river rock bench startled the attractive young woman walking by. A frightened noise escaped from her perfect lips. She jumped sideways, looking angrily down at Kevin.

"Oh, I'm sorry," He said. "Just amusing myself. Kind of in my own little world, you know."

"No, I wouldn't know." Her fright / flight / fight juices worked well.

A little testy for a beautiful woman.

She paused and recovered nicely. "Look, I am sorry." She smiled. "My reaction there was a little over the top. I was deep in thought and you scared me."

"That's okay. I was deep in thought and I scared me."

She giggled. "Well, I'd like to chat, but I've got to get to a meeting." She smiled bigger. "You have a nice day ... in your own little world, okay?"

"I'll do it. Bye."

She did a little finger wave. "Bye."

He finger-waved back at her. *Wow, what a great smile.*

As she walked away, she nibbled on her lower lip. *Oh, my goodness, he's adorable.*

Kevin enjoyed watching her walk away. She had an unbelievably cute nose, a movie star smile, glistening blue eyes, and perfectly shaped, short, "business casual" blonde hair.

After a few yards, curiosity made her look back and ... *oops, he's looking at me. And he's just as cute as I remembered.* She smiled again, gave another little finger wave, and then continued on at a faster, slightly unsettled pace.

He guessed late twenties, older than most of the coeds. She wore a tailored light tweed skirt and blazer over an executive-quality, very feminine, white blouse with subtle pink undertones. Everything exuded professionalism. Nothing hid desirability.

Hmmm ... confident ... classy. Definitely the type a successful university professor like me could go for.

When she turned and headed down a different walkway, he saw for the first time that the left rear side of her skirt was clinging due to pervasive static electricity in the air. One lacy edge of her undies showed.

Well, oops and oh my. It's a damsel in distress.

He did the "charge" melody, "Dah-dah-dah-dot-tuh-dah." He stood up, jerked the ramistat from his pocket and held it at his waist. He pointed it at the fashionable skirt. He pushed the button. Nothing happened. No lights. No whirr. No change in the clinging cloth. He shook the ramistat (a universal fix for electronic devices) and pushed the button again. Nothing. *C'mon, she's getting out of range.* He hit it three times (another universal solution) and then tried again. Nothing.

What is wrong? Even percussive maintenance didn't work. Well, when electronics fail, we must go to manual override.

Hustling to catch up, he quickly found himself on the flagstone pathway right behind the classy young woman. He considered just carefully reaching for her skirt to straighten it out, but in a rare moment of good sense, thought better of it, and fell into step beside her.

"Well, hi there. What's your name? What's your major? Do you like sipping champagne in the bathtub?"

With an uncomfortable smile, she looked heavenward. "Oh, brother."

"Your brother's here? Where? He won't beat me up, will he?"

She stifled a giggle and said, "I've really got to go. I'm going to be late"

She walked away, even faster, believing she had ended the encounter.

Unfortunately, Kevin kept up with her, still trying, in his own self-destructive manner, to do a good deed and inform her of the static cling problem. Despite his genius, Kev always became disjointed when near a potential Ms. Right. And banal banter became the "work-around" for his romantic insecurity. He couldn't just come right out and tell her about her skirt because *he* would be embarrassed. First, he had to establish a connection through a conversation and then, casually, mention the delicate issue.

"You know, my horoscope said today would be a good day for dinner after work with a beautiful new friend," he offered, smiling and letting his eyebrows make it an invitation.

She closed her eyes and shook her head.

He continued digging the hole ever deeper. "But then … I don't have much faith in that word, 'horoscope'. It sounds like new 3D technology for a chainsaw movie where you duck to avoid disgusting stuff flying into your face. Horror-scope. Yuck."

Edging toward irritated, she said, "Look, I mildly appreciate that you are trying your best to hit on me, but I don't have time for this. I am running very behind schedule."

"Okay. But I need to tell you one thing."

"What?"

"Your uh … your lacies are showing." He glanced down and tipped his head to indicate the location. She looked and saw her skirt folded-up on that side. Some frat guys looking out a window cheered. She blushed, tugged her skirt down and smoothed it out.

"How rude. You could have told me."

"I just did."

"After I flashed a fraternity." She leveled him with a look that would freeze elephant snot. "I'm sure your joyful noise is quite scintillating for all the female children on campus, but personally, I have neither the time nor the stomach for this. I am now going to walk away from you and erase this episode from my short-term memory. I suggest you crawl back into the junior high locker from whence you escaped."

She marched off to whatever she was late for.

Kevin stood there and watched her walk out of his life. He had lots of practice doing that.

13

PHELTOR HALL — TWENTY MINUTES LATER

"**N**o! Not in there. Professor Pul, this is not a scheduled stop. Mrs. Landry, please wait."

Dr. Weksler had just formed a captive microcloud in the Norton chamber, when the unexpected tour group burst into the lab.

A matronly woman from the group stared in wonder at the little cloud floating above the small-town square in the chamber. "Oh, my goodness, will you look at that. What is the nature of your experiment?"

Trying to regain control, the flustered leader of the tour said, "I am sorry, people, but we must leave immediately. We're not supposed to be in any of Dr. Weksler's rooms."

"It's quite all right, Dianne," Dr. Weksler said. "Really." He turned to answer the woman's question. "What we have created here in the Norton Chamber is the genesis of a small cumulonimbus." He looked at his watch. "If you wish to stick around, we're expecting a light shower in about three minutes."

The crowd smiled their approval. A male VIP in the group said, "The 'Norton Chamber? Wasn't that used several years ago for the study of artificial weather?"

For reasons sufficient to the Board of Regents, the university had kept completely under wraps, and generally ignored, all of Dr. Weksler's activities for several semesters. Having been forced out of every spotlight, he now thoroughly enjoyed this attention to his work.

"I can assure you that the weather, itself, is quite real." he answered with brightening eyes. "It is our inducement which is artificial. It's rather like today's young couples who let their baby know when it will be born instead of the other way around." The crowd chuckled, and he continued. "It is true, you know, that, to everything there is a season and—"

"Are you still pursuing the Betatron Multiplier as the prime mover?" Though mostly hidden behind the group, the face of the interrupting man seemed upholstered in deeply tanned leather covered now with lines and creases, as if he spent his entire life sunbathing in the Sahara. I couldn't place the accent, veneered by a good education.

Dr. Weksler, shaken, but not stirred to action, began to withdraw. His glow from the celebrity spotlight turned to pallor. "No, uh ... when, uh, when I, that is, when we ... developed the Betatron, the cyclical limitations of—"

This time a fortyish woman in the tour cut him off in mid-sentence. "Didn't it cause that explosion at the Geneva Symposium?"

Dr. Weksler faltered, "Well, that, that is ... uh, we were not prepared for the derivative frangible nature of the—"

A white-haired gentleman asked, "How is your wife doing?" That did it.

"Enough shop talk." The tour guide, Dianne, horrified and humiliated by the discussion, held up both hands as she stepped in front of the fumbling Dr. Weksler. "We have a schedule to keep. Everybody please exit through the same door you entered, over there to your left." She pointed to the door and then to the clock above the door. "You can see it's late. We do have to pick up the pace. Everybody out, PLEASE. NOW. Let's go"

Dianne pushed her tour out of the lab and back into her schedule. She glanced darkly at Dr. Weksler and followed the entire group out the door. At least she thought the entire group went out.

Once they were gone, leather face stepped out from a dimly lit alcove. I've never been good at guessing ages, but I'm thinking fifty-plus. Maybe a mummified forty-something. I'm not certain what swarthy means, but I'm pretty sure he qualified. Handsome. In an oily sort of way.

The lightweight, tan, suede sport coat had an athletic cut. His odd, raggedy, left ear hung too low. The thin moustache and small pointed beard completed the look. An unidentifiable odor drifted from where he stood. I didn't know the smell and I certainly didn't want to be introduced to it. As he approached Dr. Weksler, his unpleasant aroma arrived first.

He extended his business card to Dr. Weksler. "Professor Pul, United Global Administration," he announced, rolling his R's and placing accents in uncomfortable locations.

Professor Pul turned and walked briskly toward the door to rejoin the tour. Without looking back, he commanded, "We will talk." Then he was gone.

His odor had remarkable hang time.

Dr. Weksler slumped onto the nearest chair, his limp fingers dropping Professor Smelly's business card to the floor. The empty eyes returned. He dragged the yellow mirrored sunglasses off his head and onto his nose. I caught a glimpse of eye mist before yellow mirrors barricaded any further view to his soul.

I heard of the tragedy before I went to work for Dr. Weksler but, knew few details. It happened in January, about a month before I came on staff at Pas Tech. Dr. Weksler's wife died in the explosion. Rumors of negligent culpability still circulated on campus, along with a joke in very poor taste about setting up a betting pool for when Dr. Weksler would commit suicide.

* * * * *

The Craftsman style home came to Southern California around 1900. By 2003 the National Register of Historic Places catalogued scores of those houses, known colloquially as "California Bungalows". Architects Charles Sumner Greene and Henry Mather Greene designed the most noteworthy craftsman homes. Their creations included the celebrated "Gamble House", built in 1908 for Mr. and Mrs. David Gamble (as in Proctor & Gamble). Recognized as a masterpiece of the arts & crafts movement, it is too large to be a *real* bungalow and too small and wooden to be a *real* mansion. Mostly, it is simply magnificent.

The administration building at Pasadena Institute of Technology might also have been preserved as an historically significant house except that, when acquired by Pas Tech in 1949, no historical appreciation existed for such peeling antiques. It merely epitomized Pasadena's neglected old gems, flanked by crumbling neoclassical mansions, all waiting to be flattened. In 2003 the low, long, one story former home still had its craftsman-style wide eaves for protection from the warm California sun. The wood-shingled, sage green exterior walls still held shutters and trim finished in Swedish-latte-crème. A thin accent of dark Mandarin red surrounded each window like pinstriping on a classic car.

Kevin bounced up the entry steps two at a time and literally skipped across the porch. Pausing at the rather out-of-place Victorian-looking sign next to the gloss black door, he read through the listing and found his man: Dr. D. Wright, Assistant Dean, Personnel. He glanced at his watch. *Oh, my gosh. It can't be. I'm not on time. I'm two minutes early!*

He peeped heavenward, threw his arms out wide, and did a little Gregorian chant, singing, "It's a miracle."

He opened the handsome front door and stepped into his future. The once-upon-a-time parlor had become the reception lobby. To his right a functional metal desk surrounded a functional mental case. Reading her name plate, he smiled large, and said, "Good morning Mrs. Phelps. My name is Kevin—."

"Oxley," she interrupted. "Please have a seat Mr. Oxley. The Assistant Dean is perusing your resume, after which you will be interviewed, and a preliminary adjudication will determine your possible suitability for any potentially available position. Please note than an interview is not a guarantee of employment, nor that a suitable position is currently available or pending."

Kev said, "Well, isn't that special." He sat in a wrinkled, coffee-brown, leather wingback and softly tapped two fingernails on one of its tooled brass nail heads, until Mrs. Phelps glared at him with a frown that clearly stated, *if you don't stop that, I will surely kill you.*

He stopped.

He uncrossed his legs and sat up straight, hoping good posture would earn points. "So, uh... what's this gig pay, anyway?"

Without looking up from her paperwork, Mrs. Phelps replied, "Such would be determined by State Education Code, article 327.4, as interpreted by University Regents, under the Federal Grant program governing your academic discipline."

"Don't know, huh? That's okay. I'll ask the big guy when I get in there."

The intercom buzzed. Mrs. Phelps picked up her telephone. "Mrs. Phelps's desk. Mrs. Phelps speaking. — — — Yes, I'll send him in."

She turned to Kevin and motioned toward the hallway which, half a century earlier, led to the billiard room. "Dr. Wright will see you now. Right through there. Third door on the left."

"Thank you, Mrs. Phelps." He stood up and walked to the hall. Looking back, he offered sound medical advice. "You might want to get a little more oat bran in your diet."

Using one knuckle, Kev rapped politely on Dr. Wright's closed office door.

From the other side came a measured, professional, female voice. "You may enter."

Kevin tilted his head like a puppy trying to comprehend a new sound. Puzzled by the female voice, he looked again at the plaque next to the door, this time actually reading it: Dr. Dianne Wright. *Oh, wow, the doc is a girl.*

Putting on his well-rehearsed Dale Carnegie smile, he opened the door and strode confidently in. Aside from Kevin, the blonde seated behind the executive desk was the only other person in the office. Her back remained turned to Kevin as she studied her computer screen.

"Good morning," he said, cheerily. "Dr. Wright?"

She did not turn around. "Be with you in just a moment, Mr. Oxley."

Kevin stood in place; his unmoving eyes fixated straight ahead. His left foot moved about twelve inches from his right, his body weight resting equally on both. Simultaneously, he clasped both hands behind his back with the right palm facing outward. "Yes ma'am."

After a few silent seconds, she turned, looked up at him, and gasped. "You!?"

Dr. Wright was the same tailored skirt and blazer—older than most of the coeds—everything exuded professionalism—desirable, rare breed whom Kevin embarrassingly tried to assist with her static cling problem just an hour earlier. And yes, also the same Dianne that led the undesirable tour of Dr. Weksler's lab.

At ease, and almost laughing, Kevin said, "No, it can't be." He looked around the room. "Are we on *America's Funniest Home Videos*?" He looked her in the eyes. "Is this cute?" He smiled, arched an eyebrow, nodded, and answered his own rhetorical query. "Yeah, this is cute. Hah!"

Dr. Wright regained her professional composure (easily mistaken for disgust) and extended her professional hand. Her hand firmly shook his as she formally introduced herself, "Dr. Dianne Wright, Assistant Dean for Personnel and Professional Development."

"Kevin Oxley, none of the above."

As the handshake ended, his fingertips delicately caressed hers. Her internal reaction was not the recoil she would have envisaged. Instead, she surprised herself with unexpected fingertip tingles.

Not looking at him now—carefully avoiding eye contact— she motioned him to the twin high back traditional side chairs in front of her desk. "Please be seated."

Breathing a little too hard, she went around the desk and sat in her powerful executive chair. She cleared her throat unnecessarily, shuffled through papers, and continued to delay eye contact as her perfect teeth unprofessionally nibbled at her perfect lower lip.

"I have perused your résumé, Mr. Oxley."

"So formal, Dianne? We're practically old pals."

She finally looked at him. Another tension-charged pause, then she coldly asked, "Can we cut to the nitty-gritty?"

"Hey, go straight on down to the gritty."

She grabbed his resume, stood up, and walked around her desk, saying, "Please follow me." Leading him to her office door, she opened it, and handed him his résumé. "It appears you are an exceptional geoelectrophysicist—whatever that is. Nonetheless, you go from job-to-job without ever making much of a contribution. I can't imagine why you think you would fit in at the University."

"I like cafeteria food."

She flicked her hand like shooing a fly out the door. "No. Stop. Enough cuteness. A research position at Pas Tech carries a great deal of prestige and responsibility. While you may have the intellect and the skills, clearly, you do not have the self-discipline."

"Cute? You think I'm cute?"

"I do not."

"You're still mad at me."

"I am not."

"Are too."

"I am n—." She regained semi-professional composure. "I am sorry. You do not meet our minimum standards for further consideration. This interview is over." He didn't leave. She cocked her head in amazement and shooed him again.

He didn't move. Instead, he asked, "How about dinner Friday?"

A split second of stunned silence (while her subconscious mind processed the offer) and then she said, "How totally inappropriate. I cannot believe you would ask me for a date during a job interview."

"I didn't ask you for a date during the interview."

With her slightly frail ego, shaken by the possibility that she misgauged the situation, she said casually, "You didn't just ask me for a date during the job interview?"

"You said the interview was over."

As much as physically possible in a politically correct college environment, she pushed Kevin out of her office. She closed the door behind him, then leaned her back against it, closed her eyes, crossed her arms, and smiled a really, really big smile.

Muffled, from the other side of the door, came, "Hey, it was nice talking to me. I'll call you."

She stifled a giggle, which turned into a snort.

Then she laughed at her own snort.

14

PHELTOR HALL LAB — TEN MINUTES LATER

D r. Weksler went out to an early lunch by himself to recover from the unscheduled and unnerving tour group which had invaded his lab sanctum. When his surprise eight minutes of fame transformed to crushing depression, it quickly became more than the man could endure. I feared for his life, but following his orders, I remained in the lab to babysit our little newborn cirrus cloud while I ate the leftovers of a submarine sandwich at my desk.

* * * * *

In 1803 a British chemist named Luke Howard thought those thin, wispy clouds above 20,000 feet looked like curls of hair, so he named them cirrus clouds. The name stuck. (*Cirrus* is Latin for hair curl.) I always thought they just looked like thin wispy clouds. Not being as eloquent as Mr. Howard, I probably would have just named them wispy critters.

Two-hundred-years later, in early 2003, new discoveries in unrelated fields led Dr. Weksler to believe he might be able to do something the scientific community considered impossible: create a cirrus cloud in a laboratory. To that end, he fashioned a new refrigerated version of his Norton Chamber, with each of its four clear sides comprised of custom fabricated, triple-pane, thermal glazing. He developed a proprietary low-E coating with an amazing emissivity that gave each pane a theoretical U-value of less than 0.09 [Btu/(hr)(ft^2)(^{0}F)] after the half-inch gaps between the panes were filled with krypton gas.

Yes, krypton is a real thing. Discovered in 1896, it is a naturally occurring odorless, colorless, and tasteless gas. Which always made me wonder... how does one discover a gas that is odorless, colorless, and tasteless?

When Dr. Weksler first told me the proposed specs for his refrigerated Norton Chamber, I made an amusing reference to kryptonite and Superman. Dr. Weksler ignored it. When I made a second mirthful reference to Superman, his second non-reaction caused me to look up at his so-called, "motivational" sign hanging on the lab wall:

> LABORATORY
> More of the first 5
> Less of the last 7

As is my customary practice, I quickly retreated from attempted mirth.

Dr. Weksler formed his new super-cooled Norton chamber via high-output, vapor-phase compression refrigeration in conjunction with first stage cooling from an Einstein refrigeration unit. We couldn't go cryogenic—reaching absolute zero—but the chamber became cold enough, quick enough, to actually create a miniature cirrus cloud. Quite amazing.

During Dr. Weksler's childhood in the small farm town of Douds, Iowa, refrigeration had not yet arrived, so things needing to be kept cool went into the root cellar. Dr. Weksler nicknamed his new refrigerated Norton chamber, the "root cellar". Maybe that's grinch humor.

* * * * *

While I sat alone in the empty lab, worrying about Dr. Weksler's potentially terminal sorrow, Kevin walked in with the ramistat in his left hand and two dead D batteries in his right. "Hey," he said, without energy.

I mumbled a "Hey," while swallowing a big bite of cold cut combination on Italian bread. I assumed his job interview flamed out.

He spotted a waste basket, about eight feet away, and did a hook shot with each battery. Dead-center-perfect. Both times. Clenching his right fist in front of his chest, he said without conviction, "Yep. I've still got it."

He needed a cheerleader. So, I said, "Dude. If battery basketball ever makes a comeback, you're the macho man."

He slid up onto a countertop, stretched, yawned, and pretended to be at ease. "Zup?"

I said, "Zup me? No. Zup you. You're the one who had the job interview, man."

He stalled. Holding up the ramistat, he said, "My batteries died. Got any spares?"

"Yeah," I nodded. "Got some here in the desk. Toss it to me."

He flipped me the ramistat and said, "How's your sub?"

"Good, but I like the kind better where they toast the buns.

So, c'mon... how'd it go?" I took another bite and fumbled with the batteries, finally getting them into the compartment.

"Oh, man," he sighed, "Theophilus, you didn't tell me she was hotacular."

"Who?"

He looked at me like I had a brain leak. "Dr. Dianne Wright? PhD? I believe the PhD stands for pretty hot doctor. Theo... she is stone-cold deluscious. I felt something in our fingertips when we shook hands. She felt it too. Our fingertips tingled. It was electric."

"Yeah, there's a lot of static in the air today."

He sneered. "Cute. No, not static electricity. Something way finer. Is she single or married or anything?"

I shrugged. "Don't know. Anything, I guess. Only met her once, when I first got this job. Oh, and then, I saw her again here in the lab with that tour group a little while ago. That's all I know." I laid my sub down, wiped my fingers on the paper napkins, and leaned back in my creaky wooden chair. "And the sixty-four-gazillion-dollar question is, did you get the job, Nimrod?"

"No... but..." He thought deeply. "I wonder if her professional opinion of me might have been colored by the fact that, just before my interview, I tried to zap her in the quad with the ramistat."

I laughed. "Are you serious?"

"Well, I only *tried* to zap her," he said. "The batteries were dead. So, I went up to her to help with the skirt static cling issue in person. I guess I messed that up, too. You know... the reality is... that woman is just not a visionary."

"What do you mean?"

"She can't see beyond the truth."

"So, Oxman," I said, "she turned you on, turned you down, and tossed you out."

"Yeah, pretty much."

"Well, under those circumstances, what'd you expect?"

He said, "I dunno... a cushy job... exorbitant salary... key to her condo." Sliding off the counter, he puffed out a deep breath. "Hey, toss me the ramistat. I'm outta here. Thanks for the batts."

I picked up the ramistat with my right hand to lob it to him, but when I raised my arm, the wispy little white cirrus cloud rose up out of the root cellar and hovered in the air. "Oh my gosh," I said. "Look at that." I pointed with the ramistat. The little cloud flew off and bumped into the ceiling, rumbling and darkening. It really scared me. I am afraid of the unknown. "Aah," I shouted. "What's happening?" "Aiieee!"

Ox couldn't see the cloud behind him so, he didn't know what frightened me. He cocked his head, put his hands up in front of me, and said, "Ohh...kay, Theo. Just tell me what's wrong, and we'll get you some help."

Slowly, I lowered my hand, and the mini cloud came down right in front of Kevin.

He said, "Hey, there's a cloud stuck on my ramistat."

"I can't believe it," I said. "Your ramistat moved the cloud out of the Norton chamber."

"Well don't have a hissy-fit. I'll put it back."

"No. Stop," I said, fearful we might lose control of the cloud before Dr. Weksler could observe. "I don't want to move my right arm even an inch, until Dr. Weksler gets back. He needs to see this, Oxman. It is supposed to be impossible to control a microcloud outside of a Norton chamber. This is absolutely amazing, astounding, astonishing, incredulous, and miraculous."

"I like the skirt trick better."

Sweat began dripping down my temples. "Kev," I said, "Do you have your mobile phone with you?"

"What? You're gonna call your cloud?"

"I've got to send Dr. Weksler a message."

Kevin said, "I thought you weren't allowed to call him during his lunch."

"I'm not going to call him. I need you to *please* take a snapshot of the cloud hanging in the air, and text the photo to Dr. Weksler. Right now. Before my arm falls off. I bet he'll leave his lunch and be here in two minutes. Mama Norducci's Ristorante is just across the street."

He sent the photo and I relaxed a bit, even though my stiff right arm began to hurt.

Kev had me as a captive audience so, he said, "You know, Theo... maybe your Dr. Weksler might consider giving me a—"

"—Not a chance," I said. "Do not discuss your unemployment with Dr. Weksler. No way. Well, okay. I'll let you talk to him about a job."

"What?" Kev said. "You flip-flop from no way to way? That quick? Are your meds wearing off?"

"I just realized he'll walk in and see that cirrus cloud hanging on your ramistat beam, and we'll both be heroes."

"Way fine."

"But don't *you* bring up the possibility of working for him," I said. "Wait for *him* to bring it up. Dr. Weksler is very formal. He adheres to old school comportment."

"So," Kevin ventured a guess, "is that why after working with him for... how long?"

"A couple months."

"...you still call him *Dr. Weksler*, instead of whatever his first name is?"

"That is correct," I said. "And it's Francis Noah Weksler. Named for Francis Scott Key and Noah Webster, but you don't know that yet."

Ox said, "And, when do you get to call him Francis? Presuming, of course, that you would ever want to call any man, Francis."

"The old school rule is, when he starts calling me by my first name, I get to call him by his first name."

"You mean he still calls you Mr. Spivak?"

"Yep," I said. Then I moaned through gritted teeth. "Uhmmm, this is really starting to hurt. What do we call me when my right arm falls off?"

"Lefty."

"Not funny, Mr. Oxley. Your lack of compassion just might make me drop your ramistat and the cloud, and thereby destroy the universe and your potential job. I need some help here."

"Alright, alright, alright," he said. "Here's the work-around: you hold the ramistat perfectly still, while I transfer it to my hand." We did so, very carefully.

"Ohhh. Thank you, Mr. Oxley," I said," Whew!"

When I went "whew!" I bumped his arm. His arm moved, and the cloud moved, bouncing into the old metal window blinds. The little cloud didn't like that. It seethed and rumbled. Instinctively, Kevin flew it away from the blinds. His arm moved too far, too fast. The cloud went up and skimmed along the end of a fluorescent light fixture. The lights flickered, and the cloud grew larger and darker.

"Oh, no," I said, "I think glaciation is occurring."

"Right. Whatever that means."

"It means water droplets in the cloud are changing to ice particles. Get it away from those fluorescents."

Kev said, "I can't wait any longer for your doctor kook. I'm putting this baby to bed right now." He steered the seething cirrus toward the root cellar.

"No, wait," I said, but I accidentally jarred his shoulder, and the cloud flew twenty feet away. Though still captured in the ramistat beam, the angry little cloud became increasingly difficult to maneuver. Kev tried another pass at the root cellar. He overshot. The cloud ended up a foot above my sub sandwich. That's when lightning struck.

WHAM! ZAP! ZAP!

Three tiny lightning bolts hit my Italian bread faster than you could say, *arrivederci pepperoni*.

Kevin smiled. "Well, Theophilus... just the way you like them. You got your buns toasted."

"Oh my," Dr. Weksler said. We looked in the direction of the voice. Dr. Weksler stood—in awe—just inside the lab doorway. "I saw the cirrus move," he said. "I saw the lightning. This is, indeed, momentous." Walking to us, his eyes bright all the way across the lab, he smiled as if he had never smiled before. "Thank you for the texted photo. I do not regret abandoning my *spumoni*."

I introduced them, being certain to follow protocol by saying Dr. Weksler's name first. "Dr. Weksler, this is my friend, Kevin Oxley."

"Pleased to make your acquaintance Mr. Oxley. I am the aforementioned Doctor Kook."

Kevin groaned.

Dr. Weksler continued, "Mr. Spivak has told me a lot about you."

Kev said, "Well, I—"

"—Some of it was actually good," Dr. Weksler said with a rare sparkle in his voice.

We all laughed. Ox and I made eye contact. We both knew what the other was thinking: *The grinch made a joke. He must be really excited about this.*

Glaciation reached the point where our toddler cloud just couldn't hold it any longer. It sprinkled teeny snowflakes all over me. I looked like a poster child for dandruff week.

While Dr. Weksler chatted up Kevin about the ramistat, I got down on my hands and knees to retrieve my papers, books, and sub sandwich, all of which had fallen off my desk. Using the ramistat, Kev demonstrated to Dr. Weksler, how to "fly" the cloud. He made a low pass over my desk. Too low. The petite cloud had one last little lightning bolt left.

ZAP!

Right on my tailbone. "Ouch!"

"Oops. Sorry Theo," Kevin said. "I guess, in addition to cold cuts, you now also have burnt rump roast."

Dr. Weksler developed a tiny grin. His eyes twinkled, and he said, "Well done."

A world record for Dr. Weksler. Three jokes in the same year. Seconds later, the little-cloud-that-could, dissolved without ever going back into its root cellar.

Half an hour later, Dr. Weksler and Kevin wrapped up their conversation laden with potentialities.

"So, Mr. Oxley," Dr. Weksler asked. "Theoretically speaking, what do you believe maximum control radius of your ramistat to be?"

"Well, let me think... It worked in our living room. And here in the lab. And that redhead on campus was about twenty yards away."

Dr. Weksler blinked at me. "Red head?"

"Uh..." I scrambled, "That's the English translation for *Testarossa*. It's a Ferrari with red cam covers. We saw one this morning." Dr. Weksler nodded thoughtfully.

Kevin continued. "With circuitry modifications and a stronger DC power source, probably five miles."

Dr. Weksler said, "Stronger DC power source?"

"Yeah, I'm thinking maybe half a dozen car batteries."

The conversation paused while Dr. Weksler mulled over electrifying possibilities. "Of course," he finally said, "we will need to facilitate and execute a comprehensive surfeit of experiments to ascertain all achievable applications for the ramistat, as well as all possible adverse implications of utilization."

"Well," Kevin slowly nodded, "Okey dokey." Kev never had the slightest opportunity to bring up potential employment, and now Dr. Weksler appeared to be taking over the ramistat. Kev glanced at me with his questioning eyes clearly asking, *what's going on here?*

Dr. Weksler stood up with a smidgen of pompous authority, indicating the discussion had reached its conclusion. Respectfully, Kev and I also immediately stood up.

Dr. Weksler shook Kev's hand. "Congratulations Mr. Oxley. I am giving you that government-funded, cushy, no-pressure, research position which Assistant Dean Wright said you couldn't have. I'll do the paperwork, pull the strings, and jump the hoops. You start work on Monday, March seventeen. Welcome aboard."

Kev said to Dr. Weksler, "How did you know about—"

"—The walls have ears," Dr. Weksler interrupted. "And, of course, my old age and tenure tend to grease the cutting-me-some-slack wheels."

"Well, thank you, sir," Kevin said. Then he sneered and, doing his Elvis voice, added, "Thank you very much."

"You are most welcome." Dr. Weksler reached over and included me in three-way handshaking. "Let's make history together."

"We'll do it," I said.

Kevin unleashed a hardy, "Amen."

Dr. Weksler's eyebrows arched upward at the scholastically inappropriate *amen*.

Kevin, already at the door, turned back to address Dr. Weksler. "You mentioned Assistant Dean Wright. You weren't referring to someone named Dean Wright, who's an assistant, right?"

Dr. Weksler tried to parse and comprehend.

Ox tried to clarify. "What I mean is, Assistant Dean Wright is Dianne Wright, Assistant Dean Wright, right?"

Exercising his synapses, Dr. Weksler slowly said, "Yes, the very same."

"She's not married, is she?"

"Oh, goodness no. Of course not," Dr. Weksler chuckled. "I think in her younger days she may have practiced catch and release. These days she's far too serious to have a serious relationship. Her houseplants and her relationships both die from neglect."

Kevin's eyes twinkled in my direction. "So, Dr. Wright really is Ms. Right."

Dr. Weksler neither understood nor cared what that was all about. He had ramistat fever.

15

STILL ON THE PAS TECH
CAMPUS — AN HOUR LATER

Mrs. Phelps, Dr. Dianne Wright's assistant (and friend) recognized the sparkle in Dianne's eyes. So, Mrs. Phelps gave Kevin an insider tip regarding Dianne's rigid, unwavering schedule: Thursdays — 1:13 p.m. — lunch — Mars Hill.

* * * * *

The Areopagus, founded in 1952 through the joint efforts of Jorge Pheltor and his West Coast scientist, writer, and artist friends, fulfilled Pheltor's dream of a social organization for those of high intellectual curiosity, in the tradition of London's Athenaeum established in the early 1800s by Sir Walter Scott and Thomas Moore. Pheltor purposed the aristocratic, private, on-campus club for Pas Tech faculty and alumni as a haven for tolerant, unfettered philosophical and religious discussion—freedom of speech, if you will—in the tradition of the founding fathers. Midway through the 1990s, however, the university Board of Regents learned of the Bible story about St. Paul evangelizing at the original Areopagus in Greece. A Biblical background being politically incorrect, regents officially renamed the club Mars Hill, with public conversations about Christianity being deemed inappropriate.

So much for unfettered.

"Nothing in all the world is more dangerous than sincere ignorance and conscientious stupidity."

— Martin Luther King, Jr.

* * * * *

Kev checked his watch when he arrived in the classy former Areopagus foyer: 1:33. Perfect timing. At least seating arrangements were still egalitarian in Mars Hill, so he went straight to Dr. Dianne's table. She sat alone, sipping her post-lunch coffee at the reproduction Louis XIV table below the amber-colored Jacquard floral drapes of the rose garden window.

"Why, Assistant Dean Wright," Kevin said, "what an unexpected pleasure." Sitting down in the chair opposite her, he smiled big enough to have dimples. He shrugged in a boyish way that indicated *well, at least I'm trying to be friendly.* "So, Dianne," he said. "We'll probably be seeing a lot of more each other now that I'm working at the university."

"The name is Dr. Wright. And I will be certain to keep the 'seeing each other' part to a minimum. For the record, I do not appreciate you getting a job by going behind my back."

"I tried going in front of your back, but you threw me out."

"I hope to have the opportunity again very soon." She pushed her chair back from the table while doing those little nibbles on her lower lip.

Tap dancing downhill fast, Kev said, "I'm sorry about that job situation with Dr. Weksler. I can explain. Maybe over a glass of wine?"

She shook her head. Her look pierced his corporal veil all the way to his heart.

"Look, Dianne... Dr. Dianne, how about we bury the hatchet—somewhere other than my skull—and let me take you to dinner some day after work? Or at least, a cup of coffee? Maybe a pretzel at the mall? C'mon, take a chance and get to know me."

"I already know you." She carefully folded the sophisticated ochre Damask linen napkin and placed it, quite precisely, over the gold-trimmed edge of the daffodil-pattern Royal Albert bread plate. Refined and calm, she continued, "You are unprofessional, unreliable, unfocused and... unctuous." Audrey Hepburn could not have told off William Holden more elegantly. "I don't respect a lack of commitment in a professional colleague and I would never tolerate it in a personal relationship."

Kevin said, "Commitment? Personal relationship? Whoa. Slow down girl, you're moving too fast."

She blushed. And she marched away.

Surprised by what he saw at her place setting, he called out to her, "So then, you probably don't mind if I eat your fruit compote?" He just didn't know when to quit.

Her back turned to Kevin; Dr. Wright allowed herself to quietly giggle as she rolled her eyes heavenward.

16

BAHADUR AND MIKHAIL REJOICE ON
ASH WEDNESDAY — MARCH 5, 2003

As everyone in the S.O.L. knew, Southern California is concurrently the daughter of the great Satan and the mother of all sin, in the most evil country on earth. Accordingly, His Supreme Eminence decided the S.O.L. must destroy the Southern California headquarters of some well-known Christian institution. His short list of targets included the Salvation Army, Azusa Pacific University, and World Vision. It is astonishing how religious zealotry can so effortlessly create hatred of organizations whose only missions are to provide hope, help and health.

Being a movie buff, His Supreme Eminence remembered *Tora! Tora! Tora!* and shared the concern of World War II Japanese Admiral Isoroku Yamamoto that such an attack on America might "...awaken a sleeping giant and fill him with a terrible resolve."

Thus, instead of a Christian target, he decreed the S.O.L. must obliterate a world-famous, capitalist symbol of American wickedness, the Chinese Theater in Hollywood. After all, that theater had been the location of world premieres for such disgusting American filth as *The Wizard of Oz* and *Mary Poppins*.

He scheduled the event for Ash Wednesday, reasoning that attacking on such a little known and poorly understood Christian holy day would mitigate fallout while still honoring the S.O.L. *raison d'être*.

The S.O.L. also hated the Chinese, much of the S.O.L. "religion" being based on multi-cultural hatred.

* * * * *

Though not as chilly as one might expect at 4:00 a.m. on a clear March Hollywood morning, Bahadur and Mikhail nonetheless chose to bring windbreakers, just in case. (A lesson learned from their very cold night hiding on the Fox Hills Tower roof.) Sitting in their beautiful red Lincoln Town Car parked in the deserted alley behind the Chinese Theater, they put on work gloves. There were no security lights and Mikhail wore a shiny new green turban. Perfect.

Cheap five-gallon aluminum gasoline cans, filled to capacity with gasoline, occupied the backseat and trunk. Noxious fumes filled the passenger compartment. A crash on their way to the theater would have incinerated Bahadur and Mikhail.

Just before Mikhail opened the passenger-side door, Bahadur raised his palm toward Mikhail like a traffic cop and said, "Stop. You will see now, and a lesson learn."

Bahadur removed his right-hand glove, then reached out and adjusted the dashboard switch so interior lights would not automatically come on when a door opened. "Now your door you may open, and the light will not alert to our presence any peoples."

Mikhail said, "But—"

Bahadur cut him off. "—You, the door now open."

Mikhail opened his door. "See," Bahadur continued. "The light no on. Safe are we. Idiota."

Mikhail stepped out, then stuck his head back into the car and said, "Yes, but—"

"—Halt your mouth." Bahadur scorned. "Get you to work. Unload. Unload. Unload."

Shrugging his shoulders, Mikhail acquiesced and closed his door. Bahadur opened his driver-side door and took only one step toward the rear of the car before he realized why Mikhail had been trying to warn him of something. In the still of the night, the very loud key-in-the-ignition warning chime deafened.

DING! DING! DING! DING! DING! DING! DING!

Bahadur panicked and rapidly turned back to the car, slamming his forehead into the edge of his open door. Slipping on the dew-moistened asphalt he fell backwards. His head did not hit the pavement until after he loudly bounced off the dumpster. CRASH! BOOM! BANG!

Mikhail tried, unsuccessfully, to stifle a laugh.

Bahadur, slightly dazed, climbed slowly to his feet. He removed his keys from the car ignition, slammed the car door shut, and angrily shouted, "Why are not you warn me? Idiota." Then he screamed loudly, "MUST QUIET BE!"

Both got a little gasoline spillage on their gloves and jackets as they each unloaded a can. Already tired because five-gallon cans of gasoline are awkward and heavy, they immediately decided to take a brief break. Bahadur said a prayer of thanks for their safe passage. Mikhail leaned back on the trunk and lit a genuine Cuban *Edicion Limitada Cohiba* cigar.

WOOMPH!

Fumes from the trunk roared with flame. The roof blasted off straight up as the car erupted like the throat of a volcano. Mikhail and Bahadur were thrown clear, with their gloves, jackets and clothing ablaze. Mikhail's green turban became a blowtorch. Cheap aluminum gasoline cans turned into hot aluminum shrapnel. Most of the shrapnel followed the roof straight up into the night so they suffered only minor slicing and dicing.

Ripping off their clothes, they ran for their lives wearing nothing but a jockey brief and a polka dot boxer. While running, Bahadur repeatedly slapped Mikhail on the head shouting, "Idiota! Idiota! Idiota!"

The red Lincoln Town Car became a pile of gray ashes surrounding a burnt steel skeleton. The Chinese Theater remained unscathed. An S.O.L. press release issued later that morning claimed responsibility for the test attack and stated unequivocally that, had it been an actual attack, they would have reduced the depraved Chinese Theater to ashes in disparagement of Ash Wednesday.

All the usual clue-gatherers gathered clues. This time, media outlets stated that, as evidenced by burnt remains of a green turban, the S.O.L. appeared to be a new, radical, militant Muslim organization. They didn't recognize the green turban as a red herring.

Bahadur and Mikhail delighted in watching the report on multiple television newscasts. They joiced. Then they rejoiced.

17

SOUTH PASADENA — STILL
ASH WEDNESDAY — DUSK

Having never been a religious person, I didn't go along with anyone's favorite brand of mumbo-jumbo. Science and religion being mutually exclusive, I never observed a reason to believe otherwise. Ash Wednesday struck me as especially bizarre. However, if one chose to paint a cross on one's forehead with ashes, well... to each his own.

I assumed Kevin to be a Christian. He usually went to a church on Christmas and Easter. Not much on regular Sundays. He invited me a couple of times. I never went. I'm a scientist. I believe in evolution and things I can see, feel and test. Kevin also being a scientist, I really didn't get it. Sometimes he even did things I thought should be considered irreverent. Maybe just being funny, but I didn't get that either. I assumed Christians didn't have a sense of humor and that they just kinda-sorta hung out together marveling at how good they are.

When Ox came back to our apartment that Ash Wednesday, he had a large black cross painted with ashes on his forehead. He stared at himself in our hallway mirror for a long time, swaying back and forth. Then he turned to me and asked, "Seriously now, Theo... I want your honest opinion. Does this cross make my ash look big?"

It had been my observation that when Kevin made a churchy joke, he soon thereafter went into evangelizing mode with me as his conversion target. The joke would be his "warm-up act". Next, he would test the holy water to see how much he could pour on me in one session. Understand, we're not talking heavy-handed, whap-you-upside-the-head-with-a-Bible mode, just (as he called it) "interesting religious tidbits, one scientific friend to another."

Until I had enough. Then he would graciously pack his circuit rider tent and move on to a different subject.

We had just finished a very satisfying Panda Express orange chicken dinner out on our huge second story wooden deck. It would be dark soon so, like a good scout, I put new batteries in my book light. First, I planned to check out the centerfold in the latest issue of my favorite adult model magazine. Then I planned to read my newly arrived *Scientific American* magazine well into the balmy evening. Kevin determined to spend his evening developing a new tactic for capturing the heart of Dr. Dianne.

I got just a teeny peek at the centerfold when Ox man suddenly had deep thoughts that needed to escape.

"Mr. Spivak," Kevin said, "What do you think about Darwin's Theory of Evolution?"

"Well," I said, "I don't know why it's still being called a theory. Hasn't evolution pretty much been proven?"

He vocalized a wrong answer buzzer, "BUWAAANT!" I hated that sound.

"Personally," Ox said, sitting up straight and serious, "I don't even think it should still be accepted as a viable *theory*, much less a *reality*."

"Oh, please do share your unsolicited religious rantings," I said, knowing he would anyway. I enjoyed our spirited discussions. I just never concurred with his conclusions.

"Well thank you, kind sir," He said with a grin. "I just finished reading Darwin's *Origin of Species* last night and I've been thinking about it ever since."

"And...?"

Kevin said, "And... Darwin's book, first published way back in 1859, contains absolutely no science. It is merely his own observations and conjecture. Yet his one-hundred and fifty-year-old theory of evolution is mandated by government and educational institutions as dogma. I don't even like the word dogma. Sounds like something a puppy does on your carpet."

Anticipating his soliloquy, I bent the corner of the page with that centerfold picture of the beautiful model and sat the magazine on the side table and said, "And...?"

"And," Kevin continued, "after one-hundred-and-fifty years of scientists trying to find the human evolutionary missing links which prove Darwin's theory, no such missing link has ever been found. Even Darwin questioned his own theory. You gotta read his book."

"I will. Sounds interesting." I reached for my magazine. Ahhh, but we were not yet finished. Kev stood up to pace about in the breezing orange and pink sunset.

"Theo, I could give you a ton of personal true-life examples that would make you question the entire theory of evolution. Things I've seen with my own eyes all over the world." He waved his finger in the air for emphasis. "I once saw a live butterfly on display in the Kuala Lumpur... uh... I don't know... what do you call a live butterfly zoo?"

I said, "I believe the official scientific phrase is live butterfly zoo."

Kev smiled and continued. "Thank you so much. Well, this one particular butterfly flew down and landed on a bush in front of me and, when it closed its wings, it scared me."

I raised my eyebrows and looked up at him. "The butterfly scared you?"

"Yes, it did," he said. "Do you know why it scared me?"

"Uhmm... it was packing heat?"

He shook his head in feigned frustration. "No, it scared me because the full color pattern on the underside of the butterfly's folded-up wing looked exactly like the head of a big snake. It actually, truly scared me and I jumped back away from it."

"And your point is?"

Kev said, "My point is... that fake snake on the bottom of his wing scares off predator birds while the butterfly is resting.

"Very clever." I said.

"Exactly. Theo, that's it. That's the whole thing. It is *very* clever."

I didn't get the significance. "And... so?"

"And so..." Kevin continued, "if evolutionary survival of the fittest is a true thing, then why—after eons of evolution—don't all 165,000 species of butterflies in the world have a snake head on the bottom of their wings? Huh? Maybe... just maybe... none of it has anything to do with evolution. Maybe, it is the result of a *clever* creator who created that species exactly the way it is."

I grabbed my glass of iced tea, took a slow sip, and gazed off to the top of the foothills, seeking some retort to his enticing tidbit. I couldn't come up with a single logical response.

"More to the point," Kev continued, "if evolutionary survival of the fittest is a true thing, then why haven't all creatures learned... math... farming... and how to drive a car? Why don't all creatures now read, write, talk, and build atomic submarines? Why doesn't everything have an opposable thumb? Or at least a Gatling gun?" He stopped agitating around the porch and looked me in the eyes. "If you want to talk about survival of the fittest," he said, "Just imagine... instead of a great big lion with great big teeth, the king of the jungle would be a tiny little bunny with a Gatling gun."

The Ox man was on a roll. As usual, I went along for the entertaining ride. He said, "Theo, let's talk about a goat."

I shrugged. "Are you serious?"

"As serious as bacon-wrapped gifilte fish."

I melted down into my chair for the next chapter of his bluster, and said, "Okay. Just know that you have interrupted me multiple times in my anticipatory process of attempting to drool over this month's centerfold."

"Alright, don't let your flip-flops flap. I'll be brief. And I wanna see your magazine when you're done with it."

I nodded. "K."

Kev continued his sermon. "Theo, let's say I go to a petting zoo and sit down with my laptop. A goat comes up and eats a hole in my shirt. I set my laptop on a boulder and turn to look at the hole in my shirt. While my head is turned, that goat will *not* jump up on that boulder and steal my laptop. Do you know why?"

"Let me guess," I said. "He was taught not to steal at VGS... Vacation Goat School."

"No... it's because after hundreds of thousands of years of so-called evolution, the latest, greatest, brand new 2003 goat still thinks my shirt is something worth eating and my laptop is worthless."

"Well, your laptop *is* really old."

Kev shook his head. "Okay, try this: can you name a single new animal which has been created in the last ten or twenty thousand years?"

"Uh... no."

"Well shucky darns," he said, "shouldn't a new, improved, different creature pops pop up every once in a while?"

"Yeah... if Mr. Darwin is correct, I suppose so."

Kev said, "Good answer."

"Thank you. Now can I look at my new, improved, different centerfold?"

"Yes, you may, because I must go back to thinking up a way to be captivating to Ms. Wright. And, besides, I'm tired of preaching to the deaf choir." He pointed at me.

I put my spread-out fingers on my chest and raised my eyebrows. "*Moi?*" He smiled and I said, "You know I'm still not buying what you're selling."

"Understood. Your prerogative." He tipped his head to me. "Thank you for listening, bro."

"Welcome. And I am going to read Darwin."

He gave a thumb up. I opened my magazine. Then I held up the two-page centerfold for Kev to see an absolutely gorgeous photo of the new 1/32 scale model of World War II Marine Corps ace Ken Walsh's F4U-4 Corsair.

"It is mondo cool, my friend," he said. "We met Colonel Walsh at the International Plastic Modelers Society convention in Orange County, remember?"

"I remember. Awesome man. Medal of Honor winner. That model is way fine."

I forgot to remember to ask Kevin when and why he was in Kuala Lumpur.

* * * * *

By Sunday night I finished reading Charles Darwin's *On the Origin of Species by Means of Natural Selection, or the Preservation of Favoured Races in the Struggle for Life.* That original title of the book remained in place for the first five editions until they later changed it, to be politically correct. I found the changing of the title to be disturbing on many levels.

Darwin, himself, recognized difficulties with his own theory. In his book he wrote, "Why, if species have descended from other species by fine gradations, do we not everywhere see innumerable transitional forms? Why is not all nature in confusion, instead of the species being, as we see them, well defined?"

My reading also exposed Mr. Darwin as an elitist racist.

"... the civilised races of man will almost certainly exterminate and replace throughout the world the savage races. At the same time the anthropomorphous apes ... will no doubt be exterminated. The break will then be rendered wider ... between man ... and some ape as low as a baboon, instead of as at present between the Negro or Australian and the gorilla."

— Charles Darwin

18

PHELTOR HALL

Up to this point, my work environment with Dr. Weksler had essentially been Grinch Inc. But now, his lights were on, everybody was home, and a party raged. His dead eyes experienced resurrection as he shepherded my and Kevin's non-stop flurry of activity. For clarification... a "flurry of activity" in the world of scientific research is merely weeks and weeks of thinking, calculating, and writing. After which one compares notes, runs spreadsheets, and theorizes about what, if anything, has been learned. Repeat as necessary. Boring to an outsider.

However, my observations of Kevin—and Dr. Weksler's reaction to him—are worthy of sharing. Everywhere Kevin ever worked he'd been a catalyst for change (sometimes unwanted). His time at Pasadena Institute of Technology repeated that pattern. Below are my recollections of Kev's first week at Pas Tech.

Monday, March 17, 2003

I arrived at Pheltor Hall early in the morning with coffee and donuts for the awesome threesome, my treat. Remarkably, a motivated, Hawaiian-shirted Kevin actually arrived before me. Amazing. The much warmer-than-normal Southern California Spring made his wait climatically agreeable. As I unlocked the door, he shared his thinking about how he might get back into the good graces of Dr. Dianne Wright.

"And what did you figure out?" I asked.

"I figured out that 'good graces' is shooting too high and, perhaps, I could learn to be happy with mediocre graces."

Dr. Weksler arrived just as we headed in. We were all early and excited about the future. Each of our official white lab coats hung on assigned pegs inside the foyer. Dr. Weksler's "Welcome Aboard" gesture, a brand-new lab coat with "Mr. Oxley" embroidered in royal blue on the breast pocket hung on the "Mr. Oxley" peg. Dr. Weksler and I stopped to put on our lab jackets before venturing farther into the gothic facility. Dr. Weksler's established standard lab routine included "the putting on of the coats" each morning. Though Kevin watched this routine, his personality matrix automatically obviated anything "standard".

"Good morning Dr. Weksler," Kevin smiled. "It's a beautiful day in the neighborhood."

"Indeed."

Taking a sip of coffee, Kev asked, "Where's my workstation? I'm ready to roll."

Dr. Weksler pointed to the east end of the lab. "Right over there, opposite Mr. Spivak."

"Cool."

The very long granite-topped wooden workbench stretched around the entire perimeter of the lab, only discontiguous in three places to allow for doorway access. Without putting on his lab coat, Kevin took the long walk across the ancient wood floor to his assigned eight-foot section of workbench at the far end of the lab. Dr. Weksler looked hurt by Kevin not donning the prescribed white coat. Or maybe perturbed. Probably both.

Arriving at his station, Kev meticulously moved all existing items on his workbench segment to locations at the outer limits of his territory. He then went to his van and returned with a very large cardboard box crammed full of his own exotic gear, tech toys, digital doodads, tchotchkes, and gimcracks. He stood on a chair and held the box one meter above the tidy center of his workspace. He turned the box upside down. Everything went everywhere. Dr. Weksler, standing in his own office doorway, watched Kevin's every move.

For some people, removing employment constraints and schedules liberates them to joyfully work longer and more creatively. With such freedom, Kev's job turned into his passion. The box dumping empowered one of his odd self-motivation tricks. His surprise and delight at finding some long-forgotten do-dad hiding under Kevlar sheers, or lurking behind a micro-saw, springboarded his brain into hours of wonderment. That's when Kevin thought of things other people never thought of.

"To invent, you need a good imagination and a pile of junk."

— Thomas A. Edison

"Different strokes for different folks."

— Muhammad Ali

As a certifiable Hawaiiaholic, everything Hawaiian gave Kev great joy. He fully expected to someday live on the Big

Island of Hawaii with a proper Ms. Right. (A *proper* Ms. Right, of course, must love Hawaii.)

After disorganizing the workbench to his satisfaction, he went back out to his van and brought in his one piece of "art" for which he had room on the wall above his workspace. He found it a few years earlier at a thrift store in the small town of Honoka'a on the Big Island, not far from Waipi'o Valley. Three-feet-tall by two-feet-wide, the Japanese red-lacquered bamboo frame, embedded with nickel-silver silhouettes of palm trees and ocean waves, held a discolored, water-spotted poster of the Ten Commandments ink-brushed in Pidgin English. It still had a hand-written message in the margin from the artist to his mother in Nagasaki, dated August 5,1945. Kevin didn't want to restore a thing. He liked the old piece, and its implied history, just the way he found it.

Pidgin, a kinda-sorta polyglot verbal short-hand, allowed English speaking residents and non-English speaking immigrants in Hawaii to communicate by using language bits and pieces from Hawaiian, Japanese, Portuguese, Cantonese, Filipino, Spanish and English. After a couple of centuries, it became the primary language of most people in Hawaii. In 2003, locals still used Pidgin for casual conversation.

My senses told me Dr. Weksler did not enjoy anything about the Pidgin Ten Commandments. He now watched Kevin like a hawk. No... he watched Kevin like a boss collecting substantiation for immediate cancellation of an employment contract. Kevin might have already gone over the top.

— Da Ten Rules —

(I added the King James translation here for clarification)

1. Yoa God mus be da kine on'y one, to da max

   (Thou shalt have no other gods before me)

2. Do notting for make junks dat peepo tink god

   (Thou shalt not make unto thee any graven image)

3. You no talk stink wit God's name

   (Thou shalt not take the name of the Lord thy God in vain)

4. Dah no work day mus be spesho fo God

   (Remember the sabbath day, to keep it holy)

5. Respeck yoa fadda an muddah

   (Honor thy father and thy mother)

6. You no make peepo mahke

   (Thou shalt not kill)

7. No moemoe wit somebotty you no married to

   (Thou shalt not commit adultery)

8. No cockroach noting

   (Thou shalt not steal)

9. You no talk-story wit bulai

   (Thou shalt not bear false witness against thy neighbor)

10. Nevah want odda peepo stuffs

    (Thou shalt not covet anything that is thy neighbor's)

"Different steeples for different peoples."

— Kevin Oxley

Tuesday

Kevin said cheerful good mornings and walked straight through the foyer without even looking at the lab coat pegs.

"Mr. Oxley," Dr. Weksler called out. Kev stopped and looked back in time to catch the white lab coat Dr. Weksler had tossed, the one with "Mr. Oxley" on the breast pocket.

"Uh... *mahalo* (Hawaiian for thank you)," Kevin said, holding it at arm's length, his nose scrunched up.

Dr. Weksler flashed a slightly irritated, albeit, fatherly smile. He held up a pointer finger and explained, "The number one all-encompassing rule here is... 'make progress every day.'" [Another Edison quote.]

Kevin smiled. "You got it. You da kine, boss." He did a fake yawn. "No moemoe at work." [Pronounced: mo-eh mo-eh = sleep. See commandment 7, above.]

Walking in my direction, Ox made a show of awkwardly fumbling with putting on his lab coat. He arrived at my sector with only his left arm in the jacket. The remainder dangled. Dr. Weksler studied him the entire way, then crossed his arms and slowly walked to us. His head inclined up to the left, where his eyes searched for just the right words to say in this awkward situation. *Mad boss walking.* More somber than usual, he stretched his hand toward Kevin.

"Mr. Oxley, please hand me your lab coat."

"Yes sir." Kev held it out and draped it over Dr. Weksler's arm.

"Thank you, Mr. Oxley." He crossed his arms again. "Gentlemen, I am immediately instituting new labor laws, due primarily, to Mr. Oxley's unique outlook on life."

Oh, Lord, here it comes.

"Henceforth, lab coats are optional. You may dress as you please. I may even become fond of aloha shirts, myself."

What?

Dr. Weksler strolled around the lab as his new rules poured out of some living stream which had been blocked for many years. "Henceforth, there are no set work hours. I no longer care if you come to work at nine in the morning or nine in the evening, or some combination thereof. You may choose to work all night, or all day, or all day *and* all night and then take a day for goofing off. All I expect is an honest week's effort. And, of course, personal choices may not impede anyone else's progress. We are a team. And we are in this together, all the way to the Nobel prize."

Kevin shouted, "HUA!"

"Henceforth," Dr. Weksler continued, "we focus solely on our goal, not on lab protocol. The goal is controlling weather for the benefit of mankind. I no longer believe goals are achieved by fanatical adherence to predefined and predictable parameters of behavior. If Mr. Oxley can accidentally invent a ramistat, the three of us can 'accidentally' invent a way to command the climate."

He turned and began walking toward his office. Kevin and I looked at each other with our mouths open. I wasn't even wheezing.

"Oh, and one other thing." Dr. Weksler turned and stared at us with his head cocked to one side. "I believe we must all laugh—at least once, perhaps even twice—every day." He continued strolling across the long glossy floor.

Due to shock and awe, I was barely able to get out, "Yes sir, Dr. Weksler,"

Kevin did a clenched victory fist and shouted a very military, "Sir, absolutely, SIR!" He whistled. We both clapped. I cheered.

Dr. Weksler looked back over his shoulder, holding up his hand to halt our demonstration. "Anybody hungry? Let's do an early brunch."

In a pretty good Sly Stone "Rocky" voice, Kevin said, "Absolutely."

We both jumped from our desks and jogged over to catch up with Dr. Weksler. The weight of the world came off our shoulders and the challenge of the ages came on.

"I've never been there," Dr. Weksler offered. "But I understand Mars Hill has commendable eggs Benedict."

Kevin hesitated. "Umm, I don't know... I think I might be allergic to Areopagus."

"Don't you worry Mr. Oxley," Dr. Weksler said. "Dr. Wright only appears Thursdays at one thirteen."

Kev stared blankly at Dr. Weksler. "You... but how—"

Dr. Weksler interrupted with a nod and a smile. "Geezers get to enjoy geezerhood by knowing more than people think we do." He grinned. "Stay the course, young man."

I had no idea what they were talking about. It sounded like a stinky cheese. "What's Areopagus?"

"Ah, Mr. Spivak," Dr. Weksler said, "that's many decades before your time. It's now Mars Hill." He thought a moment and added, "You know what? I'm old. I've got tenure. And I don't need any more politically correct garbage. From now on, we're going to call it by its true and meaningful name, Areopagus. That's what Jorge called it and that's what it is. And we will converse about whatever we want to converse about, no matter who it ticks off."

He grabbed his mirrored, yellow-lensed sunglasses, dragged them down from atop his head, and jammed them to the bridge of his nose. "Brunch is on me."

At the door we both stepped back to let him go through ahead of us. Even if we someday arrived at calling each other by first names, and even if he never achieved another scientific breakthrough, we would always defer to Dr. Weksler. His age, his accomplishments, and his mere existence required our respect.

We followed him through the door, hopefully on our way to becoming peers.

"Hell, there are no rules here; we're trying to accomplish something."

— Thomas A. Edison

Wednesday

Dr. Weksler's voice behind me, commanded, "Mr. Spivak, do not turn around."

Then Kevin's voice. "Close your eyes tightly. Keep 'em closed. Rotate your chair so you are facing our voices."

Dr. Weksler added, "Do not open your eyes."

Sitting at my section of the workbench with my back to the lab, I had no idea what sort of catastrophe might have occurred. Cautiously rotating in my chair, I squeezed my eyes tightly shut.

"That's it. Stop right there," Dr. Weksler said. "You're on target."

Whatever that meant.

Kev commanded, "Keep those eyes closed and stand straight up. I want rigid, Mr. Spivak."

I guardedly rose up. The top of my head became moist and then, everything down to my shoulders felt weird, warm, and wet, like amorous St. Bernard slobber. "What happened? It's really getting humid in here."

I could hear the smile in Dr. Weksler's voice. "Okay, you can open your eyes now."

"Ahh... you made fog? The whole room's full of it. I can't see anything."

Kev said, "Very carefully, walk toward my voice."

I put my arms out in front of me to make certain I didn't run into anything in the dense fog. I took three careful steps and... I was out of the fog. Dr. Weksler and Kevin stood there smiling at my Frankenstein monster walk.

"Okay, I give up. How did you make the fog disappear so quickly?

Dr. Weksler grinned. "Turn around."

I did an about-face and, for the first time, saw a four-foot cube of thick, industrial-strength fog hanging, mid-air, in front of my face. "This is astounding. And you can control it?"

"Apparently Mr. Oxley can," Dr. Weksler beamed.

Ox said, "Watch out Theo oops too late," as he made the fog cube fly right through my head and shoulders like an eerily silent, cube-shaped stealth bomber.

We watched as he flew it around the lab for a minute or so and then announced he was going to park it back in the Norton chamber. On the way to the chamber, however, the fog began to lose its cube shape. The edges rounded off as the fog lost density and then... zzzsssst. Completely gone.

"What happened?"

Kevin shrugged. "We lost power."

Dr. Weksler sighed, "Guess I'll have to check again on the rather thorny issue of my request for a purchase order." We didn't know to what he referred. He continued, "It's been difficult for the University's CFO to fully comprehend my need for three dozen car batteries."

* * * * *

Ever since the lovely Dianne Wright shot him down, Kev had been working many hours each night in his bedroom, behind a closed door, on a secret computer-based project. His recently acquired, over-the-top, hardware upgrades turned his PC into a virtual thirty-two channel audio/video studio. That gave him the ability to beta-test three new software applications: *Cinema Magic & Light*, *Auditory Emulator*, and *Anthropomorphic Pro*. He also nurtured a friendship with the Pas Tech Systems Administrator. Put them all together and they spelled: Dr. Dianne Wright, desirable rare breed.

When Dianne came to work that morning and booted up her office PC, the black and white throw pillow on her office couch rose up and became Tony Bennett wearing a tux and holding a microphone. Mr. Bennett stood on her sofa and sang, "I left my heart in Ms. Wright's office." Then the holographic crooner looked deep into her eyes and said, "Kevin is really sorry. Please accept his apology."

Dianne shrieked when the hologram first rose up, which made the indefatigable Mrs. Phelps come running in to do battle on Dianne's behalf. By the time Mrs. Phelps arrived, Dianne lounged in her chair, smiling. Together, they watched a few more loops of the three-dimensional projection before Dianne once again became Dr. Wright and called the Sys Admin.

Thursday

The next morning, when Dr. Dianne arrived in the administration building, Mrs. Phelps said, "I need to warn you, so you don't shriek again. There's a spectacular surprise waiting for you in your office."

"Is it going to stand on my couch and sing?"

Mrs. Phelps laughed. "No... but it will speak to your heart."

"Ooo." Dr. Wright headed down the hallway.

Mrs. Phelps called after her, "I think you need to go out with that cute Oxley fellow."

"Ha!"

The small lavender envelope taped to her office door allowed romantic fantasies to, once again, slip into her thoughts. She hesitated a moment, enjoying the anticipation, and then, almost dreamily, peeled open the envelope to reveal Kevin's hand-written a note on a lovely Victorian floral print card,

Dianne —

I am truly so sorry. Please forgive me and please, please, please, give me just one more chance.

♡ Kevin

Almost breathless, she opened the door and walked into her office. Seemingly every square inch of the room held roses. All colors, sizes, and types... vases... arrangements... long stemmed in and out of boxes... red... yellow... pink... white... mauve. Absolutely overwhelming.

"Oh, my God." She gasped, now officially breathless.

* * * * *

Meanwhile, back at Pheltor Hall, Kevin commenced his clandestine surprise for Dr. Weksler. Not really at ease with Kev's "show and tell", I nonetheless played my part: I fearfully turned the knob and held open the supply closet door. If it all went South, I would be a co-conspirator.

Kev said, "ROVER. Look." In the dark closet, the Golden Retriever smile appeared on screen and his bright red eyes sparkled. "With me," Kev said. He walked toward Dr. Weksler's office with ROVER heeling obediently.

The strange and uncommon mechanical sounds brought Dr. Weksler to his office door where he stood, puzzled. ROVER stopped six feet in front of him.

Kevin said, "Dr. Weksler, please hold up your left hand." (Dr. Weksler is left-handed.)

Pulling his reading glasses down to the tip of his nose, Dr. Weksler tilted his head forward and looked over the top of the rims in a tolerant — are you serious? — stare.

"It won't hurt," Kevin said. "Promise."

Dr. Weksler gave me a look and then did his best at being a good sport. "Very well..."

Kev said, "ROVER. Quick Launch." ROVER's turret elevated and rotated. The launch tube extended fully. A red laser dot appeared on Dr. Weksler's left palm.

Kevin said, "ROVER. Remember the prime directive: humans are never injured."

Dr. Weksler's eyes widened. He twisted slightly to the left, keeping his right hand ready for self-protection.

ROVER squeaked, "OK".

WOOSH!

A cold can of Dr. Weather's favorite iced mocha latte arrived in his left hand. He broke into the biggest smile of the year. "Hah! Okay gentlemen, when we're done saving the world, I want one of these critters for my home office."

* * * * *

Late that morning, Kevin received a call from Mrs. Phelps. "I just wanted you to know that all those roses took Dr. Wright's breath away. She—"

"—Oh, great." Kevin interrupted.

"No, I mean they _literally_ took her breath away. She couldn't breathe. She's allergic to roses. A horrible asthma attack. She's in the hospital, all covered with red splotches."

"Oh, my Lord."

"She's at Huntington Memorial."

He immediately left for the hospital. His first thought was to stop on the way and get her some flowers. Then he thought, _Well... maybe that's not such a good idea._

Through the slightly ajar hospital room door, he apologized many times, but she wouldn't let him in, telling him to just go away.

"Dianne, I am so sorry. Look, I know that sometimes I'm a buffoon, but... at least I'm good at it."

She groaned in discomfort. "I'm calling the nurse now to have you removed. Just like any other abnormality."

* * * * *

Dr. Weksler and I met for a late supper at Mama Norducci's. It must have been about 8:15 when we left the restaurant and noticed Kevin's van still in the Pas Tech parking lot. Dr.

Weksler decided to drop in and commend "Mr. Oxley" for his late-night commitment.

Approaching Pheltor Hall, we saw one slim shaft of light being split into many tiny rays as it refracted through the huge multi-paned window. Inside, all lights were off except for a small high-intensity beam at Kevin's station. All we could see in the dark lab was the silhouette of a man hunched over the work bench.

Dr. Weksler called out, "Good Evening."

Instantly, the light went off and the silhouetted man threw himself behind a chair, his eyes sweeping the lab, ready to counter-attack. We heard continuous strange clicking sounds.

Recognizing us, Kevin stood up. "You surprised me," he shouted. "Looks like I set it off too soon. You weren't supposed to see it until tomorrow morning."

Dr. Weksler flipped a couple of light switches on. I squinted. Dominos. A dozen rows of dominos marching to a grand finale. Falling domino decibels grew exponentially louder in the big echo-filled lab, the spectacle well worth the annoyance. A cryptic domino message appeared on the floor. It read simply: *Tonight!*

We clapped at the brilliant performance, the significance of which we had no clue.

"Very impressive Mr. Oxley," Dr. Weksler said. "So, if I may be so bold, what's special about tonight?"

"Absolutely nothing."

Dr. Weksler and I looked at each other, trying as best we could to understand our strange but likeable colleague.

Kev explained, "You weren't supposed to see this until you came in tomorrow morning. So now, *tonight* actually means *tomorrow night*."

"Very well," Dr. Weksler said. "What happens tomorrow night?"

Ox said, "Well, you can stick a fork in the ramistat upgrades, because they're done. Tomorrow night, our entire workbench becomes tornado alley."

Friday

Early Friday morning Kev purchased a fire engine red, two-wheeled furniture dolly with big pneumatic tires and assembled it in Pheltor Hall. Two car batteries wired in series with Kev's improved electronic wizardry sat on a plywood shelf attached to the dolly with L-brackets. An eighteen-foot-long cable connected it all to his more robust ramistat.

Dr. Weksler, meanwhile, finished construction of his new, improved, and larger Norton Chamber. Anchored on top of a four-foot square thrift-store coffee table with eighteen-inch legs, the entire apparatus now stood just under six-feet-tall. The four-foot by four-foot clear Glasonate sides doubled the dimensions of the original chamber. Per basic Newtonian physics, that squared the meteorological capacity of the chamber, increasing our volumetric test potential from eight cubic feet to sixty-four cubic feet.

Weather, however, lives part-time in the strange world of quantum mechanics, where an element exists in two different places at once, and where it is physically impossible to know both the location and the velocity of a particle at a given moment in time. You can only *know* one (location or velocity) ... and *guess* at the other. That volatile insecurity led us to conduct our upgrade experiment late on Friday night, after the Pas Tech campus became a ghost town.

At nine p.m. we converged on the lab with everything a "go" for testing our first major prototype upgrade. Without incident, Dr. Weksler created a vigorous three-and-a-half-foot tall tornado in the larger Norton Chamber. We ran trials and calibrations for forty minutes. Everything checked out. Time to go big.

Kev fired up the ramistat, focused the beam, and the three of us watched in fascination as our tornado rose up out of its incubator. Slowly, he moved it over to the long south wall workbench, where it gently touched down. Its winds made eerie scratching noises on the antique granite surface. We remained in control.

"Whew."

"Way fine."

"Very good, Mr. Oxley."

We triple checked analytics, complex event processing, and data visualization. Then we evaluated our "flight plan" one more time, just to be sure. From each corner of Pheltor Hall, a VHS recorder, a DVD recorder, and a dedicated video hard drive archived all activity.

Ox man said, "Let's take this puppy for a walk." He eased the joystick forward. The tornado hummed happily as it tap-danced along the countertop.

Then the ramistat CRACKLED.

And then the ramistat SPARKED!

The tornado violently shot sideways across the lab, knocking over a bookcase, throwing books in every direction. It roared down onto the table where Kev assembled the dolly. The tornado cleaned the table in less than a second.

"Whoa, my kind of hired help," Kevin said. "Go girl."

The tornado picked the dolly's spare tire up off the floor. Kev shouted, "Look out. Duck!"

The fat pneumatic tire and its heavy wheel soared over our heads and crashed through the immense, multi-paned window. Broken glass and window frames showered down on us. We crouched beside the Norton Chamber.

Dr. Weksler looked at Kevin. "What's happening?"

"Dunno. Can't control it." He stared at gauges mounted on the dolly, now about ten feet away. Straining to see, he said, "Looks like an overload in the ionization transducer."

Ripping open a supply cabinet, the tornado threw test equipment to the four corners of the large room. We all dove behind a heavy old roll-top desk as glass beakers and test tubes crashed into the desk and the wall behind us.

"She's got spunk," Kevin said, with a modicum of pride.

I carefully peeked out from behind the desk. The tornado hovered right in front of the roll-top, like a raptor ready to strike. I quickly jerked my head back in. "I think it's mad at us."

"Don't be obtuse, Mr. Spivak," Dr. Weksler said. "It has no emotions. It is purely an artificially induced and manipulated entity." He stood up. The tornado launched a pencil in his direction. Dr. Weksler dodged, as it flew past his nose and stuck two inches deep into the brick wall. He jumped back down behind the desk and yelled, "It took a shot at me."

I thought of a possible solution. "Couldn't someone just crawl over there and disconnect the battery pack?"

Kevin said, "Well, yeah, that could be done. But you'd create a discharge reversal and the ramistat would explode."

"Explode? You never mentioned explode before."

"When we were using flashlight batteries it didn't matter."

At that precise moment, I realized all problems in my world were Kevin's fault.

Dr. Weksler became our voice of reason. "Alright, gentlemen, let's just calmly and rationally consider every possibility."

"Right," I said. "Let's kill it."

Dr. Weksler rolled his eyes and continued. "The first question which occurs to me is... might we simply wait until the batteries are fully drained? Would that cause the tornado to dissipate?"

Kevin answered, "Yes, it would."

"And Mr. Oxley," asked Dr. Weksler, "How long will it take for the batteries to fully discharge?

"Forty-three days."

It became clear that we had only one option for escape from the tornado: wait until it turned its back, and then run for the door. When it roared its way to the far west end of the lab, we all prairie dogged for a quick glance. Spitting out paint chips, it plowed a trough in the 1950s acoustic ceiling tile, then slowed to destroy a large, art deco wall sconce. Tiffany shards pierced everything within ten feet. The incandescent bulb exploded, exposing bare wires in a spectacular shower of electric sparks. We hunkered down, ready to run.

...zzzsssst. The tornado touched the bare wires and dissolved.

Dr. Weksler observed, "Oh my... it electrocuted itself."

All power went off in the lab. We stood in the dark, watching lights blink out all over campus. Then streetlights went out. Businesses went dark. And everything, for as far as our eyes could see, became totally black.

Nobody spoke as each of us internalized our exhilaration versus our tons of concern.

Finally, Kevin broke the sound of silence. "You know what? I'm thinking I might wanna tweak that transducer thingy."

* * * * *

Bahadur and Mikhail, observing from a grassy knoll, phoned in their observations to their leader.

19

Over the weekend, Ox man spoke with Dr. Wright's assistant, Mrs. Phelps. She let him know that Dianne quickly recovered from the asthma attack, spending only a precautionary overnight in the hospital. Mrs. Phelps also shared that Dianne's reason for not allowing Kev to visit her in the hospital had nothing to do with anger. She just didn't want him to see her all puffy and covered with red splotches.

According to Mrs. Phelps, "The lady doth protest too much, methinks."

Monday, March 24, 2003

At 7:42 a.m. Kevin dropped in at The P.I.T. Stop, a smallish, campus-adjacent coffee house where they called a tiny cup "large" and the prices were so venti the professors described it as where the buck stars. Relying on a tip from Mrs. Phelps, Kev had arrived exactly fifteen minutes ahead of Dianne's precisely scheduled weekly visit. That allowed enough time to get his mocha, get seated at a small round table, and appear to be doing something important on his laptop.

Dianne spotted him as she came in. Awkward. She nodded recognition but didn't smile. Upon her arrival at the front of the line, the barista handed her a small box artistically gift-wrapped in muted spring yellow with an ivory ribbon. He Groucho-ed his eyebrows and nodded toward Kevin. Dianne's head slowly circled on her lovely shoulders until she saw Kev display a huge smile and a hand in the air. She issued her patented tight little smile and chose to ignore.

With frothy iced java in hand, Dianne wandered a bit, looking for an empty chair. Somebody or something covered every seat in the house. A couple of male students stretched out completely across two different, comfy, old sofas. Several female students had their backpacks and/or legs on what should have been empty chairs adjacent to where they sat. Even though the theology Prof sat on a very low over-stuffed chair, he reached way up and typed on his laptop clumsily positioned on a bar stool.

Stifling a grin (frequently required when around Kevin), Dianne turned and walked toward him. He stood up and from under his table, he graciously slid out the only available sitting surface: a spindly-legged, cane-back chair reclaimed from a thrift store. It looked great to her.

"Good morning", he said brightly, opening his hand toward the empty chair. "I saved a seat for you."

"So, I see." She surveyed the room with mock resignation and sat down, placing the wrapped gift on the small table. "How did you know I would be here?"

"Let's just say... a little receptionist told me."

"Um hmm. I must have a chat with Mrs. Phelps about boundaries."

"Now, now, don't be too harsh. She's only trying to help. You have to admit she's just not the same since she started drinking Metamucil."

Dianne didn't want this conversation to end, but grasping for something erudite to say, all that came out was, "Come here often?"

"Oh... maybe. Guess that depends on you." He pointed at the gift-wrapped box. "That's from me."

"Oh my, really? And I thought the Kona Coffee Fairy dropped it off." Surprised by her sudden concern that she might have sounded mean-spirited, she grinned, insecurely. With a slightly ragged breath, she said, "I'm not certain that it's appropriate for me to accept a gift from you, Mr. Oxley."

"Mr. Oxley? Seriously? Shouldn't we be on a first-name basis? I mean, look at us. We're sitting here in public doing highly-addictive, performance-enhancing beverages."

Loosening up, really wanting to enjoy the conversation, she said, "Very well... I don't think I should accept a gift from you — Kevin."

"Well — Dianne — that's fine, because it is not a gift."

"It pretty much looks like a gift."

He explained, "It's not a gift because it is a peace offering. I'm not certain, but I think I may have offended you at some time in the recent past."

"Ya think?" Her eyes widened in amusement.

"And then, of course, there was that floriculture event in your office when I almost killed you."

Dianne said, "Oh, what's a little oxygen deprivation between friends."

"Friends? Alright. We're back to friends"

She wrinkled her nose. "Umm... colleagues."

He put up his hands. "Okay, okay, you better open your pres—peace offering, before it's too late."

She smiled at him and took the first sip of her chilled caramel Greek frappé, followed by a relaxed deep breath. She carefully peeled the pretty gift-wrapping. The box inside made her giggle.

"Fabric softener sheets?"

Kevin said, "Eliminates embarrassing static cling."

"And wardrobe malfunctions?"

"Yep."

She looked him in the eyes (she liked his eyes) and asked bluntly, "Do you now know, or have you ever known—and can you guarantee—that my acceptance of these lovely fabric softener sheets will forever eliminate your stupid, sophomoric stunts?"

He put his left elbow on the table, leaned his forehead onto his left-hand fingertips, closed his eyes, raised the three-finger Boy Scout sign with his right hand and delivered his pained response. "Under the sole stipulation that my truthful answer will not eliminate me from competition for Dr. Wright's affection, and with our mutual acknowledgement and understanding that I am merely a boy trying to attract the attention of a really cute girl with whom he is infatuated, I will truthfully answer... yes... yes... and... probably." He opened his eyes, sat up straight, clasped his hands together on the table cleared his throat and politely said, "Now will you please go out with me Dr. Wright?"

Doing a rather poor job of hiding her enthusiasm, Dianne feigned pondering and then slowly said, "Well... okay." She held up her index finger. "One date." She extended a second finger. "<u>Very</u> public venue." She added a third finger. "<u>Extremely</u> well lit." And a fourth: "<u>Hundreds</u> of witnesses." Then her thumb.

"And you don't pick me up. We take separate cars. I meet you there. Wherever *there* is."

He did a thumb up. "Done." He stuck his arm out across the table and they shared a professional albeit tingly handshake.

Despite not-too-subtle eagerness on both sides, there were still time deprivation issues. Dianne needed to put in many extra hours in preparation for close of spring semester, followed immediately thereafter by the start of a new summer school program. Kevin anticipated mostly twelve-to-fourteen-hour days at the lab, for several non-stop seven-day work weeks.

Checking schedules on their PDAs (which branded them both as tech stars of The P.I.T Stop), a mutually agreeable Saturday became nominated and accepted.

"Saturday, April nineteen it is," He said, I'll call you with the time. I know exactly where to meet. You'll love it. Guaranteed." (He had absolutely no idea where to meet.)

She stood up. He stood up. She smiled as she shook hands with him again. "A pleasure negotiating with you... Mr. Oxley."

"The pleasure is all mine... Dr. Wright."

She picked up her drink, her fabric softener, and the gift-wrapping paper she carefully folded during their conversation. "Well I must go before I regain my senses. See you on the nineteenth."

Kevin said, "Amen."

She stopped at the door and gave her little finger wave to him along with a really great smile. He finger-waved back. She stepped outside, closed the door, and walked out of sight.

The P.I.T. Stop erupted in a cacophony of cheering, whistling, and woo-hoos. Followed by a standing ovation.

Kevin stood up—crazy happy—extending thanks to all for aiding and abetting. He bought a round for the house and the crowd went wild. Caffeine can do that to you.

20

A COUPLE OF WEEKS LATER

In addition to being almost extinct in 2003, public pay telephones were... public. Cellphones retained permanent, traceable digital footprints. And CB units were just too cumbersome, awkward, and poor fidelity when trying to stimulate thousands of supporters with a bootleg radio broadcast. So, The Pirate handled his responsibility to the empathetic masses by utilizing a relatively new technology known as a prepaid, untraceable, disposable, mobile phone. Years later, it would become known as a "burner". (Especially by those who watch *NCIS*)

As the Pheltor Hall workload continued to grow, a new Pirate rant for the Gary Puckett/Hollywood Bowl crusade became long overdue. Kevin required a quicker, simpler way to rally his multitudes. FCC books and charts in the reference room of the Pasadena Public Library on Walnut Street did the trick, providing all knowledge needed to do a home-based Pirate broadcast. For Kevin, a home-based (well, garage-based) bootleg radio broadcast would be a mixed blessing, with both "good news" and "bad news" elements. The good news: he didn't have to wear his Pirate outfit. The bad news: he didn't get to wear his Pirate outfit.

Back at the South Pas apartment, he wrote a new codex algorithm which he, quite simply, imbedded in his disposable cellphone chipset. In the garage he amalgamated the burner phone with the scan/seek function of his van's old AM radio. He knew the untraceable phone would connect directly with the final transmission phase of some local AM radio station. He also knew his limited expertise algorithm would not allow him to choose which station. The scan/seek function would arbitrarily lock onto the first strong signal it detected. Unfortunately, the polyglot Los Angeles radio market included more than a hundred AM radio stations broadcasting in two dozen different languages. He prayed he wouldn't get *Tagalog*. The Pirate didn't really have many followers in Austronesian media.

BINGO!

Much to his fist-clenching delight, his scanner hijacked the fifty-thousand-watt, number-one-rated talk radio station in L.A. The Pirate's morning drive-time three-minute radio rant from Kevin's garage ended with his traditional, "Yo ho ho and a battle of fun." People all over the Southland loudly sang "Yeah... yeah... yeah..." while canceling vacation plans so they could participate in the protest at the Hollywood Bowl.

Professor Pul heard every word.

As did Lenard Ostermann.

* * * * *

The new bootleg Pirate radio rant launched another bout of self-thrashing by FCC Under-Assistant West Coast Field Director Leonard Ostermann. No closer to identifying The Pirate, ol' brown suit had already set a new personal best for contiguous days of hissy-fits. And he didn't yet know it, but at the end of the day his face would be black and blue from a broken nose.

His thick file on The Pirate contained almost no tangible evidence. Instead, it consisted of fan mail for The Pirate, a fact which Leonard found quite annoying. Except for a couple of fuzzy video recordings from illegal TV broadcasts, nobody knew what The Pirate looked like. The black ringlets of fake hair dangling onto the forehead from below a tricorne hat, along with pasted-on shaggy eyebrows, mustache, beard and gold tooth prevented a match by the newly developed digital face scan technology. The Pirate's put-on gravelly voice could be fashioned by virtually any male over the age of thirteen, so a voiceprint didn't work.

Worse still, nobody had ever observed The Pirate's vehicle, if there was such a thing. He could have been in a car, on a motorcycle, a bicycle or on even on foot. For that matter, considering the rapid evolvement of digital communication, he could have been in some remote location on the other side of Los Angeles. Or even the other side of the world.

All dead ends.

In 2003, five percent of the Southern California population either made their living from the motion picture industry or were a showbiz wanna-be, has-been, or never-was. Those nine-hundred-fifty-thousand people included Leonard Ostermann. He religiously read *Billboard* and *Daily Variety*. He only knew enough about the biz to be annoying.

Early that morning, Ostermann's frustration reached the point where he decided he had seen so many cop movies that he could just go and be a hard-boiled detective. He put on a fedora and drove to Hollywood, purposefully taking a detour through Chinatown on his way. *Chinatown* being, arguably, the best detective movie ever made, Leonard felt such a detour might more fully transmogrify him into detective mode.

His wanna-be street smarts told him The Pirate must have some connection with... pirates. So, the iconic, double-arched, Melrose gate of Paramount Pictures became his first sleuthing stop of the day. He demanded an immediate personal meeting with that most famous historic movie pirate, Errol Flynn.

The Melrose gate guard politely said, "I am sorry, sir, but Mr. Flynn is deceased."

Sensing a conspiratorial cover-up, Ostermann said, "Well now, that's a convenient answer for you, isn't it?"

"Excuse me, sir?"

Leonard twisted his head out of his car window and with his well-practiced, hard-boiled P.I. sneer, added, "I don't believe a word you're saying, but for the sake of discussion, let's pretend I do. In that case, how recently would you try to get me to believe that Mr. Flynn died? Huh?"

"1959."

Momentarily thrown off his game, Ostermann quickly changed tack. "Very well, let's say I take your word on that. Let's move on to the more important matter of Captain Jack Sparrow."

"Who, sir?"

"I read in the trades that principal shooting has been completed and *Pirates of the Caribbean* is now in post-production."

"I am sorry. I don't understand, sir. Isn't Pirates of the Caribbean a ride at Disneyland?"

"That's just the kind of side-stepping, lip-flapping, rigmarole I would expect from you people. Now listen to me: a man named Johnny Depp is the principal <u>pirate</u> in that <u>pirate</u> movie and I demand an immediate meeting—right now—with that Depp fellow."

Upon viewing brown suit's federal identification as FCC Under Assistant West Coast Field Director, the gate guard slid shut his guard booth door and hurriedly notified the executive offices.

Even though Paramount had no connection with the *Pirates of the Caribbean* movie, and despite their view of Leonard Ostermann as a looney-toon who should be sent back to Warner Brothers, there was always that latent fear of federal guns and badges. The studio's Public Relations Director arranged an immediate meeting in Paramount's largest and most opulent conference room. She gently assured Mr. Ostermann that Johnny Depp was neither a pirate nor The Pirate. Leonard became somewhat mollified when she gave him two tickets to the next Paramount premiere and an autographed picture of Errol Flynn. Prior to the meeting, she had done an admirable job of forging Mr. Flynn's signature.

The white oak triangular conference table in the Cecil B. DeMille Room at Paramount could comfortably seat five people on each of its three twenty-foot-long sides. Hollywood memorabilia and gold-framed historic photographs jeweled the walls. The overall powder blue and dusty rose décor exuded plush.

His importance sufficiently acknowledged, Ostermann rose from his executive guest chair and concluded the meeting by addressing the entire room... even though the PR Director was the only other person present. Leonard swept the space with a royal wave of his hand. He pulled out his little red notebook and projected loudly, "Know this: I am going to make a file on you people. If I ever see Errol Flynn doing an illegal television broadcast, you are all in big trouble. And, should that happen, this studio will never work in this town again."

Tracking down the origin of The Pirate's stuffed parrot became brown suit's next clever detective step. That meant Western Costume, in North Hollywood, near Bob Hope Airport. Founded in 1912 by a former Indian scout who showed cowboy movie star William S. Hart how Indians really dressed, Western Costume Company had eight miles of costumes under roof.

Western had no knowledge of the fake parrot. Once again, however, Mr. Ostermann's federal credentials ruled the day. They assigned an Executive Vice President (EVP) to accompany Leonard as he methodically walked through and inspected the entire eight miles of period clothing. Although Ostermann demanded, Western Costume could not produce either genealogical or ornithological records for any of their fake stuffed parrots. The hapless EVP became forever known to his co-workers as the company's only EVPSC (Executive Vice President for Space Cadets).

Leonard Ostermann's frustrating day ended when, to take better photographs of pirate stuff, he stood up in the boat on the Pirates of the Caribbean ride at Disneyland. Falling on top of the large woman in the bench seat behind him, he tipped the boat and dumped them both into the water. When Leonard stood up, the large woman's even larger husband grabbed Leonard's camera and smashed it into his face.

Which explains his broken nose.

21

PASADENA — THURSDAY, APRIL 17, 2003

D r. Weksler insisted the Ox man and I take a day off to celebrate Kev's one-month anniversary at Pas Tech. Kev and I decided to catch the final night of a Dodgers three-game home stand against San Diego. Dodger Blue had already lost the first two. Just killing time at our South Pas apartment before heading to Dodger Stadium (only ten minutes down the Pasadena freeway) we thought a quick drive up to Dr. Weksler's Pas Tech office might be a nice diversion. Maybe coax another stealth "war story" out of him. Maybe even talk him into joining us for the ballgame. Highly unlikely of course, but worth a shot. It felt strange when we realized we both enjoyed hanging out with our boss.

Feathery white clouds bounced off the San Gabriel Mountains as we walked toward the Pheltor Hall west entrance. The lawns were limp due to heat and drought. We climbed the pinkish sandstone steps and, at the building's front door, halted with disgust.

Ox wrinkled his nose. "What is that smell?"

I almost gagged. "Oh man, did the world's biggest rat just die inside the wall?"

Kev covered his nose with one hand and reached out with the other to grab the doorknob.

"Wait," I said. "I know that smell."

"Well, don't invite it to the game."

"No, seriously," I said. "Desert man's been here."

"Who?"

"Professor somebody," I said. "A smelly dude on a lab tour, three... four weeks ago. That same day you interviewed with Dr. Wright. He had something wrong with his left ear. Weird guy. He was out to lunch."

"Probably eating rotten food."

On the other side of the front door, loud angry voices came echoing down the hall from the direction of Dr. Weksler's office.

Guarded, Kevin quietly turned the patina-dappled brass doorknob, his eyes darting about, checking for anything unusual. When he opened the door, the unidentifiable foul odor with an undercurrent of dirty sweat became stronger. Yep, the personal scent of Professor Smelly.

"JDLR," Kev whispered. "C'mon." Silently and almost instantly, he covered the forty feet to Dr. Weksler's open office door. I hung back a bit before cautiously joining Kev to peek inside.

Desert man wore a lightweight imitation suede jacket over a frilly, loose weave, collarless shirt exposing far too much hairy male cleavage. His beard and moustache still looked satanic. This time I clearly saw what remained of his left ear: a mangled, burned, and blackened nub. He sat on the wrong side of Dr. Weksler's desk, in front of the computer, where Dr. Weksler should have been. Open file drawers all around.

Professor desert man—his finger pointed menacingly at Dr. Weksler's face—shouted, "Do you not understand that our offer will soon become deadly serious?"

Dr. Weksler, standing on the guest side of his own desk, said, "Professor Pul... our research will never be placed in your hands. It is solely for the benefit of all mankind."

Odoriferous Professor Pul stood up, red-faced. "It's time for me to end this meeting right now." His hand reached for the small bulge inside his sport coat.

Instantly airborne, Kevin flew horizontally across Dr. Weksler's desk, his head slamming into Pul's abdomen. At the same time, his left hand grabbed Pul's right wrist and yanked it out of the sport coat. Pul deflated to his knees. Kev jerked Pul back up to a standing position with both of the Professor's arms behind his back, trapped inside the peeled down sport coat. Ox held Pul captive with an extremely strong right-hand grip on the sport coat straitjacket. His left arm circled the stinky Professor's neck.

I knew Kev was in great shape but ... *oh my gosh. What's going on here?* I never before saw him do anything like that. With thirty additional pounds of adult muscle, his athletic condition far surpassed that of his teenage football stardom. I would have bet he could still throw a sixty-yard pass and hit a sprinting receiver on the numbers. I suppose that's why some women chose to stare at him.

Out of breath and in obvious pain, Pul arrogantly scoffed at Dr. Weksler. "So, is this is how you peace-loving, sanctimonious, American humanitarians end an exploratory business meeting? I only wished to hand you my business card."

Kevin said, "Theo, check the jacket."

My hand trembled (keeping time with my wheezing). I removed an ornate gold business card holder, the only thing in the jacket, and laid it on the desk. Turning my head in case of explosion ... *Yeah, that's gonna save my life* ... I used a pen to flip it open. *Oh, good. Just business cards.*

Kevin released his grip on Professor Pul and attempted to smooth out the jacket. Pul fended him off and made hate-eye contact. "Do Not Touch Me."

"I apologize," Kevin said. "Perhaps I overreacted. But... Do Not Threaten My friends."

"I don't threaten. I react to stimuli." Professor Pul grabbed his business card holder, swept me aside, and huffed to the door. Before exiting, he stopped and addressed Dr. Weksler. "You lack wisdom. When you reconsider, it will be reckoned unto you as righteousness."

He squalled out of Dr. Weksler's office, slamming the door. A lifetime supply of filthy aroma remained.

"Oh, that smell," I choked out. "Gotta get oxygen in here." I reopened the office door.

Dr. Weksler said, "That fellow is a snot bubble."

Kevin snickered, "A snot bubble?"

"Most definitively... slimy and filled with hot air."

I went to the bay window to let in more fresh air and noticed Professor Pul on the grassy knoll down below. A short obese man in orange clothing walked toward him.

I whispered, "Kev take a look."

Ox came to the window, followed by Dr. Weksler.

Softly, Kevin said, "It's the goon with the gun from the top of Mt. Wilson." He quietly asked Dr. Weksler, "Do your windows squeak?"

"Never. I give them a good drink of WD-40 every week."

Kevin quietly opened a single section of the multi-pane, louvered window.

Down below, the basketball-shaped, orange-jumpsuited, unibrowed bully snapped off a Nazi salute and shouted, "*Muerte a los Marranos.*"

Pul did not return the salute. Nor did he shake hands. Nor smile. Firmly, he said, "Mikhail, I require that you never speak Spanish. Do you understand?"

Mikhail said, "Si."

Professor Pul, in no mood to deal with his billy goat minion, clenched his jaw and said, "Listen carefully, Mikhail. His Supreme Eminence arrives from Toledo on Saturday. When you pick him up, tell him—only in person—not on the phone—that he must not use his mobile phone at all, for any purpose. I do not trust Weksler and his nerdy baud squad. They may be doing high-tech spying on us right now."

Kevin and I smiled at each other, did a silent fist bump, and continued our low-tech spying.

Pul wrapped up his instructions to Mikhail. "We must all destroy our mobile phones immediately." Pul handed him a new phone. "This is a pre-paid, disposable cell phone for His Supreme Eminence. Give it to him as soon as you pick him up. With these phones, there are no names and no records."

Kevin flashed a knowing smile toward me and whispered, "Yo Ho Ho."

Professor Pul continued, "Untraceable phones for you and Bahadur are at my office. Do you understand?"

"Si, Capataz."

"English, only," Pul said again, forcefully. "You know where to meet His Supreme Eminence?"

"Si—yes." Mikhail said. "It I got. Flaming Zeroes. 1945."

As they moved off in opposite directions, Pul squeezed his own head with both his hands, wishing it was Mikhail's throat.

Once certain they were well gone, Kevin popped open the rest of the windows while I flipped the wall switch to turn on the ceiling fan. Dr. Weksler pulled the long chain three times to get the fan on high.

My decades of model airplane building gave me historical knowledge of flaming zeroes in 1945. So, I spoke first. "I think the location they talked about has something to do with the Japanese Zero fighter plane, and 1945 would obviously tie-in as the year. The anniversary of an atomic bomb falling on Hiroshima is just a few weeks away. Something seems to fit."

"I concur," Dr. Weksler said. "And, at my age, I have personal experience in that arena. But, first..." He nodded to Kevin. "Your physical rebuke of that walking Petri dish was... charming." Thank you for coming to my defense."

"You are very welcome. We gotta keep the good guys safe."

"That having been said..." Dr. Weksler cleared his throat. "Mr. Oxley... is there something you would care to share with me about, as you so deftly described him, the goon with the gun?"

Uh-Oh. I slinked down into my chair, hoping I might disappear.

Kevin described our Mt. Wilson event. When he got to the creeper firing the machine gun, Dr. Weksler interjected, "Machine gun? Was that not of concern to you?"

"Not at all," Kev replied, "They just tried to scare us. Shooting blanks."

I said, "What? You never told me that."

"I told you there was no danger and not to worry, didn't I?"

"Well, yeah."

Dr. Weksler asked, "And how did you know they were blanks?"

"I could tell by the report," Kevin said. "The sound. And no hits registered anywhere. I went back that night and recovered a couple dozen crimped shells."

"And you didn't tell me?" I said, building myself up to some serious blaming.

"I thought it would be better if you remained scared of the goons, so you wouldn't try something foolishly brave and heroic."

Well, how about that... me... foolishly brave and heroic. Is that a compliment? Or, maybe something else? Perhaps both a compliment and a something else. I am conflicted.

Kevin finished bringing Dr. Weksler up to speed, including The Pirate details. Dead air hung over the conversation. Dr. Weksler deliberated, his chin resting on his outstretched left thumb. Slowly, he said, "A pirate. You're a pirate."

Kev proudly responded, "Well, I am The Pirate."

"I get that. I've heard of your... crusades. Have you told anyone about our research?"

"Just Mom, Newsweek, Geraldo Rivera, did you know his real name is Jerry Rivers, National Enquirer, Mad magazine—"

"—Now is not the time, Mr. Oxley."

"No sir. No mention to anyone."

"Good. Mr. Spivak?"

"Nothing. To no one."

"Very well," Dr. Weksler continued. "Keep it that way. We do not discuss our work with Dr. Wright or anyone else. The university's politically correct administration considers me a benign relic... so long as I remain invisible. If they learn what we are doing, they will absolutely put a stop to our research. For now, it's critical to keep our work totally confidential."

"Totally."

"Confidential."

Dr. Weksler burned into Kevin's eyes. "And no more, 'Yo ho ho and a bottle of fungus.'"

"Battle," Kevin corrected. "And fun. Battle of fun. Not bottle of—"

Dr. Weksler raised his eyebrows.

"—Yes sir," Kev said. "No more yo ho ho. No ho-ho's. No ding-dongs. Nothin'. And 'bottle of fungus' is cool. Fungus is good. I'm good. We're good."

The concern about confidentiality surprised us, but Kev and I felt kinda-sorta warm and fuzzy about becoming "silent partners" in Dr. Weksler's humanitarian vision. The next surprise came from the Ox man himself. He assumed total command of our situation, something I had never seen him do (except on a football field). His easy-going, blue-gray eyes transitioned to laser-crisp steel blue. He stood up, silently walked to the door, then did an abrupt about-face. He waved his left hand in Dr. Weksler's direction. "Uh... tell me more about your 1945 personal experience."

Dr. Weksler briefly evaluated receiving a "command" from Mr. Oxley, and then complied. "My father's kid brother, my

Uncle Jake was only a few days older than me and we joined the Marines together in 1945. They rejected me on a critical need deferment, figuring they'd want eggheads like me around to create the next generation of weapons. Uncle Jake became the hotshot kid, a leatherneck fighter pilot wanting to make up for lost time."

Like fighter pilots from all wars and all countries, Dr. Weksler continued his story with his two out-stretched hands representing planes in a dogfight. "Uncle Jake shot down three Japanese Zeroes in his Corsair, in just the last few weeks before Pacific theater combat ended. The Marines racked up a 12-to-1 kill ratio. Jake told me, 'Everybody was flaming Zeroes.'"

The lower of Dr. Weksler's two diving airplane hands exploded and the victorious one (the upper hand) flew away.

"I'll give Uncle Jake a call if you think it worthwhile."

"I don't yet know what's worthwhile," Kevin said. "Yes, call him for whatever insight he might have."

"Well, I know he'll tell me a lot of the same stories again. I don't mind, of course. He's worth it. It'll be nice to reminisce about Mable Grable."

He lost me on that one. I said, "Mable... what?"

Dr. Weksler smiled. "Uncle Jake's girlfriend, Mable. After the war she became my Aunt Mable. He always told her she had legs like the movie star, Betty Grable, the number-one pin-up girl of World War II. You may recall, Betty Grable's movie studio insured her legs for a million dollars. Jake named his plane, *Mable Grable*. He mailed her a black and white photo of the plane from Iwo Jima in 1945. She had the photo in her hand when she died three years ago. Very proud of her fighter plane." Dr. Weksler sniffed.

"How about an aviation museum?" I tossed out. "Like, Planes of Fame in Chino? Maybe they've got a Zero, or someone who can figure out a connection. And there's that new Palm Springs Air Museum."

Kev said, "Call them first thing in the morning."

"I'm on it."

Kev thought aloud, "Professor Slimeball said the 'supreme eminence'—whoever or whatever that is—is coming in from Toledo. That's close to the Air Force Museum in Dayton."

Dr. Weksler said, "I have very old friends in very high places at the Museum, the FAA and the TSA,". "I'll call them all. They can check for red-flagged scum."

Definitely in charge, Kev walked to the big bay window and gazed out at the parking lot beyond the grassy knoll. He turned back to face us. "Got another idea. I'm being creative here so, just go with me. You know I've got a hot-rodder's heart, and I'm thinking flaming zeroes might have something to do with racing. Zero-zero is the number of a race car well-known for a flaming crash. Pomona drag strip can have times ending in zero zero, with enough flames to roast all the coffee in Kona. 1945 could be a position on the starting grid. The NHRA museum is next door to the drag strip, and Irwindale Speedway is right down the road. I'll hit 'em all tomorrow morning."

Dr. Weksler nodded. "A credible hypothesis, Mr. Oxley."

Ox sat on the back of his maize yellow barrel chair with his feet on the seat cushion. "Now, what about the Spanish? I know how to say burrito and that's about it. Either of you pick up on any of the Spanish?"

Dr. Weksler shook his head.

"Yeah," I said, "I took a couple of years of Spanish before grad school. I caught one thing from the little round orange guy. Sounded like... *muerde a los...* I believe that's murder or kill something. That's all I got. Oh, and... *Capataz...* which, sounds like maybe, captain."

Ox made a summary announcement. "Our next step-up in the ramistat testing is tomorrow night. I'll only need an hour or so to do final tweaks tomorrow afternoon. Let's all spend tomorrow morning doing our research and then get together to compare notes. Theo, along with everything else, please see if you can figure out what the little orange doofus wants to kill. Let's hope it's a bottle of Jose Cuervo."

"I'll drink to that," Dr. Weksler said. He stood up, pulled out his gold pocket watch, and surprised both of us by announcing, "It's late. I'm heading to the Dodgers game. Would you gentlemen like to join me?"

Dr. Weksler likes baseball?

Kevin answered for both of us. "We would love to! We dropped by your office just to see if we could talk you into going to tonight's game with us. We assumed you'd never been to a Dodgers game, so we already got three tickets in the right field bleachers. Let's do this."

Dr. Weksler smiled and ushered us to his office door. "We'll go in my car," He said. "I have free parking at the stadium."

Wow. How'd he swing that?

"Some kind of a Pas Tech perk?" I asked.

"No, I bought my first season tickets forty-seven years ago when they still called the stadium Chavez Ravine. Four box seats. Just to the left of home plate. Right above the dugout."

Whoa.

Dr. Weksler held up his hand. "Oops. Almost forgot." He went back and opened his lower right desk drawer. Pulling out a frayed and faded *Brooklyn* Dodgers baseball cap, he snugged it on his head. When he bent down to lock his office door, we got a good look.

Concerned, Kevin said, "Uh... Dr. Weksler, I don't know if you noticed. Looks like somebody scribbled all over the bill of your cap."

"Yes, I know. That is a 'thank you' note from Jackie Robinson."

Kev and I almost skipped down the elegant, pinkish, well-worn sandstone steps.

Nearing the staff parking lot, Dr. Weksler said, "Mr. Oxley, you appear to be a Mopar man. Would you care to be our chauffeur?" He tossed his keys in the air. Ox caught them over his head and then looked where Dr. Weksler pointed. Kev's jaw dropped. He gazed reverently at the old, brand-new, jet fighter plane-inspired, cream-colored car with gold on its tailfins.

Dr. Weksler said, "Mine is the '57 Plymouth Fury."

Kevin walked toward the classic gem passionately, as if going down the aisle in Notre Dame Cathedral toward his true love. With new understanding, he smiled at Dr. Weksler, and said, "I get it... 'Hell hath no *Fury* like mine.'"

"That is quite correct. The yearbook staff always forgets to capitalize Fury."

Arguably, the most exciting new car of 1957, the Plymouth Fury, had high performance and unprecedented handling for a midcentury American car. The Fury served as low-priced flag-bearer for Chrysler Corporation's "Forward Look".

Motor Trend magazine surprised the automotive world by announcing their prestigious "Car of the Year for 1957" as being the <u>entire</u> Chrysler Corporation lineup. Such an honor never happened before or since.

Dr. Weksler bought his Fury new in 1957 and, after a couple of months, garaged it, taking it out only for special occasions. A financially astute decision, the $2,925 car became worth at least a hundred-thousand-dollars.

When we settled into the stunning collectible, Dr. Weksler remarked, "As a point of reference for our sojourn, know that I consider Dodger Dogs and nachos an obligatory, gourmand experience whether the Dodgers are winning or not, which is a healthy attitude to cultivate because the Dodgers have infrequently been victorious for the past seven years."

* * * * *

That night Todd Hundley came off the bench as a pinch-hitter in the bottom of the eighth with two outs and two on. Slugging a three-run homer, he lifted the Dodgers to a 4-3 win over the Padres. Dr. Weksler took it as a presage of blessings for our awesome threesome.

22

TOLUCA LAKE, CALIFORNIA — THE NEXT AFTERNOON (FRIDAY)

"**L**ooks like we have diddly and we also have squat," Ox said, as he peppered his already salted and ketchupped freedom fries. According to plan, the three of us gathered for a two o'clockish lunch in Toluca Lake at Bob's Big Boy, a hamburger restaurant built in 1949. Its architecture, the precursor for midcentury modern coffee shops, led it to being named an official "State of California Point of Historical Interest". Seriously. Only in California would a burger joint be an historical monument.

Because of its proximity to the studios, the small neighborhood of Toluca Lake became home to more celebrities than you could shake a shtick at. Toluca Lake residents in 2003 included Steve Carell, Kirsten Dunst, Billy Ray Cyrus, Denzel Washington and scores more. Back in the day, Frank Sinatra and Bob Hope lived up the street from Bob's Big Boy. William Holden's house, just down the street, hosted the wedding reception for Ronald and Nancy Reagan. On weekends in 2003 the Bob's Big Boy parking lot filled up with cool old cars brought in by their cool old owners, including Jay Leno.

Kevin learned nothing of value at the three racing venues that morning. Same non-result for me with my aviation-related research.

"Yeah, I got nothing." I said.

"Uncle Jake sends his regards," Dr. Weksler added. "but he didn't have any ideas for us. He did say, 'If you run into those thugs, blow 'em out of the sky.' None of my associates at the FAA, TSA or anyplace else had a clue."

I took a hot, juicy bite of my double-decker cheeseburger and looked around the large dining room. Always loved the place. Not a 50s-*themed* restaurant, but an *actual* 50s restaurant. The walls presented movie posters, autographed movie star headshots, and vinyl record albums devoted to surfing, hot rods, and young love, all such topics well covered in the *Jan and Dean Golden Hits Volume 2* album hanging above our heads.

"So where do we go from here?" I asked, taking another bite.

Kevin, still in charge, said, "Well, we all found no leads, but we also all found a lot of interesting factoids from 1945. Let's just throw 'em on the table."

Dr. Weksler said, "From an historical viewpoint, 1945 was an astonishing year."

Nods all around.

He continued, "The most well-known events, of course, being the surrender of both Germany and Japan, ending World War II, and, as Mr. Spivak mentioned yesterday, two atomic bombs being dropped on Japan."

I said, "I couldn't find a single item online that would connect Japan to Professor Pul and the little round guy in the orange jumpsuit. The whole history of Japan in 1945 seems to be just one fanatical ego after another leading the country ever closer to annihilation."

While Dr. Weksler drizzled more secret sauce on both his salad and his double-decker, he said, "You want to know about ego-fanatical? On January 27, 1945, even though every German knew Germany would soon lose the war, Adolf Hitler went on the radio telling all his countrymen to continue their sacrifices because Germany would be triumphant. Shortly after that, he and his mistress both committed suicide. German radio, of course, announced that he died in battle, heroically fighting to his very last breath. Now there's an object lesson in why an honest free press is crucial to freedom itself.

"Roger that," Kevin said, nodding. "On a happier note, in 1945 Jackie Robinson signed his contract with the Montreal Royals, the Triple-A farm team for the Brooklyn Dodgers." "Anybody see a Professor Pul or an orange McDoofus connection there? No? Me neither. Okay... next?"

"I've got a good one," I said. "In 1945 a new invention—the ballpoint pen—went on sale at Gimbels department store in New York City. It was the cool, high-tech gift of the Christmas season and it wasn't cheap. A ballpoint pen cost a whopping $12.50. In today's money that's two hundred dollars. The ballpoint pen was the Apple computer of 1945."

The early delivery of our desserts allowed me to alternate bites between double-decker cheeseburger and hot fudge cake with ice cream. I could do that because I was an adult.

"I made no headway with the 1945 angle," Kevin said, "so I researched Professor Pul and his company, United Global Administration. You may have noticed his business card had no address, just a phone number. That number is a defunct mobile phone and United Global Administration is a hollow shell Delaware corporation owned by another empty shell in Vegas. They've got more than two dozen up-line bogus corporations stretching across the U.S. and then on to Western Europe. They're like nesting Russian Matryoshka dolls—where little ones keep popping out of bigger ones.

"The Pas Tech IT department didn't have enough processing power to determine where that big boy's HQ really is so, I turned it over to a friend at the Fed with immense megabytes. He thinks they may not even have enough muscle to dig out the root. United Global is cloaked deeper than a Klingon Bird-of-Prey.

"And, Professor Pul is a piece of work. If he's a professor, it must be at Ghost University. The only Pul I found is Tiglath-Pileser III, an ancient blood-thirsty King who carried North Israel into captivity in 734 B.C. His empire stretched as far west to what is now Spain. Pul was his personal name."

"What the heck is a personal name?" I asked.

"Fascinating," Dr. Weksler said. He turned to me with a large chunk of desert on his spoon and said, "To answer your question, Mr. Spivak, in ancient times a personal name was similar to a nickname, but far more potent. If you knew the king's personal name and you could actually say it without being impaled, you had major juice."

Kevin said, "I found a couple more bits of 1945 trivia that keep jumping around in my head like they're saying, look at me, look at me. One is that, in August of 1945 discussions were already taking place with British officials about founding the State of Israel."

Dr. Weksler shifted to intense mode. "And the other?"

"At about the same time in 1945, during the post-war chaos, anti-Semitic Nazi officers were being secretly smuggled through Spain into various Spanish-speaking South American dictatorships."

Dr. Weksler said, "That... may be... the connection."

Ox turned to me. "Theo were you able to figure out what the oompa-loompa said to El Capitan Professor Pul?"

"Actually, it was, *Capataz*, which is more appropriately translated as 'foreman'. And yes, as a matter of fact, with extraordinary assistance from the P.I.T. language department, I think we figured it out. The round ogre's attitude, tone and body-language were all consistent with a compatriot greeting, and what he shouted in Spanish was, 'Death to the hogs!'"

That's when I remembered to be scared again.

23

PHELTOR HALL — EVENING, THAT SAME FRIDAY

I could barely hear Kevin's shout above the roaring wind outside the lab, "Theo, please get the door for me, stat!"

Inside the lab, I parked my cloud in a holding pattern, put my new ramistat v3.4 in its holster and jogged along the aisle toward the closed northwest door.

My yell, "I'm on my way." echoed off the faceted blonde and dark wood-paneled walls leftover from a more gracious era. My shoulder and legs struggled against the huge door, attempting to hold it open while Ox dialed down his wind velocity. Stretching my neck and tilting my head, I could see the seven-foot-tall tornado turn the corner on the stairwell landing and move down the remaining half-flight of steps to the corridor floor. Kev followed ten feet behind, holding his shiny new ramistat v3.7 out in front of himself, blissfully driving his remote-control tornado.

I braced a chair under the door handle and got behind the heavy door. I wasn't scared, I just wanted to make certain the door didn't get away from me and impact on the tornado. Well... okay... I was hiding behind the door. At that moment, I generated a large supply of FUD (Fear-Uncertainty-Doubt).

Kevin successfully steered his tornado down the aisle between the folding chairs.

A spontaneous, "Who-Hoo." escaped from my throat.

Kevin clenched a fist. "Yes."

Scampering across the back of the auditorium, trying not to trip over all the chairs, I pulled my ramistat from its holster as I ran. Racing carefully down a narrow aisle, I stopped, turned on my ramistat, and pointed it at my six-by-nine-by-three-foot glowing white cloud hanging just below the twenty-five-foot-high ceiling. *Right where I left you. Good girl.*

* * * * *

Our complex three-way ramistat test had been scheduled on the Pheltor Hall master calendar for at least a week, which meant it had also been automatically entered on all faculty and administration calendars via the university intranet. Yet, upon our arrival, we found the big room reconfigured for a liberal politician's speech to be held the next night. The event had nothing to do with the physics department and Dr. Weksler hadn't been notified.

Now don't get me wrong. I have no problem with any university hosting a liberal political event. My issue is that virtually every university that permits liberal political events on campus also steadfastly refuses to allow conservative political events on campus.

As a personal sidebar, I don't get it. If the ideas of the educational elite are so profoundly correct, why then do they fear any expression of competitive views? To me, such a policy wafts the aroma of a wacko religion that prohibits followers from attempting to explore truth. Verboten.

I guess Kevin had much the same negative reaction to the auditorium issue because the next morning his van sported a new home-made bumper sticker:

> Radical Liberals Support Freedom of Speech Unless You Disagree with Them.

Two-hundred wooden folding chairs filled Pheltor Hall. They faced a temporary stage planted in front of the eastern wall. We decided to just consider the hindrances as a component of our experiment. As Dr. Weksler said, "If we truly have control of weather, then we will not be thwarted by something as common as a phalanx of goose-stepping chairs."

* * * * *

I carefully piloted the rectangular cloud around and between twelve massive air-circulation fans, each hanging down from the ceiling on a 15-foot-long wrought iron shaft. Every fan had nine huge, intricately carved, dark wooden blades sprouting from a gothic black hub. Collectively, they looked like a medieval torture machine.

I brought my cloud down to hover about ten feet above the floor. So far, our calculations held true. It appeared that, given enough power, we could create and control a cloud of any size, but only as a three-dimensional orthotope (more commonly, but incorrectly, called a three-dimensional rectangle), and only by maintaining a nine-by-six-by-three aspect ratio.

We looked at each other from opposite sides of Pheltor Hall, put our ramistats in their holsters, and jumped and cheered as if we had just won the World Series. While celebrating I noticed my cloud start to drift toward a large light sconce on the wall. I grabbed my ramistat. We didn't need another out-of-control encounter of the electric kind.

I yelled, "Ox, we've got some instability." I pointed a threatening finger at my cloud. "Oh, no you don't." I regained control just before a sizzling catastrophe, using the joystick to steer it to the center of the big hall... all the while avoiding those lethal ten-foot fan blades.

Kevin shouted back over the roar of his tornado, "That's an easy fix. We'll do it in the next step-up. Where's Dr. Weksler?"

"Don't know."

"I want him to see our stupid pet weather tricks."

Glimpsing back at the auditorium doors, I said, "He should be here by now."

Kevin scurried between two of rows of chairs to come over to me. "How's the lateral drift issue?"

"No major difficulty," I said. "But she has her own idea of what constitutes proper behavior. I need to be alert."

"Good. The world needs more lerts." He smiled with dimples and twinkled his eyes.

"You're sick."

Opening a side panel on my ramistat and looking at the gauges, he said, "Duracination on the integral realignment shift sub-assembly looks good. Seventy-three percent and cookin'. We are on it." He reengaged his own ramistat. "After you my dear," he said with a wave of his hand. He guided his tornado up the steps on the left of the stage while he ascended the steps on the right.

Smoke seeped into the auditorium all around the edges of the closed rear door. *Oh, my gosh. Is there a fire in the hallway?* Before I could react, the door flew open and Dr. Weksler ran in with his ramistat v3.5 held in both hands out in front of him like a divining rod. He grinned like the Joker.

"This is fantastic," He shouted. "Look." He turned to look back at the doorway as it slammed shut. "Oops." He opened the door again and pushed it against the wall until it chunked into the antique brass door holder.

Not smoke. Fog. Very thick fog. Dr. Weksler marched down the aisle in our direction. With his right arm stretched above his head, he flung his hand in a 'wagons ho' gesture and shouted, "This way." His fog followed him, billowing through the open doorway.

Cool. Dr. Weksler has become the Fog Whisperer.

From the stage, Kev shouted, "Dr. Weksler, please wait right there, sir. It's show time." The tornado met Ox in the middle of the stage.

Dr. Weksler shouted back, "Careful Mr. Oxley. You're dancing with disaster."

"Hah." Kevin loudly hummed *The Blue Danube* waltz as he and his seven-foot-tall tornado did a brief meteorological dance recital. He then put his voice into Barry White mode. "You've got some fine moves," he said to his tornado partner. The wind whipped open Kevin's shirt, popping a button off and untucking it from his jeans. "Behave yourself, girl." The tornado whirred seductively. "Umm, me too," Kevin said.

Then they both bowed.

Dr. Weksler, who had stopped to watch Kevin's stage extravaganza, sat his ramistat on a nearby chair and clapped. "Bravo, Mr. Oxley."

Kevin held up his right palm to Dr. Weksler, and announced, "But wait. There's more." He unfurled his left arm in my direction, saying, "Weather and gentleman, I give you... Theophilus Spivak. Maestro, if you please."

I hesitated. We had never attempted this before. "Uh, Kevin, I... uh... I, I don't know. You sure this is the right time and place?"

"This is the perfect time and place. Just do it."

I took a shaky breath, looked up at my shiny white cloud and pushed L-3. "What do you think?" I asked. "Is a four too much?"

"Dial it up all the way, bro. Make it a ten."

I grunted my throat clear. "Okaaay." I turned the ramistat secondary potentiometer to max and we all looked up. In approximately 3.23 seconds my cloud became dark and roiling, precisely within its orthotope perimeters.

"Now!" Kevin shouted.

I pushed the left "fire" button. It rained ... in a nine-foot-by-six-foot rectangle on the floor. Then the rain converted to an overabundance of hail. The sound of hail bouncing off wooden folding chairs on a hardwood floor slammed our ears... cacophonous... LOUD!

Dr. Weksler stared with his mouth wide open.

Kevin shouted over the din, "It's confirmed. A ten makes hail."

Little hailstones collected on Dr. Weksler's lower lip. He didn't react. He just stared, looking like he was foaming at the mouth.

Kev pushed a ramistat button to make his tornado spin in place. He pointed at it, winked at it, and flirtingly said, "Don't go changin.'"

As he jogged over to me and Dr. Weksler, the industrial strength fog skulking in through the other hallway door joined the fog already in the room. It all crept irrepressibly toward us.

Dr. Weksler grabbed Kevin's hand with both of his own hands and shook warmly. "Kevin," he said. "Congratulations."

Ox said, "Thank you." He turned off his ramistat v3.7. His tornado fizzled out. Zzzsssst.

Dr. Weksler turned to me and vigorously shook my hand. "Theo, congratulations."

"Thank you, sir."

Wow. We are now on a first-name basis with the legendary Dr. Francis Noah Weksler.

Dr. Weksler put his arms on our shoulders and turned the three of us around to walk up the aisle toward the door. Fog engulfed us. Earsplitting screeching noises made all three of us jerk our heads to look straight up in an effort to determine the source.

One bank of three monstrous ceiling fans shrieked maniacally as it wrenched free from struts and brackets.

Dr. Weksler shouted, "Duck!"

Kevin said, "Quack... quack-quack-quack."

"Not now, Mr. Oxley."

Darn it. We're back to surnames.

We all hit the floor, squeezing under chairs for protection. My cloud shot a lightning bolt into the fog, making it glow just enough so we could see the gigantic torture machine's shadow of death gyrating above us. Then came the shower of sparks, followed by a loud KRAAAACK! All three fans crashed into our improvised bunker of old wooden folding chairs.

Thank God they don't make 'em like they used to. Those antique chairs, heavy, hefty, and built to last for eternity, saved our lives. We all crawled out, brushed off, and exhaled. Nothing broken. Except fan blades. And chairs.

My cloud fritzed out, but the fog continued condensing. Dr. Weksler said, "Kevin, I believe our fog is experiencing free-agent tangential drift."

Well alright. We're back on a first-name basis!

Kevin replied, "You are correct sir, and that's an easy tweak. But first, we need to completely turn off the fog. Any idea where your ramistat is?

We couldn't even see our hands in front of our faces as we touched our way slowly through the thickest fog in Pasadena history.

"I know exactly where my ramistat is," Dr. Weksler smirked. "It's on one of the two-hundred folding chairs somewhere in this vicinity. But we don't need to worry about finding it right now because right now we are celebrating a giant step for mankind."

CRASH! BLAM! CLATTER! Dr. Weksler crashed into and fell over a folding chair, taking eight additional chairs down with him.

"Ouch!"

"Dr. Weksler?" I yelled.

Kevin shouted, "Are you okay?"

We couldn't see him, but we heard the warm smile in his voice as he said, "I am marvelous."

* * * * *

In the parking lot just beyond the grassy knoll, Bahadur and Mikhail stood in the dark, leaning against their new car.

Bahadur watched through binoculars as fog rolled out of Pheltor Hall windows and skylights.

Mikhail answered into his prepaid mobile phone, "Si. Oops, I mean, yes. Perdóname. Oops, sorry, I mean pardon me. Smoke, maybe. Fire, think no. Supreme Eminence tomorrow. Flaming zeros. I will there be. Si. Oops. Byegood."

24

NORTH OF BURBANK, CALIFORNIA — LATE THAT SAME FRIDAY NIGHT

A sixteen-foot-tall by forty-foot-wide stucco arch the color of boiled shrimp stretched above and across both sides of the gate-guarded entryway, which had not actually had a gate nor a guard in thirty years. Missing chunks of stucco exposed the weather-worn cheap plywood construction. Rough, hand-crafted, metal letters bolted to the arch wore sun-faded flaking turquoise paint. The letters spelled out:

> Kagel Can on Estates

The "y" went missing in 1971 and nobody ever bothered to replace it.

Estates? Really? That's a bit of self-puffery.

We were surprised to learn Dr. Weksler lived in a single-wide house trailer. Not that there's anything intrinsically wrong with either trailer parks or single-wide mobile homes, but as a relatively well-paid professor at a prestigious university for forty some years, we expected, perhaps, a goodly-sized craftsman in a prestigious community like

Sierra Madre or San Marino. Instead, he lived in a run-down trailer park several miles from the 210 freeway, in the foothills east of Pacoima, on the southwest edge of Angeles National Forest.

He had the farthest space in the last cul-de-sac at the north end, the nearest "neighbor" being the equivalent of almost two city blocks away. His mobile home, carport, and detached single car garage all sat side-by-side in front of a parched brown hill which rolled into a mile of isolated barren land before the beginnings of forest.

Following our immensely successful indoor weather trilogy, Dr. Weksler invited us to his place for celebratory coffee, tea, and munchies. The three of us sat at his small dining table next to his small kitchen. Centered on the table, a platter of semi-homemade nachos beckoned. Then I spied a can of *SpaghettiOs* (my favorite culinary sin) in an open cupboard. Dr. Weksler kindly poured them into a paper bowl and nuked them for me.

"Thank you for the late supper." I said. He nodded and raised his glass of iced tea toward me. "Dr. Weksler, you cook a mean can of *SpaghettiOs*." I raised a forkful in a return salute.

"Thank you, Mr. Spiv... uh... Theophilus." He chuckled. "First-names will take some getting used to. And yes, I admit to being adroit at microwaving. I was cooking with a microwave when everyone else still thought it was just radar."

"Seriously?" Kevin said.

"Yes, seriously. The first microwave oven came on the market in 1947. I knew Percy Spencer, the man who invented it. A World War Two radar guy." Dr. Weksler smirked. "I remember being in Grand Central Station, New York City, winter of '48. Bitter cold." He shivered. "Brrr. Believe it or not, I got a microwaved hot dog out of a *Speedy Weeny* vending machine. Just about the highest technology on the planet at the time. I loved it. Still love nuke dogs."

Ox and I looked at each other, intrigued. He asked, "Did your radar-slash-microwave experience have anything to do with creating stealth technology?"

Dr. Weksler nodded, "Corn on the cob ."

Ox and I looked at each other again. This time, worried that Dr. Weksler's brain had spent too many years in front of his old radar oven.

Gently and caringly, I said, "I saw a can of creamed corn in the cupboard. I could get it down and heat it for you, if you want. I'm sorry sir, but I don't see any corn-on-the-cob."

He looked at me as if I had two heads and didn't use either one. "Corn on the cob supplied the inspiration" he explained. "One night for dinner I put some leftover steak and a leftover cob of corn on a plate and nuked them both for ninety seconds. The steak came out barely above room temperature, but the corn on the cob came out too hot to handle."

"So...?" Kevin said.

"So, there had to be a reason," Dr. Weksler said. "There is always a reason, you know. For everything. Just like you, Theophilus, I don't believe in chaos theory accidents. Things happen because someone or some power makes them happen. So, I repeated my leftovers experiment multiple times, and I always got the same results."

"And...?" I said, still not getting the point.

"And, I proved to my personal satisfaction that the exterior shape of a vehicle made a profound difference in radar detectability. The test vehicle—in this case, the corn on the cob—trapped the microwaves instead of bouncing them back. All those little pockets between the rounded surfaces of the kernels absorbed the waves so they could not rebound. That's why the corn got hotter, quicker. I deduced that if this had been radar searching in the dark for invading flying food, the steak would be shot down. The corn on the cob, however, could slip through without detection. That was the beginning."

Kevin and I sat absorbed in wonderment with our silent mental equivalent of gasps.

"Wow, what a story," I said.

Kevin, shaking his head, added, "Really." He looked around the trailer, which possessed welcoming elements of feminine decor, and started to ask a question, "Uh, Dr. Weksler—"

"—First names please." Dr. Weksler cut him off.

"Oh, right. Sorry. Okay. Uh… I'm sorry, again… what is your full name?

"Francis Noah Weksler."

"Now I remember. <u>Francis</u> Scott Key. <u>Noah</u> Webster. Right?

"That is correct."

"There must be a story there, too."

"Indeed," Dr. Weksler said. He scratched an earlobe as he reminisced. "*The Star Spangled Banner* didn't become our national anthem until March third of 1931. My parents led the movement which finally made it happen."

"Really?"

Nodding slow and proud, he said, "Yes. Even though they were immigrants—" He paused, looked at our faces, wondering how we might react. "—*legal* immigrants, they were highly patriotic, and they loved this country. They learned English as fast as they possibly could and studied hard to become citizens. They learned about and assimilated into the U.S. culture because *this* was now their country and they wanted to be fully part of it, unlike many today who want to replicate the decayed culture from which they escaped. My parents were grateful for their opportunity."

I wasn't expecting Dr. Weksler's brief personal history lesson. But the goal being to get to know each other, I decided to launch my own feelings on the subject and see if they touched down softly.

"I really respect your parent's attitude, Dr. Weks—Frank," I said. "Kev and I have a shared ancestry and I'm proud to say both sides of our families came to the United States as legal immigrants. They waited for their turn in line and they followed all the laws."

"Hear, hear," Kevin said.

"Which brings up one of my pet peeves," I added. "I do not understand why we allow unlimited numbers of illegal immigrants to remain in our country. I'm wondering if so-called "immigration reform" might ever specify the maximum number of illegal aliens we will tolerate. Maybe... fifty million? One-hundred million? Two-hundred million? Unlimited? At what point will some honest person in charge say, enough?"

That certainly got their attention.

I continued, "What about safety? We know next-to-nothing about the millions of illegals sneaking in. They could be violent criminals or carriers of deadly diseases. They could be terrorists carrying suitcase atomic bombs. They could be democrats."

"Hah!" Kev and Dr. Weksler both laughed.

"At the very least," I continued, "illegal aliens take jobs away from American citizens, especially Americans of color. I cannot comprehend why black leaders support illegal immigration when the unemployment rate among black youth hovers around 20%. Simply removing all the illegal aliens in the country would virtually guarantee full employment and higher wages, instantly."

They both nodded in agreement. That gave me courage to continue.

"Allowing illegal aliens to stay here obviously has nothing to do with compassion. Those millions of illegal aliens are not here as refugees from war. They're not here as refugees from a natural disaster. And they certainly are not here as political refugees because both Mexico and the United States have the same kind of government. Both of our countries are democracies in which the people are free to vote for their favorite corrupt politician."

Dr. Weksler laughed out loud, pointed at me, and said, "I'd vote for him."

When the smiles died out, Dr. Weksler said, "By the way... Kevin... just curious... how did you come up with the word, ramistat? Forgive me, but it sounds old-fashioned and not at all scientific."

Kev laughed. "That's because *it is* not at all scientific. I named it for Harold Ramis. He wrote my all-time favorite movie, *Ghostbusters*. He also played Egon Spengler. I love that movie."

Dr. Weksler nodded and smiled. "Me too."

Kev made intense eye contact with me and announced, "Okay, Mr. Spivak, it's time to play Fab and Famous Physical Facts."

He used the "M" word —*Mr.*—followed by my last name.

"Really? You're gonna try to evangelize me again? Here? Now? In a social setting with our boss? In his home? After midnight?"

"I don't mind at all," Dr. Weksler said. "Sounds like another lively topic."

I put my face into both my hands and mumbled, "Then may I please have more SpaghettiOs?"

"Coming right up," Dr. Weksler said.

"Okay Ox man. Hit me with your best shot. Remember, it's already past my bedtime."

He raised his index finger. "First question. Multiple choice. When were we mere mortals first told the earth is round? Was it in 1492 by Christopher Columbus? Or 1522 by Ferdinand Magellan? or 1577 and Sir Francis Drake?"

Playing along, I raised my hand. "I know. I know."

He pointed at me. "Theophilus Spivak, do you have the answer?"

"I do. And it's a trick question. The answer is, none of the above."

"You are correct."

"The real answer," I said smugly, "is Eratosthenes, in about 240 B.C.

Kevin vocalized his buzzer sound effect. "Buwaaant! I am sorry Mr. Spivak, but the correct answer is not Eratosthenes. He came many centuries late to the party. The correct answer is—tah-dah!—the Bible."

"What!?"

Dr. Weksler grinned and chimed in. "That is absolutely correct, Theophilus. Almost three-thousand years ago, the Bible clearly described the earth as round and suspended in space. Actually, theologians had to do a little interpretation on the word, *space*, because such a word didn't even exist three-thousand years ago. The original Hebrew word used in the Bible, *belimah*, means *nothingness*. Close enough, I should think. And rather profound."

The Ox man added, "And remember, Theo, at the same time when the Bible taught us about a round earth hanging in space, other religions of the world taught that the flat earth sat on a gigantic turtle atop a humungous elephant, or some other nonsense."

I had never heard of such a thing, but I quickly recovered from my mild astonishment. Sticking to my own belief system (which, I guess, was a non-belief system), I said, "Okay, are we done now?"

"Nope. Question number two: when were atoms discovered?"

I knew the answer. Any physicist knows about the unseen building blocks of the entire world. "A lot of scientists contributed to our body of knowledge," I said, "but in the early 1800s, John Dalton conceptualized atoms and then in 1897 physicist J. J. Thomson discovered the electron."

Kevin said, "All true. Good answer."

I radiated.

He added, "However... more than two-thousand years ago this was written in the Bible: 'All things were made by God and they were all made from things that can't be seen.'"

"Whoa." I raised my palms facing Kevin. "No more. This is bordering on spooky. And ancient aliens."

Dr. Weksler slid a new paper bowl of freshly nuked SpaghettiOs my way, keeping a portion for himself. I said, "Thanks," and stuffed my mouth full so I wouldn't be able to answer any more questions.

"Mr. Spivak," Kev said, "I can see you are unable to safely vocalize, so I will submit just one more Fab and Famous Physical Fact, to which you need not respond."

"Goh fah wit," I said with tomato sauce on it.

Concerned by my deep involvement with SpaghettiOs, Kevin said, "Please don't make any more comments. I don't want you choking to death before you're converted." He shuddered. "Ooo, death by tiny pasta."

Dr. Weksler smiled.

"I'm sure you know, Mr. Spivak, it was only in the 1800s when we discovered that the stars in the constellation of Pleiades move together, in unison. That's because gravity binds the cluster of Pleiades."

"Yeth, ah know."

"Around that same time in the 1800s, physicists also discovered that the three stars which comprise Orion's Belt in the constellation of Orion do *not* move together. They are not bound by gravity or, anything else. The stars in Orion's Belt are just..." —he waved his fingers in the air— "...loose."

"Know thawt too."

"What you don't know is what the Bible said about those scientific facts four-thousand years ago when no human in the entire world knew anything about them. In the Bible, God refers to His own power over the universe by asking a mere human, 'Can you bind the cluster of Pleiades, or loosen Orion's belt?' Mr. Spivak... how did that knowledge get written down in the Bible four-thousand years ago?"

That one gave me goosebumps. My mind came up with no explanation for how such knowledge could be in a four-thousand-year-old document. I gulped down a big bite, and said, "Dunno, but I'm still not buying what you're selling."

My eyes sought pity from Dr. Weksler. "That stuff really bothers me," I said. "And, anyway, I can't see living my life based on four-thousand-year-old scraps of goat skin. JDSK."

He looked quizzically at me.

"Just Doesn't Sound Kosher."

He smiled like Mona Lisa.

I continued, "You seem really at ease with all that, that" —I did quotation marks with my fingers— "Bible science."

"Oh, I've read it many times. It's all there in the book."

"Are you one of them?" I closed my eyes tight, trying to think of a less offensive way to ask my question. "Uh... you know... a churchy guy?"

"All my life." He smiled warmly. "Sometimes my walk's been a little wobbly, but I always stumbled my way back home."

Kevin finally changed the subject by asking Dr. Weksler about his name. "Francis Noah Weksler is such a cool name. And you've got cool initials: FNW. Can we call you FNW? Or, maybe just FW? Or would you prefer Francis?"

"Please just call me Frank."

"So... Frank..." Kevin looked around again at the interior of the small trailer home. It had a woman's touch. "Is there a Mrs. Weksler?"

I gave him a concerned look and mouthed, *NO*, which he ignored.

Dr. Weksler said, "There was. That's her in the article." He pointed to an old framed newspaper clipping hanging beside the aluminum front door.

Kev got up and went over to examine the framed story. "Nobel prize? Wow. Dr. Sarah <u>Norton</u>?" He rejoined us at the table. "Norton... as in the Norton Chamber?"

"Yes," Dr. Weksler said. "Sarah and I shared the same dream."

I moved my eyes back and forth at Kevin and mouthed, *NO*, again.

"Will she be joining us this evening?"

"She was killed in the Geneva explosion."

Ox let out a deflating breath. He actually seemed to shrink. "Oh my gosh. I'm sorry."

"Me too." Dr. Weksler said.

"I'm stupid," Kevin said.

"You are," I agreed.

Picking up the frosty pitcher, Dr. Weksler poured himself an iced tea refill. He walked the few steps it took to arrive in his single-wide kitchen, took a sip and sat the tumbler on the aluminum framed, yellow Formica counter. Still silent, his back turned to us, he busied himself with wiping up a bit of spilled salsa and bean dip. He pointed to a small piece of embroidered cloth mounted in a wooden frame perched on the corner shelf above the small metal sink. "Sarah made that herself," he said. "Her hobby for a while, when we were younger. She did that piece when we were grad school newlyweds in Greeley, Colorado."

He took it off the shelf and read it aloud, "Cookin' lasts. Kissin' don't." He sat it back on the shelf. "It's an old country saying. It's not true. After fifty years of marriage, I still liked kissing her." His voice frayed around the edges. "She was my best friend." He turned his back to us for a few moments. We said nothing. Cleaning things which didn't need cleaning, he reflected a bit longer before saying, "Gentlemen, let's move to the living room for some shop talk."

Ox and I silently walked the short distance to the feminine sofa, upholstered in a country plaid of Navajo-white, pine green, tobacco brown, and pale cobalt. It sat under the front window, which had mid-fifties full-size Venetian blinds. The sofa was comfortable. We were not.

Dr. Weksler grabbed his drink and watchfully followed us, ambling his way to the worn black leather recliner.

"To use a baseball metaphor," he said, "developing stealth technology was nothing more than a bush league hit into shallow right. Not that difficult to execute. The last fifteen years of my life, however, have been devoted to the control of weather. That is the real deal. That, is something which will change the world. Perhaps even save it."

He took another sip and went silent. He made long, intense eye contact with me, as if trying to read my mind. That ended when he nodded and said, "Theophilus."

He moved the intense eye contact to Kevin, as if trying to read his soul. Finally nodding his head, he said, simply, "Kevin."

I sat up straighter and concentrated, fearful I might not hear the coming pronouncement due to my loud pulse booming in my eardrums.

Slowly, clearly, dramatically, he asked, "How long will it take... for us to have... a fully operational... full-scale prototype?"

Well that wasn't so bad.

I exhaled my captive breath. "Six months, maybe."

Kevin said, "Twenty-three years."

Dr. Weksler asked, "How about five weeks?"

"Impossible," Ox said. "Even if I wanted to finish the project and put an end to my favorite job."

Dr. Weksler revealed his plan. "If we can have a complete system up and running in five weeks, then I'm taking us to Paris for the International Environmental Studies Conference."

"Dr. Weks—Frank, that's fantastic."

Kevin didn't even want to consider it. "Sounds like a great adventure, but you know how I hate deadlines."

Understanding and wisdom sometimes do accompany age. Dr. Weksler knew the precise words to motivate the Ox man. "Kevin, a successful demonstration at the I.E.S. will guarantee you cushy research grants for the rest of your life."

"Well shut my mouth and pack my bag."

I said, "Yes! Everything's chicken."

Dr. Weksler perked up. "Everything's chicken? How on earth did you come up with that?"

We explained about our grandfather.

Dr. Weksler raised himself up out of his recliner. He leaned against the front door with a huge smile and said, "My, my. Long-ignored memories. Back in the day, as is the current vernacular —World War II, to be precise— *everything's chicken* became a really *hep* expression used by all us *hep cats*." The laugh lines around his eyes celebrated. "*Hep*, you understand, came before *hip*, which came before *cool*, which preceded whatever's out there now."

We were privileged to enjoy another of his stories.

He continued, "What you probably don't know is, there's more to that expression."

"Really?"

"No, we don't know."

"Well," he said, "when all is good, then us hep guys said, 'Everything's chicken.' And when everything's GREAT... you know... you get paid, the arrogant Lieutenant gets court-martialed, you have a three-day pass to spend with your girl in Paris... then you said, 'Everything's chicken but the gravy. And you know what the gravy's made out of... more chicken.'"

We loved it.

He stopped leaning. "Gentlemen, please join me in a toast."

We stood up and raised our iced tea glasses, proud to be doing so.

He tipped his glass toward me. "To Theophilus, a loyal, tireless associate steadfastly dedicated to our goal."

"Hear, hear." Kevin said.

Dr. Weksler nodded his tumbler toward Kevin. "And, to Kevin, whose unique perspective on... everything in the world..." He smiled. "...led to our breakthrough."

"Hear, hear again." I said.

Kevin said, "Aw shucky-darns."

Dr. Weksler continued. "During the previous, rather tough, few months, I had made up my mind I would not live to see the kind of progress we've made. Thank you, gentlemen, for my... resurrection." His eyes went moist again.

"My turn," I said, raising my glass with a tilt to Dr. Weksler. "To Dr. Weksler, a man who will be remembered up there along with Louis Pasteur, Jonas Salk, and Bill Gates." As a quick afterthought I added, "And Thomas Edison." We all grinned.

Kevin added, "A man whose name will go down in the history books, boring eighth graders well into the twenty-third century." Dr. Weksler enjoyed that as well. Then Kevin pretended to scold me. "C'mon Theo, you didn't use his first name." He waved his hand in the air. "Don't worry, I will fix that right now. Raise your glasses on high, gentlemen." We did. Ox continued, "A toast of respect and admiration, to our friend... Dr. Frank N. Storm."

We talked and planned and then finished the late evening with some respectable coffee Frank made in his forty-year-old stainless-steel percolator. As Kev and I exited his aluminum front door, down onto the trailer's retractable metal step, and then out onto the cracked carport concrete slab, Frank said, "Good night, gentlemen. It's time to wind the cat and put out the clock." We laughed. Our grandmother used to say that. Everything felt warm and fuzzy.

Except that religiosity stuff.

25

SATURDAY — KEVIN & DIANNE
FIRST DATE 1.1

A geeky new outdoor recreational activity called geocaching became popular in 2003. Appallingly, the blowing up of a civilian jetliner twenty years earlier made it possible. Russia shot down Korean Airlines Flight 007 (a Boeing 747 jumbo jet carrying 269 people) in 1983. No one survived.

As a direct result of that ghastly Russian mistake, President Ronald Reagan issued—for the common good of the world—a presidential directive making the U.S.-created and owned Global Positioning System (GPS) freely available to civilians everywhere, once it became sufficiently developed. The final stage in creation of GPS came on May 2, 2000, thus allowing civilian users all over the earth to receive a signal using wholly American-owned satellites and technology.

To geocache, a player employed his or her GPS-equipped PDA or mobile phone to search for a "treasure", using only navigational coordinates. The treasure (a cheap toy or trinket) would be in a small waterproof container located at the coordinates. The finder would sign and date a logbook kept in the container, and then trade a new bauble for one of those inside.

* * * * *

Based on Dianne's comfort-level with her PDA, as demonstrated at The P.I.T. Stop, Kevin decided it would be mundane to simply call her and say where to meet him for their first date. Instead, he sent her a text:

Let's meet at 34.171959, 118.31893 – 5p – Field #1 – very public – hundreds of witnesses – look for the Starfighter in the sky.

She texted back:

OK. What about attire?

He responded:

No need to bring a tire. I have a spare.

She texted:

LOL. Over.

Kevin didn't know whether Dianne's LOL meant "Laugh Out Loud" or "Lots of Love". As opposed to "Loser of Losers. Over."

The blue and white Lockheed TF-104 Starfighter named *Spirit of Burbank*, a retired jet fighter/trainer perched like a gigantic model airplane atop a pedestal twenty-feet in the sky at the edge of George Izay Park in Burbank. If Dr. Dianne Wright figured it out, the coordinates would take her right to the base of the Starfighter. Kevin's five-year-old niece, Shari Michelle, would be playing her first-ever T-ball game at the park's softball field #1, almost in the shadow of the Starfighter. Kevin showed up early because he coached Shari Michelle's team, the Bad News Bunnies.

Dianne didn't even own jeans or a sweatshirt. Even for a casual outdoor date she had a serious need to look professional (not that she was uptight or anything). She chose an exquisite short-sleeve pastel yellow top over a neatly pressed white skort.

Despite all her time spent getting ready, she still managed to show up early (not that she was anxious or anything). Geographic coordinates and Starfighters were simply not an issue for the cute Assistant Dean who grew up as an Air Force brat. It appeared she passed Kevin's first test. Or, perhaps... Kevin passed *her* first test.

Upon arrival at Field #1, Dianne saw Kevin on his knees, teaching Shari Michelle how to swing a bat. This being a facet of Kevin Oxley Dianne would never have suspected, it thawed a goodly portion of the remaining frost on her heart.

Kevin placed the ball on the tee as Shari Michelle absorbed his instructions with intensity. He told her how to swing the bat level in order to hit the ball solidly. Then he told her how to hold the bat with her elbows bent, ready to uncoil and get a solid hit. Shari Michelle concentrated, listening carefully, hanging onto Uncle Kevin's every word, because she really wanted to get a solid hit for him.

He said, "Now, when I say 'okay'... you swing just as hard as you can, okay?"

She swung just as hard as she could, solidly hitting Kevin's forehead.

Ox woke up, flat on his back, with a circle of kids, concerned parents, and Dianne above him. He blinked and rotated his eyes. His comprehension muddled at first, he soon figured out the odd cyclorama above him. A burly male assistant coach held up three fingers and said, "Kevin. Kevin, look at me. How many fingers am I holding up?"

Kevin squinted and said, "White Zinfandel."

Those who knew Kevin laughed. Those who didn't were even more concerned.

Burly coach said, "Ox man, seriously. Are you okay? What do you need?"

"I need a kiss on the boo-boo."

Burly coach said, "Well, if you insist," and leaned down toward Kevin.

The crowd laughed.

"No." Kevin crossed his arms up in the air to ward off the encroaching evil. He looked at Dianne. "I need a kiss on the boo-boo from a fair maiden."

Immediately, two pretty young women got down on their knees to kiss him. Dianne didn't know what to think about her own emotional reaction. Dare she even consider it as... jealousy?

In mild panic, Kevin waved-off the two pretty young women. He shouted, "No, not you two." He pointed at Dianne. "Her."

Laughing, they both stood up.

Kev said. "Sorry sis and sis, but sibling aid is not called for in this situation," They knew that, and they also knew about Dianne. That's why they laughed as they teased their older brother. He gave a pretend disgusted flip of his hand toward the two. "Dr. Dianne Wright allow me to introduce you to my insufferable sisters, Nurse Julie and Dr. Lori."

The three women exchanged standard pleasantries, which lead to delightful exploratory small talk.

Kevin, still flat on his back, interrupted the chit-chat. "Excuse me but... I am the injured party here. Still on the ground. Wallowing in pain."

Sister Lori looked down at him, pointed at Dianne and said, "Brother Kevin, I am perplexed by what you told us. Dr. Wright doesn't seem at all like a cold fish."

Everybody laughed except Kevin. "I never said that."

Sister Julie, giggling, told Dianne, "That's true. He never said anything like that. Just kidding."

"Laugh at my expense if you must, but I am still wounded, and I am still in need of a boo-boo kiss from a fair maiden."

Five-year-old Shari Michelle leaned in and kissed him on the forehead.

"There you go, Uncle Kevin."

Still on his back, he grabbed Shari Michelle with both hands and lifted her in the air twirling her up and down as he said, "Oh, thank you, princess." Everyone laughed and clapped as he sat her back down on her feet and she took a bow.

The crowd stared at Dianne, chanting "Boo-boo, boo-boo, boo-boo." Her heart now completely defrosted, she let out a calming breath, shook her head, got down on her knees, and lightly kissed Kevin's forehead.

The crowd woo-hooed.

Raising her head back up with a smiling nibble on her lower lip, she made astonishing contact with his deep glacier blue eyes. "Oh, what the heck." She leaned in and gave him a warm full kiss on the lips. *What am I doing?*

The crowd, now numbering about 80 people from three ball fields, cheered and clapped.

Dianne gracefully stood up, daintily brushing the infield dust off her hands and knees. She put her hands on her hips and stared down at Kevin as if he were a vanquished villain. "Take that," She swaggered.

Still stunned by what just happened, Kev didn't move. He didn't respond.

After a few seconds she said, "You can breathe now."

He gulped large air. And the crowd went wild.

When he stood up, the umpire yelled, "Play ball."

As the throng dispersed, breathless Kevin said to Dianne, "If you don't mind, just have a seat in the bleachers and I'll see you after the game. It'll only be about 40 minutes. Then I'm taking you to the zoo and then I'm taking you to dinner. Well lit. Multiple witnesses. Cheap prices."

"Sounds good." She took a seat right behind the Bad News Bunnies dugout.

Still a bit dazed as he walked to the dugout, Kevin knew his symptoms were mostly emotional, not physical. *Wow, T-ball is far more exciting than I ever expected.*

* * * * *

By the way... the Bad News Bunnies won their very first T-Ball game with a final score of 54 to 53. About an average score for a forty-minute game in which all sixteen players on the field chased the ball at the same time and, once they got to it, the best any player could do was throw the ball four feet in the wrong direction.

26

STILL SATURDAY — KEVIN & DIANNE
FIRST DATE 1.2

D riving from the T-Ball field on Victory Boulevard, then passing by the Autry Western Heritage Museum, and ending up at the L.A. Zoo in Griffith Park, took only nine minutes. A lot of history in those nine minutes.

America's first singing cowboy, Gene Autry appeared in 200 movies and television programs, wrote the song, *Santa Claus Is Coming to Town*, sung the original hits of *Rudolph the Red-Nosed Reindeer* and *Frosty the Snowman*, and founded the *Los Angeles Angels* major league baseball team. The only person ever awarded five different stars on the Hollywood Walk of Fame, Mr. Autry himself established the Western Heritage Museum in 1988, a museum almost as remarkable as his life.

In 1924, Los Angeles named one of the longest streets in the world, Victory Boulevard, as a tribute to America's World War I soldiers. The twenty-five-mile-long street ends at Griffith Park, where Colonel Griffith J. Griffith donated seven square miles of his land to the City of Angels as a Christmas present in December 1896. After his release from prison (for shooting his wife) Griffith set up a trust fund to construct the Greek Theater, the Griffith Observatory, and other projects dear to his felonious heart. In comparison to New York City's Central Park, Griffith Park is much larger and much wilder. It is, basically, undeveloped small mountains in the center of a huge city.

The hundred-acre Griffith Park Aerodrome, home to aviation pioneers such as Glenn Martin and Jorge Pheltor, eventually became the L.A. Zoo parking lot, right next door to the Autry Museum.

Per their P.I.T. Stop covenant, Dianne and Kevin drove separately from the T-Ball game to the zoo's palm tree-festooned main entrance. They were met at the zoo by a balmy, almost tropical, remnant of an ocean breeze coming up from the Palos Verdes peninsula. Though unintentional, Kevin and Dianne looked like a color-coordinated couple with her soft yellow top and his light-yellow Bad News Bunnies T-shirt.

They walked and talked, sharing popcorn and munching churros, all the while paying more attention to each other than to exotic animals. They made a social call at the Meerkat Colony, bestowing amusing pet names on several critters, strolled completely around the Gorilla Reserve, scoped out the Komodo Dragons, and spent quality time in the Australian Pavilion with the Koalas, Double-Wattled Cassowary, and Yellow-Footed Rock Wallaby.

They both wanted to spend some time at the "Fun Fair" event raising money for the Wounded Warrior Project, a new organization just launched in February of 2003. So, they headed back toward the Children's Zoo, where the fund-raising mini carnival occupied open space.

Dianne went straight for the merry-go-round, where they had sloppy fun trying to share an iced-tea on their side-by-side carousel steeds whose ups and downs were not mutually synchronized. The iced-tea, in a Styrofoam to-go cup, had an exceptionally long straw sticking out through the flimsy plastic lid. At one point, Kevin raised the cup to take a sip. He misjudged the apogee of his horse, and the straw went up his left nostril. She saw it happen and giggled.

Kev went with the moment. He turned his head to face her with highly arched eyebrows, crossed eyes, and a totally goofy smile which made the straw sticking out of his nose point straight at her. He then dragged it out of his nose and offered her a drink through the straw, which she merrily refused. When he attempted to remove the straw from the lid, the lid popped off. And that's how things got sloppy. They laughed even more. Much to her surprise, she didn't mind the iced tea spilling on her. Dr. Wright began emerging from her emotional coma.

When finished mopping up spilled tea, they headed to the electronic shooting gallery tent. Dianne went first, scoring one hit out of twenty-four shots at the moving targets.

She smirked. "I bet you couldn't tell I've never shot a gun before."

"Really? I hadn't noticed."

She laughed and raised her right hand to testify. "Absolutely true. Never in my entire life. Are you any good at this?"

"Aw shucks ma'am. Yep, I guess I'm... kind of a marksman."

"Really? Can you show me? What do I need to do first?"

"Okay, the first thing you need to do is kiss me on the boo-boo."

She gave him *the look* and said with feigned displeasure, "Lean forward." He leaned in. She kissed him on the forehead. "Now, the shooting demonstration, please?"

Kevin bought a double electronic reload. Forty-eight shots. "Which line do you want me to shoot at?"

"I guess, uh... just start with the top row."

"Okay. Wish me luck."

"You don't need luck," she said. "You got a kiss on the boo-boo. Remember?"

He studied the rows of targets, mentally assembling subconscious notes on size, speed and spatiality. The top row of targets moved to the right. The next row below moved to the left. That alternating direction of travel continued for all four rows. Each row had fifteen moving targets always visible.

Assuming a stable shooting stance, he gently squeezed the trigger. The first target in the first row fell. He kept squeezing and targets kept falling. He went 48 hits for 48 shots.

The booth operator and Dianne were both stunned. Speechless. Neither had ever before seen such a thing.

The booth operator said, "Uh... Yeah."

Kev said, "Well thank you, kind sir, for your exuberant affirmation. By the way, I didn't center the first three because the sight is out of zero. It needs an eighth inch click to the left.

"Uh... Yeah."

Dianne put her hand in the crook of Kevin's arm and began walking away with him. "How did you do that?" she asked.

"Actually, it's not too difficult. The number one rule is you don't shoot at the target."

"Excuse me?"

It's a moving target. You don't shoot at the target. You shoot at where it's going to be. Ya gotta lead your target."

"Uh... Yeah."

The booth man shouted, "Hey guy, you forgot your unicorn. You won the biggest unicorn we have."

They stopped and turned around. Kevin looked at Dianne with a question mark face. Softly, almost pleading, because she didn't want to hurt Kev's feelings, she said, "If you don't mind, I don't need a unicorn. Let them use that money for the wounded warriors." Kevin's turn to have a melting heart.

Kev shouted back, "You can keep it. Save the money for the vets."

"You got it, man. Semper Fi."

Kevin nodded and quietly said, "Roger that."

They waved goodbye to the Meerkats and continued down the very wide cement pedestrian path toward the zoo exit.

A male voice shouted, "Yo. Ox man."

Kevin's face lit up. He high-fived in the air with a huge smile on his face, grabbed Dianne's hand, and almost dragged her to the pop-the-balloon-with-a-dart booth. He leaped over the counter and bear-hugged the buzz-cut, camo-geared, twenty-something booth operator.

Kev said, "Eugene, where have you been, man?"

"Saving the world, buddy, just like always."

They yakked a bit, not really saying anything specific other than how good it was to see each other again. Then Kevin paused the celebration, saying, "Dianne, I'd like you to meet my friend, Yoo Jin Kim."

Eugene said with a giant smile, "Dianne, it's a pleasure. Any friend of Kevin Oxley is... in trouble."

They laughed and Gene continued, "Listen, Ox, I'll be back to L.A. in a couple of months and I'll have Melissa with me. Let's all paint the town red, white and blue. We could start with dinner at our old chomping grounds, the Pasadena Panda Palace." Gene turned to Dianne. "You like Chinese?"

"They're some of my favorite people."

"Hah!" Gene pointed his thumb at Dianne. "She's a keeper. I'll call you in a few weeks and we'll get 'er done. That work for you?"

"Sounds like a strategy."

"But right now," Eugene said, "I need a really big favor. Immediately if not sooner."

"Sure. What?"

"I've been in this booth for four hours without a break. My relief didn't show up and, believe me, I need relief. Can you man the booth for a couple a minutes?"

Ox said, "You got it, bud. It just needs to be really quick. We have an eight o'clock dinner reservation."

"Not a problem." He handed off the booth apron and looked at his watch. "I'll be back by 7:40. Promise. And it's three darts for a dollar." As he straddled the booth frame for a quick getaway, his right pants leg rode up revealing a carbon fiber blade prosthetic leg. Heading to the head, he patted both sides of his waist and said to his kidneys, "Don't worry guys. We're on our way. Hang in there."

With Eugene out of range, Dianne asked Kevin, "What happened to his leg?"

"Afghanistan."

Kevin tied on the booth apron, saying, "Well, when in booth, do as the boothians." He became a barker. "Hey, here's where you win the big ones. Step right up folks. Three darts for a dollar."

A very young boy timidly laid a quarter on the counter. "Can I play?"

Kevin pretended he hadn't noticed and looked out over the boy's head. "Hey, special offer right now for the first kid to step up here and lay down a quarter. It's three darts—only a quarter—for the first kid here. Any takers out there?

The boy tugged Kevin's apron. "Mister, I think I have a korder. But I'm not sure."

Still pretending he hadn't seen the child, Kevin looked down and did a googly-eyed double-take, making both the kid and the Dianne giggle.

In his W.C. Fields voice Kevin said, "Ahh yess... how's the weather down there? Let me see the color of your money, my boy."

The child sheepishly held up his quarter. Kev examined it, holding it up to catch the fading sunlight. "Ahh yesss, those are the right colors... shiny, silvery, and roundy. Here are your darts, my lad. Be careful. They're loaded."

"Thanks mister."

Kevin dove for cover when the little boy threw all three darts at once. Two went wildly into the ground and one bounced off a balloon without popping it.

Kevin analyzed the situation and shouted, "You did it. You won the grand prize."

"I did?"

"Yes, you did, young man. I saw it with my own eyes. You are the first person to ever dent a ba... well... I better check just to be sure..." While the little boy worried, Kevin rotated the balloon on every axis, thoughtfully inspecting each centimeter of its spheroidal topology. "Umm-hmm. Yes... I think I see... Yes, there it is. I see a dent in that balloon. Ahh yess, congratulations, you are our new champion."

Kevin handed the boy a huge stuffed animal. The kid's eyes lit up and so did Dianne's, as the euphoric lad ran off to his parents. Kevin fished in his pocket, pulled out two $20 bills, and put them in the apron pouch.

Removing the apron as Eugene walked up, Kevin said, "Hey Gene. Had a big winner while you were gone, but I put forty bucks in this wearable cash box to cover the loss.

"Ah thanks, man." Gene said. "All the money gets to the vets. Like they say... the greatest casualty is being forgotten." He glanced at his big military watch. "Hey, what'd I promise you, huh? Look, I'm right on time. It's 1940 hours."

Kevin went quietly reflective for a split-second and then shouted, "Military time."

"Well, duh."

"No, I mean it's not a year, it's the time."

"What?"

Kevin jumped out of the booth, grabbed his mobile out of his pocket, and sent a text to Theo and Dr. Weksler:

1945 is not a year. It's the time: 7:45 P.M.
Still don't know about flaming zeroes.

Stupid. How could I not have thought of military time?
The reality of the situation was, knowing the time resolved only half of the unknown, and it didn't put them any closer to intercepting His Supreme Eminence. So, Kev went a little easier on himself as he stood there, out in the middle of the forty-foot-wide sidewalk, thinking... twisting... contemplating... looking this way and that. *What do I do now?*

Something subliminal u-turned into his cognizance. He snapped his head around to look at the signpost on the edge of the walkway:

← Flamingos

He looked left, to where the wide cement path went uphill. A couple hundred yards away, right beside the path, stood the outdoor exhibit of at least 50 spectacular pink flamingos he and Dianne strolled past not twenty minutes earlier.

The oompa-loompa pronounced flamingos as flaming zeroes!

Kevin took off running up the walkway, his goal being to reach—as fast as humanly possible—the large orange ball he spotted in the distance. He shouted as he ran up the gentle slope, "Stop that shuttle! Stop them! Stop the shuttle!"

Zoo patrons on the walkway gave a very wide berth to the running, shouting, crazy man in a Bad News Bunnies T-shirt.

About a quarter mile uphill beyond the Flamingos, near a zoo shuttle tram station, Mikhail nervously met His Supreme Eminence for the first time. Mikhail clicked his heels together, raised his right arm in a Nazi salute and shouted, *"Muerte a los Marranos."* Supreme Eminence fluttered a weak left-handed acknowledgement. They boarded the tram and it disappeared over the crest of the hill, out of Kevin's grasp.

His Supreme Eminence carried a large belly and softness around his edges. Longish gray hair accompanied his white mustache and goatee. Like all good Assassins at an important meeting, he wore a white suit, accented by a flamboyant red sash flowing around the waist and flipped over his shoulder. He pretty much looked like Elton John pretending to be Colonel Sanders.

27

STILL SATURDAY — KEVIN & DIANNE
FIRST DATE 1.3

Emotionally absorbed and mentally self-deprecating, the Ox man gradually ambled back toward Dianne and Yoo Jin. Of the many action options which came to his mind, none appeared worth a rip. Putting his hands in his pockets, he turned and looked back up the hill to where Mikhail and His Supreme Eminence so effortlessly departed with neither concern nor delay.

"What just happened?" Dianne asked.

Eugene added, "Who were those guys?"

Kevin pondered before answering. "Just a couple of creepers. Planning evil."

Dianne said, "You okay?"

"Yeah, I'm fine. I'm just uh... I don't like it when my situational awareness lets me down. I'll get over it, right after I alert the zookeepers and the CDC."

Eugene said, "The CDC?"

"Yeah, they were a couple of diseased animals." They all smiled, Kevin not so much. He did rekindle a tiny bit of twinkle in his own eyes. "Seriously," Kevin said, "It's not a big deal." He did a Joisey gangsta, "Fuhgeddabout it."

Kevin grabbed Dianne's hand (she didn't resist) and began walking to the zoo parking lot. He shouted back to Gene, "Tell Melissa I'm really looking forward to painting Pasadena. Right now, Dianne has a date with a pineapple princess."

"I do?"

* * * * *

Kev had reservations at his favorite tropical-themed eatery—Five Oh!—about a fifteen-minute drive east of the zoo, in Old Town Pasadena. Dianne knew her way around Old Town, making it easy to honor their vow and take separate cars, again.

She parked in the three-story gray cement parking structure around the corner from Five Oh! and he parked in the four-story adobe color building which housed the restaurant on ground level. Though built into the parking structure, clever exterior decor made the restaurant appear as a free-standing building. Easy to spot even from a block away, it looked like the Warner Brothers themselves had decorated the set, sparing no expense.

A smallish forest of real palm trees and lush tropical plantings thrived all along the outside of Five Oh! partially hiding the hand-carved koa wood entry door and old ripple glass windows. The exterior, covered with weathered dark green shiplap siding, looked for all the world as if it had been salvaged from a 200-year-old sunken whaler in *Ke ala i kahiki* (road to Tahiti) channel off Lahaina Town. An ersatz rusty corrugated tin roof overhung the sidewalk all the way to the street, protecting pedestrians from stray typhoons. Holes raggedly cut in the roof accommodated the real palm trees whose bright green fronds hung out over the front edge of the corrugated gray metal.

Knowing he would take her to Five Oh!, Kev wore a very classy mauve and gray floral print Hawaiian shirt. Walking from opposite directions, Dianne and Kevin arrived in front of the restaurant at the same time. She smiled. He smiled. They both said "Aloha" at the same time and grinned at their own infatuated cleverness. Kev opened the deeply polished door and said, "Welcome to Honoka'a Town."

She said *"Mahalo,"* (thank you) and walked into a tropical paradise wrapped in the heavenly scent of plumeria. He didn't notice the cold suspicion that hit her eyes when he mentioned Honoka'a.

Sixteen artificial geckos walked around high up on the Five Oh! interior walls and ceiling. As they crawled along, they subtly changed colors to match the background, just as in real life. A very up-scale burger restaurant, Five Oh! only took reservations for parties of eight or more. Kevin had a reservation for two because he created the robot geckos.

The young woman standing in the thatched roof hostess hut greeted him, "Good evening, Sir. May I please have your name?"

Kevin said, "Well, I'm not sure. Are you going to give it back?"

She giggled.

"On second thought," He said. "Kevin is not really a good name for a girl. Why don't you just take my mom's name: Herman. She probably won't even mind if you keep it. You know, you can get some really great nicknames out of Herman. You could be called, Her. Or Man."

The grinning hostess said, "No thank you, Mr. Oxley. I'm just going to stick with Leilani, the name mom and dad gave me. By the way, they said to say hi to you and your guest."

"Well, Herman, please extend my aloha right back to your parents."

She rolled her eyes and smiled at Dianne, extending her hand as Kev introduced them. She led them to a wonderfully cozy and tropically secluded booth with a gently gurgling bonsai-sized fountain. As she left to get their beverages, Leilani leaned over to Dianne and, in a stage whisper, said, "By the way his mother's name is Evelyn. She is a delightful lady. We all hope you get to meet her."

Kevin and Dianne settled in, nervously exchanging placid niceties. The so-called conversation degraded to inanities about the zoo, the weather, and, "By the way, when is the start date for the fall semester?" Dianne knew the answer and that question didn't lend itself to discussion, so dialogue crumbled to an awkward halt, swiftly replaced by a dreaded lull, not aided by Dianne's apprehension.

Fortuitously, Leilani delivered a complimentary *Pu-Pu* platter (Hawaiian appetizers) just in time.

Dianne said, "I need to ask you something very important. No joking around. You have to give me a truthful answer."

Wary, Kevin said, "Okay..."

She gazed at their surroundings. "I love this place, and I love Hawaii, but why are we _here_? And why did you mention Honoka'a? Did somebody tell you something about me and Honoka'a town?"

Kevin's meerkat-in-the-headlights stare indicated he hadn't a clue about whatever bush she was beating around. *Is that anger?*

"I'm sorry," she said. "It's just that, it's obvious you arranged our 'accidental' meetings at Mars Hill and the P.I.T. Stop. And, yes, I was flattered. Now... if you're just doing the Honoka'a thing to woo-hoo me, that would be too personal and too phony."

No, not really anger. But edgy. And confusing. "I have no idea what you're talking about," Kev said. "We are here because this is my favorite restaurant and I wanted to share it with you. My mom and Leilani's parents are best friends. I love Hawaii. I've been there a dozen times. I've been to every island and my favorite place in the world is the Big Island."

Now it was her turn to breathe through the mouth. Her eyes were glistening, in anticipation of his next answer. "And Honoka'a?" she asked.

"I really like Kailua-Kona on the Big Island. I've got friends there. But there are too many tourists and too much traffic. So, I explored the windward side and found Honoka'a, an old sugar plantation town. I love it. It feels like home. That's where I'm going to live when I grow up."

Dianne let out a breath. "Okay, I apologize for the drama. That's uh... a pretty good answer." She paused. "And, if it's totally true then it's a *great* answer."

"Totally true." He raised a Boy Scout salute. "If I'm lying you can wash my mouth out with ginger soap and poi."

"Yuck." She smiled and, for some reason, felt comfortable unleashing personal information. "Hawaii and I go way back to my fifth grade when my dad got transferred to Hickam Air Force Base on Oahu, right next to Honolulu International Airport—did you know they share the same runways?"

He shook his head.

"Well they do, because..." She did a wave off. "Sorry, that's another story. Anyway... dad piloted a C-135 Starlifter. He delivered people and things all over the Pacific Rim. The 15th Air Wing also did support for the Space Shuttle. I met astronauts. I met pilots. I was inspired."

He was engrossed.

She continued, "I wanted to be just like daddy, flying off into the wild blue. I got my pilot's license at sixteen. I soloed to the Big Island at seventeen. When I was in college at Hilo, I hung out weekends on the leeward side in Kailua-Kona." She paused, as if it was the end of her story.

Kevin's head tilted as his mind scrambled, hoping he hadn't rudely missed her point. He didn't remember her saying anything additional about Honoka'a. Taking a chance, he said, "And... Honoka'a?"

"Oh, sorry. Just deep in thought." She sucked in a breath. "My dad is retired in Honoka'a. And that's where I want to live when I grow up."

Whew. Good. I Didn't miss anything. They both went silent, each trying to diagnose inferred karma. Things had become too multi-leveled too quickly for just a casual first date.

The dinners arrived. As Kevin anticipated, Dianne had ordered the restaurant's signature, "Pineapple Princess", a third-pound Angus burger glazed by a secret teriyaki sauce, topped with a pineapple ring and a butter-grilled portobello slice on a freshly baked sweet Hawaiian bread roll. Kevin ordered the "Pineapple Prince", essentially the same thing as Dianne's, but with a full half-pound of beef and the addition of a wasabi smear on the bun to make it manlier. They shared the famous never-empty *Waipio* Bowl of seasoned sweet potato fries and breadfruit chips, both munchies crisped to perfection.

Because he really, really, really liked her, Kevin misplaced much of his remaining cool. He looked around, admiring the tropical splendor while mentally groping for something which might resemble an actual light-hearted conversation. Finally, something came to him. He looked at her and said, "You may find this hard to believe but I have never before gone out with an Assistant Dean."

She said, "Hey, what a coincidence. Neither have I." (She really was cute.) "So," she asked, "if not Assistant Deans, what kind of girls do you usually go out with?"

"Hmm, good question. Let me think." He became extremely serious. "East coast girls are hip. I really dig those styles they wear. And the southern girls with the way they talk—"

"—they knock you out when you're down there?" She laughingly finished his sentence, a line from the Beach Boys' golden oldie song, *California Girls.*

"Yeah." He smiled. "You got me."

She gently sang the bass singer's intro to the chorus, "Duh dooby doo." (She was killing him softly with her song.)

They both leaned in a bit toward the center of their table and, together, not wishing to disturb other patrons, quietly harmonized the last line of the chorus...

"I wish they all could be California girls."

They unsuccessfully tried to smother their giggles. Now in their own little world, they were quite surprised when all diners and wait staff within thirty feet applauded.

You may recall that a couple of weeks earlier they were applauded by Kevin's co-conspirators at The P.I.T. Stop. So, including the baseball field crowd, she and Kevin had now received three standing ovations in three different venues in two weeks. Wow. They might wanna take this show on the road.

When refills of their non-alcoholic, umbrella-enhanced, papaya and passion fruit-flavored tropical iced-teas arrived, Dianne asked, "So, no serious romances? Ever?"

He looked up to the left, thinking. "Ah... well... there was this girl a few years ago who looked like she might be a possibility, but our worlds kept getting in the way."

"Sort of star-crossed lovers?"

"No, more like *Star Trek* lovers."

Not certain she heard correctly, she said, "*Star Trek* lovers?"

"Yeah. She was an unknown species."

Dianne smiled, shaking her head.

"But she had a whole bunch of really cute noses."

She laughed out loud, then let out a satisfied sigh. "That was so bad." She beamed.

The Leilani express delivered perfect Kona coffee and complimentary desserts of individual chocolate lava cakes with a hint of coconut flavor (as a result of the chef replacing some egg in the batter with coconut oil).

Kevin said, "I am still in awe—jealous, actually— that you got to go to high school in Hawaii. That is just... I don't think high school could get any better. Were you like a colorful Hawaiian social butterfly?'

"Hah. Me?" She pointed to herself. "Tomboy. Never signed up for girly-girl. All I wanted to be was up in a plane." She shook her head. "Definitely not colorful social butterfly. More like drab anti-social moth."

With a bit of coquettish challenge in her voice, she asked Kevin, "So, what do you think makes a good relationship?"

He replied, "Midget mathematicians."

"What?" She looked at him with furrowed brows and palms turned up.

"Midget mathematicians. You know... its those little things that count."

"Oh my gosh," she groaned. "Alright, Mr. Oxley, you asked for it. My turn. Ya ready? Ya sittin' down?"

Not knowing what she meant, he shrugged and said, "Uh, I guess so."

She said, "I went to a really tough Catholic school. My teacher was Attila the nun." She punctuated the punch line with a finger rim-shot on the edge of the table.

"Hah. That's funny." Kevin said.

She said, "I once dated a guy who was so old that he went to college with a grant. Ulysses S. Grant." Another rim-shot.

"Ha."

She said, "I'm in a gang that races hamsters and never cuts their hair."

He dutifully played straight man. "Your gang races hamsters and never cuts their hair?"

"Yep. We're called the fast and the furriest."

"Hah," He groan-laughed.

She held up both hands with palms facing Kevin and said, "Okay. Okay. That's it. I'm done."

With a bewildered chuckle and a colossal smile, he said, "Where on earth did all that come from? You do stand-up on weekends?"

"Grandpa was a twenty-one-year-old vaudeville comedian in 1933, after all the stars had already left for radio and movies. He never made it to Hollywood. I learned his jokes before

I learned to fly. Made up a few of my own. More useless knowledge."

"It isn't useless. It's priceless. I wanna hear more."

"Next date," She said, then instantly blushed. Uh, oh, she let the meerkat out of the bag.

Kevin jumped on it. "So, there's going to be a next date?"

Glowing red, she said, "Well... yeah... I guess... maybe, we could give it another try."

After a long evening of deliciousness, they finally exited Five Oh! to the outside world of Old Town Pasadena.

Dianne had a durable, etched-in granite, personal rule: never kiss on a first date. But... as she had already kissed Kevin at the baseball field (under duress) and at the shooting gallery (ibid, sort of) and because he had really broad shoulders, she decided she needn't have an internal debate over that edict. She also did not condone public displays of romantic affection. But she made exceptions to her rules—right there outside Five Oh!—for a brief and remarkably warm goodnight kiss in full view of the starboard plumeria bush.

They happily agreed to see each other again, soon. At that moment though, she needed to hurry to her car and get home, because she still had reading and paperwork to do, and had to be up early in the morning to finish prepping for her Sunday school class.

"Your Sunday School class has homework?" Kevin asked.

"No, my Sunday School class has me as their teacher, and I'm not prepared."

Kevin moved to walk with her, but she said, "No, don't walk me to my car. It's just around the corner and it is perfectly safe here." She waved to a pair of police officers on bicycles who nodded. After taking a few steps, she came back and gave Kevin a timid little kiss, then scurried away. She called back to him, "I had a really nice time today. Thank you."

He shouted back, "You're welcome. Me too. You're adorable."

She rounded the corner and—out of Kevin's sight—she finally got to happy-nibble her lower lip.

28

STILL SATURDAY EVENING — JUST A FEW MOMENTS LATER

Inside Five Oh! Under-Assistant West Coast Field Director, Leonard Ostermann finished his dinner and ordered his Kona coffee. He knew he deserved to relax and recover from his Pirate quest and his long day of being very important, so he leaned back and sifted through the *Pasadena Star-News* in his peaceful booth cloaked by huge green elephant ears and other profuse tropical foliage. A section two headline captured his attention...

> BOMB AT PASADENA RADIO STATION FIZZLES
> S.O.L. STATEMENT: JUST A WARNING!

Outside Five Oh! Kevin soared in his afterglow, doing mind reruns of his day with Dianne. He graciously opened the door for an exhausted couple with four exuberant children heading into the restaurant. The herd of wild munchkins, excited to see geckobots again, tried their best to trample Kev. Dodging the little crazies led Ox to personal entanglement with a potted six-foot palm.

"Arrgh!" he said in his Pirate voice.

Ostermann dropped his newspaper and sat up straight, his ears wishing they could swivel.

Still in Pirate voice, Kevin said, "Avast there mini-maties."

Ostermann parted the tropical leaves behind his booth and peered out, wild-eyed, seeking a person to match up with the Pirate's voice. He caught a glimpse of the distinctive mauve and gray aloha shirt as the front door shut. With his napkin still tucked into his shirt like a bib, Leonard jumped up, knocked-over the waiter carrying his pot of coffee, ran past the hostess hut, dropped sufficient cash at the front desk, and shouted, "Out of the way. Everybody out of the way! This is a Federal emergency."

He ran out the front door, looked left and right, then ran to the near corner, and then ran back to the far corner. Nothing.

He couldn't have disappeared that fast on foot. He's got to be in the parking building.

Ostermann jogged into the structure. He ran up to the attendant, an elderly rock 'n' roller who never left the 1960s. The hard-of-hearing attendant, whose ears became irrelevant during the legendary four-hour Led Zeppelin concert at The Tea Party in 1969 still had what remained of his long white hair in a ponytail.

Ostermann shouted, "I'm looking for a man... mauve and gray shirt."

The attendant said, "You're booking for a band? Marvin Gaye's hurt?"

Leonard blinked and blankly stared. "No. The Pirate. The guy with the big bird."

"Snow? The tyrant? The sty with the pig herd? Right on, man."

Ostermann's blank stare continued as he trotted away.

Seeing a fleeting hint of Kevin's aloha shirt seven rows of cars away, Leonard Ostermann shouted, "Hey you! Yo ho. Are you a pirate? Can we talk about pirates? Do you know any pirates?"

Kevin didn't know who was shouting and had no intention of finding out. He simply said, "Plate. Texas". Instantly, the van's front and rear license plates changed to Texas plates. He decided not to wait for a break in traffic that would allow him to exit to the left and head toward home. Instead, he immediately pulled out to the right, immersing the van in slow Saturday-night-dinner-and-a-movie traffic creeping eastward on Colorado Boulevard.

Officer Ostermann wrote down the bogus Texas license plate in his little red book. Then he jumped into his car, conveniently parked in a handicapped spot next to the exit. Leonard always felt his important business activities deserved federally mandated access to handicap parking and that congress just hadn't yet gotten around to it. Really ticked by the parking citation under his windshield wiper, he tore it up and threw it out the driver's window, shouting to nobody in particular, "Next time look at my license plate, you mugwumps. I'm on official business."

The semi-aware parking attendant turned his head and saw Ostermann's vanity license plate: FCC #1. He thought perhaps the strange fellow was pastor of First Congregational Church.

Looking out his window at the crumpled pieces of his parking citation on the cement floor, Leonard shouted, again to no one in particular, "And clean up your parking lot. It's disgraceful."

Ostermann thundered out into traffic without bothering to even look at the traffic, cutting off a rental car driven by a female Japanese tourist. She and seven drivers behind her were all forced to swerve and/or slam on their brakes. It looked like a NASCAR restart gone bad. She grumbled, "American drivers." She shook her fist at Leonard. "What? Does a windshield make you blind? You should be arrested for D.W.A. — Driving While Arrogant."

Weaving back and forth between the two northbound lanes, Leonard finally spotted Kevin's white van with the Texas plate three blocks ahead, as it turned into the driveway of a small strip mall just outside the Old Town historical district. Ostermann repeatedly banged the rear bumper of the car in front of him while mercilessly honking his horn.

Just as Kevin hoped, at that time on a Saturday night, no delivery trucks were parked in the commercial zone behind the strip mall. Completely empty. Kevin only needed six seconds to make the transition, so he went for it.

He announced, "Four twenty-six", the cubic inch displacement of the big V-8 in a 1970 Plymouth Hemi 'Cuda, one of his personal favorites. Four-twenty-six was also his voice-activated computer command to initiate the van's instant hot water heater and bring water up to the correct temperature for the transition. In two seconds, hot water sprayed from all those mini nozzles imbedded all over the van. In four seconds, the van exterior white paint changed to a perfect match for Panther Pink, one of the Mopar special High Impact colors available in 1970. In the fifth second since the entire process started, John Wayne's voice came over the sound system announcing, "Four twenty-six complete. Saddle Up".

Kevin said, "Plate. Minnesota." The license plates and frames changed to Minnesota. He then parked his bright pink Minnesota van in the strip mall's customer parking lot. "Way fine," he said. *We have seriously elevated the art of hiding in plain sight.*

His parking spot gave him a great view of flashing red and blue lights on the roof of the Pasadena police car that followed Leonard Ostermann into the strip mall parking lot. Kev watched the officer get Mr. Ostermann's autograph. Catching a break in traffic, Kev waved bye-bye in his rearview mirror, and headed west on Colorado Boulevard toward Arroyo Parkway and, eventually, back home to South Pas.

When thermal color-changing Hot Wheels© diecast model cars came on the market, they inspired Ox to develop color-changing for his van. The process began, of course, by reverse-engineering the model cars, not difficult for an accomplished geoelectrophysicist. As usual, Kev went way beyond what he considered would be ordinary, humdrum, every day, garden-variety color changing capability. He formulated a series of colors, each of which emerged from the van's basic white paint at a specific water temperature. Once those formularies worked flawlessly, it became a simple matter of reprogramming the water heater to deliver instantaneous hot water at requested precise temperatures.

A chosen color remained stable for 24 hours, or until changed by a Kevin voice command. When he said, "Ambient", his California license plate instantly reappeared and the van's color returned to white, remaining so until he instructed otherwise.

On his way home that night, Ox made one quick stop in an alley as dark and desolate as an undiscovered crypt. He said "Ambient", and his technology delivered precisely as programmed, returning the van to white with Cali plates in two seconds flat. He pumped his fist, shouted, "Everything's chicken," and happily slapped the dashboard, which made the mirrored disco ball drop down. The Bee Gees sang, "Stayin' alive, staying' alive..." and Kevin smiled.

29

BETWEEN IRAQ AND A HARD PLACE

A Brief Timeline of How Professor Smelly Became the S.O.L.
Creeper-In-Chief

Holy Toledo!

On June 12 in 1124 A.D., *Hassan-i Sabbāh* (Hasan, son of Sabah), known worldwide as the Persian Old Man of the Mountain, died at the age of seventy-three. He left behind no heirs because he murdered both his sons.

A Muslim, and the self-proclaimed earthly incarnation of god, Hasan did not actually believe in the religion he practiced. Born without the heritage required to attain wealth and influence in his ancient Arab homeland, he nevertheless became the most powerful and feared human on earth.

Hasan could lie as much as necessary without putting his eternal soul in jeopardy because he practiced the Islamic principle of *taqiyya* (pious dishonesty). Hasan, himself, perfected the "Doctrine of Intelligent Dissimulation" (lies) to a smoothly polished art. He taught that same skill to his initiates.

Hasan purchased unwanted male children from their parents. Those boys then spent their childhood learning absolute obedience to Hasan, for he was god. He employed astonishing, bloody, and ruthless means to mold all those pliable young males into stealth killers. As adults, they joyfully murdered when instructed to do so, with neither hesitation nor fear. For they knew paradise would be their reward for following Hasan's will.

Marco Polo, in his book, *The Travels of Marco Polo*, testifies to having learned the following about Hassan-i Sabbāh, and his acolytes, "... all deemed themselves happy to receive the commands of their master and were ready to die in his service. The consequence of this system was, that when any of the neighboring princes, or any others, gave offense to [Hasan], they were put to death by these disciplined [followers]; none of who felt terror at the risk of losing their own lives, which they held in little estimation, provided they could execute their master's will. ...Thus, there was no person, however powerful, who, having become exposed to the rancor of the Old Man of the Mountain, could escape."

> *"Those who are being initiated do not so much learn anything, as experience certain emotions, and are thrown into a special state of mind."*
>
> — Aristotle

Hasan's brainwashed killers became the most ruthless, cold-blooded, and effective secret military force in history. Hasan had a pet name for his 70,000 followers. He called them *Assassiyun*, (i.e., people who were faithful to the foundation of the faith). It did not take long before the world realized that Hasan had invented *assassins* and by extrapolation, *assassination*.

By the start of the third Crusade (1189 A.D.), Hasan, the Persian Od Man of the Mountain had been deceased for three generations, but kings and caliphs still cut deals with his Assassins. Both King Richard's Christian Knights Templar and the Muslim army of *Saladin* (Salah al-Din Yusuf) made huge payoffs to the Assassins in exchange for a guarantee of no Assassin attacks. Thus, Crusaders and Saracens could battle each other without concern for their six (back). Such machinations were the seeds, and Persia the rich soil, for the roots of the S.O.L.

Believe it or not, *Jihad* had mostly non-violent meanings for many centuries. Of course, *Jihad* can also be a "holy war" against unbelievers. The question then becomes, who gets to decide which people are the unbelievers and whether the war is holy? Simple, really. Whoever attacks first, declares the people they are torturing and killing to be unbelievers. That makes their war automatically holy. Different Muslim sects sometimes decide that men, women and children of some other Muslim sect must be tortured and killed because they do not live their lives properly. Repeat as desired.

To put it into a Western perspective, approximately thirty-five percent of all Baptists consume alcohol. A U.S. "jihad" would be analogous to one Baptist denomination deciding that members of a different Baptist denomination are unbelievers who must be tortured and killed because they drink alcohol. Or... because they do not drink alcohol. If that happened in the United States, *all* Christians would publicly condemn such obscene religious radicalism, and would join with secular government forces to put an end to it.

No free passes. No sadistic serial killers pretending to be holy.

On a bright blue 711 A.D. spring morning, slow but useful winds up from the south helped Muslim General *Ṭāriq ibn Ziyād* land his men on the shore of what became Gibraltar. The name, Gibraltar, survives to this day, derived from the Arabic, *Jabal Ṭāriq*, which translates to Mountain of Tariq.

Both Christian supporters of the recently deceased Visigoth King of Spain and marginalized Spanish Jews had requested military assistance from the Muslims in North Africa. The Muslims happily sent aid, seeing it as an opportunity to conquer Spain. *Ṭāriq's* seven-mile voyage through the straits northward from Morocco went undetected. It took only eight months to subdue Spain, and most of the country became the Islamic state of *Al-Andalus*. Therein, as subjects of the Caliphate of Cordoba, Christians and Jews were protected peoples who paid taxes and were permitted internal autonomy. Medieval Spanish Muslims became known as Moors.

At that time—when only fifteen percent of the world could read and write—Al-Andalus became an educational, cultural, and scientific hub for Europe and Mediterranea, a brilliant jewel of the Islamic golden age. Knowledge and culture were freely exchanged in a cooperative environment among Christians, Jews, and Moors.

After seven-hundred years of war with Christian kingdoms, the fall of Granada in 1492 ended Muslim rule in Spain. King Ferdinand II of Aragon and his Queen, Isabella I of Castile, took over. The Spanish royal couple had amassed enough gold to finance the *Tribunal del Santo Oficio de la Inquisición*, more affectionately known as the Spanish Inquisition. Jews and Muslims were given two choices: convert to Christianity, or permanently leave Spain. Many converted to Christianity because Moriscos (new Christians of Moorish origin) and Marranos (new Christians of Jewish origin) considered themselves Spanish and considered Spain their home.

The Holy Garduña soon became silent partners with the Spanish Inquisition. The Garduña supplied excellent counterfeit documents and perjury. Even Christians loyal to the King and Queen were tortured and killed as the Inquisition transitioned from vetting converts to making money. The more "heretics" murdered, the more gold for the church, as well as for Ferdinand and Izzy. The Garduña could be trusted because they always kept their promise to torture and murder innocent people at the agreed upon time, for the agreed upon price.

The Holy Garduña eventually did become an embarrassment for the crown and the church. The last (supposedly) *Eminencia el Supremo* (Supreme Eminence) and sixteen of his *Capataz* were publicly hung in the Seville town square in 1822. That, of course, had no effect on those Garduña members who had already immigrated to South America.

About a hundred years later, Francisco Franco won his bloody Spanish Civil War in the spring of 1939. In typical compassionate leftist manner, he immediately murdered three-hundred-thousand former political opponents, suspected former opponents, and suspected friends of suspected former opponents. Also murdered in his *limpieza* (cleaning the country)—his euphemism for extrajudicial executions— were union members, businessmen, educators, and Catholic priests who had the poor taste to minister rites for conservative Republicans.

As a personal sidebar, I find it interesting that no communist government has ever been established by free election.

What's good for the people must be forced on them by torture and murder.

As World War II wound down, Nazi officers with enough stolen money began their clandestine escapes from the fatherland, relocating to South America with the assistance of... you guessed it: The Holy Garduña. The Garduña leadership included descendants of the Moors who shared Nazi loathing of Jews. By now, the pejorative double entendre, *Marranos*, not only meant Jewish converts to Christianity during the inquisition, but also... hogs.

Persia changed its name to Iran in 1935. Being born in Iran made Professor Pul Persian/Iranian with both Spanish and German blood. As his German grandfather often said about those bloodlines, *"Macht nichts* (doesn't matter), as long as there are no Jews in the bushes. What does matter is learning to control the people."

After graduation from *Dabirestân* (Iranian high school) in 1978, Pul stuck around to help overthrow the last Shah of Iran, and then moved to Argentina where his kindly old *Opa* (grandpa) amalgamated Pul's slightly confused Iranian theocracy into a wildly-confused evilocracy. Pul's grandfather had been a Nazi SS Officer. The nut didn't fall far from the tree.

Accompanied by his comrades Bahadur and Mikhail, each of whom migrated to Argentina from his own revolution-racked country (both spoke Spanish poorly and English strangely), Pul brought his brand of Garduña to the United States in 2002 on a Thanksgiving weekend party bus returning to San Diego from Tijuana, Mexico. It only cost two thousand pesos (about one-hundred-and-seventy-five U.S. dollars) to buy phony documents and illegally ride the bus across our porous border.

Settling on the acronym S.O.L. for use in the United States because he knew it had some unknown (to him) populist meaning, Pul created his own meaning: "Sons of Liberty". Although his agenda had nothing to do with liberty, he knew such a name would be well-received in American media. By way of example, consider oft-praised non-republics with such names as Democratic People's Republic of Korea, Republic of Cuba, Union of Soviet Socialist Republics, etc.

The South American Garduña operated out of a green, orange and magenta seaside resort on the Argentine coast. That branch of the Garduña (from whence Pul emerged) dedicated themselves to turning all the Americas into holy communist countries. Yes, *holy* and *communist* are oxymoronic, but such people have a way with words. Their rationale? Melding communism into a religion will make control of the masses easier, which means less expenditure for bullets and greater wealth for the fearless leaders.

The original Garduña sect, headquartered in a fifteenth-century Moorish castle near Toledo, Spain and their leader, His Supreme Eminence, were basically, the Spanish mafia. His Supreme Eminence flew from Toledo to Los Angeles on a mission to meet with Professor Pul and smooth out the tumultuous relationship between the two branches of Garduña. Professor Pul did not wish to smooth anything out, but successfully pretended he did by practicing *taqiyya* ... lies and deception being a holy means to achieve one's pious goal. Pul believed murdering His Supreme Eminence to be a pious goal, because Pul could then personally control both Garduña sects. He hoped his green turban ploy had sent *norteamericano* authorities on a wild noose chase.

Pul had only two followers in the U.S. (Bahadur and Mikhail) and no followers at all in either Spain or Argentina where *sospechaban que estaba loco* (they suspected he was insane).

As a personal sidebar, I'm thinking a world-wide standard of decent behavior might be a good thing. Perhaps call it something catchy like, "The Ten Suggestions".

"In some societies mass murder is the basis of job security."
— Dr. Francis Noah Weksler

"Christopher Columbus courted Isabella
Because she had the gold and he was her fella"
— Kevin Oxley

"Different versions for different Persians."
— Theophilus Spivak (Hah! I just made that up.)

When in full dress uniform, Assassins wore white garments with a red sash around the waist, their "holy colors of innocence and blood". These are the same colors worn on special occasions by The S.O.L.'s Supreme Eminence, Professor Pul, and underlings. For they still practiced the ancient ways.

A thousand years ago, Hasan's power stretched from China to Spain.

In 2003 it reached Los Angeles.

30

PASADENA INSTITUTE OF TECHNOLOGY
— MONDAY MORNING AFTER "THE DATE"

Dark, cherry wood trim in the former Pheltor Hall library (now the media center) nicely complemented the burled walnut paneling and gold-leafed ceiling rose. Though constructed in the 1950s, the architect designed it all to mimic an 1890s high-class Victorian Estate. None of it went at all well with the flat screen TV bolted above the sculpted-plaster fireplace.

Dr. Weksler kindly indulged Ox each time he retold his Five Oh! magic. It wasn't until almost 8:37 a.m. when Dianne deliria diminished to the point that Kev could focus on the work at hand. Dr. Weksler and I were most attentive to any details Kevin might recall from having witnessed the meeting between little round orange guy and His Supreme Eminence. The only truly known specifics were the Nazi-flavored salute and the outlandish red and white uniform. When we googled his outfit, we learned His Supreme Eminence could have been either an ancient Assassin or Saint Nicholas. Neither seemed likely.

Our next planned ramistat step-up would be the big one: a full-scale test outdoors. If successful, it would punch our ticket to the I.E.S.C. in Paris. Dr. Weksler knew we still had enormous obstacles to overcome in a short timeframe.

For my status update presentation, Dr. Weksler and Kevin settled into a couple of the media center's old Louis XV bergère chairs with floral-patterned heavy fabric and painted beech frames. My laptop wirelessly connected to the flat screen for a slow and clunky (state-of-the-art in 2003) slide show presentation. Kev had a difficult time paying attention. Apparently, that is a symptom of severe infatuation, even for a super-hero pirate.

I would finally get to use my new combination three-color ballpoint pen and three-color laser pointer which I purchased expressly for the presentation. I could switch the laser beam from blue, to green, to yellow, with yellow being the coolest part because, in 2003, yellow lasers were rare and unstable. My laser pen even came with its own super cool clear-vinyl pocket-protector.

The first slide, showing yellow circles on mountain tops throughout the world, utilized a simple transverse Mercator meridian projection map with sixty-degree stripes. With my pointer pen in my left hand, I moved a blue laser dot from mountain top to mountain top, all over the planet, summarizing the daunting mission. Kev and Dr. Weksler were impressed.

"To recap our conjectural hypothesis," I said, "conventional wisdom dictates that a global weather controlling system requires thirty-two ramistat transmission towers, located on key mountain peaks throughout the world. Right?"

Dr. Weksler nodded. "Yes."

I changed the slide to a photograph of Los Angeles with Mt. Wilson on the horizon. Switching to my impressive green laser, I said, "Our proof-of-performance prototype for the L.A. basin will require construction of a large tower here at the pinnacle of Mt. Wilson." I pushed the page down key on my laptop and the Eifel Tower appeared on top of Mt. Wilson.

Dr. Weksler, stroking his chin, nodded. "Regrettably, that appears to be the only option."

I said, "That will cost at least three million dollars."

Kev added, "And take six months to engineer and construct. A different solution is mandatory because Theo and I can't wait that long." He switched to a French accent. "We have a need to say *parlez-vous anglaise?*"

Dr. Weksler shifted his eyes from me to Kevin to me. "Are you suggesting there is another path we may follow?"

Kevin said, "Absolutely."

Kev and I took turns explaining while I quickly advanced through several pages of simple graphics illustrating each step of our plan. The first page displayed only a red disk near the bottom of a blank white slide. I converted my laser color to yellow, so it would show up on the red disk. Now, Kev and Dr. Weksler were *really* impressed.

I showed off a bit by holding my left arm out and shining the yellow laser dot all over the media center. But then, instability seized the day. The pen got very hot and melted itself into a mini police Taser gun. It zapped my left wrist. "Ahh!" I dropped it onto my lap. "Aiieee!"

For the remainder of my presentation, the fingers of my left hand looked like Wolverine. And I ambled with an embarrassing pain.

Except for bodily harm, I really liked that old three-color laser pointer-pen, and the new ones they have now are stable.

I'd actually like to buy another one, if I could remember where I got it. Probably got it at Geeks-R-Us.

Kevin continued with his description. "That red disk represents our new, improved, ramistat which we will connect to a larger, powerful mobile transmission device."

I added, "The ramistat signal travels through an intensification unit, which streams an even stronger signal to an uplink dish, where it is beamed to a satellite in a geosynch orbit."

Kevin wrapped it up. "And the satellite narrowcasts it back down into the troposphere. By using an existing communications satellite, we can create weather anywhere in the world with the extremely powerful mobile transmission device we already own"

Dr. Weksler said, "We already own a powerful mobile transmission device?"

"We do," I said, "The powerful mobile transmission device is Kevin's van."

Kevin said proudly, 'It has a Hemi."

It took only a millisecond for Dr. Weksler to get it. "Brilliant," he almost shouted. Then he turned pensive. "What will it cost to link with a communications satellite?"

"Absolutely nothing," Kevin said.

I explained, "There are currently 3,219 manmade satellites in orbit. One hundred forty-seven of them have geosynchronous orbits at approximately 22,236 miles above mean sea level. Eighty-five of those are U.S. government downlinks which we can use at no cost."

Dr. Weksler asked Kevin, "How do we obtain permission to use a Federal satellite?"

"We don't ask."

Dr. Weksler ruminated with grave concern. "Seriously? You are suggesting we covertly engage a United States government satellite merely to save six months and three million dollars?

We both nodded and said, "Right."

Dr. Weksler said, "I like it."

31

THE POWERFUL MOBILE TRANSMISSION DEVICE SLIDE

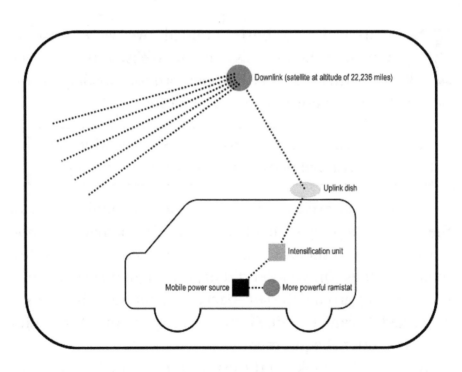

32

OUTSIDE PHELTOR HALL — THREE DAYS LATER — 8:00 A.M.

Bright-eyed and bushy-brained, we were close to launching the big mission. Dr. Weksler arrived even earlier than us, his bumper proudly displaying the new sticker Kevin created per his request:

> If Social Security is running out of money, why aren't congressional pensions running out of money?

We were all excited about our first-ever outdoor test of the ramistat, loosely scheduled for one o'clock that afternoon at the Gorgonio shoetree. Kev and I touched up the last few interior details. Dr. Weksler did his pre-flight inspection and, while looking around the jam-packed van interior, rhetorically remarked, "I can't imagine how on earth you made room for all this additional equipment."

Kevin said, "I took out the espresso machine."

Dr. Weksler nodded approval.

I finished re-channeling the HUD video display maps. "Ox man, I hope you can live without donuts." He whined sufficiently. I pushed two glowing amber buttons and announced, "Hey, take a look. No donut shops, but a lot of heavenly bodies."

They looked up. The windshield HUD's new three-dimensional projection capability showed crowded intersecting paths of satellites orbiting earth.

I said, "All eighty-five federal satellites are now in the system," I dialed in a new setting, flipped the mini-toggle, and pushed the silver button. The global projection debanded, replaced by Southern California with icons representing the three satellites we calculated as being appropriate for our experiment. "There they are gentlemen. Our SoCal stellar ramistat connections. Cosmologically speaking, that's how we roll."

Down near the floor of the van, a small storage compartment lid popped open and Kevin's Pirate outfit dropped out at Dr. Weksler's feet. He held up The Pirate suit and inquiringly raised an eyebrow at Kevin.

Kev said, "Previous engagement."

Dr. Weksler timidly touched the stuffed parrot attached to the Pirate jacket shoulder. "Your bird died."

Kevin and I decided to head out first because we needed to make a stop on our way to the Mojave Desert. Dr. Weksler would hit the road in his rented jeep after his morning lecture concluded. Our plan called for a noonish lunch rendezvous at the China House Cafe in the heart of Lucerne Valley. Close to the intersection of California state highway eighteen and Old Woman Springs Road, the historic restaurant made a logical stopping off point.

The few roads (mostly dirt) in the desolate region had all been wild west horse, wagon, or foot trails. Locals advised city folk against following the old paths. Any such trail might lead to a timeworn pioneer shack or mineshaft, but most often it ended in deadly nothingness. The hot, painfully bright blue desert sky could be both unforgettable and unforgiveable.

Piute, Serrano and Chemehuevi Indians recognized the dangers for centuries. A trail named Old Woman Springs Road, for example, went from the mountain down to Old Woman Springs, so named because while young bucks went up the deadly mountain portion of the trail to gather *piñon* (pine) nuts, women and elderly tribe members remained safely behind at the springs.

After lunch we would head up to the shoetree for the big test.

* * * * *

For our outdoor ramistat test, we analyzed multiple potential sites, each with its own pros and cons. Regarding the local L.A. mountains, Dr. Weksler said, "That area obviously has a lot to offer, both topographically and meteorologically, but the entire southern face of the mountain range can be seen by nineteen million people."

"I guess we'll have to do the test in Hawaii," Kevin said.

"Guess again," Dr. Weksler said.

We smiled.

Dr. Weksler made the decision. "Theo, I like your Gorgonio Canyon shoe-tree suggestion. It's on the other side of a mountain, out of sight from the high desert, in uninhabited terrain." He nodded thoughtfully. "The shoe-tree appears to be as good as it gets."

* * * * *

My elementary school model rocket club held their annual, three-day weekend launch at Lucerne Dry Lake in the high desert. After the Monday morning awards, my family would head back to Los Angeles—but not on the freeway. Instead, Dad took the winding road up the uninhabited side of the mountain and then over the top and down through the beautiful resorts of Big Bear Lake and Lake Arrowhead on the southern (populated) side. On the way up the mountain we always stopped at the shoetree, a place most people never knew existed.

Yes, I know, model rocketry is not a "normal" interest for a young African American from the inner city of Los Angeles. Sort of like a black teenager saying he wants to be a NASCAR driver when he grows up. Nothing wrong with it. Nobody would try to prevent it from happening. But it didn't fit the cultural mold. I really never did fit the cultural mold. I was a geek then and I'm a geek now. Works for me.

Which kinda-sorta makes me think about being African American. If I was born in Germany would I be African German? If I was born in Brazil would I be African-Brazilian? If I was born in Africa would I be African African? I'm just an American. Maybe I have more melanin than you. Maybe I have less. Who cares? I embrace Dr. King's dream for people to "... not be judged by the color of their skin, but by the content of their character." I don't know anybody from Africa and don't expect I ever will. I'm black. So what? Far more importantly, I'm an American. Thankfully.

"Say It Loud – I'm Black and I'm Proud."

— James Brown

The custom of tying old shoes together with their laces and tossing them up into a tree, may be a descendent of ancient "rag-trees". In the case of rag-trees, peoples of the world hung bits of clothing or rags onto trees while sending up prayers. That practice dates back a thousand years or more. My last summer in the rocket club—the fifth grade—I tossed my worn-out fourth grade tennies onto the same shoetree to which we would be going for our ramistat test.

Our planned route would take us up through Cajon Pass above San Bernardino and out to the high desert. A right turn at Victorville (home of the Roy Rogers–Dale Evans Museum for thirty-five years.) would take us east on the eighteen to the far side of Lucerne Valley, and then south for a steep climb up the mountain. Sadly, for Kevin and me, the Roy Rogers museum had moved to Branson, Missouri just a couple of weeks earlier, on March 28, 2003.

Finding the unmarked and barely drivable hundred-year-old "road" known as Gorgonio Trail could be problematic. Concealed by a mix of scrub oak, Joshua trees, manzanita ("Little Apple"), yucca plants ("Our Lord's Candle"), and creosote bushes, the trail did not appear on any map, and was unknown to the early civilian GPS. But we wouldn't miss it because the van's extremely accurate (Kevin created) digital *altimeter* didn't know anything about maps, roads, and GPS. Instead... at precisely 2,316 feet, the altimeter's synthesized female voice would order us to turn into the scrub.

Our Gorgonio Canyon test site, many miles into the wilderness, had no homes. No civilization. No worries.

For good luck, I would bring along my worn but still serviceable Nikes to hang on the shoetree.

* * * * *

"Ready to motor?" Kevin asked. We were in his van, parked on the grass up behind Pheltor Hall.

"Let 'er rip," I said, trying to sound confident. When he released the parking brake my instant all-purpose anxiety took over. "Kev, I'm really concerned. Do you really think this test is going to work?"

"Don't know. That's why it's called a test."

He put the transmission into drive, looked in his side-view mirror, and slammed on the brakes. The lovely Dr. Dianne Wright appeared at Kevin's window with a happy sunshine smile. "Good morning guys. I heard you mention a test. What kind of test?"

Sworn to absolute secrecy, we groped for an answer. Kev put the transmission back into park.

"Blood test," He said at the same time I said, "Driver's test." Mild panic.

He quickly said, "Driver's test. And I quickly said, "blood test."

Dianne scrunched her eyebrows. "What?"

Always good under pressure, Kev's brain worked incredibly fast. Without hesitation he explained, "Well, you see, Theo has a rare blood disorder. And the DMV won't let him drive if we don't get him tested.

She leaned forward, so she could see me on the other end of the bench seat. With warm, sincere concern, she said, "Oh dear, Theo, I am so sorry. What are your symptoms?

Not knowing what to say, I stuttered. "Well... I... uh... uh... I... I... I... uh... it... it...

Kev said, "It makes him stutter."

He made eye contact with me and, with a wicked smile, said, "And it makes him very hyper." He nodded at me, eyebrows up.

I caught on and felt compelled to save the day by bouncing up and down in the seat, tapping out non-rhythms on the dashboard, and banging my knee on the door as I said, "I... I... I... uh... uh... uh..."

Ox really enjoyed it. Giving Dianne a worried expression and, as if embarrassed for me, he loudly whispered, "And then, suddenly, he will just start making that horse sound by flapping his lips."

I stopped banging and stuttering and switched to making that worrisome horse sound with my flapping lips.

"Yeah, that's the one," Kevin said. He made a rolling motion with his hand, indicating I should keep it up and speed it up. "C'mon Theo. Don't be shy. You know the nurse said it's good for you to just let it out."

I leaned toward Kevin and did an extremely loud and boisterous flapping horse lips sound. Kevin wiped my horse slobber off his face.

He told Dianne, "The symptoms are, of course, controlled by the medication he took just before you arrived." He looked at his watch. "Yep, everything should be fine in two seconds. One Mississippi. Two Mississippis."

I stopped all symptomatic expression.

"Well, I hope you feel better, Theo," she said. "Good luck with your blood test. And your driver's test." A little suspicious, but not certain why, she said, "I'll see you later." She did her patented little finger wave and walked toward the administration building.

Kevin once again put the van into drive and stepped gently on the accelerator for a non-conversational ride down Los Robles Boulevard and then onto the two-ten freeway.

Once we were safely on the freeway, I said, "Horse lips?"

"Well, it doesn't matter now, Theo," he said. "Because you didn't do it right anyway."

"I did it perfectly." To prove my point, I made the best horse lips sound ever.

He said, "Naw. You need more air behind it and looser lips." He did his own amateurish version. It was lacking in everything except moisture. He obviously needed a lot more practice. He threw in a couple of whinnies, to which I objected, declaring them out of bounds. We did dueling horse lips for at least ten miles.

I still think I won.

33

HOLLYWOOD — SAME DAY — LATER THAT MORNING

Instead of driving straight to the high desert, Ox and I took a longcut through Hollywood to visit a hobby shop that just got in a new series of Hot Wheels. Traveling north on Highland Avenue we came to a dead stop about two blocks from the Hollywood Bowl. Northbound slush hour didn't start until mid-afternoon so, something was wrong.

"What's going on?' I said, trying different head orientations to get a clearer view. "All I can see are wall-to-wall cars. This is mondo ugly."

Kevin said, "Up scope. Zoom: two hundred percent."

The electronic periscope unit whined as it rose up out of the van roof. Live, high quality video displayed on the HUD, in front of the windshield. No worry, because the bizarre California legislature hadn't yet passed a no-periscope-while-driving law.

We analyzed the video feed. "Something's up at the Hollywood Bowl," he said. "Can't tell what. There's police and a bunch of people carrying posters."

"I can't make out the signs." I said. "Can you do more zoom?"

He guffawed. "Can I do more zoom? Hah. Can a bear run naked in the woods?"

I nodded. "Yes, it can. But it will get very cold in the winter."

He issued a voice command. "Zoom, five hundred percent—bearing: nine degrees Port." Looking at the HUD image, he smiled large. "Wow. Look at that."

The Bowl marquis read:

ROCK LEGENDS

Tickets on Sale Now

The demonstrators, fans of The Pirate, carried home-made signs:

Pirate/Puckett POWER!	We Want Gary!
The Pirate Rules!	Yeah! Yeah! Yeah!
Yo Ho Ho!	And A Battle of Fun!

Now I knew who to blame for the gridlock. "They're picketing the Hollywood bowl because of _your_ Pirate."

"Guilty as charged," Kevin said, smiling cosmically, basking in his own glow. "Woo Hoo. Down scope." The periscope silently slid back into its roof well. He turned and looked at me and, with a rare sense of urgency said, "Quick, help me find a place to hide the van."

"What?"

"I need six seconds in a dark alley."

"You need a shrink."

He made a sudden left turn, crossed the yellow center stripe, and shot into the underground parking of an out-of-business former neighborhood market. The top of his van barely cleared the large FOR SALE sign on front of the boarded-up building. He drove down to the lowest level, made a U-turn in the farthest corner, and looked around. Empty. No windows. Only two fluorescent bulbs still alive and clicking.

Kevin said, "Plate. North Carolina."

I had no idea what was going on.

He said, "Forty-three." (The car number of NASCAR's most famous driver, the "King", Richard Petty.)

I asked, "What are you doing?"

"Fulfilling our destiny."

Another cryptic answer that provided no data. I did, however, notice he said _our_, another of those _group_ words. A bad sign.

In six seconds the van exterior paint color changed to Petty Blue.

John Wayne's voice announced, "Forty-three complete. Saddle Up".

I just sat there blinking in the dark, wondering what alien species had captured me. I had never seen this before. Didn't know anything about it. Didn't know what to do with it. At least I finally knew what all those stupid little micro nozzles were for.

He pushed a quick-release pin and flipped the steering wheel/control yoke over to me, which I didn't even know was possible. He said he needed to take care of something in the "back office" (Kevin code for the van's cargo area) and that I was now the co-pilot.

Oh, why not. I'll just co-pilot all the way into police custody.

I shouted back to him, "Where are we going?"

"Into the history books." Another cryptic answer. I despise cryptic answers.

Turned out he was right, though, about the history thing. It was the first protest ever organized by text messages. Official count showed more than two-thousand people participated in the protest. He told me to exit the parking facility, and he guaranteed there would be a clear path to follow.

Handing me a Captain Hook mask he bought in Fantasyland, he said, "Better put this on."

"Why?"

"To thwart facial recognition software."

Made sense to me. A much better idea than prison.

I drove up out of the dark parking ramp into the sunlight and stopped at the edge of Highland Avenue. With northbound traffic heading toward the Hollywood Bowl still completely blocked due to the protest, nobody moved. I heard mechanical buzzing in the back office. Demonstrators at the Bowl pointed in our direction. People cheered. Southbound traffic came to a stop as cars and protestors cooperated to clear a path for the van.

In his Pirate costume, Kevin stood on the van's internal equipment hoist platform as it rose up through the van's center sunroof. He waved, and the crowd went wild. They all parted like the Red Sea for the van to pass through unimpeded. I got into the mood for a few moments and gave a royal wave out the window with my left hand, the one on which I wore the Captain Hook hook. It came with the mask. Regaining my senses, I rolled up my window and locked the doors.

I slowly drove the North Carolina-licensed, Petty Blue van through the cars and the exuberant crowd toward the Hollywood Bowl entrance. Like gigantic schools of fish moving as one, the multitude cleared space for the van in front of the

Bowl marquis. They repeatedly chanted, "If Puckett's a no, then we won't go." — "If Puckett's a no, then we won't go."

The throng suddenly hushed when a brawny, unyielding, crowd-control police officer marched toward the van, obviously on a mission. The policeman stopped beside the van. He used his megaphone to address the protestors, saying. "I will handle this." He looked up at Kevin the Pirate and sternly shouted, "Hey buddy."

The Pirate pointed to himself and feigned misunderstanding. The Pirate people smiled.

The policeman tossed his megaphone to the Pirate and shouted, "Give 'em heck pirate dude." The crowd went wild again.

Using the megaphone, The Pirate greeted his people. "Avast there maties."

It being The Pirate's first-ever personal appearance, nobody knew how to respond. Some shouted back, "Avast." Some, "Yo-ho-ho." Some sang, "Yeah... yeah... yeah." Most just cheered.

The Pirate, on the megaphone, asked, "Who sold more records in 1968 than any other artist, including the Beatles?"

They shouted, "Gary Puckett."

The Pirate asked, "Who's first five hits were million selling gold records?"

The crowd shouted, "Gary Puckett."

The Pirate said, "Who is the greatest living voice in rock 'n' roll history?"

The crowd answered, "Gary Puckett."

The Pirate said, "Who do we want at the Rock Legends concert?"

Everybody screamed, "Gary Puckett." And a two-thousand-voice chorus sang, "Yeah... yeah... yeah. — Yeah... yeah... yeah. — Yeah... yeah... yeah."

Kev and I both noticed a Channel Eight television news truck. I put on the emergency flashers and slowly drove through the multitude, hoping to escape video scrutiny. Kev immediately went into his wrap, as I carefully drove away.

Still using the megaphone, with fans cheering for each sentence, The Pirate said, "I am so proud of you. You could be at work, or at school, or watching Oprah, but instead you came here to stand up for what's right and true. You're beautiful. I love you. And remember: Yo! Ho! Ho! And..." — He spread his arms, beseeching audience participation.

Two thousand admirers completed his signature line, roaring, "A Battle of Fun!"

With clenched victory fist, The Pirate shouted back, "Booyah!" Using the megaphone for the last time, he said, "And let's hear it for Hollywood's finest." He tossed the megaphone to the peace officer, pointing and smiling at him. Everybody cheered, clapped, and then sang, "Yeah... yeah... yeah — Yeah... yeah... yeah. — Yeah... yeah... yeah."

Kevin the Pirate waved goodbye as he descended into the van. The Channel Eight camera tracked us heading up Cahuenga West. The cheering crowd flowed onto both sides of the street, purposefully blocking the television truck. They continued singing, "Yeah... yeah... yeah."

From the back office, Ox shouted, "Help me find a place to hide the van."

34

GORGONIO CANYON — SAME DAY — EARLY AFTERNOON

Where the little-used mountain dirt road turned further south, we pulled off and got out to marvel at the lone, nineteen-foot-tall California Black Oak sharing dry soil with tufts of straw-colored grasses and twisted red manzanita. More than hundred pairs of shoes swung from branches growing in all directions out of the contorted, multi-forked trunk. Someone had ringed the tree with a white picket fence at the perimeter of its canopy, and put up a sign:

> This is a tree of the people, by the people, and for the people. Please do not climb on it, carve on it, or harm it in any way. We hope your hopes expressed by the shoes on this tree come to pass. The shoes will be gently removed twice a year and given to grateful people who have no shoes. May the Lord bless and keep you and give you peace.

Standing outside the picket ring, I tossed my Nikes up and watched them embrace a high branch. Who knows, maybe there really is something spiritual about hanging shoes on a tree. I mean, I did it as an eleven-year-old geeky kid from south-central and I became a physicist at a prestigious university working to make the world a safer place. Who knows?

The old dirt road continued left, back toward the next small chunk of civilization, but we continued to the right, up the mountain face for another twelve-hundred-feet on what could only be described as a barely discernible path. At an altitude of precisely 2,316 feet, Kevin purposely drove past the turn-off to Gorgonio Trail because he wanted to experience the reaction of his digital altimeter.

The altimeter's irate, condescending computer-generated female voice said, *"What just happened? You missed the turn, didn't you? Are you a freaking idiot? I can answer that. Yes, you are a freaking idiot. Make a U-turn right now and I don't even care if it's a legal U-turn. Just do it. You freaking idiot."*

By the time Ox turned around, Dr. Weksler had assumed point. He lead us slowly up through the dust. Four-wheel drive, though not mandatory, might have been encouraging. Even so, the van's extra-duty suspension kept us somewhat sure-footed. A slow-going hour later, we arrived at our selected clearing, a patch of rocky high ground above a dry creek bed. Beyond that point, the trail became nonexistent, unless one were driving an M46 Patton tank.

We all got out, checked our space, and then rearranged parking so the rear of Kevin's van had a line-of-sight to halfway up the mountain. Surrounded by lodgepole pine, which does well on a northern slope with infertile soil, we were, interestingly, also surrounded by cactus, due to the climate zone. We all paused, for a brief moment, to appreciate breathtaking views with mild pine scent whispering through clean, dry, hot mountain air.

With his binoculars, Dr. Weksler did a three hundred-sixty-degree scan. As expected, he saw no sign of humanity. "So far so good," he said. Lifting up his white-framed, yellow mirrored sunglasses, he pulled out a handkerchief, and wiped his head, temples, and neck. "Whew. We picked a sizzler." He went back to scanning through his binoculars.

"It's perfect," I said. "Hot and dry. Not a cloud anywhere."

"Yep," the Ox man agreed. "Sure, Sure looks like rain to me."

Dr. Weksler let the bi-nocs fall onto his chest, held in place by the leather strap around his neck. "The only thing related to homo sapiens I can find is that dilapidated miner's shack and outhouse where the dry creek bed bends around the boulder."

He pointed. We looked. The derelict shack, on the far side of the gully, about a hundred yards uphill, leaned seriously against a fallen oak. The pine stand, though thicker over there, still had a lot of scrub brush and cactus. The old shack hadn't started off as a lean-to, but a hundred years later that's about all that remained. Much of the weathered-gray, home-made, pioneer lumber had rotted away. The outhouse, in slightly better condition, still had a recognizable quarter-moon "window" in its door.

"What do you think?" Dr. Weksler asked.

"Well, the lights are off," I said.

"And nobody's been home for a hundred years," Kevin added.

"I concur. I doubt anyone's been there since the last fleck of gold came out of these mountains in 1896. Gentlemen, we are a go. Tell you what… I know it takes ten minutes to open the van and set up the equipment. Please get started without me. I'll join you to help, right after I do one final, extreme visual of the entire mountainside, sector by sector, back and forth, up and down. If I spot anything on two legs, we cancel the test."

He climbed onto the rock outcropping above the gulch and began his systematic sectoring toward the southeast. Kev and I walked to the rear of the van. I reached for the door handle in the middle of the two back doors, saying, "Please allow me to open your doors for you, sir."

He stopped me. "Excuse me, Mr. Spivak, but this is my van. Those are my van doors. They are my responsibility. I shall be the one to open them."

I stepped back. "Well, if you truly feel that way, be my guest, kind sir."

He held up his keys in his right hand and pointing to them with his left, said, "And these are my keys. And this is my key fob with a remote button."

"I can confirm that, sir. I recognize it as your very own personal key fob, Mr. Oxley. I have great fondness for that key fob."

Thinking our conversation, a mite odd, Dr. Weksler turned to look. Now assured that he had Dr. Weksler in the audience, Kevin melodramatically pushed the remote button on his key fob and launched our newest van upgrade, one which we had kept secret from Dr. Weksler: automatic everything.

All van doors and panels unlocked, including the new sliding section of the roof.

The two back doors swung open, revealing new controls and displays on the door inside faces.

Support braces deployed from the van's frame and attached themselves to the back of the back doors, holding them steady.

Struts under the van extended, lifting the rear wheels off the ground to give the van a stable, automatically leveled, rock solid stance.

The roof panel slid open, and the four-foot diameter uplink dish rose out of the van on its articulated arm.

Two collapsed control room swivel chairs came down from the ceiling, opened up, and snapped into position in front of the master consoles.

A two section, diamond tread pattern, steel platform slid out from under the van, unfolded, and slotted itself into position, covering the space between the two open back doors.

A third collapsed swivel chair rolled out from a shelf built into the rear of the chassis and sprung open, ready for action, on the platform between the back doors.

Everything powered up and lit up, ready for action.

Instead of ten manual minutes, the entire process took only thirty-two robotic seconds.

In Gloria Swanson's voice, the van computer announced, *"All right, Mr. DeWeksler, I'm ready for my close-up."*

35

SAME DESOLATE SPOT — A FEW MINUTES LATER

Inside the van, Kevin and I sat at the two new master control consoles. Dr. Weksler stood outside behind the van, so he could observe dish movement as well as auxiliary gauges and monitors now in the back doors. We all had headsets with voice-activated mics. At Dr. Weksler's insistence, we each wore a white helmet with a clear Glasonate visor and individual HUDs. Kevin customized his helmet with a buccaneer black flag on the front and hot rod flames on both sides. It caught Dr. Weksler by surprise, but he just went with it.

"Power's up." I said.

Kevin said, "Dish is live."

The status light on our consoles glowed amber.

Kevin typed in a command. "We're hot and searching."

Full color flat screen monitors on the A and B consoles, and inside the open left back door, displayed the earth with three satellites above. One satellite blinked blue.

Looking at my readout, I toggled through the three choices, and said, "Sys Command calls SatCom Nine best bet, Frank."

"Got it," Dr. Weksler said. "Any issues? Any reds"?

Kevin and I did swift visuals.

I said, "No reds."

Ox said, "Green as a jolly giant."

Dr. Weksler said, "Anchors aweigh, my boys."

* * * * *

One hundred yards away, on his belly, inside the remains of the abandoned miner's shack, aspiring cult monster Bahadur peered through his own bi-nocs. He and Mikhail, wearing camouflage, had been waiting in place since before noon. Bahadur watched every move we made. Mikhail hid in the outhouse, occasionally standing on the bench to peek out through the bottom of the quarter moon.

* * * * *

I flipped open a latch, pushed the encapsulated button, and said, "Securing ... ... SatCom Nine ... ... now."

Kev and I watched our screens while Dr. Weksler watched the actual dish. The articulated arm whirred and snicked as it rotated, tilted, and locked onto the satellite 22,000 miles up. A beautiful thing.

Dr. Weksler returned to his station at the rear of the van.

Ox typed, hit enter, and said, "Channel sixteen on standby. Waiting... Waiting... Waiting... Waiting... Waiting... We are... locked."

"Yes." A jolt of ecstatic adrenalin rushed through all of us.

"Coordinates, Frank?" Kevin asked.

Dr. Weksler, now intent on his own back door display, said. "Let's target four-thousand feet below the pinnacle. Make it 35.46 to 35.47, north."

Ox confirmed. "35.46 to 35.47, north. Got it."

Dr. Weksler said, "I wish to start small, just to be prudent. Do a surface plot with a total of 2.5 square kilometers ... just under a square mile. Please give me perimeters of 118.25 to 118.26.

Kevin confirmed as he entered coordinates. He put his hand on the chrome-plated T-bar control to activate the ramistat but... didn't do it.

He turned to Dr. Weksler and said, "You should have the honor, Starbuck."

Dr. Weksler smiled and nodded. I thought he was going to cry. "Thank you." He stepped forward and grabbed the T-bar. He paused, bathed in anticipation and perspiration. It looked like he might have said a silent prayer. With his thumb, he pushed in the black plastic interlock button on the chrome T crossbar. And pulled.

An eerie hum told us the invisible ramistat signal went dynamic. The red digital countdown display showed 00:00:00:20. Twenty seconds. Countdown beeps (one per second) began.

If we wished, we could watch the readouts. If we wanted to, we could listen to screeches as digital devices agreed upon a common language and then shared their needs with each other. Other than that, we could only wait. Twenty seconds sure seemed like a long time... fifteen... ten... five... four... three... two...

Dr. Weksler loudly shouted into his headset microphone, "CONTACT!" He scared me half to deaf.

The tones changed again. Kevin said, "SatCom's solar wing is repositioning."

Finally, we heard what we had all been waiting for, a sound like the hyper, irrational, foolish cousin of a fax modem. The scratchy, squeaking din with multiple muted beeping tones meant SatCom Nine sent an amplified ramistat beam back to earth.

The glowing red countdown clock reached 00:00, but nothing happened. Total silence. We looked at each other. Wonder and worry.

CRAA-BOOM! The thunder was LOUD and STARTLING. "Aiieee!" Yes, I squealed yet again.

We scrambled out of the van like kids rushing to the bouncy house at a birthday party. We cheered as a dramatic, flawless, three-dimensional rectangular (that 3D orthotope thing) storm cloud formed, grew dark, and hovered, perfectly still, in one spot at the side of the mountain. It started raining and we started celebrating. It only rained within the programmed ground surface rectangle and nowhere else. Though we stood less than fifty yards away on our promontory, not a drop fell on us. Handshakes and hugs. Back pats and woo-hoos.

Kevin said, "Wow, I think maybe ramistat satellite connections will actually work."

Mildly alarmed, Dr. Weksler said, "I thought you *knew for certain* it would work?"

"Well, I knew for certain that it would either, A, work, or B, blow up the satellite."

Dr. Weksler said, "What?"

Kev said, "Or blow up the van."

I said, "What?"

In an Australian accent, Kevin said, "And we'd lose half of Australia. Aye mates, now there's a real chuck-a-wobbly."

He was pushing our legs. Of course, it would work. Kevin only made mistakes with women.

Mostly.

* * * * *

Rain also did not fall at the old miner's shack. Bahadur heard the thunder but knew of nothing else other than our celebration he watched through his binoculars. Looking up, he saw dry tree branches and no hint of the astonishing storm. Mikhail remained in the outhouse peeking through the moon. The thunder scared him.

* * * * *

Within the stormy rectangle, rain rolled off the dry pine boughs and fell to the parched ground which, unaccustomed to heavy precipitation, quickly became saturated. Water began to run downhill in rivulets on the hard, dry earth, as it sought drainage to the flatlands.

The Ox man heard it first: a distant slushing noise, soon followed by what sounded like hundreds of twigs cracking. He shouted the alarm, "Flash flood! Theo—help me engage. I can't just cut power; we still have to do a half-step power-down to prevent the discharge reversal."

Kev jumped into the van and began adjusting controls. "Frank, get to high ground. Wish us luck."

"Oh, my Lord. I should have foreseen this," Dr. Weksler said, beating himself up. "The ground is far too dry and hard." But he didn't run. He stayed behind to help close up the van which, regrettably, still had to be done manually.

* * * * *

Water from thousands of rivulets hurried into the normally dry creek bed and rapidly filled the gulch until, a half mile later, it became a deafening flashflood. The overflowing creek swept away the miner's shack and outhouse, carrying them and their occupants down the mountain in the raging water.

* * * * *

We had already canceled our cloud and were still buttoning up for evacuation when the flash flood roared past us, right below our stone ledge.

"Oh—my—goodness," I said, again filled with FUD (Fear-Uncertainty-Doubt). "We dodged a water cannon."

"Wow. . . look up there," Kevin pointed. "No more miner's shack."

We looked, troubled by implications.

Enormously disturbed, Dr. Weksler let it out. "Our impact in this vacant setting underscores tremendous responsibility. All potential negatives must be precisely anticipated. We cannot play God."

In totality, we did not unleash an extraordinary volume of water, just a fair amount all at once. The short-lived flood ended as soon as it started. When we eliminated the cloud, we eliminated the water. Like turning off a heavenly spigot. Portions of Gorgonio Trail became slippery mud slopes, but we slid back down the mountain with no additional drama.

* * * * *

The creek flowed to the east and Gorgonio Trail angled to the west, so we never saw Bahadur riding the crest of the flash flood sitting on the closed outhouse door, holding his breath, and holding tight with both hands. A white knuckles session.

From inside the outhouse, Mikhail wiggled his fingers through the quarter-moon cutout and shouted, "Out of here get me. *Por favor.*"

Bahadur, having no intention of loosening his grip on the outhouse, said, "Mikhail, worry do not. Safe I am."

36

SAN FERNANDO, CALIFORNIA — TWO HOURS LATER

In the bedroom office of his red tile-roofed, mission-style house, Professor Pul debriefed Bahadur and Mikhail, neither of whom smelled very good. Especially Mikhail. They stood in front of Pul's desk dripping remnants of flood water on the dirty carpet. Mikhail tilted his head to pound water out of his ear.

The Professor didn't notice their vulgar odor because he had his own. His apocrine bromhidrosis (not B.O. but a close relative), generally confined to his always bare feet, directly resulted from years of sharing filthy wall-to-wall carpeting with two large, and filthy dogs. The dogs smelled better than him.

Pul held court at his nicked and stained wooden desk. A four-foot by six-foot map of the United States, tacked to the warped wood-paneled wall behind him, showed California, Arizona, Nevada, Utah, Colorado, New Mexico and Texas highlighted in dayglow yellow. Large magenta letters above the map spelled *Aztlán*, the Spanish name for the U.S. lands he believed should be reclaimed by the Holy Garduña.

"Dr. Weksler must be delighted with his extraordinary new capabilities," Pul mused with his peculiar educated accent. "But not nearly as pleased as I shall be."

Mikhail and Bahadur bobbled their soggy heads in agreement, eagerly awaiting their next assignment for the cause.

"Si, Capataz. We wish to you please," Mikhail said bowing slightly in a show of respect.

Long-repressed anger toward Mikhail simmered in Pul's eyes. He opened his upper right desk drawer and removed the oddly proportioned MSP, two-shot, silent pistol. Tan colored with a black muzzle, the KGB-developed weapon for agent personal protection made no sound when fired. Unique in all the world (silent shooting without a silencer) the engineering break-through came in the ammunition. The MSP projectile cartridge used a plunger to propel the bullet, and all gases remained within the shell. Mikhail got a good look at the small Derringer-type pistol, because Professor Pul held it two inches in front of Mikhail's nose.

"Capataz?" Mikhail said, wild-eyed.

"Mikhail, my little Billy goat," Pul said. "How many times have I told you never to speak Spanish while in this country? How many times?"

"*Ocho.*"

Mikhail panicked. "Eight. Eight."

Bahadur moved sideways, wisely not wishing to be part of whatever happened next.

The hatred in Pul's eyes boiled over as he stood up and added his left hand to steady his grip on the MSP. He rolled the back of his head on his tense neck muscles. After having calmed himself ever so slightly, Pul looked again at Mikhail, leaned forward, and shouted. "Bang!"

Bang, one of Pul's two, stinking, muscular, 130-pound bullmastiffs, jumped to attention—ready to kill, a Jekyll &

Hyde change from his nap on the dirty loveseat Bang shared with Supreme Eminence.

Professor Pul snapped his finger and pointed at Mikhail. In a hot L.A. second, Bang pinned Mikhail to the floor, growling savagely with his deadly teeth above Mikhail's face, upon which Bang drooled abundantly.

Although relieved at not being dead, Mikhail immediately transitioned from merely frightened to superbly terrified.

"Mikhail," Professor Pul said gently, "I do not wish to shoot you now."

"Thank you, sir."

"Oh, no Mikhail, I am afraid you misconstrue. I would be very happy to shoot you later; just not now. These are very special bullets. Far too expensive to waste on you. If I want you dead now, Bang will simply eat your throat."

Mikhail reached his free hand up to cover his throat. Bang growled and moved his fangs closer to the windpipe. Mikhail's hand retreated.

"What do me you want me to do?' Mikhail asked.

"I want you to blend in with the people in this country, so you are not so noticeable. I want you to burn that stupid orange jumpsuit. You stand out like... (He groped for a metaphor) ... pumpkin man. I want you to think before you talk. I want you to think before you act. I want you to think before you think you are thinking."

Mikhail paused to think. "Okay, that will I can do."

Professor Pul continued, "Yes is not *si*. It is yes. Commander is not *Capataz*, it is Commander. Spanish is Spanish, and English is English. Do not speak Spanish. Do not speak Spanglish. I want you to never again speak Spanish in this country until we take over this country.

"S... yes, Commander."

If you speak Spanish again, I will send you to back to Pamplona where they will grind you up and feed you to the bulls. Do you understand?"

"Yes, Commander."

He looked at Mikhail thoughtfully, and shook his head. *No, I will not feed him to the bulls. It would make the bulls sick. And they would grow up small and round. And stupid. And Orange.*

"Mikhail... I am going to purchase a very cheap gun. If you screw up again, I will shoot you with a very cheap bullet. Do you understand?"

"Yes, commander."

"Bang, down! Mikhail, up!"

Bang returned to his loveseat. Mikhail gracelessly stood up.

Professor Pul issued orders to Bahadur and Mikhail. "You may kill Weksler and his entire baud squad if you wish. I don't care. Just bring me that van."

37

ARCADIA, CALIFORNIA — TWO MORE HOURS LATER

Following the outdoor ramistat test—about which Dianne knew absolutely nothing—Kevin and Dianne had a date to meet at 5:18 p.m. in Thoroughbred Mall, a somewhat upscale shopping center squeezed in between Santa Anita Park Racetrack and the Los Angeles Arboretum (where they shot the TV series *Fantasy Island*).

The Gorgonio Trail muck got cleaned off both Kevin and his van in time for the date. Normally having no concerns about the van's secrets, Kev never-the-less sought additional security, just to be sure. While still in his garage he said, "Plate. Iowa." Then, happy as a Kauai clam, the Ox man headed east on Huntington Drive through ritzy San Marino.

Three cars back, Bahadur and Mikhail tailed him.

* * * * *

Signature colors of Persian Green and Chiffon Yellow adorning streamline-modern architecture made Santa Anita Park an instant jewel of the San Gabriel Valley when it opened in 1934, way out in the small country town of Arcadia.

Hollywood had a long and storied relationship with Santa Anita Park. Legendary personalities Bing Crosby, Joe E.

Brown, Al Jolson, Harry Warner, and Hal Roach each owned a piece of the track. Horses owned by Alex Trebek, Spencer Tracy, and Errol Flynn raced at the park. Roy Rogers's thoroughbred, Triggairo, won the 1975 El Encino Stakes at Santa Anita.

> Geek Alert — for those who are trivia laden like me: A 24-foot tall fiberglass replica of Trigger was created for the Roy Rogers Museum. Mr. Rogers allowed the NFL Denver Broncos to use the mold to create Bucky the Bronco which stands above the scoreboard at Bronco Stadium. After Bucky was completed, they, literally, broke the mold.

Kev chose to wear the same handsome mauve and gray aloha shirt he wore at his Five Oh! dinner date with Dianne. Unfortunately, that shirt built an indelible link to the mind of Leonard Ostermann. Ever since that night at Five Oh! Ostermann had cruised the foothills trying to find the van with the Texas license plate and the driver with the Marvin Gaye shirt.

A wide, lushly landscaped, center divider decorated stunning Huntington Drive, a ten-lane boulevard that stretched from South Pasadena all the way east to Santa Anita Park and the Thoroughbred Mall. Stopped for a red light on Michillinda Avenue, Ostermann angrily watchdogged traffic passing by on Huntington. Upon seeing the distinctive mauve and gray aloha shirt drive through the intersection in a white van, he gave chase.

Well, that's not quite accurate. He tried to give chase, but his red stop light interfered with official business so, he ran the red light and edged out into the fifty-miles-per-hour traffic, honking his horn and shouting out his window, "That's the shirt. That's the pirate van. That's him. Get out of my way. This is official business. That's him. Do you hear me?"

He drove his two left tires up over the curb and onto the median, forcibly creating his own lane by making legal traffic crowd over to their right. He lowered the passenger window and yelled, "Get out of my way, you maniacs. Can't you see I am chasing a pirate?"

Five lanes of east-bound Huntington Drive traffic skidded to a stop amidst blaring horns and cursing. By keeping his two left tires on the median and utilizing continuous honking and screaming, Ostermann made it all the way to the mall without crashing his car.

Seven other people, however, crashed their cars.

Arriving in the congested mall parking lot, Leonard methodically drove up and down each parking aisle searching for a white van with a driver wearing that Hawaiian shirt. Ostermann's intense, small, bright eyes continually flicked back and forth across the parking lot like the tiny red lights on his frequency scanner, or a Cylon Centurion.

He happily muttered aloud, "I've got you now, you petty pirate perpetrator." Oh, he liked that. He smiled at his accidental alliteration and tried to think of more as he drove. "You... you buccaneer broadcast bandit. — You... pedantic parrot person." He was so very pleased with his own cleverness.

When police officers arrived on Huntington Drive to take statements, the first question asked of each of the seven crashed motorists was, "Did the airbag go off?" Each motorist gave the same answer: "Yes he did and he's probably still yelling."

* * * * *

Inside the mall food court, Kevin sucked up the last drop of his iced tea. Grabbing a small packet of ketchup and a couple napkins for future use, he ambled to their agreed-upon meeting spot in front of the electronics store. Kev knew he was early for their date, but Dianne was worth it and... she worshipped punctuality.

He also got to watch the 1950s, black and white, oxymoronically titled horror movie, *Zombie Heaven*. That "classic" played 24/7 in an endless loop on a flat-screen TV in the store window. More shoppers joined him because large flat-screen televisions were still something new to behold, and *Zombie Heaven* was so old and bad it didn't even play on late night television. Everyone stared at the big screen with their backs to the mall's main promenade.

Kevin had calculated it far in advance, but just to be sure, he confirmed with the electronics store manager that the current *Zombie Heaven* would end at 5:18 p.m. Counting on Dianne's always-right-on-time arrival, Kev reached into his pocket for the ketchup packet mere seconds before she walked up to his back and tapped him on the shoulder. She whispered intimately, "Hi stranger."

Kevin turned around in a zombie pose with thick red blood oozing from his mouth.

Dianne recoiled. "Oh!"

He held up the empty ketchup packet, wiped off the ketchup blood, and grinned. He didn't know what a zombie voice might sound like so, with a pretty good Bela Lugosi vampire accent, he said, "Greetings. Might I be the first to bite you today?"

Dianne broke into a huge smile and rushed to embrace him. With his strong left arm behind her waist, he dipped her theatrically while they shared a melodramatic kiss. After a few seconds they remembered to stand up and breathe. Dianne gazed deeply into Kevin's eyes, licked her lips, and said seductively, "Mmm. Heinz."

The small crowd of shoppers laughed and broke into applause. The shoppers were all on foot, of course, so it was—officially—a standing ovation. Despite it being only their second date, Kev and Dianne now had four standing ovations to their credit.

As they walked to the multi-theaterplex, she held his arm just above the elbow, consciously enjoying the large bicep. With a big smile she said, "My, aren't we in a good mood today."

"Yes, we are. Definitely celebrating. That's for sure."

"Let me guess," Dianne said, "You got a Hawaiian shave ice machine for your van?"

"Ooo, good idea. Then, in his Nazi spy voice, he said, "This is much bigger. We have made stupendous progress in our experiments."

Her smile went rigid. "What do you mean?"

Still doing his German accent in time with his wriggling eyebrows and sneering, Kev said, "I have been sworn to secrecy Fräulein, but the precise nature of our research will soon be revealed to the entire world.

She didn't smile.

* * * * *

In the mall parking lot, Bahadur used his lockout tool to open the driver's door of Kevin's van. He climbed in, closed the door, and got down on his knees to see if he could figure out how to hot-wire a van. Couldn't be too hard. He saw it in a movie.

Mikhail, not being nearly as sophisticated as his hero Bahadur, just pried open the back doors with a mini crowbar. Grabbing a handle on control console B to pull himself up into the rear of the van, he accidentally turned on the master power switch. The van went live. Mikhail went star struck.

"Is Enterprise Starship." His eyes gleamed. Being a Trekkie of little brain, he forgot the task at hand and began to role play, declaring, "Log of the Captain, date of the stars, four five six seven eight nine." The adorable looking, but nauseating, little man hadn't had this much fun since ripping wings off his first butterfly when he was eight. "Klingon prey of the bird, decloaked, it just did. Up your shields."

He pressed another random button on the console. The ramistat dish rose up through the roof, aimed at the mall.

"Scottie," Mikhail announced, "Speed of seven warps, now we need." Then he tried a strange Spanish-accented version of a Scottish accent, "Aye Captain. Get you will seven warps, but may it destroy the Prize of Enter."

Mikhail swung his chubby little body and arms around looking for another button to push. He found one. He pushed it. Mikhail yelped in delight at the cool electronic sounds as the activated ramistat whirred, hummed, and shrilly went deet... deet... deet... deet... deet... deet...

* * * * *

The ramistat signal traveled through a mall clothing store, making shirts and skirts on racks rise in sequence as if doing the "wave". Deeper inside the mall, Dianne and Kevin's conversation became so intense that neither noticed the ramistat's effect as it traveled toward them.

Chewing on her thumbnail, Dianne said, "So, both you and Theo are helping Dr. Weksler with his personal windmill project?" She crossed her arms and looked away. "Oh Kevin, I am so sorry. You're going to get hurt."

"What are you talking about?"

She replied, "Dr. Weksler's Quixotic weather fantasy. Kevin, he's being kicked out at the end of the semester."

"What?"

"The Board of Regents voted to cancel Dr. Weksler's tenure. His grant is not being renewed. The whole department will be closed until more trustworthy leadership can be found."

Kevin said, "More trustworthy leadership? Is that liberal college speak for someone who shuts down his own cognitive functions, genuflects to political correctness, and only believes what he's told to believe?"

The ramistat signal reached them, flipping up the hem of Dianne's skirt. Kevin finally became aware of shrieks and confusion throughout the mall. He looked back and saw clothing behaving badly. His eyes went wide. He banged the heel of his right hand on his forehead. "Ahh! I forgot to set my alarm. Somebody's in my van." He held up wide-spread fingers of both hands in front of Dianne. "Uh... just... uh... just stay here. I'll be right back."

He ran toward the mall exit, leaving her alone to deal with disruptive emotions.

38

SIXTY-SECONDS LATER

Seeing Mikhail in the back of his van, messing with a console, Ox jumped in and shouted, "Hey. You. What are you doing in my van?"

Like a firefighter entering a room, Kev always immediately calculated all possible escape routes. Like a police detective, he constantly knew the position and demeanor of all persons on a scene. But, in his middle-of-an-uncomfortable-situation-with-Dianne frame of mind—neither guarded nor prepared— he got slammed in the face with the butt plate of Mikhail's assault rifle.

Dazed, in a great deal of pain, his nose draining blood everywhere, Kevin sprawled backwards out of the van. He landed awkwardly, hitting his head on the parking lot cement. An ordinary human would have gone unconscious. Ox fought against incapacitation and simply refused to allow encroaching mental darkness to win. Struggling up onto hands and knees, he vaguely recognized the situation and forced his body to roll out of the way as Bahadur chirped tires in reverse, missing Kevin by two inches.

Three rows away, Leonard Ostermann heard the tires chirp. He spotted the white van moving too fast and too erratic for normal parking lot courtesy. Throwing his transmission into reverse, he shouted, "Gotcha!" Driving backwards in the wrong direction on the one-way row, he snaked in behind the van as it emerged from the other aisle. Leonard honked, shouted and waved.

In Kevin's van, Bahadur, seeing Ostermann behind him, rhetorically asked, "Why is monkey brain in such a hurry?"

Mikhail answered, "The sale of white at Penney's?"

Leonard whipped his car around and stopped it in front of the van. Bahadur hit the brake. Mikhail hit the dashboard. Mikhail's nose bled all over his side of the van interior.

Ostermann jumped out of his car, leaving his door open, and ran to the van's driver window.

"Alright now," Leonard said smugly, "It's about time. Oh, there are two of you. Well, double my fun. We finally meet... perky perverted pirate perpetrator people. Hah!"

Mikhail looked at Bahadur and shrugged. "He is tick of a lune."

Bahadur said to Leonard, "Monkey brain, your car is cowardly. Look, it runs away."

That's when Leonard remembered he did not put his transmission into park. Moving at idle speed, his car headed toward two cars parked at the end of the aisle. He decided to continue his presumed possible pirate pursuit *after* saving his own car. Running to his car, he shouted, "Stop. Stop. Stop." His car ignored him.

Bahadur drove the van up onto the sidewalk to get around Ostermann's car.

Puzzled by such a blatant display of inappropriate driving, Ostermann stopped running for a moment and shouted at

Bahadur, "Hey, you're not allowed to do that." Leonard then jumped into his driver's seat as his car did a slow-motion crunch into the two parked cars. He, once again, immediately drove away from the scene of a crash. Stepping on the gas, he rammed a car backing out of a parking space. That lady driver shouted, "What are you doing, you jerk?"

Leonard complained loudly, "Civilians. That's the whole thing. This country just has too many civilians." Backing up to get around that car, he immediately ran into a car behind him.

He and all other drivers got out of their cars. A muttering crowd of crashed car owners surrounded him. Realizing he had an attentive audience, Leonard took the opportunity to make an official announcement regarding the situation, saying, "What is the matter with you fools? Can't anybody drive around here? Move those cars now. You are obstructing government business."

A red-faced, burly driver stomping toward Ostermann said, "I'm gonna obstruct his face."

Disgusted by burly driver's lack of respect, Ostermann pulled out his pen and little red notebook. "That does it. I'm starting a file on you."

At that very moment, Ostermann saw the van, one row over, heading toward the parking lot exit. Making a split-second executive decision on whether to start a file or capture the van, Leonard abruptly dashed off after the van.

Not far away, Kevin stood up slowly, clearing his head, and peeling crusted blood from nose, lips and chin. Gazing around, he spotted his van and gave chase, using every bit of his athletic ability in an attempt to arrive at the van before it left the parking lot. Kevin and Ostermann both caught a break. An endless stream of girl scouts, giggling their way through the crosswalk, blocked the van, some attempting to sell cookies to Bahadur and Mikhail.

"No cookies," Bahadur shouted. "No. No. No. Go little girls away."

Mikhail said to a scout, "*Uno* box would I like. Mints of the thin, *por favor*."

Before Mikhail could pay for his cookies, Bahadur rolled the windows up and locked them. Looking in the side mirror, he saw Ostermann running toward the van. "We are followed by monkey brain!"

Bahadur hammered the horn and accelerated. Shrieking girl scouts scrambled to safety as the van raced through the stop sign. An incoming car, swerving to avoid collision, drove straight into the huge J.C. Penney display window. Bahadur slammed on the van brakes. The van bounced off a cement retaining wall, decapitated a fire hydrant, and skidded sideways into a light pole, which snapped in half and crash-landed on the car sticking out of the Penney's window. The broken hydrant's twenty-foot-tall geyser soaked everyone and everything.

Inside the van, Mikhail pointed at Penney's. "Look! Is true. A sale of the white! And they have old facefull! I love this country!"

Leonard Ostermann ran toward the bedlam, shouting, "You are history, pirates."

Three police cars, sirens blaring, Christmas trees in full bloom, thundered into the parking lot.

Bahadur said, "I think another time we van steal." They both jumped out the front doors and ran like squealing wild boars.

Ostermann pounded on the van's rear doors and shouted, "Open these doors, right now.". The doors popped open. "Oh. Well, thank you." He climbed inside. "Aha. I knew it. A remote broadcast facility... or... something."

Seeing nobody home, he jumped out and ran to the front. He sat in the driver's seat and began his own forensics. "Left the scene, huh? Not a problem, Mr. Pirates. Got all the evidence I need, right here. I will send you both on the big cruise." He looked around and pushed a button. Whipped cream squirted all over him. "Yuck. What a sicko." He pushed another button. The mirrored disco ball dropped from the ceiling and the Bee Gees sang, *Stayin' Alive.* Ostermann screeched, "Aiieee!"

Three police cars, a crowd of vehicular victims, and a hundred looky-loos surrounded the van. The Lieutenant and a patrol officer from the first black and white cautiously approached the van driver's side while an officer from the second black and white moved toward the passenger side with her hand hovering above her holster. The officer in the third squad car, using the built-in megaphone, told the crowd to back away and take cover. He got out, crouched behind his door, and leveled his red laser dot on the van door.

The Lieutenant at the driver's door said, "Please step out of the vehicle, sir."

Lenny Ostermann happily exited the van. "Officer am I ever glad to see you. Thank you for your fast back-up." He shook the Lieutenant's hand, squishing out whipped cream. "You would not believe what has taken place in this parking lot. It has been just absolute chaos."

The Lieutenant didn't know whether to shoot or throw up. He nodded for his partner to take over while he wiped off his hand.

The officer said to Ostermann, "Identification, sir?"

Ostermann said, "Yes, that is an excellent idea. Give me your names and badge numbers. I'll start a file." He reached into his jacket for his notebook. Both policemen tackled him. After the pat-down, they allowed him to stand.

The officer asked, "Is this your van, sir?

"Of course, it's not my van. Don't be ludicrous."

"Then, can you please explain, sir," the Lieutenant said, "how you happen to be in possession of this vehicle that is not yours?"

"Because it was used in the perpetration of a federal crime."

"Sounds like a confession to me. Up against the van. Spread 'em."

"What are you doing?" Leonard asked. "Don't you know who I am?"

"Yes sir, we do know who you are." That response greatly tickled Leonard's ego. The officer continued, "You are our grand theft auto perp."

Kevin made his way to the front of the crowd, hoping to claim his van.

An officer walked up to the Lieutenant and said, "You better look inside the back of this van. There's enough high-tech stuff in there to launch a space shuttle."

Kevin backed away into the crowd. *Well... yeah... maybe a small space shuttle.*

The officer continued, "And there's blood all over the equipment."

Another officer shouted from the front, "Got a lot of blood up here, too. And we found this stashed behind the driver's seat." He held up Mikhail's weapon.

"An assault rifle? Whoa. We've got more here than just a car thief." He rapidly issued directives. "Have dispatch call tow. Put the van in lock-up. Get SoCal Edison here, now. Call fire, meds, and mall management. Get statements from anyone who heard or saw anything, or even think they heard or saw anything."

Kev assessed the situation. *Better get the heck out of here.* He slipped deeper into the crowd, and then away... back to the mall.

The lieutenant jerked his thumb toward Ostermann, saying, "And put the whack-job on ice."

Ostermann looked around to see who the whack job might be, just as an officer cuffed him.

"What are you doing?" Ostermann said. "I'm a government official."

"Okay, sir," the Lieutenant said, taking a calming breath, "May I please see your identification?"

"What a thickheaded question. I don't have any identification. It flew out of my hand back on Huntington Drive."

The Lieutenant issued more instructions. "Contact San Marino. See if there's a connection with that traffic multiple. And PLEASE, get the nutball out of here."

Still looking for the whack-job, and now the nutball, Leonard became especially perplexed when told to watch his head as they placed him in the rear seat of a squad car. Pointing at all the officers as he raised up to shout a complaint,

Leonard hit his head on the doorframe. His last words as a free man were, "I'm going to start a file on each of—Ouch!"

* * * * *

When Kevin returned to the mall, Dianne was gone.

39

BACK IN PASADENA — 6:00 P.M. — SAME DAY

Other than salient details, Kevin hadn't talked much after I picked him up at the mall and brought him to Pas Tech. The Pheltor Hall Media Center had become the "War Room". He slouched in one of those elegant old bergère chairs with his feet on a bookcase shelf. I paced, waiting for Channel Eight news at six to come on. Dr. Weksler hunkered down in his office, preparing his part for later that night.

Kevin had left six messages for Dianne in the previous ninety minutes. He went for attempt number seven. "Hello, Dianne's, answering machine, this is Kevin's tongue. Come on, you can't be that mad at me. I'm sorry I left you stranded at the mall. I can explain. We really need to talk. Please... please... call me."

My worst television fears came true. "Kevin, you better come look at this."

He clicked off his phone as I turned up the sound. A film clip of protesters at the Hollywood Bowl, the Petty Blue van, and The Pirate, filled the screen. The TV voice said, "That's the scene at the Hollywood Bowl this morning when an estimated two-thousand rock 'n' roll fans gathered to protest the upcoming Rock Legends concert."

"Now you've really done it," I said. "We're on television."

Kev moaned, "Look on the bright side. It's our first legal broadcast."

Under different circumstances his comment might have been mirth-provoking. Under these circumstances, I just wheezed.

The TV voiceover continued. "Disgruntled protestors are upset because sixties singing sensation Gary Puckett is not included in the show. Hollywood Bowl officials say they are inundated with letters and phone calls demanding Puckett be added to the Rock Legends lineup. But the big excitement at the Bowl? A surprise personal appearance by The Pirate. This is the first time the urban folk hero has ever been seen in public."

A gloomy Dr. Weksler walked into the room. I turned off the TV. Without a hint of camaraderie, he said, "Did we find out where they're holding the van?"

Kevin jolted his feet off the bookshelf and immediately sat up straight like a teenager caught by the high school librarian. He nodded. "Foothill Wrecking & Impound in Azusa."

Very squeamish about Kevin's entire plan, I pleaded, "Ox man... are you sure this is the right thing to do?"

"Yes, I am absolutely certain. Theo, we're boy scouts. We clean up our own messes, remember? We can do this."

"Theophilus," Dr. Weksler said, "I am truly sorry to say I have even less confidence in the other options we discussed. We must be there before the forensic examination tomorrow, and we must retrieve the van before the thugs find it."

"Oh, I understand." I fidgeted. "But we've got to be really careful. We don't know what kind of people we're dealing with."

"The kind who bring an Uzi to the mall," Dr. Weksler said.

"Frank, if you're not comfortable and onboard with our plan, that's alright," Kevin said. He attempted to provide a way out for Dr. Weksler. "You don't have to be part of this, Frank. We can modify details, so you're not involved."

"Am I comfortable? Not at all. Am I onboard? Yes. Because we have no other options, and we certainly can't go to the police." He stared at me and then Kevin. "I still can't believe you children put our research in jeopardy over yet another infantile pirate prank."

Kevin said, "Frank... I am so... "

He never finished his contrition because Dr. Weksler walked out of the war room.

* * * * *

Essentially a junk yard, Foothill Wrecking & Impound contracted towing and storage services for several small municipalities at the edge of civilization, in arid, sandy terrain which did not quite qualify as high desert. As opposed to a police impound facility, the privately-owned Foothill yard provided many advantages to Dr. Weksler, Kevin and me, the most important being that no vehicle title, plate, or record search of any kind happened until a police unit filed a cause of action and then sent officers to obtain needed information at the impound facility.

Minimalist construction at the storage yard meant unleveled ground crusted with a meager layer of peeling sunbaked asphalt, in turn covered with a thin, balding layer of whitish gravel. The nine-foot-tall chain-link perimeter fence would be our biggest challenge.

* * * * *

At our earlier war room strategy session, I pulled the short straw, so I had to play the female lead (like Jack Lemon and Tony Curtis in *Some Like It Hot*) for the upcoming awesome threesome "midnight theater" production. We rented most of our gear from Western Costume, a more efficient choice than piecing together outfits from multiple ordinary clothing stores.

Kevin got to be over-the-top glitzy and gold-chained street boss, looking as if ready to film a hip-hop video. My role required me to wear five-inch platform heels, silver fishnet stockings, brown leather miniskirt, and a mellifluous red, brown, copper and gold silk blouse over a molded female body form strapped to my torso. Having had no practice in the art of make-up, I did a sloppy job, especially with the lipstick. Oh, and I had some pretty cool earrings from the Hollywood Magic Shop.

* * * * *

We drove to the impound yard in Dr. Weksler's daily-driver, a nondescript four-door sedan appropriate for an elderly college professor. He parked in the shadows.

Two guards took turns doing a cursory yard patrol every half hour. Kev and I needed to walk up to the entrance just before either guard left on the twelve A.M. patrol. Then we had to detain them both for as long as necessary. Accordingly, a few minutes before midnight Kevin and I began our long stroll up the dark sidewalk toward the chain-link front entrance gate.

The wrecking/impound yard needed to operate at a profit, so they reduced costs where possible. Thankfully, that included fewer and lower wattage lights. Perhaps in the dim light our ruse might work. If I didn't pass out from high anxiety.

Still agitated by my attire—for which I blamed Kevin—I spoke softly so as not to be heard by the guards. "This is the most humiliating thing you've ever made me do."

"Naw..." Kevin replied. "You looked far more stupid last Christmas in the salamander suit."

"Well I look pretty stupid right now."

You smell lovely." He said.

"Thank you. We're going to go to jail. You know that don't you? I am going to jail in a brown leather mini-skirt."

"But it goes nicely with the blouse."

"Really? It's not too busy?"

Kevin gave me his most sincere look ever. "Oh no. Not at all. And those are good hues. Have you ever had your 'colors' done? I think you're a summer."

One of the guards, observing our approach, arched his eyebrows toward his fellow guard, saying, "Uh boy. Get a load of this."

* * * * *

Meanwhile, a wino clumsily shuffled along outside the razor wire-topped, nine-foot-tall, chain-link fence framing the rear alley at the far end of the impound yard. Except for some shadowy spill-over from the yard's sparse lighting, the rear alley had no light at all. The wino wore a winter trench coat, perfect for Chicago in February. But this was Azusa, during a heat wave, and still almost ninety-degrees at midnight.

He stumbled toward the rear gate without bumping into it, and though his head and extremities wobbled, he had no trouble visually inspecting the padlock. The faint sound of tires on distant gravel heightened the bum's concern that he had, perhaps, not sufficiently dirtied and roughed up the new trench coat he purchased that afternoon. *Too late now.*

The private security patrol car drove up and stopped. The window came down and the driver lit up the wino with his nine-hundred-sixty-lumen tactical flashlight. The bum (Dr. Weksler) took a deep breath, purposely making it shaky.

The rookie private patrol officer spoke with a friendly voice so as not to aggravate a potential situation. "Say buddy, what are you doing out here tonight?"

Dr. Weksler took a swill of cheap something from a screw top bottle, then turned around and gave an eyelids-at-half-mast blank stare straight into the flashlight. To avoid explanation, Dr. Weksler pretended he didn't speak English and, instead, mumbled his reply in a strange accent and language that he simply made up as he went along. "Manangahela farquar doshi tunafish."

The officer opened his door and stepped out of the car, keeping Dr. Weksler in the flashlight beam. "I'm sorry buddy... what did you say?"

Rubbing his belly as he staggered toward the private cop, Dr. Weksler said, "Izvestia pavarotti chechwandee Kung pow moose."

The patrolman raised his palm in a "stop" motion and took a step backwards. The officer clicked off his flashlight. "Look, buddy. I get that maybe you're hungry?"

Dr. Weksler said, "Chai tea grundig machiota loves chachi."

"Right. I'm gonna pat you down now," the security officer said. "And then maybe we can get you a donut or something. Okay?"

Dr. Weksler unsteadily stood in place, obediently awaiting the frisk. The private patrol officer, on personal high alert, kept the weird wino at arm's length, stretched out his left hand and cautiously touched him.

Dr. Weksler giggled and wiggled as if a child being tickled. "Oooo... lockie dunda pressy body yunga noony neena."

The Patrolman jumped back, shouting, "I am not frisking your noony neena." He backed away into his patrol car, keeping his raised palm toward the bum. *Forget it man. He's just a harmless alien derelict. He sure ain't gonna steal anything in his condition.*

The officer took a five-dollar bill from his pocket and tossed it to Dr. Weksler. "Here ya go, buddy. Get yourself a double McTriple." As he drove away, he courteously tipped his head and said, "Have a nice evening, sir."

Dr. Weksler acknowledged his departure with a rubbery "attention" stance and a shaky military salute, saying, "Heisenberg principle, Norton chamber, Samsung widescreen. Kinko's, Krakatoa."

The patrol car exited the alley and vanished around the corner. Relieved, fully focused, and efficient, Dr. Weksler pulled very long cable cutters from inside his brand-new dirty trench coat. On his first try, he cut the padlock shackle in half.

When he carefully slid open the chain-link gate, it made a grating sound as it briefly scraped on the asphalt. Panic time.

At the front entrance, Kevin and I reached the two bored guards just when we all heard a brief metallic scrape in the far distance. Both turned their heads to face the messy property filled with rusted cars and pulled parts.

The first guard said, "What was that?"

The second guard, walking away, said, "I'll check it out."

I rushed up to the gate and spoke in the best female sounding voice I could muster. For some reason it came out country. "Excuse me you big strong rangers. Would y'all mind given' me your opinion of my new gazonkies?

Guard #2 did an immediate about face and walked briskly back to the gate. Kev and I were outside the chain-link fence, so the guards had their backs to the yard while they looked at us. Just as we planned.

Kevin chastised me. "Why Trixie LaRue, these fine gentlemen don't have time to settle our silly little quarrel."

Guard #1 said, "Oh, we don't mind helping, ma'am."

Guard #2 excitedly chimed in, "No, not at all. Always glad to help a lady, ma'am."

I said (in my female voice), "My gazonkies are both just entirely too small. Now y'all can see that, can't you?"

The guards starred at my chest. With both of my index fingers I pointed to the sides of my head and said, "Why, I declare, y'all... my ears are up here."

Surprised and embarrassed, they both looked up to where my palms were now cupping my earrings. "See. My new gazonkies are just too small.

Kevin said, "But they are very special gazonkies. Watch."

I returned my hands to the pointing-at-both-ears position while Kevin activated a remote control in his pocket. My earrings began moving back and forth while bobbing up and down. Then both of my earlobes stretched to about seven inches in length, all the way down to lay on my shoulders. They laid on my shoulders for three seconds, then shot back up to normal with an audible cartoonish "whoosh" and "boing". The rubberized theatrical appliances from the Hollywood Magic Shop, (with special effects by the Ox man) worked beautifully.

Both guards stepped back in fear.

Guard #1 said, "Say, uh... you got some kinda weird muscle control there, lady?"

In the distance, behind the guards back, Kevin and I saw his van silently roll down the slight grade and through the impound yard open rear gate, with wino Weksler at the wheel.

Kev said, "I just bought these gazonkies for her today. They are what you call a novelty item."

Totally amazed, Guard #2 said, "The miracles of modern medicine."

Kevin looked at me. "See, I told you so. They're fab. Okay, let's leave."

We turned and began walking back down the sidewalk. I looked at the guards, gave them a clown lipstick smile and said, "Bye y'all."

Guard #1 said, "Hey. Wait a minute."

We continued walking, but faster now, as Kevin apprehensively looked back.

Guard #1 said, "Where can I get some of those?" Then after Guard #2 gave him a questioning look, Guard #1 added, "Well, I thought, you know, maybe for Mother's Day. Or Christmas."

"Try the Dollar Gazonky store," Kevin shouted. We kept walking.

"Okay. Yeah. Thanks, man."

My left earring shot out a spark and began smoking. I reacted with an "Ouch." We continued walking, very quickly, as my left gazonky continued to spark and began rolling up and down. I said "Ouch!" with each spark.

Guard #1 shouted, "What's going on?"

Kevin shouted back over his shoulder, "It's time for her three-thousand-mile check-up."

Guard #2 shouted, "But I thought you just got them today."

Kev rolled his eyes at me and shouted, "They're still under warranty. They are <u>certified</u> used gazonkies."

"Well that's good." Guard #2 said, nodding his satisfaction to Guard #1.

In my cowgirl voice, I shouted, "Hey, goodnight all y'all. I am very late for a Tupperware party. Ouch. Bye-bye. Aw. Ow!"

We walked faster and, after arriving in the shadows, began to run. I broke a heel and ran lopsided, my left ear lobe rolling up and down, sparking and smoking all the way to Dr. Weksler's car hidden in the shadows.

Clip. Clop. "Ouch." Clip Clop. "Oh. Ouch." Clip. Clop "Oh. Ow!"

40

SOUTH PASADENA — SAME TIME

The Garduña Billy goats broke into our South Pasadena apartment at the same time the three of us rescued Kevin's van from the impound yard.

Using a Smyth-West MXS-207 lock set with twenty picks and seven tension tools designed specifically for American locks, Bahadur compromised our apartment deadbolt and unlocked the knob in less than twenty seconds. Bahadur and Mikhail each carried a Mexican-produced SEDENA version of the German MP5 machine pistol in the rear of his waistband, with his squared-off shirttail hiding the grip. Stepping into the dark living room, they pulled out their weapons and held them at the ready. Bahadur silently closed the door.

Mikhail said, "Is cake piece."

Carefully, they walked to the center of our large living room. They froze when they heard John Wayne say, "Don't take another step, pilgrim."

Behind their backs, the wall-to-wall HD television came on with life-size video of John Wayne standing guard, holding his Winchester Model 1876, lever-action, repeating rifle. Kevin, in camo paint, holding an airsoft M-16 replica, stood shoulder-to-shoulder with the Duke.

The video Ox man said, "We've got you covered, and police are on their way."

John Wayne said, "If you twitch a finger, it'll be the last body part you ever twitch."

Bahadur and Mikhail, despite personal ineptitude, possessed some military skill. Trained, fanatical, and brainwashed to die for a cause they didn't even comprehend, they used eye blinks, to coordinate timing. Synchronized, they dove forward, rolled onto their backs, and sprayed machine pistol bullets in the direction of the enemy voices.

They both screamed in confusion and fright as the wall of harmonized sixty-inch TV screens exploded. When they recovered their wits (miniscule though they may be), they quickly planted a couple of deadly surprises before running from the scene, bleeding from plastic shard and metal fragment cuts.

> *As a personal sidebar,* I have a difficult time understanding suicide bombers. I am not religious, but if I was, and my religious leader told me that, in order for me to be the most spiritual and blessed person possible, I must blow myself up, I'd say to him, " Cool. Show me how. You go first."

Per Kevin's stratagem, we drove separate escape routes from the impound yard, Dr. Weksler in the van, Kev and me in Dr. Weksler's sedan. We rendezvoused in the Pas Tech staff parking lot where we parked Dr. Weksler's car, and then headed out in the van for a debriefing celebration at our South Pasadena apartment. Kevin drove the van, after changing its color to black. I sat in the middle of the single bench seat. Dr. Weksler had shotgun.

"Oh, my goodness," Dr. Weksler said, "I thought I was doomed when that chain-link gate scraped on the pavement. How on earth did you keep them occupied?

Kevin said, "Theo seduced the guards."

I said, "If you got it, flaunt it."

"You needed a diversion, Frank, so..." Kev shook his index finger at me three times as he said, "He came. He saw. He gazonkied."

We laughed, woo-hooed, and laughed some more. Recalling a similar victorious feeling from my childhood, I sang, "We are the champions."

"Whoa," Kevin exclaimed. "Big Blue Wrecking Crew."

Dr. Weksler jumped in, "Oh my, yes. The 1981 World Series."

"Ox and I were seven. It was the first time we ever went to a Dodgers game."

Kevin said, "We beat the Yanks in six games."

"Sarah and I were there too," Dr. Weksler added. "It was a great time."

I tried to recall their names. "I know Rick Monday was one of the Dodgers who recorded *We Are the Champions*, but I can't remember the others."

With his finely tuned Dodger memory, Dr. Weksler added, "Steve Yeager. Jay Johnstone. Jerry Reuss. They had a hit with it. And all the money went to charity. Yes, gentlemen, I believe that is an entirely appropriate... chorus for us." He smiled at his rhyme.

We all sang, "We are the champions... we are the champions... we are—" The siren cut our performance short. We could almost feel the flashing red and blue lights as Ox pulled over to the curb. Palpitation time.

A paramedic van wailed past, followed by a South Pas Police cruiser. Both turned left onto Raymond Hill Road. We sat still and quiet until we could no longer see flashing emergency lights.

Dr. Weksler broke the silence. "Isn't your apartment up on that hill?"

"It is."

We circled up Raymond Hill, where a carrot color glow swayed in the sky. Turning the final corner, we saw our apartment building in a new light. The light from a blazing inferno.

We had to stop at the cordoned-off police perimeter. Fire trucks, hoses, and equipment cluttered the street. Spectators stared and pointed. Scrambling out of the van, we approached the female police officer on the other side of the yellow caution tape strung across the street between sawhorses and light poles.

She respectfully said, "Gentlemen, please stay back, for your own safety."

"What happened?" I asked.

"Two firebombs."

* * * * *

The next morning, Ox and I woke up in Dr. Weksler's living room. Disoriented due to waking in an unfamiliar environment, I blinked a couple times and remembered I slept in Dr. Weksler's recliner. Blinking again, I noticed that I still wore the leather miniskirt and blouse of many colors. "Ahh, it wasn't a dream."

"No, it was a nightmare," Kevin said, groggily stretched out on Dr. Weksler's couch, still wearing his glitter jacket from the night before. He got up on his knees on the couch and turned to face the closed venetian blinds. A ceramic skunk with a clock in its belly shared the shelf below the blinds with binoculars and souvenir coffee mugs. Kevin rotated the blinds open. Having never been to Dr. Weksler's home in the daytime, we scoped out the environment.

His house trailer squatted on the edge of wilderness at the farthest uninhabited corner of Kagel Canyon Estates. The ramshackle carport more-or-less sheltered his well-worn ten-year-old brown Ford sedan. Farther back, at the end of the cracking concrete slab, his 1957 Fury hibernated under a soft tarp.

Using binoculars to look beyond the carport, we confirmed that the old trailer park had not experienced fresh paint since before we were born. Every leaning termite-infested mailbox, former chicken coop, bullet-hole-riddled sign, and rock border with most of the rocks missing had at one time or another been painted in a "Southwestern" motif of turquoise and shrimp. The turquoise long since lost its luster and the shrimp had gone bad. Tall-haired ladies in muumuus walked their little yappers. Short-haired men in denial were the little yappers. One wore a T-shirt proudly emblazoned with "Trained Service Dog".

Ox closed the blinds and dropped down on the couch, shaking his head.

"Why does Dr. Weksler live like this?" I said. "He must have a decent income. What does he spend his money on?"

Holding up the ceramic skunk with a clock in its belly, Kevin said, "Art?"

Moments later, Dr. Weksler, jam-packed with enthusiasm, blustered in through the aluminum front door with coffee and donuts.

Kevin said, "Caffeine."

I said, "Sugar."

"Good Morning Kevin! Good morning Theophilus!"

We both yawned, "Good morning, Frank."

He put a drink carrier and the "Pacoima House of Giant Donuts" box on his small kitchen table. Kevin gratefully received his steaming styro cup of black and sat at the end of the table. I seized my larger-than-standard maple bar, grabbed my coffee (the one with excessive cream and sugar) and sat in the dinette chair closest to the donut box.

Coffee already in hand, Dr. Weksler leaned against his microwave. "Much work ahead of us today gentlemen," He smiled with happy eyebrows. "Kevin, the van is a little banged-up. Nothing more than bumps and bruises. I'd like a damage assessment with anticipated time frame for repairs as soon as possible."

Kevin nodded. "Got it."

Obviously, Dr. Weksler began consuming caffeine while still at the donut shop. Way ahead of us. "Theo, please use the PC in my bedroom to acquire overnight alpha-numerics. Don't need a full report, just preliminaries. It's under Ramistat Data. The subfolder is AlphNum."

I stared vacantly at his incomprehensible enthusiasm.

He looked at his watch. "Still early. I should be able to reach Dr. Matthias Liechtenwalther in Varenna to work out details for our Paris presentation." He headed for the door. "I'll go out to my car to make the call so as not to disturb your work."

I lost my cool. Actually, I never had any cool. But I did get myself in a snit. Well, maybe not quite a snit, but it was at least a fret.

"Excuse me," I said. "What is wrong with this picture?"

"What's wrong with what picture?" Kevin said.

"I'm sorry..." Dr. Weksler said, "...what? Oh, no problem. Dr. Liechtenwalther and I have been friends for many years. Matt will take my call, even if it's late at night there."

I closed my eyes and rubbed my forehead. *Oh, my freaking gosh. These are smart people. What is their problem?*

Not understanding why I had to explain something that seemed so obvious but, keen to do so, I said, "In the last twenty-four hours, a maverick bureaucrat from the lunatic fringe of the FCC tried to send Kevin to Alcatraz, our equipment got hijacked by two rejects from the Muammar Khadafy Explorer Scouts, half the Arcadia police department captured and quarantined the van, and while you, and I, and the King of Bling here (I pointed to Kevin) were out playing Grand Theft Auto with our own van, the maid came in and tidied-up our apartment with a flame thrower!"

Kev said, "So, what's your point?"

I stood up and waved my giant maple bar for emphasis. "My point is, these are not common, ordinary events in the life of your average university research assistant. Something has gone awry."

My maple bar bent over, and a large chunk fell off. I caught it in my mouth, midair. Very impressive. *Guess Kevin's not the only athlete around here.*

My rant gave Dr. Weksler pause. He sat his cup on the microwave and folded his arms. "Maybe Theo is correct. Maybe we should delay the I.E.S. until next year. Perhaps we need to slow our pace for a while."

"We don't have a while," Kevin said. He looked at Dr. Weksler with sad eyes. "Frank... the last time I saw Dianne, she told me your research grant isn't being renewed. At the end of this semester, we're all out of work. Out of the University. Out of time."

Dr. Weksler sat down and did not move.

I said, "Frank, you've been tenured for over forty years. You ended the cold war, for God's sake. You must have some juice."

"I do... but it's prune juice."

Ox displayed a tiny quarter-inch gap between his thumb and forefinger. "You both know we're this close to controlling the weather. We can't just give up now."

I sucked in air past my gnashing molars. With my teeth clenched tighter than a bad ventriloquist, I said, "Okay, yeah. I guess we go for it. Now or never."

We all thoughtfully nodded in agreement. Dr. Weksler looked exhausted. His labored breathing gave Kev and I concern about his health.

Dr. Weksler said, "Gentlemen, I have a very bad feeling about going back to the University. We are far too visible there. A better alternative is to work right here."

Kev and I looked around the small trailer, trying to comprehend what he had in mind.

"No, not in here," he weakly chuckled. "I have a home laboratory in my garage." He pointed out the kitchen window. "I believe it will work just fine for us."

We looked out at Dr. Weksler's garage, in front of the dry brown hill lightly populated by dry brown weeds and the dry brown remains of a long-ago vegetable garden. The beat-up, one-car garage sat at the end of his pot-holed driveway. Thinking of the scorpions, tarantulas, and snakes that lived out there scared me, but I knew they only came out at night when it wasn't so scary for them. Because they knew the muumuus would be asleep.

We're going to work there? In the Munsters garage? Oh... not good. Dr. Weksler has flipped his crazy switch.

41

L.A. CHINA TOWN — SAME TIME

Unless you're a criminal, you probably never heard of LA's other Twin Towers. Officially named *Twin Towers Correctional Facility* (this is a true thing) they buttress Chinatown like a fortress, just off the one-ten freeway, halfway between Ostermann's downtown L.A. office and our burned-out South Pasadena apartment. After his arrest at Thoroughbred Mall, Leonard Ostermann came to know residents of those twin towers up-close and personal.

Jammed in a cell filled with unsavory dudes, Lenny, out of his element but, too arrogant to shut up, filibustered all night long about injustice and his own importance. Now, early in the morning, he looked terrible. Even his shoes were wrinkled. His fellow inmates, dressed in diverse dirty street attire, some sporting semi-fresh vomit, looked better than little Lenny. Many cellmates wore orange jumpsuits courtesy of L.A. County. Mikhail would have fit right in.

A couple dozen arrestees scoped out Ostermann while he looked down his nose. The leader of the pack, Mad Man Malvern, of the blue Mohawk and massive tattoos school, wore black leathers laden with chrome zippers and chains.

Respectfully addressed by his peers as "M3", Malvern stood six-feet-four, seven feet when you count his five-inch Mohawk and three-inch biker boot heels. Built like a brick linebacker.

Little Leonard looked puny next to M3. Then again, Leonard, only five-foot-six on a good day, looked puny regardless of who stood beside him. Seeing Ostermann's crumpled brown suit with no tie, M3 snarled, "So, what're you in for? Impersonating a stockbroker?" All the prisoners laughed, except those who were stoned. The stoners were already heavily invested in staring dreamily at the green-painted cement block wall.

Ostermann didn't have the good sense to either laugh or be afraid. Instead, he snubbed M3 like an annoying insect and grabbed the cell bars once again to wail at the guard. "Guard. Guard. Did you even hear me? I have repeatedly stated I wish to see the police commissioner."

M3 growled at Ostermann, "Hey, you. Little annoying person. Be quiet."

Ostermann, trying to comprehend the situation, pointed to himself and asked, "Me?"

M3 shouted, "Yes, you, Mickey Mouth."

Ostermann turned back to the cell bars, banged them, and shouted, "Officer. Officer. This has gone too far. I now demand to speak with the mayor. Do you hear me?"

M3 gripped his leather jacket's chrome chain, wondering if it might fit around Ostermann's neck. Alas, it did not. M3 raised Ostermann up by the armpits and yelled in his face. "Everyone hears you, you whining hyena. Shut your mouth."

Mystified, Leonard cocked his head and said, "Look, Mr. M and M and M, I don't think you understand my situation. I must leave." Leonard wriggled free and shouted to the guard, "You there. Guard. I simply demand to be released."

M3 hit the heel of his hand onto his own forehead and said, "Well, gee whiz, why haven't I thought of that before? He grabbed bars and said, in a prissy voice, "Oh Guard, I simply demand to be released."

M3's associate, Ralphy Boy, grabbed some cell bars, put on M3's affectation and said, "Oh Mr. guard, sir, I also simply must leave."

Enveloped in laughter, other inmates got into the act, grabbing bars and saying, "Oh my, me as well." and "Please do set me free." and "Would you mind terribly if I escaped?"

Leonard, emphatically stated, "Okay, Mr. Smart guys, I've had about enough of all of you. Listen to me. I am serious."

"I am so scared," M3 mocked. He made a googly face while doing a "loser" sign on his forehead with his right hand and pretending to gag himself with his left index finger.

The prisoners laughed it up. Now surrounded, Leonard came closer to bodily harm than he could have ever imagined.

A police officer unlocked the holding tank door. "We heard from your office, Mr. Ostermann," the officer said. "You're free to leave. NOW, PLEASE."

Ralphy Boy stepped in front of Ostermann. "Oh, little Lenny, don't go now. You'll miss the squash tournament.

"Squash tournament?"

M3 said, "Yeah. We're going to take turns squashing you."

Leonard stormed through the open cell door.

M3 called after him, "Hey, brown suit... don't forget your tie. We washed it for you".

Ralphy Boy pulled Ostermann's tie from the community toilet bowl and held it out to him. Leonard jerked the tie out of Ralphy Boy's hand, slinging water all over himself.

"That rips it." Leonard said. Using both hands, he pointed at each prisoner. "I'm starting a file on you, and you, and you, and you, and especially you, and... all of you." The hyena had spoken.

They all went, "Oooo."

42

PACOIMA — A LITTLE LATER THAT MORNING

The Ox man and I made a quick Pheltor Hall run to pick up the Norton Chamber and electronic odds and ends. Upon our return to the trailer park, the three of us disconnected, disassembled, and carried all gear from Kevin's van into Dr. Weksler's overcrowded single-car garage. As we unloaded the final oh-my-gosh-that's-heavy item from the van, I noticed a satellite dish on the hill behind the garage.

"Hey, you've got a dish," I said to Dr. Weksler.

Kevin looked up at it. "In lovely southwest colors."

Dr. Weksler groused. "I had to fight the HOA for a year before I finally received permission to install it up there. Very strict covenants regarding appearances and color schemes."

"Well thank goodness," Kevin said. "You wouldn't want the neighborhood to get tacky."

The hot day and hard work gave us concern about Dr. Weksler's health, concerns not unfounded. Remember me telling you about how weird his eyes looked in the yearbook photo? Well, it didn't mean manic, as had been my original assumption. Turned out he had a lazy left eyelid that often drooped and a right leg that wanted to drag. Both conditions resulted from a minor stroke in his fifties. The eyelid only became cosmetically startling when he posed for a photograph and tried to compensate for the droop. Photos invariably came out with either the wrong eyelid raised or both eyelids unnaturally wide-open, as if he had just grabbed a live wire.

The first indication that Dr. Weksler might be experiencing a health episode in the brutally hot garage came when we leaned the main control console against a stack of orange crates in a back corner. Sweating profusely and breathing hard, Dr. Weksler worried about the old crates, and then made us move the console five feet to the left, where it could lean against other equipment. Weird.

Dr. Weksler closed the garage door with his remote and we paused to look around. The scrap of light struggling in through a single grungy window revealed nothing more than a filthy garage stuffed with junk. Flotsam on a workbench proved to be a messed-up first-generation Apple computer. With stacks of van stuff added to garage clutter, we could hardly move.

How can we ever work in such a place?

Panting and blinking, Dr. Weksler puffed out, "I find it quite valuable to copy data from my Pheltor Hall computer and store it on a computer here at my home office."

His synapses are not firing in the correct order.

Kevin made alarmed eye contact with me. For a moment, I tried to figure out who to blame, but quickly got past that. Too hot to care. Too worried about Dr. Weksler.

Kevin said, "Uh, Frank..." He groped for gentle words. "The space in this garage... it uh, well, I think... there may not be quite enough room in here for us."

Confused, Dr. Weksler said, "Oh, my. Really?" He glanced about and sighed deeply. "Very well. Perhaps we may have to find another lab." He slowly and spookily sang, "Hi-ho, hi-ho, it's off to work we go," as he shuffled off, his right leg dragging noticeably.

Kevin and I followed, ready to catch him.

Stopping near the pile of antique orange crates, Dr. Weksler said, "They are rather attractive, don't you think? Did you notice how artistically they are arranged? I did that myself; you know."

We needed to get him to an emergency room.

Kevin said, "Frank,—"

Dr. Weksler held up his index finger to make Kevin pause, and then said, "Young master Ox, you are not the only one who knows how to customize a remote control." He held up his garage door remote and pushed a button. Smoothly, with a vault-door clunk and a graceful whir, the stack of antique orange crates rotated one-hundred-twenty-degrees, exposing a very dark cave. We couldn't see more than two feet inside.

Doing a great Count Dracula voice, Dr. Weksler made the syllables in "laboratory" sound like five distinct words as he announced, "I have an emergency lab-or-a-to-ry." He hunched over like Quasimodo and entered the passageway, letting his left arm swing aimlessly, while purposely dragging his right leg. His Dracula-voiced, "Walk this way," erased any lingering fear about health.

Kevin shouted, "You son of a donkey!" He softly punched Dr. Weksler on the swinging arm. Dr. Weksler made his arm swing around three times in a complete circle.

We replicated his monster gait, and "walked his way" through the dark opening. He pushed his remote again and the orange crate door swung shut behind us. KLUNK.

"Aiieee!" Yes, I squealed.

Total darkness. Kev and I became aware of a throbbing buzz in the totally blacked-out distance. We didn't recognize the sound, and we couldn't see a thing. The dark completely swallowed Dr. Weksler, who stood only a few feet away.

At least, we hoped he did.

43

STILL IN THE DARK

Kev and I took only a couple more tentative baby steps and then stopped in the black unknown. Trapped like rats. Involuntarily, I loudly sucked in a large volume of air, apparently in subliminal preparation for some serious wheezing.

Off in the black we heard CLICK, CLICK, CLICK followed by heavy, rotating metal. Multiple tiny points of red, green, amber, blue, and white light appeared in the dark, like a distant unknown galaxy.

Somewhere out there in front of us, the faint greenish-gray ghost of Dr. Weksler appeared. His outstretched phantom left arm held his open cellphone up into the cool moist air. He had a ringmaster smile in his voice as he announced, "Tah Dah." Lights blazed on and we were in neo-geek nirvana.

The clicks we heard came from Dr. Weksler punching in his security code and swinging open a large red metal door at the end of the very dark tunnel.

His home office turned out to be roughly the size of a six-bedroom, two-story house. Now that I think about it, "roughly" made a good descriptor. The walls, coarsely hewn out of the natural rock, curved inward to meet at the top center of the cave ceiling twenty-five feet above us, supported by steel and concrete beams. The damp, musty air smelled like Grandpa Keppel's old cellar in Keokuk, Iowa. We were inside the large hill behind Dr. Weksler's garage.

Thirty-feet away on the right, a black steel circular staircase led from Dr. Weksler's "coffee break corner" (his "man cave" inside his real cave) up to a black steel catwalk ten-feet above our heads. The catwalk stretched around three-quarters of the second story. A long aluminum extension ladder went from the catwalk almost straight upward to a steel hatch in the top of the curving rock ceiling. It all felt like a big, weird, stone submarine.

Sunk into the cement floor at the far end of the great room, a hydroelectric generator continuously pulsed. About a third the size of those at the Hoover dam power generation facility, red wire mesh screening held together by a shiny black steel bar framework stopped things (and people) from falling into the whirling generator blades. Above the generator, at the end of the catwalk, a heavy iron chain hung on a large ratchet wheel mounted in a track suspended from the stone roof.

In addition to the throbbing generator, the constant background "white noise" included the sound of running water. Dr. Weksler had tapped into one of the many underground tributaries of the Los Angeles River, so he could always cook up homemade electricity.

Kevin expressed my shock-and-awe precisely, whispering, "Holy Batcave."

"I'll take that as a compliment, Kevin," Dr. Weksler said. "Thank you." He casually added, "This all makes it easier to work on weekends and it's really a nice little tax write-off you know, having an office at home."

"Well, sure," I said, breathing through my mouth.

"Of course," Kevin added. "This is what I plan to do with all my caves."

We wandered about, ooing and ahhing. Far better equipped than Pas Tech, Dr. Weksler's "home office" had every conceivable piece of electronic apparatus, and the river-powered generator made it fully self-sustaining, regardless of circumstances in the outside world. The remarkableness even extended right down to a bowl of fresh oranges and apples on a little red table next to the black circular staircase.

Seeing a really huge video monitor mounted on the distant wall, I said, "Oh my gosh, Frank. Is that a terrain-following satellite imager 136XK with RADAC?"

"No, it's a big screen TV with remote. I like to watch the Dodgers when I'm working."

Kevin exhaled. "Wow. And back in your garage we thought you were about a hundred clicks short of a Geiger counter."

He grinned and pointed at both of us. "Gotcha."

I spread my arms, encompassing the astonishing view. "How? Why? When?"

At first not understanding, Dr. Weksler then said, "Oh, right, the lab. Well, I originally built this as a small bomb shelter back in the 1960s. As the Cold War wound down, I just kept excavating and expanding until... I ended up with a lab."

Kev said, "Well, shucky-darns. I only turned my bomb shelter into a sewing room."

Just the equipment we could see cost many millions of dollars. I couldn't imagine what construction costs and unseen things in other areas of the compound might be worth.

"This must have cost a fortune." I said.

Dr. Weksler nodded. "A small one, yes."

"Please forgive me for asking, but where did you get the money?"

"From George."

"George?"

"Well, Jorge." He clarified.

"Jorge? Jorge who?" I asked.

"Jorge Pheltor."

"As in Pheltor Hall?" Kevin asked

"Yes."

I put my face into my hands, trying to wrap my brain around it all. "You mean Pheltor Hall as in Pasadena Institute of Technology Jorge Pheltor? Pheltor Hall Pheltor? Him Pheltor?"

"The very same."

"I don't get it."

"Jorge befriended me," Dr. Weksler explained. "One of many mentors who blessed my life. He left the University a lot of money when he passed, but he left me enduring royalties on thirty-seven patents. He wanted me to use the money for pure research without meddling from University politics and government bureaucracies. I try to fulfill his wishes.

"Jorge loved to fly more than anything on earth. If the three of us can learn to control the weather, then air travel will be as safe as a walk to the mailbox. And, in the future, perhaps we can develop safe commercial space flight for everybody. Theophilus... Kevin... we have all the resources we need to make his dreams come true."

Ox and I stood in stunned silence while the entirety of it all sank in.

As an afterthought, Dr. Weksler threw in, "Oh, and then of course, there are the WD-40 monies."

Once again, we had no idea.

Addressing our gapes, Dr. Weksler looked up into his memory and continued. "Back in 19... 53—when I became a full professor—Pas Tech placed me on sabbatical loan to NACA. Our emerging space program needed help developing an extraordinary formula which had capabilities like nothing else ever before. It took a bit of time, but we eventually created WD-40. The WD stood for Water Displacement. The 40 referred to the fortieth formula we tested. The previous thirty-nine did not work. Other folks thought we had thirty-nine failures in a row. I never saw anything as a failure because I always believed what Uncle Tom taught me."

"Who's Uncle Tom?" I asked.

"Edison. Thomas Edison."

"Oh, well, sure." Kevin said. "Of course. Just about everybody gets a little advice now and then from their Uncle Tom Edison."

Dr. Weksler smiled at Kev's cute, but well-made point. Dr. Weksler's unique life had truly been mentored and blessed.

"Because I was on loan from Pasadena Institute of Technology," Dr. Weksler said, "I couldn't participate in the patents. But I had stock options. I exercised them as soon as permissible. WD-40 first went on sale to the public in 1958, the same year NACA became NASA, the National Aeronautics and Space Administration. The first cans of WD-40 hit the shelves in San Diego. By 1993, we were selling a million cans a week. And, it hasn't slowed down a smidgeon.

"Welcome aboard my dear friends. Everything's chicken."

"I have not failed. I've just found 10,000 ways that won't work."

— Thomas A. Edison

44

AN HOUR LATER

After his release from county lock-up, Leonard Ostermann went straight to his office without wasting tax-payer time and money by going home for a shower, shave, and change of clothes. He chose not to wear his tie. In his movie memorabilia-filled ninth floor office, with a forged-autograph Errol Flynn 8 x10 as his inspiration piece, Lenny now conducted business on a black 1940s desk telephone.

"They lost the van?" He said into the phone. "Stupid, incompetent bureaucrats. — That's not funny. — Apology accepted. — Now... I want to know who owns that van with the phony Iowa and/or Texas license plate. On second thought, just fax me a list of all vans with phony license plates. — What do you mean the DMV doesn't have a list of all vans with phony license plates? Isn't that what computers are for? — Okay, listen to me. I want to know everything about the owner of that van. Where he lives, what he does for fun, what he does for malice, how often he flosses." Leonard slammed down the phone and stared out his window at Chinatown and the "Hollywood" sign in the hills beyond.

Cleo entered with a cup of coffee. "Good morning, Mr. Ostermann. Looks like you had a rough night. I thought some decaf might calm you."

Taking the coffee mug without breaking his absorbed gaze through the window, he said as if reciting dialogue from an old detective movie. "It was, indeed, a rough night in the bare-naked city. I've been patrolling the savage underbelly of the urban beast for a week. Just for the record, doll, I find being calm improbable while a deranged sociopath runs amuck in our village, pretending to be a pirate. Who knows what deadly, diabolical deed he is committing at this very moment?"

* * * * *

Kevin shot his straw wrapper and hit me in the shoulder. In retaliation, I turned and fired my straw wrapper at him. He dodged my shot and caught my wrapper mid-flight. He rolled it into a ball, made it "disappear" with some grade school "magic", and pretended to put the wrapper in his mouth. He did his usual "magical" misdirection and tossed the rolled-up straw wrapper onto the countertop behind him. Putting his tongue against the inside of his cheek, he made it appear that he was chewing a wrapper into a spit ball.

Raising his eyebrows, he showed his hands empty, and mumbled, "Huh?"

"Yeah," I said, "you've really got that trick down. I've liked that one ever since you first showed me in the second grade."

He mumbled as he chewed, "Ever see how I can spit it out?"

I called his bluff. "No, don't believe I have." I put my straw into my Classic Coke can and stood up with my chest puffed out. "Show me." I tapped my chest. "Right here. I double dare you." We both knew there was nothing in his mouth.

"Naw, not now. Some other time."

"C'mon dude," I said. "Hit me with your best shot. If you've got one."

He blew out the marble he had hidden in his mouth. A surprise variation on his decades old trick. The marble hit my Coke can with a loud KLAK!

"Aiieee!" I jumped.

"Gotcha."

We both laughed, as did Dr. Weksler on the other side of the cave, working with the generator control panel. We were making good progress and finally having fun doing it. Kevin went behind the central command console with a handful of nylon zip ties to bundle the last of the cable connections. He mumbled something to me.

I looked his way. "What?"

He stuck his head out from behind an equipment rack and shot three more marbles out of his mouth. I got hit by all three.

I whined, "Mr. Weksler, Kevin is shooting spit marbles at me."

"Children, behave. We have serious work to do."

"Actually," I said, "looks like we're finished cabling the video array. Kev?"

"Yep. The ineez and outeez from the former van console are linked to the lab's video board. We have unlimited World Wide Web and satellite access. And, I finally lost my marbles".

I said, "Check it out, Frank. Let's test... uh... I know, Southern California Doppler weather radar map." I moved a potentiometer to zoom-in on the large screen high-def.

Dr. Weksler nodded. "Very nice."

Kev said, "If all is well, we should have total international capability." He turned a clicking knob 29 degrees and selected one of two dozen thumbnails on the video monitor. *Gilligan's Island* came up on multiple big screens with opening credits written in Chinese and the theme song sung in Chinese.

Kevin did a fist clench. "Yes, it worked. OK... let's—"

"I'm getting some kind of interference here." I interrupted.

Gauges on the generator control panel fluttered wildly.

Dr. Weksler shouted, "Everyone into the garage. Now."

Though clueless, Ox and I stopped what we were doing and followed him out of the lab. As soon as we emerged into the garage, Dr. Weksler hung a tarp across the entrance to the dark tunnel. "That horrible, horrible woman," He said.

Kev asked, "Excuse me... who are we talking about?"

Dr. Weksler squinted out the garage dirty side window. "The manager of the trailer park, Ms. Zambini. Every time she gets near my lab, all the equipment goes haywire. She's a walking magnetic phase inverter."

* * * * *

A twenty-something by-the-book babe, Ms. Zambini ran the trailer park like a mafia boss running a preschool. She also owned Kagel Canyon Cuties, the park's hair salon located in the guest bedroom of her own trailer, the source-code for muumuu lady tall-hair. Ms. Zambini's ever-present personal pyramid of metal hair curlers atop her head affected everything electronic when she passed by. At night, residents of Kagel Canyon Estates always knew Ms. Zambini's location because television screens flickered, and lights dimmed wherever she walked.

* * * * *

It seemed like a simple issue to me. "Why don't you just ask her to stay away from the lab?"

"She doesn't know about the lab," Dr. Weksler answered. "Nobody in the world knows about it except you two. My lab is a blatant violation of the trailer park codes, covenants and restrictions, subsection nine, paragraph fifty-three which, among other things, forbids excavation, irrigation, and the raising of livestock."

Kevin said, "So what's she after you for today?"

"I don't know. I got rid of the kangaroo."

Bam! Bam! Bam! Ms. Zambini knocked on the door.

Dr. Weksler said, "Pretend you're doing something normal." He put on a sham smile and opened the garage side door just a bit. "Ms. Zambini, Good morning. And how are we today?"

"*We* would be a lot better if *you* would follow the rules, Weksler."

"Why, Ms. Zambini, is there a problem of some sort?"

She curled her index finger, summoning him outside. When he opened the door just enough to slip out onto the narrow-gauge sidewalk, she craned her neck to peek inside. She caught Kevin and me playing tic-tac-toe with our fingers in the deep dust. She gave us both a serious skunk-eye.

Pointing at Kevin's van, she stated, "That vehicle is parked in your driveway."

Dr. Weksler nodded. "Yes, it is."

"It should be in the designated visitor parking area at the west end of Winnebago Way."

"Why, yes, of course, that is where it should be. I will take care of it."

"If you don't move that vehicle A-sap, I will personally cut off your shuffleboard.

"Ouch," Kev said.

"Know this, Weksler," Ms. Zambini continued, "I am not your personal baby-sitter. If I have to come all the way out here again, I will be kicking some serious butt."

I sneezed mightily, kicking up a dust cloud which surrounded my head.

She stepped around Dr. Weksler and looked in at me. "And who is that?" She demanded.

"Just some friends."

Kev said, "It's normal for us to play tic-tac-toe in the dirt."

She pointed at me. "What's the geeky one's name?"

I said, "Me?"

"You see any other geeks around here?"

"Well, actually there are—"

"—Never mind, dust bunny." She pointed two fingers at her own eyes and then pointed them at my eyes. "I'm watching you."

She did an about face, shook her head at Kevin's van, marched down the driveway, and continued her foot patrol up Doublewide Drive.

Kev said to me, "Ah, don't worry about her. I think she has a crush on you... dust bunny."

45

MID-DAY, MID-CAVE

All chairs in Dr. Weksler's lab were red, a pleasing, unexpected accent to the gray, black and beige cabinets and fixtures. Most importantly (as it would prove out) all the red four-wheeled desk chairs were custom-manufactured to Dr. Weksler's specifications. At his age, bending over and grabbing a handle to raise or lower the seating height of a chair could be problematic. So, he had special "air pump" fittings installed which raised the seat by putting one's foot on a small platform where the adjustment handle would normally be and then pumping it with your leg. The seat could be instantaneously lowered to the shortest setting by simply stepping on that little platform with one's full weight.

Peering up, I could see Dr. Weksler through the opened metal hatch in the cave roof. On top of his dry brown hill, he checked the newly installed cables which went from his satellite TV dish through holes in the hatch down to the lab below. Satisfied, he closed the hatch, and whirled the submarine-style locking wheel tight. With a satisfied grin, he shot me a thumbs-up.

Kevin, on his cell phone, finished another monologue in Dianne's voicemail. "Dianne, we really need to talk. Please call me back." He pushed "end call" and deflated into his chair.

I asked, "Do I detect something here beyond your standard, short-lived, school-yard infatuation?".

"Oh, Dianne's okay. You know, if you like that type... beautiful... witty... confident... intelligent." He spun himself in a circle on his red, four-wheeled chair.

"Intelligent?" I said. "That's finally something that appeals to you?"

He stopped his chair. "Well, yeah. Of course. Duh."

"Wait a minute, aren't you the guy who says a woman's vocabulary should be smaller than her gazonkies?"

"Oh, please. That was my undergraduate phase. I'm more evolved now." He spun himself around in faster circles, and accidentally fell over backwards. Four-wheeled chairs are not as stable as five-wheeled chairs. Even if you are more evolved.

Dr. Weksler clanked down the last two metal stairs of the catwalk. "All is well at the transceiver. How are we doing here?"

"All systems one-hundred-percent." I pointed my elbow toward Kevin. "Except for our chief cook and heart-throbber."

Dr. Weksler looked to Kevin, "I am truly sorry about the Dr. Wright situation. I know you don't want to hear platitudes from a geezer, but..." He gave Kevin a reassuring fatherly nod. "...it will work out. Give it time."

Kevin stood up, hooked his thumbs in the rear pockets of his khaki cargo shorts and wandered aimlessly. "Yeah. Hope so. Thanks."

"But right now," Dr. Weksler said, "we need to know— absolutely for certain—that my TV dish will work as an uplink."

"Absolutely for certain it will work."

"With no little glitches that may destroy the western hemisphere?"

"No glitches at all. With your world's greatest uninterruptible power supply from that generator, and your lovely formerly turquoise dish, we can do our magic anywhere from Denver to Honolulu."

"Magnificent."

* * * * *

For lunch, we ordered pizza delivery. Kev googled and found a local pizzeria that agreed to construct a large pizza to our detailed specifications and deliver same.

We call our version of a Hawaiian pizza, which the Ox man and I invented in 2001, the "Monsoon Moon". It has small chunks (not slices) of ham, gobs of pineapple, bacon crumbles, and extra sauce. Then, we do our "top secret process". We cover the entire pizza with a thick layer of cheese. When that cheese melts together, it hermetically seals the toppings inside and turns the whole thing into a hot grease sandwich. For the exquisite finale, we paint the cheese with creamy sriracha sauce. It comes out of the oven as a dusky yellowish disk... like a monsoon moon.

A Thai housewife in the Chonburi Province of Thailand created sriracha sauce in the 1930s. In 2003, almost nobody in the U.S. had ever heard of sriracha sauce. Kevin, however, brought back several bottles from eastern Thailand in 2001. He kept a bottle in his van for emergency dining situations just like this.

I never knew why he was in eastern Thailand. We kinda-sorta had our own "don't ask, don't tell" policy.

* * * * *

In the garage driveway, Kev happily sniffed the hot and suitably greasy pizza box as the joyful high school delivery boy drove away in his unfinished rat rod. Ox gave him a twenty-dollar tip to assist with his cool project car, a rust-color, chopped and channeled 1926 Essex two-door sedan proudly wearing a Chevy 409. Ox watched the rod rumble away and reverently whispered, "Praise the lowered."

That's when the disgusting duo, Bahadur and Mikhail, drove up and squeezed their car in at an angle, next to Kevin's van. Bahadur made a statement by using the car to threaten bodily harm. Kevin made his own statement by refusing to move. Bahadur roared the engine. He stopped the car an inch from Kevin's kneecap.

With a huge, friendly smile Kev said, "Hi there! Hey, you're the dudes who dented my van. Well, halleluiah shucky-darns, nice of you to drop by. Let's exchange insurance cards."

Bahadur and Mikhail got out of the car and, as they walked to Kevin, each raised the front of his shirt, revealing an MP5 machine pistol stuck in his waistband.

Kevin smiled again. "Well those are certainly more impressive than insurance cards. Ahh, you know what?" He made a dismissive wave. "Just a bumper-thumper." He turned and walked toward the garage. "Forget about it. No harm. No foul."

That's when Professor Pul got out of the backseat.

With his FAMAS F1 submachine gun.

* * * * *

By the way, it's been a while since I first mentioned the FAMAS F1. Just in case you've forgotten, it's a cheaply made French machine gun. The acronym, FAMAS, stands for *Fusil d'Assaut de la Manufacture d'Armes de Saint-Étienne* (Assault Rifle from the Saint-Étienne Weapon Factory). The F1's plastic parts broke frequently, and the weapon often jammed due to the poorly designed disposable magazine.

Though officially compatible with NATO standard 5.56x45mm brass-cased cartridges, using NATO bullets exceeded safe operational limits, the only safe ammunition being the much more expensive French manufactured steel-case SS109 cartridge. Fraught with problems and unreliable, but still a deadly weapon, the F1 became a cut-rate deal on the gray market.

Pul and his thugs had three. More than enough.

46

A MINUTE LATER

The mouth-watering aroma of our custom-built pizza floated into the cave, accompanied by the repellent odor of Professor Pul. As our precise pizza construction specs included neither limburger cheese nor putrefied sweat socks, the olfactory challenge confused my nose.

> Geek Alert — for those of you who are trivia-laden like me: Limburger cheese is fermented with the same bacteria which creates stinky feet. It is scientifically correct to say Limburger cheese smells like dirty feet. And vice-versa.

Juggling the large pizza box, Kevin stumbled into the lab, as if pushed. Dr. Weksler and I jumped to our feet to help him. Before we could assist, Bahadur and Mikhail followed Kevin in with their MP5 machine pistols drawn. Professor Pul then swaggered in with the arrogance and confidence that accompanies complete evil. "It is so good to see the awesome threesome together again," he said. "Good afternoon, gentlemen."

"Professor Pul?" Dr. Weksler raised his voice. "I demand to know the meaning of this." He stood up and walked angrily toward Pul, who pointed his weapon at him.

Kevin said, "Frank, sit down. Now." Dr. Weksler returned to his command chair, in front of the main console.

Pul said, "Thank you, my friend The Pirate. Your boy scout instincts just saved his life."

What? Pul knows about The Pirate? And that Kev had been a scout? And our private nickname, the awesome threesome?

Dr. Weksler, reacting to an apparent personal relationship between Kev and Pul said, "Kevin, are you part of this?"

"Just to relieve your concern Dr. Weksler," Pul said, "the playful pirate child has nothing to do with this particular event. However, he will soon have a role to play." He looked at Kevin. "Won't you... Ox man?"

Kevin said, "Frank, I have no idea what he's talking about. Consider the source."

Pul continued, "And I have not forgotten, Dr. Weksler, that you _demanded_ to know the meaning of this. Hah! We'll get to that in a moment. But first we need to prepare for contingencies."

Bahadur gave his MP5 to Mikhail who stood guard while Bahadur patted down each of us, confiscating all personal communication devices.

Pul said, "Should anyone have the heroic notion of grabbing Bahadur and using him as a human shield, please know I will joyfully shoot right through Bahadur in order to kill an infidel hero." Pul smiled. "And Bahadur simply won't mind at all."

Bahadur agreed. "It true is happy to be martyr. Thank you." He gave our cellphones, walkie-talkies, PDAs, and pagers to Pul, and retrieved his MP5 from Mikhail.

Professor Pul dumped the pizza out onto a desk, dropped all our phones, etc., into the empty box, and carried the box with him to the nearest computer workstation. He said, "I have a few minutes of housekeeping. Please eat your pizza now. You must maintain your energy level up for our very busy day today."

He deleted all email and social media accounts from the first PC. Looking up and seeing we were not eating, he said, "Did I not say to eat your pizza? Bahadur, if they do not start eating by the time, time I count to five, shoot the old one. One Mississippi... two Mississippis... three Mississippis..."

We ate. It was really good. I threw up.

Professor Pul methodically deleted all messaging accounts on all computers, followed by violently ripping all landline telephone cables out of the walls. Without talking, he strolled among consoles, cabinets, and equipment, looking and touching like a teenage girl turned loose with daddy's credit cards on Black Friday. Meandering past the steel circular stairs, he sat the pizza box on the wooden workbench. With both hands, he picked up a heavy four-foot-long pipe wrench lying on the floor and, swinging harder than necessary, shattered each communication device. He appeared to receive great joy from destroying things.

From the bowl on the little red table, Pul grabbed an apple with his left hand and an orange with his right. He held them palms up, arms outstretched, squeezing, and determining heft, as he thought-stared into space. His smirk said he came to a decision. He put the apple and orange into his pockets, picked up the hefty pipe wrench and walked back to us.

All eyes followed. Where Dr. Weksler sat, a couple of feet from a black steel catwalk support beam, Pul pulled the orange out of his pocket, tossed it up in the air, and swung the wrench like a baseball bat. SMACK! The raggedly split-open orange flew over our heads drooling wet orange gunk. Professor Pul glared unblinking into the eyes of Dr. Weksler, raised his eyebrows, and said, "Fascinating."

He repeated with the apple, swinging so hard that small chunks of mangled apple soared to the catwalk on the other side of the room. Pursing his lips as if wanting to kiss his own brilliance, he began his lecture.

"Interesting, indeed. We completely mutilated the orange as you saw. Very messy." Pul shook the juice off his fingers and wiped them on his jeans. "The apple on the other hand, not unlike the human skull, somewhat retained its shape so as still to be recognizable as part of a former human even though it had been rendered extremely dead and bloody." He leaned in toward Dr. Weksler. "Oops, I meant, juicy." Pul giggled.

Dr. Weksler crossed his arms and swiveled his chair to face us. With his back to Professor Pul, Dr. Weksler never saw the blow coming.

"Very well then," Pul said. Let's proceed." He grabbed the huge wrench handle with both hands and reared back like a vicious Sultan of Swat, with Dr. Weksler's skull as his baseball.

Kevin stood up, knocking his chair over, shouting, "Pul! No!"

I closed my eyes.

Professor Pul swung the heavy wrench powerfully. KLANG! A solid hit on the catwalk support beam. The soul piercing sound reverberated around the two-story bunker. Pul leaned in close to the beam, touching and examining. "Hmm... not bent, dent, or damaged in any way. Very nice, Dr. Weksler. This is maraging steel. High nickel, cobalt, and molybdenum content. Perhaps a splash of manganese. Good weldability. Super strength." He looked over his shoulder to Dr. Weksler. "Nitrided?"

Dr. Weksler slunk in his chair, and said softly, "Yes, it is."

Pul said, "We are impressed. Somebody spent a lot of money here." He promenaded across the room and hung the wrench in its outlined space on the peg board up behind the workbench, and shouted back, "Mr. Oxley, Mr. Spivak, shame on you. You scouts must remember to put your tools away in their proper place. Take care of your tools and they will take care of you."

Dr. Weksler said, "*I* left it on the floor."

Pul shouted, "And I would expect nothing less of you." He turned to Bahadur and Mikhail. "Who wants to be the one that gets to shoot Dr. Weksler?"

They both raised their hands. A very excited Mikhail said. "Me do. Me do. Me do."

Pul held up his palm, curtailing continued exuberance from the dumb deadly duo. "Fine. Thank you. That will do." Addressing us, he said, "Kevin, Theophilus, here is how it will work. If at any time I feel either of you are a hindrance, or are out of my control, I will let Mikhail shoot Dr. Weksler."

Bahadur lowered his head, stuck out his lower lip, and kicked the floor with his heel.

Pul said, "Oh I understand your disappointment, Bahadur. Tell you what... if Mikhail doesn't kill Dr. Weksler with his first burst, then I'll let you shoot him as well." Pul reflected for a moment and added, "Aww, what the heck. We're all friends here, right?" Bahadur nodded, smiling eagerly. "Even if Mikhail does kill him with the first burst, I will still let you shoot Dr. Weksler after he's dead."

Bahadur wriggled, excited as a puppy.

"Now, to answer your earlier query, Dr. Weksler... No, actually, I believe it was a <u>demand</u>." His eyes burned as he recollected. "Yes, yes, yes indeed... you <u>demanded</u>. You said, and I quote, 'I <u>demand</u> to know the meaning of this.' Well, my goodness, I thought for certain a genius like you would have received a clear message from the unfortunate fire at the scout's apartment."

"You're responsible?"

Pul pointed at Dr. Weksler. "Amazing. He is so astute."

"Why?"

Professor Pul resumed his walkabout, heading back toward the main console. He spread his arms wide, in admiration of the facility. "This... this will do very nicely, Frank. Thank you for sharing your lab with us."

Dr. Weksler rose up in anger, but Kevin put a hand on his shoulder and held him down while Mikhail salivated over the potential joy of shooting him.

Pul swaggered back and sat down in front of us. Putting his feet up on an auxiliary panel, he said, "To address your dreadfully naïve question, Frank... you ask, why? I answer, why not? What you have developed here is the most powerful weapon ever known. No army, no country, no religion can withstand the forces of nature. He who rules weather, rules the world."

"World conquest? That's your agenda?"

"Not the world, Frank. Don't be plebeian. I only want to restore what belongs to my people."

Kevin said, "And that would be...?"

"*Aztlán*. Seven of your united states, including those you call, California, Colorado, and Tejas... all Spanish words. You even had the nerve to call one of the territories you stole, *New Mexico*. How would you feel if we stole your land and called it, New United States?"

"But you don't have to steal our land. Just sneak in illegally and we'll give you everything you want for free."

"What I want is what belongs to the Holy Garduña—*Aztlán*—promised to us in the visions of *Apollinario*, the sanctified hermit of the Sierra Morena. We are the S.O.L. The Sons of Liberty. Yet the United Nations still refuses our petition to restore the royal family to the throne. All our lands, everywhere, our entire country, my royal family, were all seized by other countries, by infidels, and by the United States of America."

Kevin said, "We stole your whole country? Wow. That's heavy, man. Did I ever tell you about when somebody stole my Gameboy? Well, I suppose this is much bigger, of course."

"Don't even offer sarcastic sympathy, Kevin," Dr. Weksler said, "The Garduña, his royal crime 'family', ruled by torture and murder."

Kevin looked at Pul. "Whoa. You must have killer family reunions."

* * * * *

At frequent opportune moments, Pul made it clear that he loved, respected, and wished to emulate Libya's Muammar al-Khadafy and Iraq's Saddam Hussein. Both used domestic violence as one of their loving options for brotherly leadership. Pul dreamed of replicating in his new land of *Aztlán*, the iron-fisted control of Khadafy and Hussein. Both had already provided their blueprint for successful leadership: private torture and public execution.

Yes, Professor Pul was psychotic, with secondary delusional beliefs which could never be altered by facts or truth. Just another apprentice megalomaniac. Also, not the brightest bulb on the Hanukkah bush. But, then, one need not pass an intelligence test nor a sanity hearing to be admired and respected by fellow terrorists.

* * * * *

Standing on top of the master control cabinet, Pul delivered a proclamation to his captive audience. "We claim this facility in the name of the Holy Garduña. This laboratory is now the embassy for the Sons of Liberty. We have cut off all your communication with the outside world. Nobody knows where you are. You are isolated and the Garduña now controls the weather. Accordingly, we will give the United States and the world a demonstration of our power. Go to your workstations. You will create weather the world will never forget."

"The equipment isn't ready." Kevin said. "We're not finished."

Dr. Weksler and I exchanged a glance.

Pul said, "Then do what you must. Now. Get to work. Finish it. Now. NOW."

Kevin's stall tactic gave us a tiny bit of stress relief because it meant Pul didn't know as much about our abilities as we had feared. We headed to our workstations, but Pul intercepted Kevin. "Not you," he said, "For you, there are special plans. Come with me."

"Well, I hope this won't take long. I have a dentist appointment this afternoon."

"You won't be needing that. You will be a star in my attention-getting public spectacle."

As he walked with Professor Pul, Kev said, "You don't understand. It takes three months to get an appointment with my dentist." He opened his mouth wide and pointed to a molar. "This tooth needs a cap." He pointed to a molar on the other side. "And this one needs a gown." He grabbed an eye tooth between his thumb and index finger and pretended to wiggle it. "And this little tooth cried whee, whee, whee all the way home."

47

FIVE MINUTES LATER

A bloody machete in the hands of a black-hooded executioner interrupted the regularly scheduled television program. In a few seconds, the slightly blurry, hijacked, KLOS-TV Channel Six broadcast picture came into sharper, but still not perfect focus. No audio yet, but the clearer view revealed the executioner as a computer-generated graphic image superimposed on live video of a red chair positioned in front of black drapes. Word rapidly spread throughout Southern California. Nobody knew what to expect.

Professor Pul made certain every monitor in the lab carried Channel Six. He also made certain Dr. Weksler and I watched. Automatic weapons settled any debate.

Pul marched Kevin into the ground floor utility space just left of the large red, steel, bunker entry door, where Mikhail set up the television camera, microphone, red metal folding chair, and black drape background. With Kev and Pul only twenty feet away from our workstations we saw and heard everything.

Professor Pul, hideously gleeful, said, "I was delighted to learn that you had this other career as The Pirate."

"Oh, it's really more of a hobby."

Pul continued his train of thought, "You are an excellent spokesman. Your pirate persona receives instant attention from the media. Our broadcast will show the people of California just how dreadfully serious the S.O.L. must be taken."

Kevin said, "Actually, you know, I've been thinking about it, and we're really too far away from the Channel Six broadcast tower for a good quality transmission. I'm going to come out all fuzzy."

The Professor raised his FAMAS and sited the after-market, retrofitted, red laser dot on the Ox man's nose. Kevin crossed his eyes, so he could see the red dot. "Fuzzy is not automatically a bad thing. There's worse stuff than fuzzy."

Pul commanded, "Destiny awaits. Sit in your chair. Now."

As did millions of Southern Californians, we watched it live on television. Society almost came to a full stop. Virtually every television set in every home, office, and public building tuned to Channel Six. Frightened by the disturbing broadcast, hushed Pirate fans gripped their armrests and gasped for breath.

"Those who do not love me do not deserve to live."

— Muammar al-Khadafy

In full Pirate regalia, complete with the fake stuffed parrot on his shoulder, Kev walked into the TV picture in front of the black drapes and sat down on the chair. Awkwardly raising a sheet of paper in his zip tie-bound hands, Kevin, The Pirate, read the official declaration exactly as Professor Pul wrote it:

"It is me. Yo. Ho."

Kev The Pirate looked at Pul offstage and said, "Nicely written greeting. You really captured the warmth." Then he looked back at the camera, did googly eyes, and continued reading Pul's script:

> "I come to you today through the benevolent courtesy of the S.O.L., more accurately known as the Sons of Liberty. Our goal is to promote the common good and insure liberty for all peoples of the world, regardless of—in most cases—race, creed, or religion. As such, the S.O.L. demands immediate world-wide capitulation to the following:

> "1. Restoration of our rightful ownership of Aztlán, our soon-to-be homeland;

> "2. Recognition by the United Nations that Aztlán is a sovereign nation;

> "3. Unlimited economic and military support from the United States of America;

> "4. Acknowledgement of and confirmation that the following deplorables have no right to exist: The nation of Israel, as well as all Jews, some Muslims, most Christians, a lot of Hindus, and certain Buddhists we don't like very much.

> "The S.O.L. is now in possession of the world's only WRMD, Weather of Really Mass Destruction. It is a weapon that controls the weather. This solidifies the S.O.L as the most powerful benevolent organization on Earth.

"As proof of our power, the S.O.L. will—today—create a snowstorm in Hollywood."

Surprised, Kevin looked again at the off-camera Professor Pul. "You will? Really?" Kev did a rolling-eyes-they're-all-crazy shrug into the camera and went back to reading Pul's manifesto.

"If the S.O.L. demands are not met, the Sons of Liberty will wreak havoc on the world until the world in general, and the United States of America in particular, collapses to their knees."

Pul cut the microphone. He cut the camera. He left the executioner graphic on screen for five seconds and then he cut the bootleg broadcast. Thankfully, he did not cut anything else. He remained silent for a few moments, debriefing in his own head, then said, "Excellent job, boy scout."

"Well I hope you're happy because this is going to just ruin my folk hero image."

* * * * *

Thirty-minutes later, deep in clandestine, whispered communication, Ox and I sat on the cement floor behind the main equipment rack. Dr. Weksler, holding a soldering iron and a small coil of flux-core solder occasionally flamed a snippet of solder to produce smoke and smell. We wired and moved stuff, then removed and rewired the same stuff again, pretending to work so that we looked like we were actually working and not actually pretending to work. Well, that was a stupid description. Let me try again. We were doing busy work, so it would look like we were busy doing work. Never mind.

Dr. Weksler whispered, "What are we going to do?"

"Well... I think I have a plan," I said, timidly.

Kevin said, "Alright Theo."

"Here's my idea... Dr. Weks... Frank, you excuse yourself to go to the bathroom. I'll stay here and pound on this cabinet to distract them. Then, Kevin, when they're all looking at me, you run out to the van, get your baseball bat, and come back in here and hit someone."

Dr. Weksler asked, "What do I do in the bathroom?"

I said, "Call the police." Dr. Weksler and I got excited about my plan.

"Okay, but there's no phone in the john."

"Well, see if you can borrow Mikhail's cellphone."

"Good idea."

I said, "Just tell him you need to make a personal call."

"Right."

Kevin interrupted our zeal. "Hold it, hold it, guys. Moe. Curly. This is a stupid plan."

We considered his candid assessment and concluded that yes, perhaps, it might have been a stupid plan. I never claimed to be a military strategist.

Professor Pul approached. "Coffee break?"

We silently continued imaginary tasks as Pul admired the equipment. "By the way, Dr. Weksler," he said, "I must congratulate you on your successes. The Board at Pasadena Institute of Technology sees you as an embarrassing joke and, yet, look what you have accomplished. Even though I always believed in your dream, I admit there were times over the years when I, too, questioned your rationale."

"Over the years?"

"Oh, yes. We've monitored you and Sarah Norton for at least a decade. I remember well, her speech at the Geneva Symposium this past January. You and she spoke with such passion. What exquisite irony that what you two envisioned is now my army."

Dr. Weksler seized Pul. "You will not degrade her dream!"

Kevin inserted himself between Pul and Dr. Weksler, waving his palm at Bahadur to dissuade him from shooting. Even as Kevin put himself into the line of fire, Dr. Weksler shouted at Pul, "I won't allow you to use this as a weapon."

Kevin calmed Bahadur and tugged Dr. Weksler off Professor Pul, literally ordering, "At ease, Frank. Stand down."

Taking advantage of the distraction, I quickly went to Mikhail and said, "May I please borrow your phone for a moment? I really need to make a call... and go to the bathroom."

Mikhail, overwhelmed by the complexity of my request, slowly said, "I think so not." He brandished his machine gun, which quite effectively changed my mind.

Highly insulted by the elderly Dr. Weksler's physical affront, Pul's machismo took over. "Brave words from a feeble old clown. But words don't mean much at this point." He raised his FAMAS F1 and pointed it at Dr. Weksler's face. "Say goodbye, Frank."

Kevin waved his hands in the air. "Whoa. Whoa. Whoa. Hey, hey, hey, hey. You need all three of us to get the job done. Nobody needs to get hurt."

Pul rammed the heel of his custom pistol-grip assault rifle stock into Kevin's stomach. Ox doubled up and fell to the concrete. "Unh. Maybe I didn't explain that concept clearly."

Kevin wasn't hurt. He saw it coming, tightened his abdominal wall and rolled with the blow, hoping his acting would soothe Pul's blood thirst.

Professor Pul shouted, "I am becoming intolerant of you offensive infidels." He looked down at Kevin, still writhing on the cement floor. Pul pushed the barrel of his F1 into Kevin's stomach. "You appear to be valuable and yet you are a joker." He twisted to Dr. Weksler. "And I don't like old clowns, either." He backhanded Dr. Weksler's face, drawing blood with his ornate ring.

Increasingly crazy Professor Pul turned on me. "And this one..." Pul said, touching the F1 muzzle to my chest directly in front of my heart, "...is such a nervous little mouse. Are you of any value at all? Perhaps we should kill you just to provide a little show and tell."

"Professor Pul," Kevin interrupted, "all equipment is up and running. We're A-OK. Where do you want your snowstorm?"

Pul turned away from me, wearing the condescending smirk of the negotiator who did not blink first. He nodded to Mikhail, who immediately exited the lab on a pre-assigned reconnaissance mission. The nutty professor then weirdly sang, "He's off to see the blizzard, that wonderful blizzard of ours." He giggled. Psychotically.

Kevin looked at me and compassionately asked, "Theo, how's your FUD?"

"Call me Elmer."

Then I fainted.

48

THIRTY-FIVE-MINUTES LATER

"Telbird Five is in a geosynch," I announced. Kev and I worked at our usual stations, but Dr. Weksler had to roll up a chair and function from an auxiliary control board and small split-screen array because Pul chose to observe from Dr. Weksler's master control console. A purposeful professional affront to Dr. Weksler. Not only psychotic, but childish.

"Uncluttered channels?" I asked.

Dr. Weksler said, "Thirteen and... twenty-eight."

"I'm pinging twenty-eight."

Ox said, "Redirecting."

Pul drummed his fingernails on the sheet metal body of the FAMAS lying across his lap, his feet up on the master console in front of him. "I am becoming impatient again."

Kev said, "I hate when that happens."

We pushed buttons, entered codes, and flipped switches in the correct sequence, hoping our ramistat tweaks would produce snow instead of merely slushy hail. Or deadly hail. Or something else. Or nothing at all.

Targeted coordinates enveloped the Hollywood Chinese Theater. We certainly would have preferred to attempt our first snow day in an isolated area rather than the epicenter of Los Angeles tourism.

"My readings are good," Dr. Weksler said.

"We are locked," I said.

With his hand on the old Mustang chromed T-bar, Kev offered it to Dr. Weksler, who shook his head and said, "There is no honor in this."

What an emotional double whammy. We were about to create a remotely-controlled snowstorm—something never previously accomplished by anyone, anywhere—but we were doing it for the wrong people, for the wrong reason.

Pul shouted, "Show the world our power. Now."

Kevin pulled the T-bar.

All the digital bleeps deets, and screeches communicated perfectly. In twenty seconds, it would either snow at 6925 Hollywood Boulevard on the hottest afternoon of the last thirteen years or... we didn't know what.

Averaging two million visitors a year, mostly in the summer, the Chinese Theater became a tourist mecca in 1927 when silent screen stars Norma Talmadge, Mary Pickford and Douglas Fairbanks became the first Hollywood royalty to sign the cement. Per Professor Pul's orders, Mikhail did his mental best to blend in with hundreds of tourists by changing how he dressed. Instead of his usual dirty orange jump suit, he wore dirty orange shorts and an XXXL dirty orange T-shirt.

Standing next to William Shatner's footprints in the forecourt cement, Mikhail pointed down and said to a female sightseer, "Is Kirk the *Capataz*." Realizing he spoke a Spanish word, he panicked and tried to erase it from the air with wild hand gestures, shouting, "*Captain* of the Kirk. Captain. Captain." The sightseer lady ran far away.

Looking down at his hero's signature in the cement, Mikhail saw the first snowflakes land. He looked up and received a face full of snow from a gray square cloud.

"Snow. Just like must be is."

Confused vacationers stared in wonderment. The courtyard became bitter cold. Accumulated snow began to drift. Tourists, dressed for a broiling Southern California summer, needed immediate shelter from the freezing weather. So, they walked across the street to where it was still sunny and hot.

Six hundred-and-thirty-two tourists would take home amazing snapshots

* * * * *

Dr. Weksler's cave turned into tensionville because Mikhail did not call to confirm snow. Professor Pul watched Channel Eight on all monitors, his head turning every few seconds to stare briefly at the bulky satellite phone sitting beside him in its self-contained, battery-laden, carrying case. Then his heated gaze returned to the TV.

Dr. Gil, the KZLA-TV weather maven, delivered his drought update while standing in front of the full-screen meteorological conditions map, shaking his head. "Still no end in sight for this record-setting dry spell." He pointed to the map covered with happy sun faces. "No precipitation of any kind, anywhere. Agricultural experts predict a ten-billion-dollar loss to the state's farm economy if this hot weather doesn't end soon."

Pul, red-faced, looked as if he might detonate.

I gulped and, switched the master video monitor to our own computer-generated view. Our video map showed a white snowflake icon hovering above Hollywood. "Professor Pul, our computer indicates heavy snowfall over Hollywood at this very moment."

"I am familiar with computer-generated graphics. Your screenshot means nothing. If this is a lie, you will not live to regret it."

BING! BONG! — BING! BONG! Everybody jumped.

Professor Pul lifted his satellite phone out of its cradle. "Yes?"

We could hear Mikhail's excitement. "Is snow, Commander Pul. Just as will be you said."

"Excellent. Return immediately."

"It is snowing in Hollywood," Pul told Bahadur. "His Supreme Eminence will be pleased. I'm leaving now to bring him back here for finalization of our mutual demands." He swept his index finger at Dr. Weksler, Kevin and me. "Watch them. Closely."

A few minutes later the three of us once again whispered conspiratorially.

Kevin said, "Okay, now's our chance. We've got to figure a way out of this."

"There's only one of them," Dr. Weksler said. "Surely we can overpower him. He's a rebel without a clue."

Bahadur said, "No talking."

Kevin raised his hand. "May we pass notes?"

Bahadur seriously pondered the request and then, without strong conviction, said, "No... think me not."

Turning to his PC, Kevin quietly entered a line of code. *Bahadur = Not Human.*

He then clicked to select the preprogrammed commands for *Quick Launch* and *Spanish.*

The satellite phone rang. Relaxing his guard, Bahadur answered. "Is Bahadur. — Yes, Mikhail. — Commander Pul here is not." Their conversation continued as Kevin's ROVER rolled slowly toward Bahadur and stopped in front of him. Bahadur told Mikhail to hold on. Suspiciously, he looked over at the awesome threesome and saw us nonchalantly doing nothing. Curious, he leaned in to get a closer look at ROVER.

With a big video smile, ROVER said in its cute squeaky voice, *"Como se llama usted?"*

Surprised and puzzled, Bahadur answered, "Bahadur."

ROVER squeaked, *"Adios Amigo."* A can of Iced Mocha launched at flank speed into the Billy goat's forehead. He fell to the floor, out cold.

On the satellite phone we heard Mikhail saying, "Hello? Hello? *Hola?* Oopsy. Hello?"

We ran to make our escape. Ox paused and grabbed the SatPhone. Imitating a computerized voice phone greeting, he said to Mikhail, "You have reached the S.O.L. embassy. Please listen carefully because our menu has changed, and you are not too bright. For Professor Commander Pul, use 'A'. For bombings and other public relations activities, use 'B'. For Spanish, use *Dos Equis.*"

We scrambled out to the driveway and into the van. Kevin already had the ignition key in his hand as he reached for the steering wheel. It wasn't there.

"What the hay?"

We looked through the windshield and saw FCC Under-Assistant West Coast Field Director Leonard Ostermann standing in the driveway. He smirked and held up a steering wheel puller and lock plate tool in his left hand. The van steering wheel dangled from his right forearm. Although Leonard's tough-guy sneer didn't work, he had perfected looking stupidly smug. He twirled the steering wheel on his arm like a small hula hoop. It hit him in the side of his head and knocked him down.

"Ow!"

Kev threw open the van door, yelling, "You freaking federal fool." He jumped on Ostermann, grappling for control of the steering wheel. They both sprawled down onto the cement driveway as Kevin shouted, "Give me that wheel!"

"Will not. You are not getting away this time."

Ox roared, "Give it to me."

Ostermann yelled, "This is bodily assault on a federal fool. No, I mean, ossifer. No, I mean... I order you to cease and desist right now."

Bahadur arrived and angrily pointed his MP5 at them, saying "You are big in the trouble." He patted his MP5 lovingly and, in his strange accent, attempted an even stranger Cuban accent, quoting (sort of) Al Pacino: "Say hello to my friend of the little."

Kevin grabbed Ostermann's throat with both hands and looked up over his shoulder at Bahadur. "You can shoot me if you want, but just let me choke him first."

Machine pistol persuasion raised Kevin and Leonard to their feet. Ostermann looked Bahadur up and down with a sneer and said, "And just who are you supposed to be?"

Remembering Leonard from the mall parking lot, Bahadur smiled with evil in his eyes and said, "It is monkey brain."

49

STILL IN THE CAVE LAB — FORTY MINUTES LATER

"**I** demand to speak with your supervisor," Leonard Ostermann shouted.

Mikhail had returned from the Chinese blizzard, joining Bahadur in guarding us—at a safe distance—while awaiting the arrival of Pul and His Supreme Eminence. Ostermann's feet were zip tied to a chair as punishment for being obnoxious. Unfortunately, he was not tongue tied.

Lenny stood up and bellowed, "How long must I wait?" Forgetting his feet were tied to the chair, he took an angry step forward and tripped flat onto his face.

"What's the matter with him?" I said. "It's the third time he's done that."

Kevin said, "He's a little slow on the download."

Dr. Weksler nodded. "I'd say he's about one pouch short of a kangaroo."

Bahadur and Mikhail picked Ostermann up and sat him back in his chair. "You are giving me the ache of the head," Mikhail said.

Bahadur said, "Do that again and I will shoot you a little bit."

Kevin said, "Do it again Lenny."

"Oh, you're gonna pay," Ostermann said, "you... you... you prickly, pernicious, Pirate."

Bahadur moaned, "What with you two it is?"

Kev said, "He took my steering wheel."

Ostermann stuck his tongue out at Kevin.

Kevin smiled at Leonard and said a prissy, "Yo. Ho. Ho."

That did it. Leonard heatedly waved his finger at the Ox man. "I'm gonna bring you down." Furious, he stood up to lunge at Kevin, and fell on his face again.

Pointing the barrel of his FAMAS at Ostermann, Bahadur said to Mikhail "Him we will drag now." To Ostermann he said, "That it is. I now will shoot you a little bit." He and Mikhail began dragging Leonard away, still tied to the chair.

"What, wait, no," Ostermann said, finally able to recognize peril before it killed him.

Kevin interrupted the flow. "Hey, hold up there, guys—trust me on this—you don't want to go off shooting somebody without getting the blessing of his supreme whatever." Kev pointed at Ostermann. "Look, I know this guy is an arrogant paper pusher. But... Bahadur, Mikhail, listen to me." Kev proudly puffed out his chest. "He's a United States Government arrogant paper pusher. You don't want to mess there. Our government loves these guys. We collect arrogant paper pushers. It's kind of a federal hobby. We've got tons of them."

Ostermann nodded in enthusiastic agreement. "Yes, it's true."

The big red door klunked open. Bahadur and Mikhail dropped Leonard on his back (still tied to the chair) and dashed for the door, safeties off, hoping to shoot something. Professor Pul entered, wearing a 1930s Spanish fascist military uniform, similar to Generalissimo Franco, but with more medieval splendor, and a red sash. He really enjoyed gloriously riding his bi-polar express. Pul loudly announced, "Prepare for the arrival of the rightful heir to the combined thrones of Garduña and Aztlán... the Czar of Liberty... His Supreme Eminence."

Wearing his white suit and red sash, his overweight Supreme Eminence dawdled in. He looked sleepy, his "regal aura" being closer to that of an elderly accountant who didn't want to go to work, and dressed funny

Regardless, the scummy bears, Bahadur and Mikhail, bowed their heads reverently, both saying, "Your Supreme of the Eminence."

He acknowledged their supplication with a casual wave. "Yes, yes. Fine, fine."

From the far west side of the lab, where he still laid on his back, tied to a chair, Leonard Ostermann shouted, "So who's this clown?"

* * * * *

Pul sent Bahadur off to run an errand. Ostermann, still zip-tied to the chair, now had duct tape across his mouth. Thankfully.

A klaxon sound effect accompanied by a severe weather alert graphic on Channel Eight had us all riveted to the video monitors. Quirky weather guy Dr. Gil hopped and gesticulated as a snowflake appeared above Hollywood on his weather map. Dr. Gil said, "The big story we're following for you continues to be the freak snowstorm in Hollywood. What happened, folks, is a low-pressure system way over on the other side of the globe swooped down over the North Pole and stopped right here above the Chinese Theater."

Anchorwoman Audrey asked, "So, no connection between this snowstorm and that S.O.L. cult threat?"

"Absolutely none. Just a quirk of nature. Our old friend The Pirate is yanking our meteorological chain. I guarantee you there is no such thing as a weather machine. But if you believe in it, give me a call because I will be happy to sell you the bridge to Catalina Island."

Pul, in the command chair, snapped off all TV monitors. "Fools! Those senseless, irresponsible, media fools."

Supreme Eminence yawned. "Oh, sorry. Up late last night watching *The Ten Commandments* on the movie channel. Yul Brynner is awesome." He stretched and stifled another yawn. "So, perhaps there may be no throne after all, Professor Pul? It appears your grand show of power came off as a hoax."

"Power," Pul said, nodding and thinking. "Absolute power. That's the only thing that will grab their attention and make them devoted to me. And... to you... of course." He walked to my station, lifted me above his head and, with his perpetual morning breath, shouted in my face. "What's the most powerful force in nature?"

I was going to say, *your breath*, but thought better of it. Instead, I coughed and timidly said, "A tsunami?"

"A tsunami. Yes!" He tossed me into my chair and turned to Supreme Eminence, seeking accord. "An enormous tsunami will destroy a large part of Los Angeles. That will confirm and authenticate our power."

"Hmm... yes, very well," Supreme Eminence said, then dramatically added, "So let it be written."

Under armed guard, Professor Pul gathered our awesome threesome in a semi-circle. "You heard His Supreme Eminence. You will create a tsunami. NOW."

I said, "But we can't do that."

"And why not? You told me a tsunami is the most powerful force."

"It is, in nature. But not in weather."

"A tsunami is not *weather*," Dr. Weksler said. "We also can't create earthquakes, make volcanos erupt, or turn water into wine. So, don't ask."

Kevin said, "His supreme Eminem here needs to order up something a little less exotic."

Pul flipped all the way to psychotic totalitarianism. "His Supreme Eminence has decreed a tsunami, ergo, you will find a way."

Dr. Weksler, Kevin and I all made eye contact with each other, and nodded in silent resolve. We had already made our decision. We would do nothing more for the S.O.L.

"Even if we could create a tsunami," Dr. Weksler said to Pul, "we will not. You may kill us all right now, if you wish.

Kevin said, "There is no threat that can make us do this. We're done with you."

Pul smirked and said, "Bring it on home, Bahadur."

Bahadur thundered into the lab and tossed two disheveled women down onto the cement floor. Neither could break their falls because zip ties held their wrists behind their backs. They couldn't cry out in pain because duct tape covered their mouths.

The blonde had bruises on her face, arms, and legs, and a black eye. One side of her formerly professional-looking dress had a seam ripped out, and one torn short sleeve dangled from a few threads.

The woman with gray hair had multiple cuts about her arms and face, and a fairly new three-inch gash on her chin, held together with two butterfly bandages.

Dr. Dianne Wright and Dr. Sarah Norton-Weksler had put up quite a fight.

50

JUST A MOMENT LATER

"**I** sense a new spirit of cooperation," Professor Pul said.

Dr. Weksler gasped, wide-eyed, and put his shaking hand to his face, with utter incomprehension.

What is this? Some sick Pul joke? Who is that? Sarah's dead. Dr. Weksler screamed, "Sarah!?"

Pul ripped the duct tape off Sarah's mouth. She moaned and broke down, crying. "Frank, what's going on?"

Dr. Weksler sobbed uncontrollably as he ran, shouting, "No! No! No! No!" He dived into Pul, knocked him to the floor, and began choking him to the death. "You turn her loose, you freaking monster! You turn all of us loose!"

Pul squeaked out, "Bahadur, shoot the old woman, just like I told you to do."

The deafening roar of a long F1 burst made Dr. Weksler stop and jump up in total panic, shouting "Sarah." He turned and saw her standing, alive, no bullet wounds, next to Bahadur who held her securely by her zip tied wrists behind her back. Pul laughed hysterically and Bahadur used the stock of his FAMAS F1 to slam Dr. Weksler in the side of his head.

Ox and I couldn't move without being ripped to pieces by machine guns. Seeing Dianne as a battered captive tore at Kevin's heart. And explained why she had not returned his calls. Dianne cried a bit, mostly from emotional release at seeing Kevin, now believing there might be hope. Seething flowed like lava in the Oxman's eyes.

Nobody rushed to embrace or talk because the machine gun gang did not allow such. No questions allowed. No answers provided. Only the tsunami ultimatum. Pul had leverage.

* * * * *

An hour later Dr. Weksler, Kevin, and I sat, triangulated, in our wheeled red steno chairs with hatred and revenge giving us more energy than a *Venti* espresso six-pack. We needed to keep Professor Pul on an even keel while hoping for a chink in his leverage. That meant we had to move forward with creating his tsunami.

We eventually conceived a feasible plan—utilizing weather—that would probably produce a tsunami. But, at the same time, we didn't want it to actually work. *Kobayashi Maru.* A no-win situation.

Regardless, we would insert an abort code sequence into our tsunami computer programming. The tsunami would automatically cancel itself at the last possible moment, even if none of us were alive to do it ourselves. But then, of course, even the abort code needed its own failsafe mechanism, just in case something *really* weird happened. We would accomplish that by programming an "abort the abort" command and linking it to an existing glowing amber button on the master control board. We had our work cut out for us.

* * * * *

When we finished programming the tsunami, Dr. Weksler stood up and addressed Kev and me. Once again using his hands like a fighter pilot illustrating a dogfight, Dr. Weksler summarized. "So, we'll force an air pocket all the way down from ten thousand feet and have it impact on the surface of the ocean." He made the edge of one hand come down from on high and hit the flat-out palm of his other hand. Then he made the hand that got hit (the "ocean") rise up and tidal wave itself away.

"Like a gigantic belly flop," I said, kinda-sorta excited. I demonstrated with my own hands. "It'll come in at a shallow dive angle and make a humongous wave!"

Dr. Weksler enthusiastically concurred, "Yes. More than sufficient to destroy the coastline."

Ox said, "Gee whiz, guys, this is so fun. You know what? Maybe we all should get together more often and brainstorm mass death and destruction."

"Oh."

"Yeah. Sorry."

Our scientific creativity overcooked our common sense. Geeks on parade.

* * * * *

Professor Pul insisted on having Dianne and Sarah watch our tsunami launch, using their presence as a shield against our rage. Mikhail dragged Sarah Norton over to the black steel circular stairway and hobbled both ankles to the bottom step with nylon zip ties.

Bahadur lecherously grabbed Dianne's waist, pushing and pressing her to the stairway.

"Hey, slob," Dianne said. "Watch your hands. And wash your hands, too." She sniffed the air. "As a matter of fact, you should seriously consider bathing more than once a decade." She pretended to stick her finger down her throat.

Bahadur roughly zip tied both of her wrists to the stairway rail. He amused himself by nuzzling her neck. "Mmmmm."

"You mobile maggot farm!" She squirmed and hit him in the face with her head. His nose released a torrent of blood. She tried to spit in his face, but it landed on his dirty pink tank top.

Bahadur murmured a sensuous, "Ohhh," as he used two fingers to rub the spittle into his shirt while blood from his nose streamed down his lips and grimy chin.

Kevin shouted, "Pul. You're getting your tsunami. Call off el macho piggo."

Pul nodded to Bahadur. He stopped.

Weksler blinked misty, hopeless eyes. Kevin looked like a cool, calm, coiled killer waiting to be sprung.

Dr. Weksler said, "Professor Pul, we think we can give you a tsunami, but we don't know what else might happen. We could be unleashing any kind of unknown deadly, uncontrollable, weather anywhere in the world. We simply do not know what may occur. Please reconsider."

Pul said, "Okay, I'll think about it there I'm done thinking about it."

To clearly emphasize his resolve, he rested the long barrel of his FAMAS F1 on top of my head and shouted, "Give me my tsunami!" He shot a deafening two-second burst (about thirty-five bullets) into the utility space. The hot barrel sizzled hair and scalp on my head, leaving a painful cooked skin stripe.

All rounds thudded into drywall and stuff in the other room. Except one. It zinged off something metallic, hissed back over our heads, ricocheted through a red couch in the coffee corner of the great room, and shot down a framed Kirk Gibson poster which crashed to the cement floor and sprayed shattered glass. Everyone flinched. Except Kevin and Pul.

Well, they certainly aren't blanks this time.

* * * * *

"We're linked," I said. "Paired connection. SatCom Nine."

Pul observed from right behind us, without his weapon. Ten feet away, Supreme Eminence held Pul's FAMAS F1 on us, eliminating any possibility of the formerly awesome threesome overpowering Pul and snatching his gun.

Studying the equipment, Pul said, "Yes... yes, I see the application. I understand the control functions. Continue."

Kevin pulled the T-bar. We heard the ramistat signal. Kev said, "This is not a good career move."

* * * * *

One-hundred-thirty nautical miles west of Malibu, strange, unnaturally occurring winds came together at ten thousand feet above the Pacific Ocean. The accumulated forces plunged to seven thousand eight hundred feet and combined their energy to create a sixteen-mile-long invisible air pocket which split the cloud cover as it shot downward at a precise 18.73-degree angle. Picking up speed exponentially, it broke the sound barrier at thirteen hundred feet with a tooth-rattling sonic boom equivalent to a hundred thunderclaps. Seconds later, the terrifying noise of the supersonic air pocket hitting the ocean surface temporarily deafened all creatures within a three-mile radius. The surface of the ocean indented, forming a trough all the way to the horizon. A monster wave began its brief and violent journey to the coast of Southern California.

* * * * *

The video display map lit up with a dashed line of red rectangular icons out to sea.

I looked at Professor Pul and pointed. "There it is."

Kevin said, "The red rectangles are your tsunami."

Pul immediately asked when it would hit Los Angeles. Dr. Weksler pointed to the digital count-down clock: 00:00:37:00. "Thirty-seven minutes."

"It is done," Pul said. He turned and rejoined Supreme Eminence with a small curtsy. "Your Supreme Eminence... as was your desire... you have a tsunami."

Supreme Eminence spoke dramatically, "So let it be written."

Using his burner phone, Pul called the three major local television news departments, notifying each that the S.O.L. had just launched a tsunami that will destroy the Los Angeles coast. He nodded to Bahadur, who excitedly yanked a combat knife out of his boot and marched to Sarah Norton, his eyes teeming with bloodthirst. Smiling wickedly, he wiggled the terrifying blade in front of her face until she, once again, sobbed in dread. Bahadur really liked torture.

Bahadur cut the zip ties on her ankles. Confused and now free after more than three months of captivity, she turned and ran to Dr. Weksler as he ran to her. They compressed fourteen weeks of grief, sadness, and heartache into multiple hugs, kisses, and hurried conversation flooded with anxiety.

* * * * *

Attempting to address Pul as a "professional peer", Dr. Weksler maintained a semblance of deportment, hiding the rage as best he could. "Professor Pul, I beg you. Stop this tsunami. You cannot possibly comprehend the totality of consequences that will flow from your actions."

"Oh, my good doctor," Pul said. "Your absolutely marvelous naiveté continues to entertain. My comprehension is finely tuned, thank you. I instantly recognized that your Betatron Multiplier, as you and your now slightly bruised, Sarah, demonstrated in Geneva, held such promise, we just couldn't let it end up with all those self-righteous do-gooders."

Dr. Weksler took a reflective pause to reshuffle synapses. With eyes closed, he tilted his head down while a forefinger and thumb stroked the tip of his nose. It took only seconds to assemble the pieces. Opening his eyes, he slowly verbalized his weighty deduction. "You... caused ... the explosion."

"You figured it out," Pul said. "Very good. Yes, I did. I made it go boom." He clapped as he looked about the group, mockingly indicating he wanted everyone to clap for Dr. Weksler. Bahadur and Mikhail clapped with one hand against the stock of their assault rifles, not really understanding why. His Supreme Eminence merely allotted another royal limp wave.

"Yes sirree, I blew everything up, Frank," Pul continued, pointing to the side of his head. "Including my ear. And I blame you because, you are so ignorant of the real world. But, reeelaaax, Frank, it's all good. What's a little ear between friends, huh? I'm sure we'll be able to work everything out to my satisfaction. And, uh... in case you haven't figured it out yet, Sarah was always my insurance policy to keep you in line. Hah! Then, when I added Dr. Dianne to the mix, well... I had batteries in my pocket. Had this been Texas Hold 'em, I'd be an even richer man."

Seeing my and other blank stares, Pul savored his worldly superiority by clarifying his metaphor. "For those less traveled, batteries are a pair of aces—as in double A? — and 'the pocket' means hole cards." He raised both hands as if pistols, pointing at Sarah and Dianne. "Bang! Bang! Hah! You lady docs are my aces in the hole. I can't lose. Do you feel the love?"

Dr. Weksler said, "You really think you can get away with pretending Dr. Norton is dead? She's famous. Somebody will catch on."

"Already got away with it, Frank. A respected Geneva dentist and a Swiss *Canton* (county) medical examiner, both confirmed her death. Both, by the way, now live a very wealthy life-style on the Argentine Riviera." His voice went as chilling as his eyes. "You must all learn to be grateful that I no longer believe in the Third Reich."

51

Pul nodded and Bahadur cut the ties holding Dianne's wrists to the stair rail. Greatly relieved to stand up straight after more than an hour of either being bent over or having both arms stretched above her head (those having been her only choices), she rubbed her wrists and stretched. Then she slapped Bahadur harder than she ever hit anything in her entire life. Bahadur reared back a retaliatory fist but, looked first to Pul who subtly shook his head. "She is an asset."

Dianne and Kevin rushed to hug each other, apologize to each other, and explain to each other. But, no kissing, because they were in a "public" setting and it was only their third date, kinda-sorta. Then, she repeatedly "love-tapped" Kevin around his torso. "You really created a weather machine? One that really works? And you didn't tell me?"

"Well, yeah,"

She looked at me and Dr. Weksler. "And you built it at our university?

I answered, "We did."

She smiled warmly at Dr. Weksler. "So, you're really not just an old looney bird?"

Dr. Weksler said, "Yes. Uh, no. Well... trick question."

"Think of the honor this will bring to the Science Department," she said, "and the prestige for the University."

She paused, finally aware of our alarmed expressions. She leaned back onto the master control console and, with fear-filled eyes, said, "And, you really did launch a tsunami?"

Kevin immediately grabbed her with a full-body embrace, dragging her away from the console and passionately nuzzling her ear while whispering these sweet little words: "Don't touch anything. That amber button on the control board cancels the automatic tsunami abort. No, don't look at it. Just look at me."

Pul said, "Hey you two, why don't you get a room?" He giggled, shrilly. "Oh, that's right, you can't. Because you're my prisoners. Hah!" He sat down in the main console command chair. "Now that post-resurrection social minutiae have concluded, it is time for everyone to watch the next chapter. NOW PLEASE."

Bahadur and Mikhail gathered all of us around the central command arrays and consoles. On every video monitor, Channel Eight co-anchor Audrey Ishimoto referenced the three hundred eighty-five-mile-long coastal section of Southern California overlaid in bright yellow on the telemap. A bold red line blinking offshore represented the tsunami. "Mandatory evacuation is in effect for anyone within seven miles of the coast," She said, anxiously. "You must move inland immediately. All first responders from San Diego to Santa Barbara are on non-stop coastal evacuation duty. Calls to the Pasadena Institute of Technology physics department have gone unanswered. Meanwhile, scientists at Caltech state they have no idea what caused the lethal tidal wave."

The camera switched to Dr. Gil. "Bizarre weather," he said, "Bizarre weather everywhere in the southland. Palm Springs is experiencing a record high temperature of one-hundred-thirty-one-degrees while it is hailing and snowing.

A tornado is currently chewing up the runway at Los Angeles International Airport. All we know for certain, folks, is that none of this unusual weather has been created by that silly weather machine fairy tale. Back to you, Robert..."

Anchorman Robert Putnam's voice and manner supplied needed calm and assurance. "Police from beach cities have moved into downtown Los Angeles, assisting the many thousands trying to escape on foot. You must evacuate now. Remaining in a beach city will put you at great peril. Audrey..."

Audrey wrapped the hard news segment saying, "Please stay tuned for continued updates from Channel Eight, your tsunami station. But right now, we return you to the Dodgers game, in progress. Go Dodger Blue."

On high ground, far from the ocean, Dodger Stadium still had a hot, dry, sunny afternoon in the bottom of the eighth, with a score of thirteen to one, the Dodgers sticking it to the Giants.

As he came out of his wind-up, an ear-piercing thunderclap startled the Giants' pitcher. He threw the ball straight into the ground in front of the mound. A downpour followed, so heavy the catcher could not see the pitcher, and fans couldn't see anything. In less than ninety seconds, water three-feet-deep covered the field.

The TV baseball announcer described the action: "A torrential deluge here at Dodger Stadium has players running for cover. We just looked it up and, this is—officially—the heaviest rainfall in major league history to come in the bottom of the eighth with two outs, a full count, a lefty on the mound, two runners in scoring position, during a day game, prior to the all-star break, with the home team leading by more than nine runs, and neither team having green or yellow in their uniforms."

52

WHUMPA, WHUMPA, WHUMPA, WHUMPA, WHUMPA bellowed in on the Channel Eight live feed from a twin-turbine, Sikorsky MH-60S belonging to Helicopter Sea Combat Squadron HSC-4, the Black Knights, out of Naval Air Station North Island. Assigned to the *Abraham Lincoln* (CVN-72), the Black Knights successful *Operation Iraqi Freedom* deployment, had only just ended in May of 2003. Now they wondered how to battle deadly weather. California Governor Gray Davis, who would soon be replaced by movie star Arnold Schwarzenegger in a recall election (only in California) had requested military reconnaissance of the tsunami. The big war machine flew out of North Island fully locked and loaded.

With a cockpit view of the helicopter projected full screen behind her, Channel Eight's Audrey Ishimoto addressed the bird's commander. "Lieutenant Franklyn, please bring our viewers up-to-date."

Lt. Franklyn shouted into his helmet microphone. "Yes, ma'am. Present position is seventy-five miles due west of Redondo Beach. We're flying in reverse, so we can keep an eye on the tidal wave and send telemetrics back to the base."

The TV picture changed from an inside-the-cockpit shot to a full-screen view of the raging tsunami. Lt. Franklyn resumed, "This puppy is movin'. We're clockin' it at one hundred and nineteen knots. That's a hundred and thirty-seven miles per hour. Presently, about seventy feet tall. Never seen a wave like this one, ma'am."

Anchor Audrey said, "Thank you Lieutenant Franklyn."

Briefly back on screen, Lt. Franklyn nodded, "It is our honor ma'am. Thank you."

The real-time video behind Audrey switched to a Pacific Coast map with the yellow evacuation zone and the blinking bold red line. Uneasily, she said, "Authorities calculate the crushing wave's height will be one-hundred-and-forty-feet when it hits land, with a speed of one-hundred-and-eighty-miles per hour." Audrey tossed it to Robert Putnam with a nod.

Mr. Putnam, the pinnacle of L.A. broadcast journalists, continued the hard news saying, "Escaping from the City of Los Angeles has become more difficult as this frightening Channel Eight telecopter view demonstrates." The TV screen filled with video of downtown L.A. covered by fog so thick only the tops of tall buildings could be seen. "Emergency personnel are directing civilians out of the fogbound area. A most difficult situation for all. Audrey, I understand you have another update for us?"

In a close-up, Audrey Ishimoto touched her fingers to her left ear. With a big smile and a sparkle in her voice (indicting she was already in on the "fun" news) she said, "Our roving reporter, Bambi, has the latest for you on that big ice cube in Studio City."

A full-screen shot showed Bambi standing in front of an odd-looking used car lot. She smile-stared into the camera for two seconds, then chuckled and said, "Audrey, we are live here at A-1 Ace Used Autos on Ventura Boulevard."

The camera zoomed in past Bambi and focused onto the car lot. Cars, signs, and the sales office could be seen through a translucent two-story block of ice with perpendicular sides and right-angle corners. "This gigantic ice cube started only twenty minutes ago. It is growing fast, but only vertically. Nobody knows why, Audrey, but the owner of the car lot, Mr. Ace Feinstein, tells me that when this is all over, he will have some *cool* deals for people with *cold* cash." She smiled broadly. The video of Bambi shrunk to a square between Audrey and Robert. Bambi continued to smile in her video square.

Audrey said, "Thank you, Bambi for that *chilling* report." She smiled large.

Bambi held her smile for two more seconds until she heard Audrey's retort, and then wrapped with, "And, folks, don't forget your mittens." She maintained her plastic smile until her video dissolved.

Robert Putnam looked disapprovingly to his left at Audrey Ishimoto as the camera caught him wondering how his serious journalistic career got hijacked by primetime inanity. He turned to the camera and said, "Now be sure to stay right here with us because, after the commercial break, we will continue to follow this developing story for you with our exclusive Channel Eight tsunami-cam."

The TV camera caught him shaking his head before the Director flipped to commercial.

* * * * *

Professor Pul loved to talk. His constant babble allowed him to constantly hear his own voice constantly sharing his own wisdom. Worse than Leonard Ostermann.

Several times Pul shared with us that, in addition to Khadafy, he had great love and respect for Joseph Stalin, Fidel Castro, and Saddam Hussein. At the time of our captivity by Pul, the brief twenty-one-day *Operation Iraqi Liberation* had already succeeded, although Hussein's whereabouts were still unknown. Several months later, in December, Hussein would be found hiding in a hole, like all rodents. 2003 really was an extraordinary year.

Professor Pul especially adored Saddam Hussein's creative political use of ordinary devices, his favorite being Saddam's portable tree branch chipper, reserved exclusively for use by Saddam's royal guard. The one hundred sixty-five horsepower diesel engine, triple bed knives, three-quarter inch thick double-sided chip blades, and custom-made twenty-four by eighteen-inch feeder opening, made it the largest chipper in all the Middle East.

Two-wheeled, making it easily transportable to any location of discontent, citizens could be publicly and horrifically dispatched onsite by feeding them into the mulching machine. Should one be fortunate, Saddam would consent to letting him or her go in headfirst.

Pul's kind of guy.

"I know that there are scores of people plotting to kill me, and this is not difficult to understand. After all, did we not seize power by plotting against our predecessors? However, I am far cleverer than they are."

— Saddam Hussein

In Dr. Weksler's cave lab, we were all still gathered around the master control station, watching Professor Pul become increasingly consumed with his own supremacy. He especially relished the phrase, Master Control. "Once again we shall rule over Aztlán," he said, while scrutinizing and affectionately patting the exotic equipment. "My army. My power. My rules."

Kevin interrupted his reverie. "Uh, your highness... your evilness... your eliotness... please don't touch anything. Believe me Professor Pul, this is not a good time for on-the-job training."

Dr. Weksler stepped forward and tried to physically prevent Pul from touching the controls. Pul rose up in anger, using the full momentum of his body weight to knock Dr. Weksler off his feet and send him flying into my console. Pul shouted, "Stay back. I understand your technology."

Dr. Weksler crashed hard. The corner of my console gouged a gash in his forehead. Sarah screamed and ran to cradle him.

Pul looked down at Sarah Norton and the limp Dr. Weksler with disgust, like Hitler on meth, impatient to build more showers. "You naïve, foolish, seasoned citizens. Nobody needs you anymore." He savagely kicked the unconscious Dr. Weksler in the left hip, causing an intertrochanteric fracture. Fortunately, the bone cracked almost four inches away from the joint, which did not affect femoral artery blood flow. Not life-threatening. Yet. But, upon regaining consciousness (if he ever did) Dr. Weksler would suffer physical debilitation and widespread agonizing pain.

Pul purposefully and knowingly, reached up and pushed the small amber button embedded high up on the vertical gauge panel. That deleted the tsunami abort programming. Quick as a click. The enormous killer wave would continue unstoppable, toward Los Angeles and its eighteen million souls. Pul had learned more from watching us than we ever imagined.

"There is no greater danger than underestimating your opponent."

— Lao Tzu

"Isn't my technology amazing," Pul said. "Just think of it, we can all sit here together in air-conditioned comfort and watch millions of people drown on TV. Or watch the world capitulate to the S.O.L. Or watch all of you die in a mass suicide because you were so depressed about losing your jobs at Pas Tech." He shrugged. "Whatever comes first."

53

I seriously believe Steve Austin inspired both Kevin and me to pursue the physical sciences. A hit weekly TV show for five primetime seasons, *The Six Million Dollar Man* starred Lee Majors portraying astronaut Steve Austin who, following what should have been a deadly crash, had both legs, right arm, and his left eye replaced with "bionic" implants. We loved that show. Between us, Kev and I had all the action figures. (They were not dolls.)

I didn't know everything the Ox man had done or created in his life because, apparently, such was not authorized. But as I now near the end of chronicling our story—far more than a decade after it happened—I am permitted to tell you this: Kevin became intrigued when he learned of deaf talk radio star Rush Limbaugh undergoing surgery for implantation of the "Cochlear" hearing device in 2001. Kev had no hearing problem, but apparently had occasional need for undetectable, rudimentary communication while embroiled in a difficult situation. So, he created his own bionic accessory.

Implanted within his skull through the ear canal via micro-robotic surgery, the efficacy of his entire system grew out of Kevin-developed transmissionable plastic-resin components imperceptible to a metal detector. His body's own electrical impulses, naturally generated within the heart's sinoatrial node, powered his micro-miniature implant.

With the Cochlear device as a jumping-off point, Ox created an implant that received covert radio transmissions and converted them to skull vibrations that transferred to his inner ear where he heard them as sound. Although Kevin could receive clearly understood inbound radio communication, his outbound capability in 2003 consisted solely of transmitting clicks.

A jaw clench made a click. Four consecutive jaw clenches in the sequence, left, right, right, left, turned his sub-miniature transceiver on and off. After being activated, a single right-side molar clench produced a right-side click which always meant, *yes*. A single left-side click always meant, *no*. Three left side clicks meant medical response required. In all cases, three consecutive full jaw (both right and left) clenched clicks meant, stat/emergency/now.

Unbeknown to anyone, Kevin had clenched a left, right, right, left sequence to activate his stealth communication, followed by a single right-side jaw clench ("yes") in answer to the query he had just received.

BOUNG! BOUNG! BOUNG! Three loud metallic knocks on the cave's steel door startled everyone. The S.O.L. reacted instantly. Warriors on alert. Their weapons bristled. Professor Pul tightened his grip on his F1 and, using hand commands, dispatched Bahadur and Mikhail to either side of the big red slab of a door, Mikhail with a FAMAS and Bahadur with his personal preference, the SEDENA MP5 machine pistol. A nod sent His Supreme Eminence to relative safety behind a large metal parts cabinet. Pul positioned himself between the cabinet and the door.

Mikhail leaned in, tense, every muscle at attention, ready to shoot anyone as needed (or just for fun). Bahadur grabbed the large metal door handle and gave it a powerful yank, throwing the heavy steel door wide open. With full force, the door hit Mikhail in the middle of his forehead. He flew off his feet backwards. On his way down, the back of his head bounced off the last two steps of the iron staircase and then hit the cement floor. Clank. Clank. Whump.

The door impact sent Mikhail's FAMAS flying out of his hands directly toward Bahadur. Being on alert status, Bahadur instantly ducked. That put his throat at the same height as the flying assault rifle. The stock of the weapon hit Bahadur precisely in the center of his Adam's apple. He went over backwards, clutching his throat. Even his coughing and gagging had a swarthy accent. His MP5 went flying.

Two men wearing government-issue dark suits and sunglasses stood in the now open doorway, looking like a casting call for *Men in Black 5: Direct to Video*. The two strangers momentarily looked down—very puzzled—at Mikhail and Bahadur who were quite busy groaning and gagging.

The two strangers matter-of-factly introduced themselves to Professor Pul. "Good Afternoon. I am Special Agent John Randolph, representing the government of the United States, OTA." (Office of Terrorism Analysis)

"Special Agent Wayne Scott," said the other man. "Our division supports the National Counterterrorism Center in the Office of the Director, Central Intelligence Agency.

Agent Randolph summarized, "A branch... a distant branch... of Homeland Security."

Both men moved their right hands toward their inside suit coat pockets.

Professor Pul pointed his FAMAS at Randolph and Scott. "After you raise your hands, you will make no further movement until you are told to do so."

They raised their hands.

"Just going to provide identification."

"There may be a time for that," Pul said. "We shall see." His hate-filled eyes momentarily glared at Kevin. "We have unpleasant memories associated with providing identification. For now, close the door behind you and come in slowly, moving away from my men."

They prudently moved obliquely forward to the center of the lab.

"Mikhail. Bahadur. Get up. Close the door. Search them."

Bahadur picked up the FAMAS F1 Mikhail had inadvertently thrown at him and held it on Agents Randolph and Scott.

Bahadur patted them down, searched Agent Randolph's nearly-empty briefcase, and announced, "They have no weapons. They're clean."

"Oh, they are very clean," Mikhail said proudly. "I smelled them."

Professor Pul picked up the MP5 and handed it to Bahadur while keeping his FAMAS pointed at Agent Randolph. "Why are you here? What do you want?"

"We are the official U.S. government negotiating team."

Kevin said, "Way fine. We are glad to see you guys."

"Oh, thank you for being here." I said. Reflecting a moment, I asked, "How did you know we were here? Nobody knows we're here."

Agent Scott answered, "We back-tracked the assault weapons stolen in Paris."

Agent Randolph stated officiously, "We know everything, Mr. Spivak."

"You... you even know my name?"

Agent Scott said, "It's our job... horse lips."

"Oh." I sat down, disturbingly impressed.

Kevin gave me a Vulcan salute, saying, "May the horse be with you."

Pul gun-waved the agents to a six-foot-long gray metal table. "Gentlemen, please..."

They cautiously sat in two red chairs at the near end. Agent Randolph placed his briefcase on the table between them. Professor Pul bent at the waist, politely inviting his Spanish counterpart to be seated. Supreme Eminence shuffled to the far end of the table and sat down.

"This is excellent," Pul said. Putting his hands together as if in prayer, he tickled his beard with his thumb tips, and began a conquering dictator dissertation. "The American government recognizes that the S.O.L. is authoritative, unyielding, and all powerful; that our demands for justice are legitimate and manifest; that our authority cannot be surmounted by a mere country; that I... we will not be denied; and that there will be no calm in the universe until I am satiated. So, gentlemen, I... we are ardent to begin negotiations for your capitulation."

Agent-in-charge Randolph pulled out a single sheet of crisp, white paper from his briefcase and quickly reviewed his instructions printed thereon. Looking up at Pul and Supreme Eminence, he announced, "The government of the United States of America denies all your demands."

Pul said, "What?"

Kevin shouted, "What?"

The rest of us joined in with our own incredulous, "What?"

Agent Randolph explained, "It is the position of the United States government not to negotiate such threats."

"Then why are you here?" I asked.

"Because we are the negotiating team."

Kevin put his face in his hands. "But you're not going to negotiate?"

"That is correct."

Agent Scott clarified, "It's our policy."

Kevin ran over to Agents Randolph and Scott. "C'mon guys. This weather machine thing really works. They're going to destroy Southern California."

"At this time," Agent Scott stated, "the U.S. federal government is not prepared to officially recognize the feasibility of the potential existence of a possible weather-controlling device."

Kev said, "Feasibility of the potentiality of a possibility? Do you think you might, maybe, possibly, potentially, feasibly recognize it when a two-hundred-mile-an-hour, ninety-foot-tall wall of water hits L.A.?" He turned to His Supreme Eminence and began talking.

"Look, your Supreme Enema," Kev said, "you'll never get anywhere talking to these starched shorts. Talk to me, not Homeland Stupidity. I've got friends in low places. Let's make a deal."

With a royal wave, Supreme Eminence said, "You may continue."

"Good. Let's do this thing." Kev stuck out his right hand to shake, saying, "My name is Kenneth Tucky. You may call me Ken. I am the C.R.O. for Weksler Laboratories."

Supreme Eminence shook hands, saying, "Thank you Mr. Ken. What is C.R.O.?"

"Chief Ramistat Officer. I have been assigned to assist in your search for a suitable homeland."

"That is good."

"Yeah, I bet it becomes frustrating when you keep losing your foothold in every country where a democracy breaks out. Am I right?"

"Is true."

Kev said, "And these days I know that you're left with fewer and fewer geographic choices because you really don't want to live next door to Al."

"Al?"

"Al Qaeda."

Supreme Eminence nodded. "You are correct—not good."

"Exactly. You don't want terrorists living next-door. They'll steal your publicity. When confiscating real estate, the three most important things for a cult to consider about its neighbors are vocation, vocation, vocation."

"I have heard. Is true thing."

Kevin put his arm around Supreme's shoulder and continued. "So, your Supreme Impotence, what do you think? Where do you want to go?"

"I like Cali. And Fornia."

Kevin took a power stance, putting his hands on his own hips. "Oh, I hear you. But, if you like California, then you really don't want to destroy all those L.A. beach cities."

"No?"

"No. Just imagine what it does to property values when a tsunami moves in next door."

Supreme Eminence twisted his white mustache between his left thumb and forefinger. "Uhm hmm."

"But seriously, Supreme... May I call you Supreme?"

Supreme Eminence nodded.

"Okay, Supreme, let's bottom line this deal. If you agree to spare the California coast, we'll find some great beach property for you somewhere else."

"I am listening."

"Good. First choice—and this is a winner—I've noticed that you like Hollywood movies. Am I right?"

"So, So let it be written."

Kev said, "You guys need an extreme makeover and we've got it for you." He raised up his pointer finger. "One word. One place: Glamis." He spread his hands and gave His Supreme Eminence a wow-how-about-that-look. "Huh?"

Supreme said, "What is a glamis?"

"Glamis is the biggest beach in California. It's south of Palm Springs and north of San Diego. Hollywood has been shooting movies there for a hundred years. *Return of the Jedi, Lawrence of Arabia, X-files, The Scorpion King, Patriot Games...* they were all shot there. Sound good?"

Supreme nodded. "Very good."

"And the best part," Ox continued, "Nobody lives there. So, there's no problem with changing its name from Glamis to whatever you want. You could even give your homeland a good cult-sounding name, like... Gross-icky-stan." Kev flitted his eyes between Supreme and Pul. "Hey, you know what? If you two have a sibling rivalry thing happening here, we could even turn Glamis into two countries, side-by-side. Huh? Think of it... Hurt-so-covina and Hurt-so-west-covina."

His Supreme Eminence liked the plan so, Kevin went for the close. He stared from imaginary horizon to horizon and spread his hands magnanimously. "Just imagine... thousands of square miles of pristine beach. No ocean to mess it up. Unlimited sun, all day, every day. Nobody to interfere with your terrorist training camps. Absolute paradise."

"No ocean?"

"Oh no, no ocean. An ocean would spoil it," Kev said, "But just think of all that sand. You'll love it. It's like Iran, but without oil and atomic energy."

His Supreme Eminence gave it serious contemplation.

Addressing everyone in the room, Kevin said, "His Supreme Enemy needs a moment to think about this golden real estate opportunity. And I know what we can do while we're waiting— let's just have a quick public opinion poll about Iran." He went into his TV game show smiling announcer voice. "As you know, at this very moment, right now, in the ground, under their own country, Iran is sitting on a thousand-year's supply of oil. So—show of hands—how many of you truly believe Iran needs to develop peaceful atomic energy to keep their lights on? Hands? Hands? Anybody? Nobody? Okay... survey shows: Atomic bombs."

Supreme Eminence decided. "We want ocean."

"Understood. Don't worry, Preemie. We will find you some ocean property. But, listen... we need to stop that tsunami because it is really gonna tick somebody off. Oh, I got it." He snapped his finger and pointed at Supreme Eminence. "Miami Beach. Huh? Is that the ticket or what? Yep, that's it. Beautiful ocean. We put all your people up in a nice condo complex. Beach... bingo... bikinis. No strings. Well... string bikinis... string cheese... string you along."

Supreme Eminence really liked that possibility.

Agent Wayne Scott had heard enough. He interrupted, challenging Kevin. "Just what do you think you're doing?"

Kevin said, "Saving the lives of millions of innocent people."

Agent Scott said, "You don't have authority to do that."

Kevin cocked his head. "I need permission to save millions of lives?"

Agent-in-charge John Randolph laughed. "Well, duh."

Agent Randolph addressed Supreme Eminence. "There is no deal."

Supreme Eminence shrugged and walked away.

Kevin confronted Randolph and Scott. "I can't believe you guys. He was buying the package."

Through clenched teeth Agent Scott spoke in a kinda-sorta stage whisper. "We don't need your help. We are in complete control of the situation."

The Ox man finally had a revelation of understanding. He slapped his forehead and spoke to Randolph and Scott in the same kind of whispered voice. "Oh, I get it now. I'm sorry. You didn't come here all alone. You guys aren't complete morons. You've got the marines out there surrounding the place, right?"

"No. We are totally alone."

Agent Scott looked around warily. "This negotiation is a top-secret event. It never happened."

Kev said, "Okay. Now I understand. You _are_ complete morons."

54

Pul moved all of us—Dr. & Mrs. Weksler, Kevin, Dianne, Agents Randolph and Scott, me, and Leonard Ostermann into the storeroom for safe keeping. Thankfully, they didn't remove the duct tape from Leonard's mouth. They did zip tie his wrists to the chair arms, just to be sure he couldn't go crazier. Bahadur and Mikhail stood guard outside the oversized double-hung Dutch door, with the top half of the door open, and their magazines full.

In great pain, a terminally sad Dr. Weksler slumped on one of his red chairs. Sarah, beside her husband, tended to him and prayed.

Yeah, like that will solve the problem.

In my opinion, we didn't need a prayer as much as we needed a machine gun.

Kevin said, "I had him in the palm of my hand. Then—boom—the CIA called the game. Whatcha say, Frank, when we get out of this, we send a hailstorm to the Company picnic?"

Dr. Weksler didn't smile. "We're not going to get out of this, Kevin. And it's all my fault."

"What kind of talk is that? This is no time to give up."

"You are correct," Dr. Weksler said. "The time to give up was long ago." A tired breath escaped. "I only wanted to help the whole world, but I never looked at the world around me. All I did was hurt people I love."

"Buwaaant! Wrong answer," Kevin said. "You saved the world once. You can do it again. Your wife loves you. Theo idolizes you. And as for me... since hanging with you, I've actually become more ree... ree..." (Kev hated the "R" word but finally managed to spit it out.) "...responsible. And... ree, ree..." (That other "R" word) "... reliable."

Dr. Weksler cupped his hand over a faint smile. His eyes glistened.

Huddled right beside them, I said, "He's right Frank. No regrets." I turned to Kevin. "Ox man, you know how I've always complained about all those lousy, rotten things you've made me do over the years?"

"Yep, I do."

"Well, I'm an adult. I didn't have to participate. I think maybe complaining has just been part of my fun. It's been a pretty good ride, buddy. I forgive you."

Kev said, "Really? Even the jelly roll incident?"

"No."

It being self-evident that we would have to fight our way out of our situation. Kevin automatically took the mantle of leadership, saying to Dr. Weksler. "I know we're not chemists, but do you have any laboratory glassware?"

"Well... back in the early days, I had a Schlenk line over there in the corner. There's probably still a few Beral transfer pipettes left, maybe a beaker."

"Any of it plastic?" Kev asked.

"No, I only used borosilicate glass."

"Okay. We'll just have to be careful. Any tubing?"

"Uh, no tubes. There's a glass funnel with a three-inch stem."

"What's the stem bore?"

Dr. Weksler looked at his thumb and index finger as he spread them to recall the diameter. "Three-quarter inch."

"That'll have to do. Dianne, Mrs. Weksler, can you gather those and have them ready, please?' They nodded.

Ox went to the open top of the Dutch door, looked back and forth at Bahadur and Mikhail, and said, "Hi guys. Gotta talk to the boss." He shouted, "Hey Mr. Commander Professor Pul sir. Okay if I put wheels on the Norton Chamber?"

Pul looked back from the large lab monitor where he and Supreme Eminence watched the Tsunami progress, and said, "Now, why would you do that?"

"To make it portable, your supreme professorness, so I'll be prepared for your next assignment."

Pul said, "Excellent decision boy scout. You may have a future after all."

Kev added, "And we can all ride it like a big skateboard when we escape."

"Hah! Of course, you can." Pul laughed his way back to Channel Eight tsunami coverage.

"Theo, you and the non-negotiation team take the castor wheels off that media cart over there and install them under the Norton Chamber."

Kev explained to us that a verbal signal for a team to jump into action is a trigger word. He decided, and we all felt confident that "Trigger" would be an easy-to-remember trigger word.

Sticking his head out the open half-door again, Ox shouted, "Please excuse me again, Professor Pul, sir. Permission to speak freely."

Pul and His Supreme Eminence smiled at each other and swiveled their red chairs to face the storeroom door. Pul said, "What is it now boy scout?"

"Me and my buds want to pray for deliverance from this prison. You okay with that?"

Pul and Supreme both laughed hysterically. "Well, don't count on a miracle from that pacifist God of yours. Hah! He shrugged. But, hey, whatever blesses your messes. "

Even though I knew the old saying, 'There are no atheists in foxholes', everybody wanting to pray still surprised me. I rolled my eyes. "OMG. I'm surrounded by Bible-thumpers."

Dr. Weksler said, "I think you're right, Theo. I believe you are surrounded with Bible-thumpers precisely for this very moment."

"Seriously? I haven't prayed since Vacation Bible School when I was five."

"This won't hurt a bit," Kevin said. "Promise. I'll do the heavy lifting."

He reached out his hands to Dianne and Dr. Weksler. Sarah lovingly took her husband's hand. Reluctantly, I held Dianne's. We all closed our eyes.

We all opened our eyes when we heard unintelligible mumbling. Looking toward the noise, we saw Leonard Ostermann wagging his head and wriggling. His mouth still duct-taped shut, he could only mumble in a pleading way, with soulful eyes.

Kevin said, "Lenny? You want a piece of this?"

Ostermann nodded.

We all moved to Leonard, whose wrists were still zip-tied to the chair and let him awkwardly join in the hand holding.

Nobody had any inclination to remove the duct tape from his mouth. He could pray silently.

Special Agents Randolph and Scott joined our circle, which was now, due to intrusion by shelving and equipment, an acute irregular polygon.

We all closed our eyes and bowed our heads.

I can't believe I'm doing this.

The Ox man prayed, "Father God, you have promised that when two or three are gathered in your name, you will be with them. Well, here we are Lord. Thank you for joining us to provide comfort and courage during our storm. You know the beginning from the end, so our situation is not a surprise to you. In the Bible you say, 'knock and the door will open.' Well, Lord, we are really knocking. We say these things in the name of your son, Jesus Christ."

Everybody said, "Amen." Including me. It felt good, I guess. In a kinda-sorta strange, uncomfortable, foxholish way.

55

"What's going on here!"

In the great room, every light on every console rapidly flashed off and on. Every gauge fluctuated wildly.

Professor Pul shouted again, "What is going on!? What is happening? Weksler! Get out here right now."

In our storeroom prison cell, Dr. Weksler's eyes twinkled. A wry smile emerged. He stuck his head out the open top half of the storeroom door and shouted, "Good God! It's the Zambini effect!"

Not understanding Dr. Weksler's statement, I softly said, "The Zambini effect?"

Kevin made the fingers of both his hands into circles and stacked them on his head like hair curlers. He tossed me a look. I caught it.

I screamed in pretend horror. "Oh. Zambini. Bad. Aiieee!"

Kevin shouted, "Dreadful!"

Limping from significant pain, Dr. Weksler left the storeroom and rush-hopped to the main console. In a well-simulated panic, he shouted, "Professor Pul, I am sorry. I should have anticipated this. Kevin, take the bridge. Theo, the crypto-analog module."

We rushed to our standard posts, creating a splendid sense of danger which felt so real I scared myself. Bahadur and Mikhail stood erect and threatening, on either side of central control with their FAMAS F1s at the ready.

Dr. Weksler stood right beside Pul, who sat on one of the wheeled red chairs. With his bloodied hip, Dr. Weksler bumped Pul aside and gasped in severe pain, slightly ashen. "For God's sake man, get out of our way. This is serious."

Pul rolled his red chair a couple feet to his left.

I shouted, "Shield your eyes."

Kevin shouted, "Hold your breath."

Rapidly developing his own panic mode, Pul's eyes widened and he looked from station to station as he once again said, "What's happening?"

Dr. Weksler said, "We must disengage the current power structure. It's deadly."

"What?" Pul said.

Bahadur shouted, "Oh no."

Mikhail shouted, "*Oh Dios mío.*"

Kevin shouted, "Lions and tigers and bears and other football teams!"

BAM! CLANG! The huge red steel door flew open. Ms. Zambini stormed in with the metal curler pyramid on her head. Highly irritated by all the illegally parked vehicles on and around Dr. Weksler's driveway she shouted, "That's it, Weksler. You're outta here."

With the unholy Garduñas, surprised, distracted, and totally off-guard, Kevin clicked his computer mouse. A full-screen video of Trigger reared up and whinnied on every video monitor. Kevin shouted, "Trigger!"

He leapt onto his console for a nanosecond and then, with his strong legs, launched himself horizontally at Bahadur. Right on target, Kev's three stiff fingers at the end of a professional grade football stiff-arm went into Bahadur's neck just below and to the right of the larynx. Bahadur stitched a dotted line of automatic fire up the red metal door and into the two-story high ceiling as he fell sideways to the floor, bleeding from the throat. Totally out of the fight.

At the same moment, Ms. Zambini screamed and tried to retreat out the door, but it had closed, the lock mechanism hopelessly jammed by an imbedded and smashed 5.56 caliber from Bahadur's FAMAS F1. She dropped to the floor and crawled to cover in the nearby storeroom.

At the same moment, Dr. Weksler stepped on the small height adjustment platform of Professor Pul's red steno chair and put all his weight on it. The seat instantly dropped eighteen inches. Another extremely painful hip bump from Dr. Weksler sent Pul and the unstable four-legged chair flying over backwards. Pul's head hit the cement floor like a melon, eyes rolling back into his head. Out cold.

At the same moment, I put my hands on the six-feet-tall, now wheeled, Norton Chamber and ducked my head below the top of its clear Glasonate panels. Time for me to be fearless. Kevin calculated—but could not guarantee—that the Glasonate would be bullet-proof when shot by a FAMAS F1 in close proximity. If I was to be killed, it would be while trying to save my friends. I pushed the Norton Chamber toward Mikhail as fast as I possibly could. Still, he had enough time to point his FAMAS at me and fire.

Terrified by the ricochets flying back at him off the Glasonate, Mikhail stopped firing and let go of his FAMAS a half-second before it blew apart. That saved his fingers. Instead of the specified and more expensive, French steel-case SS109 cartridges, the S.O.L. used inexpensive standard NATO cartridges which, as often happens, caused a blowback pressure malfunction due to the F1's cheap construction.

In addition to torso injuries from the exploding FAMAS shrapnel, Mikhail took three ricochet rounds, two in his right thigh and another in the left shoulder. I smashed the Norton Chamber into him at full speed. He collapsed to the concrete, his injuries instantly debilitating.

All the Glasonate panels spider-webbed and crashed to the floor in a thousand pieces. Thank God they held together as long as they did. *Odd. Why do people like me thank someone they don't believe in?*

I turned to see who else I might need to fight to save Los Angeles.

At the same moment, His Supreme Eminence, seated on a red loveseat in the coffee corner, calmly observed bodies flailing and flying. Agent Scott approached him, reading from a three-by-five card. "I am required to inform you that actions occurring in this event are neither mandated by nor reflective of United States posture in this specific situation and are not to be regarded as an act of aggression."

Supreme Eminence nodded and smirked, haughtily.

"Furthermore," Agent Scott continued, "you should know that as a representative of the United States agency known by the acronym, CIA, I am forbidden by federal law to conduct covert or paramilitary operations on United States soil."

Supreme Eminence smirked again, knowing he wouldn't be touched by the politically correct Americans.

Kevin yelled, "Hey Scotty. When the swamp scum made this lab their embassy, it became foreign soil. You may kick his Supreme Arrogance in his big fat *Aztlán*."

Agent Scott instantly rammed the professionally hardened heel of his left hand onto the side of Supreme's head. The head snapped to the right and Agent Scott met it full force with the hardened heel of his right hand. A double-tap knockout.

Not-so-Supreme Eminence landed on his substantial belly and lost his lunch. Agent Scott secured Supreme's wrists behind his back and hobbled his feet with ubiquitous nylon ties.

Scott shouted to Kevin, "Sir! Thank you! Sir!"

Damage to the tracheobronchial tree, essentially the windpipe and associated plumbing, is medically annotated as TBI (Tracheobronchial Injury) and is usually the result of trauma to the neck. That's why a "clothesline tackle" (outstretched arm in front of a runner's neck) is a serious personal foul in the NFL, accompanied by a serious financial penalty. Pro football Hall-of-Famer Dick "Night Train" Lane was so feared for his clothesline tackles (prior to it being banned by the NFL) that sports reporters often referred to the tackle as a "Night Train Necktie".

In the event of severe penetrating trauma just below the voice box, possible complications of TBI include *death* (which Kevin would not inflict); *brain damage* (which Kevin also would not do, though in the case of Bahadur it would not be noticeable); and *oxygen deprivation resulting in unconsciousness*. That last medical complication being Kevin's goal, is why he pulled his punch. The Ox man could have easily landed a death blow. He chose not to do so. However, as Kev feared might happen, he punctured the thin, undernourished and unhealthy epidermis of Bahadur all the way into the windpipe. Without a clear pathway for oxygen flow, Bahadur would die from asphyxiation.

Kevin shouted, "Dianne, piping please. Need it now, or we're gonna lose the goon."

Dianne, ahead of the game, had already bravely rushed out of the storeroom. "You got it," she said, handing Kevin the glass funnel. Kevin stuck the three-inch stem into the hole in Bahadur's neck while she secured it in place with nature's most perfect accessory, duct tape.

Dr. Weksler turned toward the storeroom door and said, "All clear." He gave a relieved come-to-me wave, and Sarah arrived with happy tears.

From the storeroom, Special Agent John Randolph thinly shouted, "Major Oxley. Injuries, sir."

Puzzled, we all looked at Kevin. For a fleeting moment he appeared displeased. One breath later, his composure regained, he handed a FAMAS to me and another to Dr. Weksler, saying, "Watch the slime. I'll contact MC." (Medical Corps) While on the run, he clenched his left jaw three times. Kev code for *MC required.* In a corner of the storeroom, he found Agent Randolph lying in a pool of blood at the foot of circular metal stairs that went up to the catwalk. Two stray bullets had gone through Agent Randolph's left lung, inferior lobe. Agonizing, yes. But, a few inches higher and he's already dead. One counts one's blessings.

Kev gave a reassuring nod to Leonard Ostermann, still trapped in a chair with duct tape over his mouth. He didn't have time to deal with Lenny, so he left him as he found him... quiet and unable to annoy. He then set about providing comfort and lifesaving first aid to the wounded agent. Hopefully, help would arrive before Randolph drowned in his own blood.

Meanwhile, in the great room, we were all relieved and thrilled to be alive. I shouted, "We did it."

Dianne said, "Thank God."

Dr. Weksler said, "Amen to that. Game over. The home team won."

Professor Pul jumped up and grabbed Sarah while pulling an MP5 machine pistol out of his rear waistband, from under the shirt. Holding the weapon to Sarah's head, he backed away.

"Reports of the visiting team's loss have been greatly exaggerated," he said. "Ladies and gentlemen, the game has just gone into sudden death." He glanced toward Dr. Weksler and with a crazy smile said, "Huh? Good sports metaphorical double entendre, right? Sudden death? Get it? Hah!"

His left arm tightly around Sarah's neck, he backed all the way to the whirling generator in the floor, keeping her as a shield between us and him. "Gentlemen lay down your guns and kick them over here to me. Thank you very much. Now, Dr. Norton," he said, "please undo the cage."

Sarah replied, "So this is how your benevolent totalitarianism will function, Professor Pul? Murdering defenseless old women?"

Pul slapped her viciously, reopening the cut on her cheek. "How dare you call me a murderer? I am NOT a murderer. If you call me a murderer again, I will kill you."

The short, defiant, gray-haired Dr. Sarah Norton said, "And if I choose not to open the screen door?"

He rolled his eyes, shook his head, and exhaled with a big cartoony show of exasperation. "Then I will shoot your husband and your friends, and you can watch them wriggle and moan and die before I shoot you. Okay?" He violently jerked her to the large hinged screen door in the generator cover. "Now open the cage, female."

Keeping Sarah as a shield, Pul made her twist awkwardly to reach up and unclasp the red wire mesh door. He threw it open. It noisily bounced a couple of times on the adjoining black iron support bar of the generator's protective screened cover.

Pul said, "Now stick out your pointer finger and stick your hand inside."

"Pul, no."

"Don't."

"Relax," he said to us. "The generator blades are almost two feet away. I wouldn't let her get chopped to pieces ... right now. Unless you force me to." He smiled. Then he shouted into Sarah's face. "Stick your hand inside." With a wincing, frightened grimace she did so, just a bit.

As a tease, Pul bumped her toward the blades. She screamed. He laughed hysterically as he jerked her back out of harm's way.

"Ladies and gentlemen," he announced, "had this been an actual execution, she would have already lost a hand. Well, maybe only a few fingers. I wouldn't push her that hard for the first chop. Please note: as your benevolent and beloved leader, I have now stopped the entire process. In the trade we call it *tormento interruptus*. He laughed again and then had a sudden creative thought. "Ohhh... you know what would be fun? One of you toss a coin to see whether we do heads first or tails first. Huh? Hah!" He went wild-eyed, looking at each of us. "Huh? Huh? Huh?"

"What do you want?" I asked.

Still using Sarah as a shield, he lugged her over to where Bahadur lay gasping on the floor. "The first thing I want," he said, "is to check on my injured man."

Bahadur looked up at Pul, barely able to maintain consciousness while breathing through the glass funnel in his neck.

Professor Pul looked down at his loyal servant and said, "Bahadur, just in case you don't survive, I wish to personally reward you for your performance in the line of duty."

Bahadur's countenance brightened a bit as he looked up at his loveable leader.

Pul said, "Bahadur, your performance has been pitiful." He kicked Bahadur in the neck, breaking the glass funnel that kept him alive. A garbled, bubbly sound oozed out. Pul looked at him and said, "Tsk. That's going to leave a scar." Showing teeth like a mad dog, he shouted at us, "What do I want? I want _my_ country. I want the righteous of the world to be rewarded and respected for rejecting gutter religions. I want President Hussein restored to his rightful throne. I want a country where rubbish the unbelievers call law is superseded by divine wisdom and holiness. A holy land where those who do not love me will suffer deprivation of existence. I want to be the old man of my own mountain..." His voice trailed off when he noticed that all eyes were focused _above_ him.

He looked up just in time to see Kevin swinging toward him on the heavy black chain hanging from the ceiling-mounted track.

Kevin yelled "Son of Trigger!" and kicked Pul in the face with both feet. Full force.

Two of Pul's teeth squirted out. Two streams of blood and drool on his satanic beard below the missing teeth, made him look like a very clumsy vampire. He lost his grip on Sarah. His MP5 fell to the floor. He flew sideways into the generator's protective screening and then noisily bounced off, striking the cement floor face first. More blood.

Kev landed on the floor beside Pul and picked up the dropped machine pistol. He looked down at the nauseating monster with utter revulsion. Keeping his eyes on Pul, Kev nodded toward us and said loudly, "Dr. Weksler, are that chain and those ratchet wheels and that track up there in great condition?"

"They are indeed. I give them a good drink of WD-40 every week."

Kev locked eyes with Pul, shrugged, and said, "Well, there you have it."

Pul didn't understand.

The Ox man explained, "That's why you didn't hear me coming. They didn't make any noise. It was just like you taught us."

Pul still didn't get it. He slowly refocused his eyes in bloody bewilderment.

Kev said, "Take care of your tools and they will take care of you."

"Oh my, Professor Pul," Dr. Weksler said. Pul slowly turned his deformed-jawed, broken-nosed, lacerated-eye, bleeding face to gaze vacantly at Dr. Weksler.

Dr. Weksler pointed at Pul's face, gave him a reassuring nod, raised his eyebrows and said, "Yep, that's going to scar."

56

Within scant minutes, Medical Corps arrived. Nobody died. Due to Kevin's foresight, even Bahadur survived. Injured bad guys went to the nearest trauma center under powerful military guard.

Dr. Weksler refused to leave with the ambulances. Other than a blood-congealing tourniquet dressing and a painkiller cocktail that would not impair faculties, he deferred medical attention. When clearly informed he would hemorrhage to the point of death in ninety minutes, he said, "In *nine* minutes L.A. will be at the bottom of the ocean."

Dianne cut Leonard Ostermann's zip ties and removed the duct tape from across his lips. But only after he repeatedly nodded "yes" to her insistence that he put a cork in it.

I pointed out what Ox and Dr. Weksler already knew. "We can't re-program the tsunami code sequence. There's not enough time."

"Well, when electronics fail," Kevin said, "we go to manual override."

Dr. Weksler, resting his gray stubble chin on his right thumb, contemplated implications as he looked over the top of his reading glasses at Kevin. "Manually?"

I said, "That computer does over two-thousand calculations for target imaging."

No alternative existed.

"I'll get readings," Dr. Weksler said.

Checking telemetric, I confirmed, "Still on SatCom IX."

With a hint of rekindling arrogance, Ostermann, shouted, "Are you using one of my government satellites?"

Kev said, "Yes, Lenny. Thank you very much for helping us save the world."

Ostermann mumbled, "Well, considering circumstances... I suppose I could conditionally authorize that. But no future easement is implied." It didn't really matter what he said anyway because everyone ignored him.

Dr. Weksler announced, "Bearing is 34.01 and 119.35 when the countdown reaches a minute fifty-six and... stretching down to 33.56 and 118.53."

"What's happening?" Dianne asked.

"Not many option plays this late in the game," Kev said. "We're going to attempt a massive lateral vaporization."

The tsunami countdown clock read 2:20. Two minutes and twenty seconds to disaster.

* * * * *

On a bluff above Malibu, Channel Eight's tsunami-cam delivered a frightening scene to the lab's coffee corner hi-def. Beyond the empty beach, far out on the horizon, a two-hundred-foot tall wall of water rushed toward the empty movie star colony and abandoned Pacific Coast Highway. Civil Defense emergency sirens wailed nonstop.

* * * * *

Kevin briskly entered data. Agent Scott watched carefully. The countdown clock read 1:59. Ox gripped the T-bar tightly and said, "I'd hate to see your electric bill next month."

At precisely 1:56 he pulled the T-bar. We watched the master control computer monitor. A narrow blue rectangle icon appeared right on top of the blinking, fast-moving, bold red line. Everything looked perfect.

We all turned to view the Channel Eight live video on the coffee corner TV. A huge splash occurred in the ocean *behind* the tsunami. Close but no cigarillo.

"No."

"No."

"No!"

On the master control monitor, the blinking bold red line of the tsunami moved out from under the blue rectangle. The blue rectangle dissolved. The deadly red line continued marching.

Dianne said to Kevin, "It... didn't work?"

"Just missed."

I began my preliminary panic. "It... it... it... mi - mi - mi – missed?'

Dianne sweetly said, "Oh, Theo, do you need your medication?

Kevin shouted, "New coordinates."

Dr. Weksler said, "Coming up on 34.03, 119.26 and 33.58, 118.44 when we reach a minute nineteen, soonest time."

* * * * *

Only seagulls saw the shocking new ocean view from Redondo Beach Pier. No humans allowed. The "beach" now stretched miles out from what used to be a shoreline. The ocean frantically withdrew as if sucked down a drain. Boats and fish flopped on wet sand which minutes before had been the bottom of the sea.

* * * * *

Tension in the lab flowed like sweat on a Kansas City Fourth of July. Kev finished data entry and looked at the clock. Four seconds left. He took a deep breath and grabbed the T-bar. "I hate deadlines."

Right on schedule, at precisely 1:19, he pulled the T-bar.

We all looked at the Channel Eight television picture. Another long splash *behind* the tsunami. Missed again.

"Oh, my Lord," Dr. Weksler gasped.

Dianne cried, "It's still moving."

Looking at the countdown, I said, "L.A. goes underwater in one minute."

Kevin slammed his fist on the console, got up, walked in a circle, hands on his hips. Head down. Eyes closed. "Dr. Weksler... give me coordinates for precisely two seconds before impact."

A pulsing obnoxious tone shrieked in sync with the countdown clock.

I shouted, "Twenty second warning."

"Frank, where are my numbers?"

Dr. Weksler called out the metrics. "The tsunami will reach 34.08 degrees, 119.09 and 33.64, 118.38 precisely two seconds before impact."

On the coffee corner TV, we all saw the huge wave ready to crush the coast. The water's terrifying roar drowned out civil defense sirens.

At his console, Kev entered data. Last chance.

Dianne squeezed his shoulder. I crossed my fingers. Then, although personally embarrassing, I said a silent prayer. Foxholes can do that to you.

The clock blinked down... 11 seconds... 10... 9... Ox grabbed the T-bar, ready to pull it one last time, two seconds before impact... 8... 7... He took a steadying breath. "Time to rock and roll." Then he pulled the T-bar with four (4!) seconds left on the clock

"Ox! You're two seconds early."

We joined in Kev's penetrating stare at the monitor. Our blue rectangle appeared in *front* of the tsunami icon. Missed again! L.A.'s a goner.

All turned to watch live video on the coffee corner TV. The ramistat-generated invisible air pocket hit the gigantic wall of water dead-center perfect. The tidal wave blew apart heavenward, instantly vaporizing into beautiful, fluffy clouds.

On the master control monitor, the countdown clock and the irritating alarm both stopped with two seconds remaining. The blue rectangle and the blinking bold red line vanished.

Dr. Weksler breathlessly exclaimed, "It worked."

Hyper-stunned, Dianne asked, "How did you know to do it two seconds early?"

Ox smiled. "Remember? Ya gotta lead your target."

Dianne said, "You're wonderf—" She didn't finish the *ful* because she was already kissing Kevin. In public.

He came up for air, put his index finger in front of his lips and said to Dianne, "Don't spread that wonderfulness rumor. You'll ruin my reputa—." She went back to kissing.

Agent Scott grabbed a notepad from inside his jacket and began jotting. "Fascinating. This technology is not covered by any arms limitation treaty."

Dr. Weksler and I exchanged alarmed glances.

Agent Scott, excited as a kid in a combat store, spread his arms magnanimously, and gawked at the three of us with admiration. "We could install one of these in each tactical theater. Think of it... Eastern Europe... Pacific Rim... Western Mediterranean... Persian Gulf..."

Kevin barked, "Lieutenant Scott, this is civilian property. Stand down sailor. Now."

"Sir! Yes, sir!" Scott backed off. He continued scribbling notes.

The ox man hated the thought of losing life-long grant money, but he also knew what had to be done. "We can't let them have this."

Dr. Weksler nodded. "Everything must be dismantled."

"Better do it before any more acronyms show up," I said. "They will confiscate, quarantine, and plausibly deny."

"Just as they did with all of Tesla's research back in forty-three," Dr. Weksler said. He let a huge sigh escape. "We need to start a full deconstruct right now."

I added, "It's gonna take many hours."

Kev's eyes sparked. "Or... we let it destroy itself."

"A discharge reversal?"

Dr. Weksler said, "Cut the power?"

I felt it necessary to clearly state the consequences. "Cutting the power at this energy level, might cause a discharge reversal of extraordinary proportions. The system might implode."

"Not might," Kevin said. "Absolutely. Positively. It *will* implode. And explode. And more things yet unknown." He deliberated a moment, then made a command decision. "Get everybody into the storeroom. Move cabinets, chairs, and shelves in front of you." We followed his instructions while he ran to the workbench at the back wall.

Dr. Weksler shouted, "We don't have time for a proper disconnect. That's heavy usage mainline electrical."

Ox shouted back, "Got it covered." He clutched the long-handled cable cutters, the same ones Dr. Weksler used to break into the impound yard and grabbed a pair of densely insulated, high-tension work gloves. He threw open a section of diamond-pattern treadplate covering the floor channel where the massive power cable trailed out of the generator.

Straddling the channel, Kevin poked the sharp jaws down onto either side of the thick electric cable, and whispered, "Though I walk through the valley of the shadow of death, I will fear no evil." With every bit of his upper body strength, he slammed the cable cutter handles together, brazenly cutting the high-voltage line.

He screamed in grotesque pain, "Awwwwwww!" And then he went silent. The failsafe mechanism brought the generator to a screaming stop as the command console vibrated and radiated sounds not of this world. The ramistat signal abruptly disengaged and, with eerie, banshee noises, the retrogressive beam forcefully withdrew—against its wishes—back into the satellite dish. The steel hatch on the cave ceiling glowed. Cables coming down through the hatch sparked violently.

We all peered into the mammoth shower of sparks and saw Kevin's ferocious, horrifying electrocution. All muscle control vanished. The cable cutters clanged to the concrete floor. His rubber band legs collapsed. His limp body slithered down like an oozing stream of spaghetti. The gloves meant to protect his life burned with nineteen-inch-long flames.

* * * * *

So much for Kevin having not inherited the responsibility gene.

57

The gloves performed to spec. Kev breathed. Struggling to rise, he raggedly said, "Shelter. Now."

Dr. Weksler and I shoved our shoulders under Kev's arms and semi-dragged him into the storeroom. Dr. Weksler groaned, putting more pain and more blood into each step.

Cables everywhere flamed and shriveled like extra-crisp bacon. The command console cabinet wrinkled and then shot out twenty-foot-long sparks ricocheting off cave walls.

Leonard Ostermann, hiding deep in the storeroom, afraid to peek out, bellowed, "Hey, what's the problem?"

Ox weakly said, "Sounds like the carburetor, Lenny."

"Okay," Ostermann said, pleased that everyone knew he was on top of the situation.

A fierce, Tesla-quality electrical storm erupted, crackled, popped, and hurled sparks from one end of the black steel catwalk to the other. All three control consoles folded in on themselves, followed by all metal cabinetry doing the same. Enormous electric arcs launched from the generator's mega-storage capacitors shot across the room accompanied by ever louder crackles, pops, sizzles, and an occasional, BANG!

Then total quiet. And total darkness. We had only sense of smell to delineate the conflagration's progress. The acrid odor of O_3 (ozone), produced by electrical fire, attacked our nostrils.

The brief silence ended when the entire facility rumbled and shuddered, forestalling our debate about making a run for the red steel door. The top centerline of the stone ceiling ripped open as the roof hatch shot straight down to clang against the catwalk and then bang and rattle on the concrete floor.

The transceiver dish on top of the hill glowed fluorescent red like NASCAR disc brakes in a Talladega night race and then with a — BOOM! — turned inside out to impersonate a dead umbrella. Two seconds later, it exploded violently, punching three holes through the cave's outer wall, and slashing a gaping crevice into the hillside. Cracks in the ceiling permitted streaks of daylight and clean air to filter in through the thick gray smoke.

After sparking ceased and debris stopped falling, we cautiously stepped out from our make-shift shelters. Without warning, the master command console roared straight up through the hole in the roof, trailing a ten-foot flame. We all jumped back into hidey-holes.

We waited a good long while in comforting silence before detecting a soft pitter-patter sound. Kevin, by himself, guardedly approached the center of the great room and looked up. He held out his arms with his palms up and smiled, enjoying the drops on his skin.

"Dr. Weksler, I think you ended the drought."

As it turned out, he had.

A few minutes later, on top of Dr. Weksler's brown hill, we enjoyed the peaceful easy rain falling all over Southern California. A perfect rainbow stretched from the mountains to the sea. After our short breather, we decided to climb back down into whatever remained.

* * * * *

Special Agent Lieutenant Scott, about to leave the scene, did a swift, professional-eye, situation appraisal. He addressed Kevin. "You gonna sanitize?"

"Yeah, I'll detail it."

"And you're not coming with us?"

"Correct. Mr. Scott, this is my new life." Kevin looked at Dianne, me, Dr. Weksler, Sarah, and Ms. Zambini. "I am going to be a college professor." He arched his eyebrows at Dianne. "Maybe in Hawaii? I am going to be in love. And we will all live happily ever after."

Agent Scott angled his head at Kev. "Major, you sure you don't wanna come in?"

Kev stared at Scott. "Over. And out."

"Alright, Ox. HUA. Semper Fi."

"Semper Fi."

Scott accompanied Leonard Ostermann out the red steel slab of a door, now hanging by one hinge and propped open by a red chair. Ostermann exited, but Agent Scott stopped, stood straight and tall, facing Kevin, and said, "Sir. It has been my privilege, sir." He did a slow, precise, and incredibly respectful salute.

Kevin snapped off a respectful salute in return. As Scott turned to leave, Kevin called after him, "Hey Scotty."

Scott looked back. "Sir?"

"My regards to POTUS."

Special Agent Lieutenant Scott nodded his head crisply and smiled. "Roger that." He rotated smartly and left the premises.

Ms. Zambini smiled at me. Well, at least I think she did. I'm not real astute with that stuff. Just in case, I smiled back. Without her hair curler head gear, she was kinda-sorta cute.

I thought about it and realized it had been a couple months since the last time I went on a date. I couldn't even remember that girl's name, but it had been our first date and it was all good for most of the evening. But then, when we kissed goodnight, my eyeglasses got completely fogged up and I couldn't see hardly anything. When I leaned in to nuzzle her ear, I swallowed her diamond earring.

My insurance deductible totaled $512. We never had a second date.

The rusty brown blood stain on the left hip of Dr. Weksler's khaki slacks continued to grow, as did his agony, but he knew meds were on the way. The six of us were alone in the remains of the lab. Dianne, Sarah, Ms. Zambini, Dr. Weksler and I were on one side of the large, partially destroyed, great room. Kev stood alone on the other side, leaving a huge sound of silence between. Questions that nobody wanted to ask floated in the emotional vacuum. Basically, it boiled down to... what's up with Kevin?

The Ox man brought relief. He looked at us and said, "I need to tell you three things. And then I need to never not talk about any of them ever again."

A group nod. Dr. Weksler hugged Sarah. Dianne nibbled her lip. Ms. Zambini held my hand (wow).

"Thing number one," Kevin said. "Less than two years ago, American Airlines Flight eleven left Boston's Logan Airport at 7:59 a.m. on September 11, 2001, heading to Los Angeles. On that plane were five subhuman monsters. That scum killed all eighty-seven innocent people on board at 8:46 a.m. by flying the plane into the North Tower of the World Trade Center. They also killed thousands more innocents in the building, including gentle, peace-loving, non-psychotic Muslims. I heard about it on the radio that morning while driving to meet my dad at Los Angeles International. My dad never arrived because he was one of the eighty-seven."

Some of us whispered, "Oh God." and, "I'm so sorry." Some just sniffed.

"Thing number two," Kevin said. "I have seen and done things I wish to never see and do again."

We all nodded, introspectively hushed.

"Thing number three: Ask me no questions and I'll tell you no lies."

"You got a deal."

"Works for me."

"Sounds good."

The six of us rushed together for a group hug, happy-dance, happy-chatter, and one Dianne happy lower lip nibble. Which she immediately turned into a full-frontal passionate kiss with Kevin, right there in public ... in front of God and everyone.

* * * * *

"...advanced nations, will someday be able to produce instruments of death so terrible the world will be in abject terror of itself and its ability to end civilization."

— Thomas Edison

"The scope of our technology exceeds the wisdom of our society."

— Dr. Francis Noah Weksler

"If no country can be attacked successfully, there can be no purpose in war.

I was fortunate enough to...perfect means which...will make any country ... impregnable against...attack. It will...provide a wall of power offering an insuperable obstacle against any effective aggression."

— Nikola Tesla

(All details of his invention were confiscated by the FBI on January 7, 1943 and were never made public.)

The End

EPILOGUE

Yeah, I know... you're thinking... how could someone who hates prologues write an epilogue? Well, it's because I really like it at the end of movies when they put little descriptions up on the screen of what eventually happened to each person in the real-life story. I think that's fun. And, of course, I hope an epilogue will help me figure out who to blame.

* * * * *

The court convicted Mikhail on one count of hottubbing with a goat. Deemed consensual, he only received three weekends of home confinement. The court released the goat on its own recognizance. Mikhail's sentence required wearing a GPS tracking device on his ankle. So as not to be cruel and unusual, the court stipulated that Mikhail could remove the tracking device anytime he felt it infringed on his illegal immigrant right to pursue whatever he wanted.

Mikhail will have a recurring role as an alien creature in a new *Star Trek* series.

He is still about two wheels short of a tricycle.

* * * * *

A carefully selected liberal judge overturned the conviction of His Supreme Eminence, citing that the jury did not constitute a jury of his peers, because there were no terrorists on the jury. The judge also ruled Dr. Weksler's Pacoima lab to, indeed, be the Consulate of The Holy Garduña, or the S.O.L, or somebody (the judge didn't care who) and the awesome threesome owed somebody a lot of money for blowing up their consulate. The judge then declared a mistrial, dropping all charges against His Supreme Eminence.

Supreme Eminence, worried that decent people of the world might someday combine their strength and destroy his sick brand of evil, retired from terrorism. With the $200,000 he received from the court (an apology for the anguish of an unbefitting jury), he moved to North Africa and launched Khadafy Fried Chicken. So let it be written.

* * * * *

Leonard Ostermann received a huge promotion on his last day of work in order to insure that his federal pension from early retirement would be at least twice that of an equivalent private sector pension. His pension followed federal guideline, considered fair recompense for someone who devoted his life to protecting a country he loved (frequently the United States).

Ostermann took early retirement to accept the lead role in a Paramount-produced television series about a "Hard-Boiled Pirate Detective in China Town". Titled, *The Egg and Aye*, Lenny wrote the script and, much like Sylvester Stallone with his *Rocky* screenplay, would not allow any studio to produce the show unless he got the starring role.

A former pro wrestler with a five-inch blue Mohawk became his TV sidekick.

* * * * *

Because Bahadur illegally lived in the United States more than ten years on an expired student visa, immigration officials required him to sign a "Promise to Appear" for the mandatory deportation hearing required by law. To the great relief of all agencies, Bahadur did not appear. His whereabouts remain unknown.

Speaking anonymously, an immigration official stated, "Hey, there are millions of guys like Bahadur in the country illegally. How are we supposed to keep track of them all? And besides, it's not like he's a criminal or anything."

* * * * *

Designer tennis shoes with hollowed out compartments in the soles, along with M112 demolition blocks (military grade C-4 explosive packaged as clay-like cakes) were found in the stinking home of Professor Pul. Charged with terrorism, kidnapping, attempted murder, and hate speech, Pul's conviction on all counts appeared to be a slam dunk. However, the *Council Representing Arabic Perpetrators* (CRAP) portrayed him as a poor misunderstood immigrant merely trying to earn a living for his family (the two smelly dogs). As a result, the sympathetic liberal judge threw out the terrorism, kidnapping, and attempted murder charges.

Pul did get convicted for hate speech. But, the Ninth Circus Court of Appeals overturned, declaring it is impossible for there to even be such a thing as hate speech toward white guys. Especially if they're Christian.

Having no educational credentials recognized by California, Pul, nevertheless, had a foreign accent which made his English difficult to understand. That being a lecture hall requirement, UC Berkeley granted him full professorship with tenure. Today, "Professor" Pul uses his university classroom as a platform to promote *reconquista*, establishment of Aztlán, and the overthrow of the U.S. government. A large number of California legislators are sympathetic to his views.

* * * * *

I marveled at the astonishing coincidence of Ms. Zambini bursting into Dr. Weksler's secret lab at precisely the right moment to save our lives. Dr. Weksler reminded me that I don't believe in coincidence. He viewed Ms. Zambini rushing in as a direct answer to our group prayer in which Kevin pleaded, "In the Bible you say, 'knock and the door will open.' Well, Lord, we are really knocking."

Dr. Weksler explained that answers to prayers aren't usually "miracles".

"God works supernaturally in very natural ways."
— Pastor Chuck Smith
Founder of Calvary Chapel

I also wondered why I had always been so willing to impute spirituality to things like old shoes on a tree, or crystals, or an Indian fakir who is actually a faker, but I always rejected any consideration of the Bible. I never figured out the answer to that question, but I knew lots of people just like me in that regard. Very odd.

"Man will believe anything, as long as it's not the Bible."
— Napoleon Bonaparte

Much to my surprise, I began attending church with Kevin, Dianne, and the Wekslers. That happened because Ms.

Angelina Zambini said she would like me to go to church with her. I happily agreed. It didn't hurt at all.

As a scientist, the Bible impressed me as the only holy book which tells followers to question everything in order to learn what is true. I respected being able to ask tough, probing, religious questions and have my questions discussed and answered without me being booed, beaten, or beheaded. Christians are not supposed to turn off their brains.

Just like Kevin, Dianne, Frank, Sarah, Angelina, Thomas Edison, Albert Einstein, and hundreds of millions of others, I'm now certain everything was created. Not accidental goop.

> *"I believe the science of chemistry alone almost proves the existence of an intelligent creator."*
>
> — Thomas Edison

* * * * *

Although Kevin and Dianne continued dating and were madly in love, Dianne had issues with that "M" word (marriage). But, that's another *mo'olelo* (story). As a matter of fact, that story will be told in *WILD GREEN: Hawaiian Honeymoon*. If they survive their cruise ship being hijacked by an insane band of pirates.

Kevin celebrated our escape from mad man Pul with his new homemade bumper sticker:

DON'T judge all Muslims by the actions of a few.
DO judge all gun owners by the actions of a few.
(Journalism Training at Most American Universities)

* * * * *

The Weksler's covered-up 1957 Plymouth Fury came out unscathed. Their tired Ford sedan got many new dings that matched the many old dings. Their garage and single-wide trailer became scrap metal. Frank and Sarah restored the destroyed former lab to its original identity as a parched brown hill. Ashes to ashes. Dust to dust.

Dr. Weksler learned of a peculiar mansion for sale in San Marino. During prohibition, it belonged to gangster Bugsy Siegel. The adventuresome Dr. Sarah Norton-Weksler thought the strange gerrymandered house seemed like great fun, so they bought it, and Dr. Weksler "set up shop".

Yes, we all lost our jobs at Pas Tech but, Frank wasn't yet finished inventing things for the good of the world. With a little help from his friends (Kevin and me) he would resurrect one of Nikola Tesla's most stunning accomplishments.

But first, the awesome threesome would have to escape from highly disturbed zombies in *WILD COPPER: Saving Humanity at the Masked Ball.*

* * * * *

Kevin called a very special phone number, and POTUS arranged for Dr. Weksler to throw the ceremonial first pitch at the next Dodgers game. Already emotional and misty-eyed, Dr. Weksler barely kept it together when four Dodger stars joined him on the mound with a teleprompter, and they all sang Harry Belafonte's classic *Banana Boat Song (Day O)* ... with new Dodger lyrics on the prompter: *"Baseball. Bay-Bay-Bay-Baseball. Tsunami come but we win the thee game. Six-foot, seven-foot, eight-foot waves. Tsunami come but we win thee game..."*

* * * * *

Oh, and three more things...

Thing number one: Should you wish to check up on whether the Bible contains fab and famous physical facts written down thousands of years before human scientists "discovered" them, please check out the following: A round earth (Isaiah 40:22) — Pleiades and Orion (Job 38:31) — Atoms (Hebrews 11:3).

Thing number two: Gary Puckett's top-billing at the Hollywood Bowl *Rock Legends* concert resulted in a sell-out. Elated fans got three encores.

Thing number three: Everything's chicken, but the gravy. And you know what that's made of.

—*finis*—

CPSIA information can be obtained
at www.ICGtesting.com
Printed in the USA
FSHW021148060520
69893FS